THE
UMBRELLA
OPTION

THE
UMBRELLA OPTION

W. F. WALSH

Library of Congress Control Number: 2013903344
ISBN: Hardcover   978-1-4797-9964-0
                     Softcover   978-1-4797-9963-3
                     Ebook   978-1-4797-9965-7

This book was printed in the United States of America.

Rev. date: 02/23/2013

To order additional copies of this book, contact:
Xlibris Corporation
1-888-795-4274
www.Xlibris.com
Orders@Xlibris.com
128066

Contents

Chapter 1:   NOISE 11
Chapter 2:   PLAYERS 19
Chapter 3:   SOFTNESS 25
Chapter 4:   INTERVIEWS 33
Chapter 5:   CONNECTIONS 43
Chapter 6:   BLUEPRINTS 53
Chapter 7:   PORTS OF CALL 69
Chapter 8:   SIDE JOBS 83
Chapter 9:   PARTS DEPARTMENT 90
Chapter 10: CONNECTIONS 94
Chapter 11: GLOBE-TROTTING 106
Chapter 12: SPECIAL DELIVERY 120
Chapter 13: SWITCHING BAIT 136
Chapter 14: MOVING PARTS 161
Chapter 15: PAID TIME OFF 175
Chapter 16: TURNAROUND DAY 188
Chapter 17: SAIL-AWAY PARTY 207
Chapter 18: PORT OF CALL 215
Chapter 19: OPTIONS 228
Chapter 20: TOT (Time on Target) 248
Chapter 21: SEMPER PARATUS 261
Chapter 22: BREAKING NEWS 278

For Janet, Frank, and Amy

Acknowledgment

Special thanks to

Janet Walsh—World's best editor and supporter
Dr. Adam Kelleher, PhD—Physics consultant and best little brother ever
Mr. Andrew Kelleher—Computer consultant and best little brother ever
Capt. Rusty Picket, USN (Ret.)—Finest submarine consultant in the business
Mr. Alan Campbell—Cruise consultant and good friend
The Cottages on Charleston Harbor—A fine spot to write
Burt Shapiro, Shapiro Media Management, Los Angeles—Agent and friend
Royal Caribbean Cruise Lines—The best in the world and another fine place to write
Mr. Edward Reynolds and Dr. Scott Curry, MD—Medical consultants and good friends
Nancy Fischer, United States Customs Service
Panera Bread Company—Another fine place to write
Ken Burger—Amazing author, consultant, and good friend
The men and women of the United States Coast Guard cutter *Vigilant*
The men and women of the 315th Airlift Wing, Joint Base, Charleston, South Carolina
The men and women of the USS *Pittsburgh*
RAYCOM Media
Litton Entertainment

Chapter 1

NOISE

THE INVESTIGATION WAS six months in the making and included trips to the Dominican Republic and Puerto Rico for Special Agent Jake Stein and some of his team. Now was the time to strike, and his stomach was about to turn upside down as he sat in a rented minivan outside an apartment complex in the Tamiami section of Southwest Dade County, Florida. He crouched his almost-six-foot frame down into the passenger seat. With a dark complexion and black hair, Jake blended in well with the largely Latino population of the Miami area.

"We've got some movement," said a voice crackling through the earpiece Jake was wearing as part of the tactical clothing he had on.

"Not until my order," said Jake in a low tone over the secure two-way radio. The minivan smelled of stale coffee as he and his partner watched the windows on the second floor of the building a few feet away from them.

"Stand by . . . stand by," said Lt. Monica Lopez of the Miami-Dade Special Operations Unit working with Jake's Immigration and Customs Enforcement, or ICE, team. "Goddamn it, one of our subjects is walking."

Jake looked up and saw a man coming out of the building, heading for the sidewalk and toward a parked BMW. The man had on dark sunglasses and an Atlanta Braves T-shirt, and he carried a small Coleman cooler in his right hand. This was not in the playbook. The team was after the people in the apartment and wanted to catch them before they acted, but now one of them was making an unscheduled exit.

"Monica, this is yours. Take him at the corner," Jake ordered. He had tactical command, seeing that it was an ICE raid. She wanted to be in on the entry to the apartment and now had to essentially play traffic cop down the street.

Monica and her partner quickly backed their unmarked Impala out of the parking spot and pulled onto the street then drove about a quarter mile down the road to wait for the guy with the cooler. A few minutes later, the BMW appeared in her rearview mirror, and she was ready to pounce. The suspect was almost up to her car when she pulled out in front of him, put on her lights, and slammed on the brakes. She and her partner jumped out of the car with their weapons drawn, pointing at the driver.

"Hands on the steering wheel," she commanded while her partner took the passenger side of the vehicle.

"Slowly get out of the vehicle. Put your hands on your head!"

The man in the car looked shocked and did as he was told. Monica's partner covered her while she slapped the cold metal handcuffs across the man's wrists. Once the suspect was secure, she opened the back door of the BMW and saw the cooler he was carrying strapped down by the seat belt. Odd, she thought as she reached to unhook the belt and see what was inside.

"Holy shit," she said, backing away from the cooler and grabbing her radio. "Jake, it's already done, it's already done, take them!"

The cooler contained a human liver, a heart, and kidneys all packed on ice. Jake immediately ordered his people into the apartment. He jumped out of the minivan and ran to the stairs leading to the second floor of the apartment building.

"Careful," he ordered as the men quickly closed in on the door.

They surrounded the door while one agent took a tactical entry tool and forced his way in.

"Federal agents with a warrant!" Jake yelled as he and the others on his team made their way into the apartment. There was a long entry hall leading to a living room. Suddenly two shots rang out.

"Shots fired, shots fired!" Jake barked into his radio while crouching down to the floor and releasing the safety on his service weapon.

In the span of around three seconds, two of Jake's agents fired their Colt M4 carbines in the direction of the living room, toward a man standing behind a table with what looked like a body lying on top of it. They missed as the man pushed the table over and ducked behind it.

"Down low!" Special Agent Will Campbell yelled. He took aim again at the guy behind the table. Agent Campbell squeezed off three more rounds, aiming at the center of the table. The hollow-point bullets blasted through the wood and into the suspect kneeling down behind it. Then silence.

"Hold your fire," Jake ordered. He and the others carefully checked to see if the suspect was down and the room clear. "We're clear, suspect down," Jake said. Two other agents checked the rest of the empty apartment and also pronounced it clear.

"My god," said Campbell, looking down on the floor next to the table now on its side. "I've never seen anything like this."

Another agent excused himself to use the bathroom to throw up. The smell alone was enough to turn even the strongest stomach.

"Monica, we need your hazmat team right away," Jake said over the radio as he looked at the cut-up body lying in a pool of blood on the floor. Along with the body were three large buckets once filled with body parts, blood, and other bodily fluids now spilled across the floor. There was so much blood and liquid that it posed a danger of leaking into the apartment downstairs. Agents had to clear out the entire building.

ICE had finally collected enough intelligence on a band of human organ traffickers from the Dominican Republic and wanted to catch them before they struck again. The dead doctor behind the table had been responsible for kidnapping then harvesting the organs of poor immigrants for over a year but had never been caught in the act, until now. Homeland Security Investigations could score one for the good guys, Jake thought as the crime scene tape was being put up around the apartment building.

"Let's get this so-called doctor out of here ASAP. You never know, he might even be an organ donor."

Two weeks later, after finishing the pile of paperwork their latest bust created, putting the human organ smuggling investigation to bed, he put on his management hat and headed to D.C. Jake Stein really was not a big fan of flying, but his job required that he jump around the American Southeast quite a bit. The worst part was having to go through the TSA over and over, bringing his service weapon paperwork and ID so he could carry his government-issued SIG Sauer P255 9 mm neatly tucked away behind his jacket for the ride in coach class. Today was no different as he left his home base of Miami for a quick run up to Washington and yet another meeting of the Homeland Security Investigations team he was a part of. Once cleared through TSA, he would be handed a small note by the agents at the gate, informing him what seats other, if any, LEOs (law enforcement officers) were sitting in should they be needed during the flight. This time he was the only one.

As an agency, ICE was fairly new and not very well known. Immigration and Customs Enforcement actually came about in 2003 when the investigative arm of the U.S. Customs Service merged with the interior enforcement elements. ICE now fell under the Department of Homeland Security. HIS, or Homeland Security Investigations, a directorate of ICE, was responsible for domestic and international illegal movement of people and goods along with intelligence operations.

As a special agent in charge of the Miami field office, Jake was responsible for his office in addition to the San Juan field office. In San Juan, the special agent in charge had left the agency for a bigger job with the DEA. Attending quarterly meetings like the one he was heading to today was a part of the job Jake didn't care for because it added more layers to his already-busy work schedule. At least he'd get to have dinner with his former live-in partner and now just good friend, Special Agent Claire Wilson.

"I'll be up on the eight fifty-five," he said over the airport background noise on his new iPhone, which he preordered when Apple decided to make the screen bigger, improve the camera, and add some other goodies. He was new to this phone, but Jake also had to keep his ancient first-edition, government-issued BlackBerry for official calls and e-mail. "Let's meet around six at Uno's if that works for you," he said while his flight was being called.

"Sure, I'll walk over and we can start there," Special Agent Wilson said as she strolled to her office just off K Street on this fine chilly April morning. She was Secret Service, but not on "the Detail" as it was known around the Service when talking about presidential or executive protection. Her job was investigating counterfeiters. She dreamed of becoming the president's special agent in charge someday, but for rookies and folks in their first few years, the closest they would get to protection detail would be as an extra body for a big event to give the impression to any would-be bad guys that there were more than enough guns around if they tried anything.

Jake noticed once again that he drew the short straw when it came to airplanes. RJs, the airline business's abbreviation for regional jets, were built to save money on fuel. As far as Special Agent Jake Stein was concerned, it might as well have been a Piper Cub. He wondered what Claire had meant when she said, "We can start there." After living together for almost a year before each decided to pursue their respective careers in federal law enforcement, he knew she would keep their dinner professional and almost ignore the romance they once had during their years at Clemson University in South Carolina. She was, after all, a Southern girl.

"Can I check that bag for you?" asked the one and only flight attendant on the little United Express jet as he climbed to the top of the few stairs it had. "No, thanks, I'll carry it on," he told her, knowing that his laptop bag was bigger than most and hoped it fit in the overhead bin. The flight attendant walked back down the single aisle, and Jake could sense that she was headed right toward him. "Okay, but if it doesn't fit, we'll have to stow it," she said in a tone that was all business.

The flight took about three hours and was nonstop to Ronald Reagan National, which in years past was simply known as National Airport. The good thing about Reagan was that it was right on the D.C. Metro and people could easily get around town without much effort. Jake's hotel of choice, and one that HSI approved, was the Hyatt on Capitol Hill, just a few minutes' walk from Union Station.

His meeting was set for 1:00 p.m., and Jake assumed it should only last around four hours tops. It was the quarterly HSI sit-down with all twenty-six offices represented. It included the usual national intel brief before each special agent in charge gave an overview of operations from each of their respective offices. He had a routine report with no major issues for his office or San Juan. Jake was thankful for a quiet report because when intel started trickling down, follow-up could create months of work chasing leads with plenty of dead ends.

After the bumpy flight around a few thunderstorms along the East Coast, the little jet landed and taxied over to the mini Jetway attached to the terminal building. Everything associated with these regional jets was mini, he thought as he walked into the main terminal and headed for baggage claim.

"So you think you have it made in Miami with Dolphins football and bikinis," said a familiar voice from behind.

"Shit, I thought I would get away from you this time," said Jake as he shook the hand and half hugged Special Agent Danny Williams of the Boston field office.

"No way. It's all me. And I still hate you," said Danny as he referred to the fact that Jake was assigned Miami and he got Boston right out of the gate from training at the FLETC (Federal Law Enforcement Training Center) in Glynco, Georgia, just five short years ago. Now both men were on the fast track, becoming special agents in charge quicker than most.

"I'll just say that it was seventy-five degrees when I left and it will be seventy-five degrees when I get home," jabbed Jake as he relished the weather at his home base, complete with tropical breezes.

"It was freezing when I left and will be freezing when I get back," said Danny, referring to the cold Boston weather even though it really had been in the fifties when he left Logan International that morning. "We have two seasons, winter and July 15 !"

"You'll have to come for a little visit or find something to come down for on business," Jake said after collecting his bag and heading for the door.

"Share a cab?" Danny said.

"I'm going Metro, faster in all this D.C. traffic. You at the Hyatt?" asked Jake.

"Yup, we all are. Camp Hyatt where all the feds come to play," said Danny. "I'll ride with you on the train."

Both men headed for the Blue Line, and each used the kiosk to buy a ten-dollar Metrorail farecard. It was a short ride over to Union Station, where they could simply walk a couple of blocks, almost across the street, to the Hyatt. Union Station was also where Jake would be meeting Claire later on for dinner at their favorite pizza place, Uno's Pizzeria, serving Chicago deep-dish-style pies. It was windy enough in Washington, where the midday temperature was in staying the fifties. Jake usually traveled light, and the only coat he owned was the Clemson Tigers jacket he wore to the football games in school.

"This is miles ahead of the T," said Danny, talking about the subway he rode to work most mornings into Boston's Back Bay Station. "Ours is slow and crammed, plus it smells like piss."

"Our nation's capital needs to look and smell good for the tourists," said Jake as both men eyed a man standing at the other end of the car. Their training was never far away in their consciousness, and this guy looked like he was up to no good. Profiling was against the rules and publicly never acknowledged in the law enforcement business, especially at the federal level. In spite of that, both agents knew it was just a natural reflex, like taking note of a passing car that looked familiar.

With one eye on the guy at the end of the car and the other on what station was coming up, the agents made small talk and looked forward to seeing fellow HSI members along with former classmates.

The hubbub of Union Station was all around them as they jumped off the Blue Line, walked up the stairs and out into the cool April afternoon in Washington, and headed just down the street to the hotel so familiar to both of them.

"We'll have to drop and run," said Danny as they walked into the lobby of the Hyatt Regency, Capitol Hill. The hotel was tucked neatly away just down from the Capitol on New Jersey Avenue and was an easy walk to restaurants, federal buildings, and just about anything else in central D.C. It housed diplomats, federal workers, business travelers, and tourists who came into town during this time of year to see the cherry blossoms.

"Yeah, the meeting is at thirteen hundred," Jake said to Danny as they took the escalator down to the lobby. "It's going to have to be lunch on the run."

Check-in would be quick today, seeing that there were only a couple of people ahead of them, and once they each got their plastic card keys and usual coupons to local eateries, they went to their rooms to drop bags and quickly headed back outside for the short walk to the nondescript building just a few doors down.

The building at 101 South Capitol looked like just another office complex and was home to some national media outlets like Fox News, CBS News, and others. It was also the Washington home to some state governments that rented office space to use when they pitched their states to business leaders and dealt with the federal government. The building's glass front and lobby were typical Washington with a high ceiling and flags of the different states adorning the walls. HSI had a special field office on the fifth floor, complete with a secure conference and communications room.

Jake made it to the building ahead of Danny, who was lagging behind with lots of elevator traffic at the Hyatt. As he walked into 101 South Capitol, he approached the security guard and presented his credentials, which indicated that he was one of the few who did not have to sign in and would walk around the metal detectors on the way to the elevator.

After a quick ride up to the fifth floor, yet another layer of security greeted Special Agent Jake Stein, but this time it wasn't a rent-a-cop like in the lobby.

"Good afternoon, sir," said the armed and uniformed agent at the desk.

"Special Agent Stein, Miami," Jake said while handing over the credentials he worked so hard to earn.

"Yes, sir, SC 3 today," said the big man at the desk. SC meant "secure conference room."

Jake waited for Danny who got off the other elevator also presenting his credentials. Both men walked down the hall to SC 3, where the door had a buzzer, a touch pad lock, and a bunch of cubbyholes on the wall next to the door. The cubbyholes were where cell phones, iPhones, and any other electronic device would be left before entering the secure conference room.

"You know, one time I actually left without picking up my cell," Jake mused as both he and Danny put their phones into the plastic cubes.

With that, they entered the code of the day given to them by the uniformed agent at the reception desk, and with a click, the door released, and they joined their comrades from other parts of the country assembled for their meeting.

"Who are we waiting for?" asked Col. Tim Felton, U.S. Army, retired, and now executive associate director, Homeland Security Investigations.

"Thompson and Bright, sir," Danny said as Felton looked at his watch showing only military time.

"Imagine that," sighed Felton. "And you guys wonder why my hair's going gray so fast." Felton had handpicked each agent who led the twenty-six SAC field offices around the country.

Within a few minutes, all agents were present and accounted for as Felton pushed a button next to the door, locking it and automatically lowering the blinds. Next, he fired up the laptop computer and inserted his common access card (CAC) then put in his personal six-digit code. The computer came to life, and Felton clicked on the secure PowerPoint that was projected on the screen. As was the case with secure briefings, each slide had the usual red banner across the top with the word "secret" written on it.

"All right, not much since our last get-together, but a couple of new nuggets," said Felton as he started off. "First, our two drug lords, Fiore and Vela, are still under surveillance with their usual distribution routes. We've dealt with this pretty well with CBP [Customs and Border Protection] in El

Paso, arresting two kingpins. The crazy thing is that the cartels don't even miss them. They just write them off as the cost of doing business."

The slide show continued for a few minutes, reviewing past data and updating cases where they had some new information. Before the September 11 attacks, interagency cooperation had been limited at best when it came to sharing information and intelligence. Now, at least in some cases, it was a bit better as each agency passed on information that might spill into the jurisdiction of sister agencies.

"CIA sent this on to us. They're getting some noise from Puerto Rico and Dominica that spiked a couple of NSA mobile reviews," he noted, as did Jake, seeing that both of these islands were within his current AOR (area of responsibility).

The National Security Agency (NSA) had computer programs that monitored cell and satellite communications in some areas overseas suspected of harboring terrorists. A "spike" meant that a real person would have to go over the actual conversation to see if there was any valid reason to step up the monitoring or engage a more focused method of elint (electronic intelligence).

"What kind of noise?" asked Jake.

"There's talk from one known TC to another person, who is unidentified, about—let me see here—'operation moving forward' were the words that the spike hit on."

A "TC" was a terrorist collaborator—someone who may have been a suspected terrorist or who collaborated with suspected terrorists or terror cells. Usually, those who collaborated also sympathized with organizations or had relationships with actual "KOs" (known operatives).

"We should be getting some more intel on these guys over the next couple of weeks, and I'll pass that along to you, Jake, seeing that's your part of the world," Felton said as Jake took a few more notes. He continued, "This TC has been seen in Pakistan and Bulgaria with former members of Hezbollah who, just a few years ago, were active members living in Beirut."

"Are they still active?" asked Jake as he continued to ponder the communications trail he was looking at on the PowerPoint slide.

"Not officially. They dropped from view about three years ago then popped up on a watch list in Islamabad, and the trail led to Varna, Bulgaria," Felton said, going over his classified notes. "You'll be in the distro now on these two and can run with whatever noise comes in."

"Copy that," Jake said.

Felton continued with his briefing as the various special agents in charge gave their reports.

Chapter 2

PLAYERS

S AN JUAN WAS like many Caribbean cities where thousands flock
every season to escape the cold and snowy winters across much of
North America. The island of Puerto Rico is bigger than most people think,
with its white sand beaches, famous historic forts, casinos, and even a rain
forest. Even though it was not a state, islanders were fond of being part of
the United States and the benefits that went along with being a territory. Jobs
continued to be tough to come by, and many people worked part-time or not
at all, collecting unemployment. One of the biggest industries on the island
was tourism accounting for around 45 percent of the local economy.

The cruise business was also a big player in the tourism industry. When
the ships came to San Juan, they brought thousands of passengers all with
money to spend. All of the cruise lines contributed to the local economy
and paid fees for each passenger they carried, which helped maintain
the terminal and services required for the big ships. They were also good
employers, accepting people from around the world to work on their famous
ships. Not all the jobs on the ships were sexy and came with big titles, but
all non-Americans were paid tax-free money, which could be wired to family
living in countries around the world. Even the lowest wage earners brought in
more per four-month contract than they could earn in five years of work back
home. Each of the big cruise lines' ships had crewmembers of over thirty
nationalities, and the industry prided itself on this fact.

Star Caribe Cruise Lines was one of the world's largest, and so was their
latest ship, the *Star Orion*, weighing in at a monstrous 159 thousand tons
and measuring more than three football fields long.

Bishar Fouad enjoyed the money he was paid at Star Caribe, working in
the bowels of the ship one floor below the first passenger deck in the sorting
room. His job, along with six others, was to sort and separate garbage such as

plastic, cardboard, glass, and other items that could be recycled from plain old trash. Bishar's roommate and childhood friend from the same village in Pakistan, Imad Patel, also worked eight-hour shifts in the sorting room, helping to keep Star Caribe's reputation as a steward of the environment intact and earning the ship last year's Green Diamond Award.

"Four hours today," Bishar said to his partner, who was sweating up a storm while putting the aluminum cans into one of the ship's three huge compactors. It was so loud in this part of the ship that all of the crew members wore hearing protection.

"Yeah, I thought it would never get here this week," said Imad, referring to the four hours of time off the ship they earned each week during the midpoint in their seven-day round trip from Miami. "We have two stops and lunch," Bishar said while wrapping up his duties for the day. "I'm going to take a shower, and we can head off," he said while walking out the door toward their small windowless cabin just one deck above. Bishar would trade his company-issued white overalls (which he had to double cuff because of his short height) for more comfortable street clothes. His dark black hair and mustache gave the forty-one-year-old a much younger appearance than most men of that age.

Lunch was in San Juan with an old friend from their school days, who was visiting the island on business. Abdul-Aziz Fahad had left Pakistan at the age of twenty in search of something bigger than himself to latch on to. Ten years later, he had found what he was looking for. He was a sales representative for a Frankfurt-based software company for which he traveled the world. The company specialized in web marketing for new products their clients were producing. Sellco was a successful company with deep pockets and clients in the pharmaceutical, dental, and medical imaging businesses. Fahad had worked hard at getting a client in Puerto Rico, and he looked forward to frequent visits during his business travels. With a client in San Juan and representing a respected software company, customs routinely passed him through without a second look.

The Sellco sales rep had come a long way from that small village a half a world away. Growing up poor was tough, and factional fighting was part of the landscape. Fahad still carried a book that his father had given him when he was only six years old. It was really just an old book of village maps and something he did not quite understand at the time. Shortly after giving his son the book, his father left on a mission with the Soldiers of Faith and never returned. Soldiers loyal to the Afghan Northern Alliance killed him along the Afghan border. Growing up, Fahad blamed his father's death on Northern Alliance soldiers and the countries who backed them like the United States and Great Britain. As a teenager, he was taken under the wing of a former Soldier of Faith commander, Mohammad Featha, who was tied to the al-Qaeda movement, along with some other radical Islamic organizations. Abdul-Aziz Fahad was a good student, learning from Mohammad Featha not only the meaning of his life, but also the mission of his life.

Now, when Fahad traveled to Puerto Rico on business, he enjoyed lunching with his friends who worked on the cruise ship. He would coordinate his schedule to be in town every so often when the ship made port calls. Lunch was never at the same restaurant and always just the three of them. This time, the three would lunch at the El San Juan Resort and Casino, where hundreds of tourists were spending their vacation days away from the realities of life at home and work. The hotel was also home to one of the biggest casinos in San Juan and a busy, noisy place to meet friends. The two employees of Star Caribe walked around the casino, not directly through it, knowing the amount of surveillance cameras that were looking down at the masses of people hoping to return home rich. The Encanto Bar was one of the hotel's restaurants situated near the pool, complete with a lunch buffet and lots of tables. Typically they would meet around 2:00 p.m., after the lunch rush, knowing that they could find a table away from others and be able to talk outside the earshot of any busy bees.

"As-salaam alaikum," whispered Fahad.

"Peace be upon you," said Imad. "Good to see you in fine health." The conversations always started with pleasantries and talk about their jobs and how the computer software business was doing for Fahad. Then it came around to business and why they were meeting.

"We've figured out a way to get weapons onto the ship, and it might be perfect," explained Bishar. "It will require one of us to transfer to housekeeping, which may take a few extra weeks to smooth over."

"Go on," ordered Fahad.

"We've been looking at all the on-loads for the last few weeks to see if there is something that does not get looked at too much in Miami. About two weeks ago, we had a bed bug problem with a few of the cabins on deck 3. So I noticed the on-load of the replacement mattresses, just by accident. I was walking down to the canteen on deck 1 for a drink, and they were coming on board through the forward cargo door. Not a single look. The beds were wrapped in plastic and went directly from the truck to the stateroom," he explained.

"Go on," ordered Abdul, who usually did not say too much when his folks were talking about a plan.

"The beds are bulky and full of foam. They are rather heavy and large. Usually they are full sized, depending on the replacement needed. These are perfect cocoons for the weapons," said Bishar proudly, noting the pleased look on his boss and leader's face.

"That's brilliant, but what about the metal detectors?" he asked, thinking he already had thought about the answer.

"They don't fit," said Imad, chiming in, hoping to get some of the credit even though it was entirely Bishar's idea. "They lift them over because they come in packs of two. So the crew just lifts them over or around, and that's it. Even if they did fit, there are metal staples holding the plastic wrap together, which would be blamed for setting off the alarm."

"This could be a solution," said a clearly excited Fahad. "We might have solved the problem of getting the weapons aboard. I will get this information to our associates in the States working on that."

The three changed the subject as the waiter came by and delivered nonalcoholic drinks, and the three men went to the buffet for food. Business talks usually only lasted a few minutes, should anyone be monitoring the conversation. Typically they picked a noisy place for just that reason.

As lunch broke up, the three men shook hands and went on their way. "Ma as-salaama," they said wishing peace be upon each other. There was much planning to be done, thought Abdul-Aziz Fahad as he headed for his next stop, a sales call for Sellco.

Federal Hill was a place not too many outside of Providence, Rhode Island, knew of. For years, this Italian neighborhood in the state's capital city was home to some of the best Italian food on the East Coast. Places like Archie's, Angelo's, Papa's and the classic Old Canteen were where locals gathered to eat and drink. The people who lived on "the Hill" were first-, second-, and third-generation Italian Americans. They spoke their native tongue with each other more often than English. Their heritage ran deep. So deep that they celebrated Italian holidays with parades down Atwells Avenue, where even the street's center line was not the typical Department of Transportation white or yellow; the line painted down the middle of Atwells Avenue in the Federal Hill section of Providence was actually three lines together in red, white, and green, forming the colors of the Italian flag.

Angelo's was Dino Tucci's favorite haunt. He hung out there pretty much every night with his friends who were all employed by the same company. Narragansett Homes & Construction was one of many builders who called Providence and Rhode Island home. They had a reputation for quality building and getting a job done on time. They also had a reputation for getting paid on time. Tucci was more than just a construction foreman. He was paid muscle and a *capo* for the other division of Narragansett H&C: the racket.

Most Americans equate the mob or mafia with the Sopranos in New Jersey or the Corleones of New York from television and film. The real mob stayed under the radar, and Providence's Federal Hill was where many of them lived, worked, and played. Two families here controlled businesses from New England to Miami. One of those was the Battelli crime family. The Battellis owned Narragansett H&C along with other legitimate businesses that they used to launder money from their main sources of income: drugs, prostitution, and extortion. They also dabbled in the import/export business with booze, clothing, and, once in a while, electronics and pharmaceuticals. Dino had deep connections in this part of the business as well as family roots with many of those he worked with from growing up and attending Central High School. His parents were born in Naples, and he was a second-generation Italian. The thirty-four-year-old worked for the Battellis all his life, and his muscular build and natural tough looks would get anyone's attention if needed.

Customers of the racket or mob didn't go to storefronts or shop off the Internet. They made personal contacts and worked them over time with the goal of getting what they wanted and were willing to pay for. Frank Castro had been working in the export department of Evergreen Shipping for three years. He moved to Providence from Canada where the rest of his family lived after immigrating from Portugal. His real name was Ali Ahamid, a Saudi-born militant and member of the Soldiers of Faith. Frank had perfect documentation as a resident alien and often talked about his Canadian citizenship and background with friends. His second life was known only to a select few.

His Canadian accent was perfected over time, and his thick black hair was carefully dyed to a dark blond to match many who lived in this part of North America. Frank wore glasses to complete the look that appeared on his forged documents.

One of Frank Castro's friends was Dino Tucci. They met while playing on a racquetball team together. He also knew Dino was involved with the other type of racket. They often stopped off at Angelo's for a cold one after a hot game, which Dino usually won. His religion forbids the drinking of alcohol, but Frank Castro, a.k.a. Ali Ahamid, had a special dispensation for operational requirements. This Monday night was no exception.

"I can always count on you to cover me for a beer," said Dino knowing that Frank owed him the brew for losing two out of a three-game match. "Mich Light," he said, looking at the bartender who knew who Dino was and that he needed to be nice to this guy.

"How's work going, Frank?" Dino said, making small talk.

"Good, well . . . you know," Frank replied, trailing off, hoping Dino would notice.

"Things going okay down there?"

"Yeah, *metza metz*," sighed Frank while sipping his beer.

"Just didn't sound like it," Dino said.

"No, you know, I've got some balls up in the air. A client needs to buy and move some stuff and can't seem to find it."

"What kind of stuff?"

"Medical stuff. Used medical equipment and some stuff for a charity," Frank explained.

"I know some guys in that business," offered Dino while taking another handful of beer nuts. "Maybe I can get you hooked up."

Frank waited a few minutes and looked like he was thinking about it.

"You know anyone who can get a hold of radioactive medical material?" he asked looking to see how Dino took this inquiry and whether he would bite.

"Like pharmacy stuff?" Dino asked.

"Yeah, sort of. Some medical procedures use radioactive isotopes in their IVs for different tests."

"Cool," said Dino without much expression. His talent for faceless expressions came with the job and was a handy skill during late-night poker games with the boys.

"This client needs to move some of that offshore along with a used CT scanner for a charity doing medical research and outreach."

The actual client was pulling together pieces of a pie that would come to be known only to a select few as the "oven."

"Let me see what I can do. Give me a list of the stuff you're looking for," Dino said, not thinking much about it.

"Sure thing. So what's up with this Red Sox trade?" Frank said, changing the subject away from his real purpose for being there.

Chapter 3

SOFTNESS

THE AIR WAS a bit chilly when Jake finished up his meeting and wandered out into the cold D.C. air on South Capitol for the short walk over to Union Station, where he would be meeting his ex-girlfriend for supper. Both had careers in law enforcement, both were self-starters and go-getters, and both wanted it all but knew that this business was hell on a relationship. Pizzeria Uno was a favorite among the Homeland Security community because of its Chicago beginnings and how close it was to the D.C. offices.

Union Station was one of the nation's largest train stations and a crossroads of life in D.C. Whether commuting by Metro or hopping Amtrak trains to and from New York, millions of people came and went from this huge transportation hub. Pizzeria Uno was located on the second floor and situated around other shops and restaurants in the main hall. Along with being a transportation hub, Union Station was also a favorite place to shop. After taking the stairs to the top where the hostess station was located, Jake saw what he was looking for. Claire was standing at the top, wearing tight jeans and her hair down, just like Jake remembered. When on duty, she had to wear her hair up, but the look was much different when she was on her own time.

"You're always on time, Agent Stein," she said, smiling and trying not to look too excited to see her former lover. "Glad you dressed up."

"Just for you," he said as he gave her a hug, but no kiss. That would be too forward after a tough breakup and move seven years ago. The two kept in close touch though. "Good to see you."

Uno's was a busy place with lots of noise as people ate, drank, and chatted about their day. The hostess seated them in a booth for two not far from the bar.

"So how's life in the fast lane?" he asked while they waited for a waitress to place a drink order.

"Not so fast, but good. I like it," she explained with a bit of hesitation in her voice. "Earning my stripes in counterfeiting and e-crimes."

"Well you don't start on the PPD. You work your way up," he said, talking about the Presidential Protection Detail and telling her something she already knew.

"Yeah, I know, Jake, but still . . . ," she countered, knowing he would pump her up with words of encouragement. "I'm working hard, and it's pretty interesting stuff."

The waitress made her way over, and the two ordered their favorite drinks. His was a scotch and water while she ordered a gin and tonic.

"Drinking on a school night," he chuckled as she gave him a dirty look.

"Me? Look in the mirror!" she said.

"How's life in Miami?" she asked while glancing at the menu and getting hungry thanks to the pictures of classic Chicago deep-dish pizza.

"Good, I'm really loving it, especially now that I made SAC. The weather, the condo, and the job, it's all good."

"You seeing anyone?" she inquired without any hesitation.

"You don't wait too long, do you?" he shot back sarcastically. "Not right now. I'm too busy at work. I love the job, but it's like chasing dragon's tails. Sometimes you run around in circles."

"I hear that," Claire said while the waitress delivered their drinks, and she had flashbacks to the days they lived together before breaking up to pursue individual lives and careers.

"So what about you?" he asked, curious to see what her reaction would be. He knew her pretty well after the almost two years they spent living together.

"I'm dating my badge and SIG," she said, referring to her job and service weapon.

Both agents enjoyed needling each other, knowing that what could have been would not be, at least for the foreseeable future. *Tonight,* Special Agent Jake Stein thought, *would be spent alone in just another hotel room.*

Dinner wrapped up with a hug and kiss on the cheek. Jake picked up the check, and they parted ways on the cold D.C. night. Jake would be back up in the capital soon enough and would no doubt be calling her again.

In the Port of Miami, the cruise ships ruled. They were the bread and butter of this port and brought billions of dollars to the local economy every year. Each passenger line paid handsomely to build their beautiful terminals and employed thousands to make sure all of their paying guests had smooth embarkation and vacation experiences. The motto at Star Caribe was, "The Guest is the Star." Working at the port was a lifetime job for most of the people who helped to get these huge floating hotels turned around in nine hours, fully stocked and ready for a week's worth of partying.

Hector Lopez was one such lifer at the port. He had been working security for seventeen years and looked forward to his retirement once he made twenty. The money was okay, but nothing special, and no one ever got rich working the overnights as a security guard. He knew all the familiar faces who came in and out on a daily or weekly basis, depending on the ship schedule. Some ships set sail for seven days and others for just three- or four-day adventures. Hector's shift started at 11:00 p.m. and ended at 11:00 a.m., four days a week. He loved the fact that he had three-day weekends every week.

"Good morning," he said to Amanda Curtis of Metro Miami Furniture & Bedding as she and her crew came through the gate. "Finally letting you get back out of the office, I see," he said, knowing that she had not been with the bedding delivery crew in a couple of months.

"Yeah, they kick me out to get some fresh air once in a while," she chuckled.

If there were bedding issues on a cruise ship based in Miami, it was a good bet that the lines did business with Metro Miami Furniture & Bedding. They were one of the largest bedding companies in South Florida and contracted with four out of the seven cruise companies who called on the Port of Miami.

"Only a handful today," she said to Hector as she handed him the paperwork for the shipment bound for the Star Caribe terminal. "Just a couple of replacement mattresses, and we're out of here."

Typically the larger, newer ships carried anywhere from 1,500 to 4,000 passengers each week which give the ship a real workout. A bed, for example, might last ten years in a standard home, but the same bed only lasted a year or less aboard these floating cities. Paying cruise customers expected the best in comfort, and that was exactly what Star Caribe liked to deliver. Once a ship made its weekly port call and turnaround, the restock took place. Along with food, booze, entertainers, fuel, and more, the hotel director's staff also had to call ahead to make sure any replacement items were ordered and would be waiting at the pier.

Amanda had been working at Metro Miami Furniture & Bedding for about five years and enjoyed her frequent trips out to the ships. Hector did his usual look around the truck, checked the paperwork, and looked at the inventory headed for the ship. "Good to go," he announced after doing his inspection, walking back up to the cab and handing Amanda the paperwork, clearing the goods for delivery on board. Her crew of four made quick work of unloading the eight box springs and mattresses at the forward starboard cargo entrance.

Crew members volunteered for extra duty, including these special on-loads, in return for extra shore time when in port. Today, included among them were Bishar Fouad and Imad Patel, who were on break from their usual garbage duty and liked to get some fresh air every once in a while. Bishar was looking for a promotion to the housekeeping team, so this was also a great way to score points with the head housekeeper. Both men, along with six others, were handed the box springs and mattresses in a line from the back of the truck to the forward freight elevators inside the vessel. The metal detectors used for passengers were too narrow for this operation and type of cargo, which were pre-cleared anyway, so they went around them where there was more room to maneuver. Once on the midship service elevator, up they went to the appropriate deck and finally to the correct stateroom, where cabin stewards were waiting to make them up before the next round of passengers was scheduled to board shortly after 11:00 a.m.

Once the old bedding was carried back to the pier, Bishar, Imad, and the others were released from extra duty and headed to the crew's mess deck for lunch, thinking that this could not be a better situation for onloading their special cargo sometime in the coming weeks.

His flight back to Miami was routine, if a tad bouncy. Jake Stein was not a huge fan of flying, but it was part of the job. He couldn't help but wonder why they couldn't have those HSI meetings by teleconference like they had other briefings. But that was above his pay grade, and he was grateful for the opportunity to use work as an excuse to see Claire. On the plane, he was flipping through some of his papers and remembered he had to follow up on the "noise," which was occurring in his area of responsibility, that was talked about in the meetings. The transcripts were from phone conversations of a possible TC on a business trip to Puerto Rico. Any excuse to spend a couple of days in San Juan was a good excuse, thought Jake as the small regional jet bounced around in the afternoon heating of the earth which causes turbulence. He knew from past experience that TCs moved around and were smart about their communications. This one seemed to be a legitimate businessman and perhaps was wrongly tagged by NSA. Or perhaps he could have had a past life and decided to go on the straight and narrow. Whatever the case, Jake tagged him and would monitor his movements and keep some notes on him over the coming months.

The airplane landed back in Miami, and Jake quickly picked up his bag and headed for the garage where he had parked his 1966 convertible Jaguar

XKE. This car was his passion and weekend toy. Jake had another car he used during the week, a government "G-ride" as the agents called it, but it was in the shop, and for this trip, he drove his personal vehicle to the airport. The Jag was cream, or as some called it, "banana." It had a ragtop and real wooden steering wheel along with spoke wheels, all of which was very tough to keep clean.

He arrived at the car, took the dust cover off, and quickly put the top down for the drive back to his condo on Miami Beach. He was headed, after all, to the famous South Beach area. *Why not ride with the top down when you can,* Jake thought as he paid the attendant and waited for the red bar to rise. The only thing he needed to watch out for were pop-up showers that the city was known for. There were none this day, though, and the drive down 195 and across the bridge to the beach was fantastic, as usual. Reaching his building on Collins Avenue, Jake pulled to the gate and swiped his card, opening it up, allowing him access to his assigned parking spot below. After a short ride up the elevator to the fourteenth floor, he was home at last. Jake's neighbor was a retired navy admiral who was married to a retired marine. It got loud next door on Saturdays during football season, and Jake was always invited to watch the games on the big HD plasma they owned. Thankfully they were great neighbors and looked after Jake's cat, whose name, Dumb-Dumb, was quite appropriate. He retrieved the cat and decided to return some of the many e-mails which had arrived while he was in flight. One of those was from the office, saying that he needed to drop over and read his secure messages sent on SIPRNET, something he planned to do during the afternoon.

It wasn't a long drive from his condo to the Miami Field Office. ICE had shared some of the space with Coast Guard Miami for the last few years. It seemed that the Coast Guard needed a downtown office to maintain close contact with those agencies they worked hand in hand with. Also being close to SOUTHCOM (United States Southern Command), also headquartered in Miami, was a plus. Most of the ICE operation, however, was on the waterfront where CBP also did much of their work. Customs and Border Protection had a few different offices because of their responsibility with both air and sea movement of goods and people.

"Good afternoon," Jake said to his assistant Rosa as he walked into the office. "Did you miss me?"

"No," she said with that deadpan tone she was known for around the agency.

"Not a bit?" he asked sadly.

"No. It was peaceful. You've got SIPRNET traffic waiting over in the intel shop," she said without even a look his way. She knew it was all in good spirit the way they treated each other. The jokes she cracked about his lack of a love life, the Span-Asian comments he made because of her Hispanic upbringing and her marriage to a guy from Korea. It was all in good fun.

"I will mosey over there then," he said while making his way toward the hall door. He could only pick up this type of secure message a few doors down, in a special room with a high-tech combination lock on the door. Just like the secure meeting room Jake had just visited in Washington, this room had cubbyholes for cell phones to be left while visiting the "intel shop."

To gain access to this room or to talk to anyone inside, there was a doorbell on the outside. A camera saw who is at the door and, if cleared, buzzed into the room.

"I've got some sipper traffic," he said referring to the secure e-mail system called SIPRNET.

"Yes, sir," said the watch officer who looked all of fifteen and should have been playing video games, not taking in sensitive documents.

"Super," Jake said as he sat at the secure computer and put his government CAC into the slot on the side of the keyboard before entering his special pass code. For this session, he would be able to access the secure e-mails that had come in about various operations in his area of responsibility. Most of them today were rather routine. There were a couple of reports from the CBP air unit based at Homestead Air Reserve Base, about thirty miles south of Miami, about a boat full of Haitians that washed up on Key Largo just the night before. There was one, though, that caught his attention, titled "PRTC," meaning Puerto Rico Terror Collaborator and was from Colonel Felton.

//////TOP SECRET/////SIPRNET/////EYES ONLY//////

TO: J Stein
FR: Felton
SUBJ: PRTC

Jake . . .

Looks like your guy was back in SJ last week. CBP tracking has him in and out within a day. Business is Sellco, based in Islamabad, Pakistan, and Frankfurt, Germany. Abdul-Aziz Fahad is the TC, but nothing in last few years to connect with any orgs or cells. He makes about one trip every one or two months and doesn't do much business on the island. No surveillance at this time. Advise if you want to put a light on him.

TF

Jake wrote back and decided to wait until there might be more activity before "putting a light on him," which meant surveillance and stretching out the San Juan offices with more tasks than they already had. It did smell a little bit, seeing that this guy made frequent trips to the island and only stayed a day or so each time. However, Sellco did have at least two clients based in Puerto Rico, which made sense.

After going through the other messages, it was time for some lunch down the street at his favorite Cuban restaurant with a view of Biscayne Bay.

Tom Sundland knew what it was like to be a celebrity. In the seventies, on a hit television show called *Murder 101*, he played a tough Los Angeles homicide detective named Sam Primo. Back then, there were only three stations on any given TV set, and his show was a hit on the NBC television network. Before moving to Hollywood to start his television career, Tom had acted on Broadway, appearing as a chorus member in the musicals *Pippin* and *Godspell*. The move out west was not all that easy, and work was hard to come by at first. He did some bit parts here and there until signing with Gold Artists Agency, one of the big representation companies he hooked up with, thanks to a childhood friend who was one of their agents. After playing a cop in a CBS movie of the week, he was tagged for a supporting role in *Murder 101*, which ended up becoming a starring role when directors caught his talent for playing law enforcement officials.

After five successful years on *Murder 101*, his luck started to change, and not for the better. *Murder* was cancelled and Tom was typecast in the role of a cop. Cop shows were on the way out, and reality shows were on the way in. During his *Murder 101* run, he started drinking because of the long hours and the stress involved with being a high-profile celebrity living under a microscope. The drinking led to fooling around with cocaine, and by the end of the run, his lifestyle was taking its toll. After the show was cancelled, he was dropped by Gold Artists and ended up signing with a small agent in Orange County who was not well connected in the business.

Being a high-profile player during those years spoiled Tom. Just being able to walk into a restaurant where there was an hour-and-a-half wait and having a good table instantly tended to go to a guy's head. When a concert was sold out, that meant for the general public. Not for someone of Tom's stature. His agent simply picked up the phone and Tom had "all access" passes to the show and went backstage to meet the artist after. After a long day of shooting on Stage 64 at the Warner lot, autograph seekers would wait for him at the gated entrance for a few moments of his time. He always obliged, knowing it was the fans that made him. This lifestyle was expensive. An American

Express Black Card was in his wallet, and Tom used it to the tune of five to ten thousand dollars a month. Tom had not hired a business manager and was not very smart when it came to saving the thirty thousand dollars per-episode paycheck he commanded. In the seventies, contracts were different, and there were very few actors with deals that included residuals. Today those residuals would set even less successful actors for life as their shows ran on cable and around the world in reruns.

Tom Sundland's celebrity life was soon left behind as producers stopped calling and the money that was left dried up. The booze and the drugs took hold, and Tom Sundland faded from popularity and public view. He did a couple of commercials and tried to get another television gig, but the business was looking for something different, fresher and younger. After hitting rock bottom and blowing most of his money on drugs, Tom ended up at a cheaper public version of a Betty Ford-type rehab center and quit the drinking and drugs. It took a while to get his life back together after the stint in rehab while trying to find his place in the world.

Thanks to a friend, Tom ended up doing some work for an ad agency in Sherman Oaks, just outside of Los Angeles. Within the last few years, retro stars had been making a comeback in commercials and other venues. The cruise industry was one such business where some of the retro stars were brought on to do special shows and theme cruises. Tom was contacted by Star Caribe about doing a few theme cruises and reprising his old character. The ad job was good, but this was just what the doctor ordered. He could do both. Work for real money at the agency and do some moonlighting in show business. Well, sort of show business. Just having the taste and, frankly, the offer, was enough to give him new life. Miller Beer also contacted him through the agency he worked for, asking if he would appear in a series of commercials, to which he quickly agreed. Commercials and the new cruise gig put him back on the map, and this time, he was not going to let booze or drugs get in the way.

The first gig on Star Caribe would be a very different experience. All he had to do was meet and greet passengers and take part in this silly game of whodunit. Tom didn't even have to stay the whole week if he didn't want to. He could do the first three days, fly home from some port, and get the same pay, but staying the week meant a free, all-expenses paid vacation! Tom Sundland, a.k.a. Detective Sam Primo, was back.

Chapter 4

INTERVIEWS

THE WEATHER IN Providence can get real cold in the winter and hot in the summer. The thing about cold weather is that it can hold on in this part of the country for quite a while, like on this April day when the high was only going to be in the forties. Dino Tucci had to see a client about a couple of late payments. Late payments when you're dealing with a banker or car dealer or any other legit business meant that you would get some nasty mail or, at worst, phone calls in the middle of the night. Late payments to the Battelli family meant that you better come up with the dough or find a hiding place for a couple of decades.

Sly Morelli ran some numbers for the Battellis up on Federal Hill. He had a place right off Atwells Avenue, which doubled as a medical supply business. The medical supply business was actually rather successful, with the elderly needing wheelchairs, walkers, and the like. In the back, Sly ran the numbers and took bets on horse races, football games, basketball games, and pretty much anything else you could think of betting on. Sly was taking two points or 20 percent of the profit while kicking back eighty to the Battellis for the right to run the games and do business on the Hill. Lately though, Sly was coming up short. Dino knew what they were taking in because he had a stool working for Morelli, just to keep an eye on the inside. For the third month in a row, Sly returned just under 10 percent. Dino and his associate decided to pay Sly a visit and see what the situation was.

"Where the fuck is he?" Dino asked the kid at the front counter of the medical supply store.

"Sly?" the scared kid asked, knowing that his boss was in the back, counting the latest take.

"No, the fucking mayor," Dino's associate, Moe "the Dentist," said. Dino did not speak much to the underlings. Moe, on the other hand, spoke for Dino during these types of visits. Both Dino and Moe knew he was in the back and had one of their own crew out behind the shop in case Sly decided to make a quick exit. Sly knew better though. Both men ignored the kid up front and walked right into the back. Ironically the door to the back, which had a buzzer and lock, was cracked open.

"What the fuck, Sly?" Moe asked as they crashed through the door. The smell of an old bar hit them as they entered the back room. Beer and liquor spilled on the floor over the years had given it an odor of its own.

"Dino, Moe . . . ," Sly said, trying to stay calm while thinking of a good excuse to leave. "What are you two guys doing here?"

"What the fuck, Sly?" Moe asked again, this time more forcefully, knowing that Sly knew why they were there. "You're making six pounds a week and sending back a point or point and a half. That's not our agreement. Third week, Sly."

"I'm keeping 20 percent on four pounds. Where did you hear six pounds?" he asked while in the back of his mind wondering if he had a snitch in his small crew.

At this point Dino had not said a word. He let his associate do all the talking. Moe's nickname, "the Dentist," did not come from spending years at Tufts Medical School up the road in Boston. Moe liked to do tooth extractions with a pair of pliers on people who didn't cooperate with Dino or other members of the Battelli organization. He was a lieutenant and didn't get there by being nice.

Finally, Dino spoke. "What are we going to do, Sly? Once. Twice maybe, but three times? I gotta figure you're either stupid or your just holding some back to give us a bonus next Christmas."

"I'm telling you, Dino, I'm doing four pounds a week, and you are getting what we talked about," he said while keeping an eye on Moe, knowing that he was like a cobra and could strike at any time.

Moe took out a cigarette, lit it, and sucked in a whole bunch of smoke. Then he grabbed Sly by the throat and forced him against the pool table that was currently being used to count money and store a large pile of paperwork.

"You have twenty seconds to get this story straight, or you'll be needing one of those walkers you sell up front to get around with," Moe said after blowing smoke directly into Sly's face from a distance of about two inches.

"God, seriously, what the fuck?" Sly said, now shaking.

"Do you want to ask him yourself?" Dino said in a methodically calm voice. Dino never raised his voice too high. Raising his voice was bad for his blood pressure, according to his doctor.

Moe decided to put his cigarette out in Sly's left eye. The scream could be heard a block away and was enough to send the kid up front running out the door. Sly grabbed his eye and doubled over in pain. Moe asked the question again.

"Sly, do you want to go over those numbers again?" he asked while taking out another cigarette and began to light it. At this point Sly had one good eye and knew if he didn't come clean, he would be ether blind or dead.

"Okay . . . okay, in the table," Sly said, pointing to the pool table. The table looked like a usual pay-for-play barroom type, but was not. This one had a special hatch just below the center bottom of the table, and with a pull from Sly, the tabletop released and opened up, revealing a secret place to store money, guns, and drugs. There wasn't room for much in the space, but it was perfect for a quick hideaway which was used, in this case, to store the extra cash.

"Now that's better," Moe said while looking into the makeshift hole in the pool table crafted below the playing surface. "I think two pounds should do it."

Sly took out two thousand dollars in cash, or "two pounds," as it was known in the rackets, and handed it over to Dino.

Dino took the cash and, in a calm voice, told Sly he had one more chance to get the payments right or he would have more than a bad eye to deal with. Both men walked out of the store and into the street, where they headed to their white Tahoe parked next to an expired meter. They were casually discussing the latest spread on the upcoming Patriots game in Foxboro like nothing had just happened. Their third guy came around to the front of the building and got into the backseat. Dino had one more stop to make on the way back to the office to check on a piece of medical equipment that might be for sale.

The government of the Republic of Georgia was broke. People were out of work and pensions once promised by the government were not being paid. They didn't even have enough money to fuel their naval patrol, which guarded the once-posh Black Sea coastline and waterways. Out-of-work government employees turned to the same black market they once protected citizens against for money, just to survive. One such employee was Sergio Levta, a Bulgarian-born scientist who studied at the University of Moscow and in Rome, where he attended grad school for nuclear physics. Sergio was a patriot and still held a great deal of pride in the former USSR. In his heyday, he was one of the youngest members of the once hailed специальное оружие, or special weapons team. Handpicked by a professor at Moscow University who saw his talent for complicated electrial conversions, Sergio was mentored and given the funds to attend grad school in Italy by the state in return for service to the government upon completion.

Government service in the former Soviet Union came with perks. Better places to shop, a car, a two-bedroom flat outside Moscow and a pass to use the special lanes of traffic reserved for high officials and Party members were just a few. Life was good for this blond-haired kid from Varna, Bulgaria, who was smart and talented. Being selected for the special weapons team brought him access to some of the most sensitve details of the Soviet nuclear program, including deployment and storage of weapons. At the time, he didn't think much about that. It was just part of the job. Years later, when the Soviet system collapsed with the end of the Cold War, that knowledge would help him and his young family survive. With the loss of the government job and benefits, Sergio moved to Georgia, where he met and married a nurse he became friends with while trying to get his life back together, looking for engineering work. Her career, not his, brought the couple a better chance at income, but it was short lived. After a very complicated pregnancy, Rina was unable to work and had to take care of the couple's new baby. Sergio was left with one income, and it wasn't much. There were not many engineering jobs in Georgia during this tough economic time, so Sergio worked as an assistant manager at a hotel in the coastal town of Batumi, just north of the Turkish border.

He and Rina enjoyed the coastal lifestyle, but money was tight, and his former income was missed greatly. The hotel business brought him in contact with people traveling from different parts of the world, including Turkey, which was just a few kilometers away. This was where he first met Mohammad Featha, who, through contacts within Russia, kept track of where the former members of the special weapons team were living. Mohammad knew Sergio was living in Batumi and working at the Hotel Azuzi, a beachfront resort which catered to international guests who flocked to this part of the Republic of Georgia, knowing that their money went a lot further than back at home.

"Good afternoon, Mr. Levta," said a voice Sergio was familiar with from previous stays at the hotel. It was fifty-six-year-old Mohammad Featha, a Pakistani businessman who has been at the hotel two or three times in the past year or so. Featha was a balding, middle-aged, bearded man who enjoyed dressing in expensive suits when traveling on business. His Russian was a bit rusty but good enough to speak to this former scientist turned hotel assistant manager.

"Good afternoon," said Sergio in the typical tone a hotel employee would use to address a guest. "And how is your stay so far?"

"Very well, Sergio, thank you. I always have a fine stay here. How is your wife, Rina, feeling?" asked Mohammad, much to the surprise of Sergio, who gave him a strange look and took pause.

"She's better, thanks. Do you know my wife?" he asked, not knowing the connection and feeling a bit strange that this guy knew her name and that she had been ill.

"I know all about you, Sergio," Mohammad said in a much different, lower tone that made Sergio's hair stand up on the back of his neck. Was the Russian or Georgian government after him for some reason? Did he pay that parking ticket from a month ago? It seemed similar to the old days when political officers would be assigned to workers and workplaces, looking for anything that may be a negative influence on the state.

"You do?" Sergio asked in a suspicious tone, not knowing really what this was all about.

"I do, and I'd like to talk to you for a few minutes, if you don't mind," Mohammad said with a look in his eye that said to Sergio this was not a guy looking for a room upgrade or wanting to complain about the bed linens.

"Is everything all right with your stay?" the hotel assistant manager had to ask, given that this was his job, and he still had no idea what this guy wanted or why he knew so much about him.

"This is not about my stay. The hotel is fine. Reminds me of places I've stayed in Moscow and Rome, two places you should be familiar with after going to school for physics some years back," Mohammad said, now showing his hand, knowing that Sergio would be on guard with what he said and how he responded.

"Who are you?" asked Sergio in a much-changed, low, and nervous monotone.

"I am a businessman from Pakistan and represent a couple of tribes. We go around the world looking for support from organizations like Red Crescent and the World Health Organization and others," explained Mohammad.

"How do you know about my past?" Sergio asked, again in that low monotone, now very suspicious of what this encounter was about. He had been doing some dealing on the black market in small items people needed or wanted-things he could get through his hotel connections. None of the contacts he used to get his hands on things like televisions, computers, or cell phones knew much about his past. The very fact that he used to work for the Soviet government as a scientist in a past life would clearly scare them away.

"Like I said, I know all about you. I also know that you're making very little money here and do some work on the side with some friends at the port. But I'm not interested in a TV or DVD player. I'm interested in seeing that you, Rina, and Alexi live the lifestyle you are used to," said Mohammad. With that, Sergio knew this guy was in the intelligence business or something similar and did his homework, seeing that he knew the name of his child as well.

"Are you former KGB?" Sergio asked, figuring that the answer would be no. Most former KGB types were interested in bigger fish to fry and not the small black market in a tiny town in the Republic of Georgia.

"No, not KGB, CIA, MI6, or anything like that. Just a businessman looking after some tribes in Pakistan and a man with enough money to pay for the things I seek for my people," explained Mohammad.

"What can I possibly get for you that you can't get yourself?" Sergio inquired, not quite knowing what this whole conversation was about.

"I have but one question for you, Sergio, on this day," Mohammad stated. "I'll only ask this question once and never again. Would you like to have enough money to retire and live a very comfortable life someday?"

"Sure, we all would. That's why we do what we do. That's why we work and save and someday. Yeah, I would like to have enough to retire someplace nice," answered Sergio.

"What if someday were today?" Mohammad asked with a very serious tone.

"I don't know what you mean," said Sergio, looking for more answers and not getting any.

"What if you were able to walk away from here today with, say, three million U.S. dollars?" asked Mohammad calmly.

Sergio knew this was something serious and had a feeling there was something deeper here. He thought he might have an idea what this guy was looking for.

Both men were silent for what seemed like an hour, but it was actually only a minute or so. Finally, Mohammad spoke.

"On this day, that is my question for you, and after today, I will never be seen here again. You will never be asked this question again," explained Mohammad while sipping his tea as both men stood away from any other person who might be within listening range.

Sergio thought and spoke carefully, still not knowing what this was all about.

"Does this have to do with my former employer and what I used to do for a living?" he asked quietly.

"It does," Mohammad answered in a cold and matter-of-fact tone.

"What can I possibly do for you worth three million dollars?" Sergio questioned.

"You have knowledge of certain things, and we need access to that knowledge," explained Mohammad. "My clients are willing to pay you three million U.S. dollars for this information and will open an account at the RBS Bank in Zurich with your name on it. Only you would have access to the funds. What you do with the money is your business. Once our business is done, you will never hear from us again."

Sergio thought for a minute. Could this be a setup? Could this be dangerous? Then he asked, "What specific knowledge are you looking for?"

"Knowledge from your old job, contacts, locations, and other things," said Mohammad, knowing that, from the tone of Sergio's questions, he might be interested.

"For what use?" Sergio quizzed this stranger from Pakistan or wherever, not really knowing who he was working for. Obviously someone with enough money to make such an offer, he thought.

"Peaceful uses. Mostly to right a ship that's listing too far to one side. To create a balance on the world stage," explained Mohammad. "There are those who feel that we who represent one side of an argument or viewpoint don't have the equal power the other side possesses."

"Who do you represent?" Sergio asked.

"People ready to pay you three million U.S. dollars, but the question is open only today. Then I take the offer and disappear, never to be seen here or by you again," Mohammad spoke while taking another sip of the tea he brought from his room, now quite cold.

Sergio knew he had been done wrong by the former Soviet system. He knew his wife was struggling with their young son. He knew this job was one of necessity, and one that he actually hated. Sergio Levta had no real religious leanings. He had been born a Christian in Bulgaria, but that was only window dressing for this smart, former scientist. Three million dollars could give him and his family a new start, perhaps in America or someplace where the dollar was strong and the currency of choice. Canada would also be an option. So many thoughts rolled around in his head, and the man standing before him demanded an answer immediately. No time to think about it. No time to discuss with his beloved Rina. Just yes or no. He wasn't giving this guy a weapon, just information Sergio thought while looking around to make sure no one else was listening or watching. With anger from the past and an eye on the future, Sergio finally spoke.

"Nothing until the money is deposited in Zurich," Sergio demanded, having made up his mind.

"Then you will see me again, and we will do business," Mohammad said while raising his cup of tea. Then in an instant, he was gone. Nothing else was said. No instructions, nothing. Sergio went back to the front desk where a guest was complaining about the breakfast served this morning in the restaurant. Something inside Sergio felt good knowing that he might soon be the guest at hotels like this, and not the complaint taker.

Everyone has a boss, including Abdul-Aziz Fahad, who actually had two bosses: his boss at Sellco and the other boss back in Pakistan. Of the latter, he was connected on many levels, including spiritually. Passing as a tribal council member whose job it was to reach out to the world for support and money from those who shared their vision, cause, and religion, Mohammad Featha knew whom he needed to talk with to get things done. He often traveled internationally, asking for material or financial help for the villages he represented. Featha would also use those opportunities to meet with his special clients who did Allah's work around the globe. This time his trip took him to Frankfurt, Germany, where he would talk to the local Red Crescent rep and then have a quiet lunch with a longtime friend whom he mentored as a teenager and young man. Lunch was at a small local place called Zur Ziegelhutte, or Corner Steakhouse, about ten kilometers outside of Frankfurt, in a small town called Raunheim. The pub was noted for its lava rocks, which people would use to cook meat they ordered at their tables. The good thing about this place was that it was always crowded for lunch and the locals pretty much kept to themselves. Conversations stayed at the small booths and tables that made up the bar and dining area. Inside, it was dark and just the type of place Mohammad liked to take these special friends.

Abdul was right on time, knowing that Mohammad would follow about ten minutes later after watching the outside entrance from the safety of his car for any tails or suspicious-looking people entering the restaurant. Right on cue, the fifty-six-year-old, dark-skinned and gray haired but balding Mohammad Featha walked through the door, allowing a rush of the cold German climate to come blowing in with him. He looked over to the right, and through a layer of cigarette smoke, in the second booth, saw his friend Abdul, the software salesman.

"How are you my good friend?" said Mohammad as he took off his overcoat and sat in the booth.

"As-salaam alaikum," Abdul-Aziz Fahad said quietly.

"How was your journey?" asked Mohammad while picking up the menu and thinking of which good German food he would choose to enjoy.

"Fine, no problem. Great to be back here in Germany and to spend time with the office people and a couple of good clients in town," said Abdul as he too looked over the menu. A waiter appeared, and they both ordered a soft drink, knowing their religion did not allow tasting the fine German beers that surrounded them.

"We have made good progress, but we are still waiting on a couple of key components to come together," Mohammad said after the waiter walked out of earshot.

"Which are you waiting for?" asked Abdul.

"The CT scanner and, of course, the 'oven' itself, which, as you know, we will be taking possession of in the weeks ahead," he explained quietly.

That the "oven" was finally going to be in the hands of the faithful, as they were sometimes called, was a miracle itself. Mohammad's people would be getting into place to make the moves needed to secure the item thanks to the intelligence they would gain from their new associate Sergio in the Republic of Georgia. After that, it would be a simple but solid plan to move the "oven" on a two- to three-week voyage across the ocean to Puerto Rico in a shipping container. Mohammad knew it was risky, but he and the organization he represented were willing to take the chance for the payoff.

"My people will be in place when it arrives. We are seeing to that as we speak to get the right broker at the port," explained Abdul with all the confidence Mohammad wanted to hear in his tone.

"That is good news, my friend. You are a key part of the success of this entire venture," said Mohammad, purposely not calling it a mission or operation. He knew those were key words that computers across continents would ping on if they were being monitored.

Abdul was not new to this side of what he called a worldwide jihad against oppression and the disgusting excesses of the West. Just two years ago, he assisted in the intelligence gathering for the bombing of the British embassy in Johannesburg, South Africa, where 283 people were killed and over four hundred injured when his associates last took aim at the West. Ten years before, he and friends gathered around a radio in that small village a world away, in Afghanistan, listening to what amounted to a play by play of the attacks on the World Trade Center on a September evening in that part of the world eight-and-a-half time zones away from Ground Zero. It was then, with the mentorship of the man sitting across from him, that the calling deep inside led to this time and place.

"We are using the usual precautions when it comes to picking our associates, I assume," Mohammad asked, knowing the answer. It made him feel better to hear it again and again from the mouth of his soldier sitting across from him, nursing a Schweppes Bitter Lemon.

"I am," assured Abdul-Aziz Fahad in a low monotone. "Good soldiers dedicated to Allah."

"How do you find these places?" asked Mohammad, changing the subject every so often in case someone might be monitoring.

"This is a favorite of some of the software engineers I deal with. They took me here a few years ago. You must try the lamb. It is clean, and you cook it on the rock they'll bring to the table," explained Fahad.

"How big is the rock?" Mohammad asked, now intrigued by it all.

"Let's order, and I'll show you how it works," Fahad said while waving his hand to call a waitress who was dressed like the St. Paulie Girl on the beer label of the same name. She was classic German in every way, right down to the shoes, which were pointed at the toes.

"Two lamb dinners," ordered Abdul in fluent German. "We will have the garlic potatoes and *gulaschsuppe* as well."

"Gulaschsuppe?" Mohammad quizzed his associate in English.

"The best soup in Germany. It takes the cold away from the inside out," Fahad explained.

The waitress brought over two rocks of lava about eight inches square and warned the men not to touch them with their hands. Then she came back with a plate of uncooked lamb and asked each to pick out which he would like to eat. Both men used the tongs supplied on the table and picked a piece of meat and set it on the stone that was so hot, it immediately began to cook. Meat cooks fast on this type of hot surface, and clearly Mohammad was enjoying this new experience. When home, he liked to cook fresh meats and vegetables found in the markets of the villages he served.

"I will have to remember this place," said Mohammad as the two cooked their meat and sipped their soft drinks while the small pub quickly filled with patrons. The weather might have been cold outside this little place, but there was a warm feeling inside which the regular customers looked forward to all day.

After the food was eaten and the drinks just about gone, it was time to head out after paying the waitress who added up each man's check. Each waitress wore an apron with a cash/change purse tucked inside so that they could take care of the charges right at the table. For credit cards, the waitress would have to return to the bar and use the card scanner, but not for these two. They paid with cash and quickly dismissed her.

"We will talk soon," said Abdul as the two donned their winter jackets and headed outside into the cold German night. Cars were parked up and down the street because the only parking was in front of the pub, and there were only a few spaces.

"We will indeed. Safe travels, peace be upon you," said Mohammad who then walked a few cars down to the rented Audi sitting with one wheel up on the sidewalk, got in, and quickly pulled away.

Abdul-Aziz Fahad did the same in his Volkswagen diesel, pleased knowing that their venture was indeed moving forward.

Chapter 5

CONNECTIONS

F RANK CASTRO KNEW that Dino could get his hands on just about anything. So when he asked him about buying a CT scanner and something called radiopharmaceuticals, he knew Dino might be able to deliver, especially when it came to cash purchases. He texted Dino that he'd be at the Old Canteen around 9:00 p.m. on Federal Hill, where they liked to hang out sometimes after a long day at work. Dino was already in the bar when Frank came in from the cold Rhode Island night, hoping for some positive answers.

"Over here," Dino said when he saw Frank coming through the door. "What are you drinking?" he asked as Frank walked toward him.

"Johnnie Walker Black and water," Frank told the bartender who clearly was at Dino's service. Even if there were a hundred people waiting in line for a drink, Dino would not have to wait. The bartender knew Dino's status in the family, as did the managers, and service was what he got.

"Long day," sighed a tired Frank.

"Same," said Dino as the two sipped their drinks and enjoyed a few minutes away from work and the pressures of life.

"The Sox suck," Frank told Dino in a very matter-of-fact way.

"Yup," agreed Dino. "They pretty much do."

"No, they really suck," Frank said again with disgust in his every word. "I might even become a Yankee fan."

"Now that's desperate," Dino chuckled while taking another sip of his scotch and water.

"By the way, did you have any luck on the medical stuff we talked about?" asked Frank quietly.

"Yeah, I can get you a rebuilt CT scanner, no problem, but it's not cheap. The other stuff, what did you call it?"

"F-18. Fluorine," Frank said even more quietly.

"That's right, it did sound like a fighter plane or something like that. I've got it written down in the Tahoe. That might take an extra couple of days, but I can get some of it. Expensive though. Bring your wallet," Dino cautioned.

"My clients are using it to help patients who can't get the testing they need overseas and are willing to pay and have it shipped."

"The other one, 'TI' or something like that, is also possible, and I'll know more by the end of the week," explained Dino as the two sat together watching the Red Sox game up on the screen over the bar.

"Just let me know," Frank said casually, hoping to keep this as low key as possible. He was asking Dino to procure two well-known radiopharmaceuticals. F-18 or Fluorine-18 and Thallium-201, better known in the medical world as TI-201. Both were radioisotopes. Both were radioactive. And both were perfect for what he and his associates wanted to use it for.

"How's thing at the port?" asked Dino, changing the subject.

"Good, but tough to keep people focused," said Frank. "The unions can be ball busters."

"That's why they're unions. I know some of those folks, so let me know if you have any real trouble," offered Dino while making eye contact with the bartender and pointing to his almost dry drink.

"We've got it under control, but thanks," said Frank. "How's your business?"

"My problem is getting people to pay on time," Dino said.

"We all know that story," Frank said, empathizing with his friend.

"I'm tired of bullshit stories and having to chase people around town for what they know is due," Dino said now starting to feel the effects of the twelve-year-old Johnnie Walker in his glass.

Frank knew how Dino collected on his debts and knew a lot more about him than Dino would imagine or would ever know he knew. His intelligence people back in Pakistan had quite a book on Dino and his family's business. It was for this reason Frank made the connection and reached out after taking months to befriend him and gain his trust.

"It all works out in the end," Frank assured his drinking buddy. "One day at a time."

"You said it," Dino sighed as he pulled out a fine Cuban Montecristo cigar and lit it up almost in the same motion.

His phone chimed with a text he quickly dismissed, knowing that one of his crew was successful on a debt collection.

The Red Sox continued to play ball on the TV screen above them while Frank continued to play ball with a member of one of the strongest organized crime families in America.

The *Star Orion*, with a staff of 1,250 people, was a 154-thousand-ton floating resort which carried a maximum of 3,400 passengers each week on their dream cruise to the Caribe. For the people who worked on the ship, "turnaround day" was the busiest of the week. That was the day that the ship off-loaded passengers in the morning and onloaded a fresh new set of faces through the afternoon before setting sail again at 4:30 p.m. During turnaround day, beds needed to be stripped, windows cleaned, cabins refreshed, provisions restocked, and what seemed like a million things to get done while docked at her home port of Miami.

Some of the crew had the opportunity to spend a few hours off the ship if their work was done and they had shore leave. Crew members rotated turnaround day with their crewmates so that that they could alternate time off the ship to take care of shopping, dental appointments, and other errands. Usually it ended up being once per month for each crew member of the environmental team.

Imad Patel's turn was today, and he quickly finished his half day of work, which had started at 5:00 a.m., so that by 9:30 a.m. he was off the ship and headed for some shopping at the Bayside Marketplace on Biscayne Boulevard, just a few miles from the cruise terminal. Bayside was a busy place, especially on a Saturday. Filled with restaurants, shops, and entertainment, locals and tourists alike flocked to the waterfront venue.

Imad was a baseball fan and enjoyed wearing his minor league caps when off duty and off the ship. The Riverdogs hat was unique in that not too many people in this part of the country recognized the logo or the team. The Charleston Riverdogs are the single "A" farm team of the New York Yankees based in Charleston, South Carolina. Their logo is a dog holding a broken bat in his mouth, and Imad picked it up from a hat store during previous visits to Bayside. Imad had a number of different minor league baseball caps that he collected and kept in his cabin on the ship. Other crew members would playfully kid him that he never made it to the majors and had to settle on the minor leagues. Imad would laugh it off, knowing they were kidding and also knowing the real reason he would wear these hats off the ship.

Bayside Marketplace housed a number of different shops including the Hat Shack on level 1, where Imad would usually stop by to see if they had any new minor league or unique hats delivered since his last visit. The place was small, but usually busy with shoppers either looking or buying. In addition to hats, they had other sports gear customers could check out and even try on if necessary before buying.

Hamid Khalid was also a frequent shopper at Bayside. He was making his way through the first level and stopped into the Hat Shack to check out some of the new University of Miami gear he saw in the window. Deep down, he thought American football was a foolish sport and a waste of the human body's strength. But for this operation, he played the fan well, sporting a Miami Hurricanes hat and looking at the different sizes of the new jerseys. The very fact that he was wearing a hat was an important signal to Imad. It told him that he had a message and that message would be left in one of a few usual spots. The fact that Imad was wearing his Riverdogs hat was also a signal to Hamid that he also had information to pass.

Imad picked out a Miami Heat basketball T-shirt, started looking at it and browsing sizes. At the very same time, Hamid picked out a Hurricanes jersey and asked to try it on. The Hat Shack only had one dressing room, and the young college student behind the counter gave him the key. Inside, Hamid did a quick scan for cameras or listening devices, knowing the exercise would be a moot point, but out of caution and training, he did it anyway. The dressing room was small and had an old wooden bench where people could sit while trying on clothes. He reached into his pocket, removed a small piece of paper with tape on it, and stuck it to the bottom of the bench. Hamid had very little time and didn't want the clerk or other customers to get worried that he was still inside. After double-checking that the note was well placed and properly stuck, he gathered up his belongings and returned to the counter where Imad was standing waiting to use the same dressing room to try on his jersey. He took the key from Hamid and proceeded to the dressing room, where he quickly closed the door and felt under the bench for the note he knew would be there. He retrieved the note, opened it, and read its contents. It was a simple sentence: "Lunch will be delivered, what do you want to eat?" Imad quickly wrote one sentence in reply. "We'll need eight sandwiches and extra fries to go with them. Ready in the cafeteria when the food is ready." After that, he stuck the note back to the bottom of the bench and left the dressing room, knowing that Hamid would need to use it again to try on a different shirt. After handing the key to Hamid and buying his jersey, Imad left the store and continued his shopping with a stop for some real lunch at Hooters, a favorite American restaurant, which in his country would be forbidden. Hamid finished trying on his T-shirt, returned the key and bought the item using cash. The college student at the cash register finished the transaction and bagged the shirt while thinking that he mostly got credit cards and this was the second cash sale in a row.

The eight sandwiches were code for AR-15 assault rifles and the fries were code for ammunition. The fact that they were ready in the cafeteria was code that his people were in place on the ship and they were ready whenever their leader was. There were a few more steps and items that needed to be in place first before the sandwiches and fries would be delivered to the *Star Orion*. Hamid headed for home and later burned the note as he built a charcoal fire to cook some dinner on the deck of his waterfront apartment in Dade County.

Rosa Lee always arrived at the office before her boss to get an early start on the day and before things could go out of control. Jake Stein was not a morning person. Early in his career with Customs and Border Protection, he was on the night shift working eleven to seven in ports such as Jacksonville, Norfolk, and Miami. As he made his way up the ladder in management, he had to adjust to working days, but he never really did. He would wander in around 9:00 a.m., knowing the world could catch him anytime on his new iPhone along with his government-issued BlackBerry. Rosa was working on the overnight e-mails and any notes from the field office in San Juan, which was still Jake's responsibility until a new special agent in charge was named.

Next door the intel folks were finishing up their morning message traffic and received a message for Jake from Col. Tim Felton in D.C. about one of the people they were keeping an eye on.

//////TOP SECRET/////SIPRNET/////EYES ONLY//////

TO: J Stein
FR: Felton
SUBJ: PRTC

Jake . . .

    Abdul-Aziz Fahad showed up in Frankfurt. Sellco has clients and office in Germany, and this is his third trip this year. Spent three days and departed via Lufthansa flt 202 to Sofia. No other contact.

TF

The intelligence watch officer put the message in a standard "Top Secret" marked government envelope and left it on Jake's desk. Also on his desk were travel vouchers that were returned from his last trip to Washington. The Department of Homeland Security, like other government agencies, had changed the way they did their expense reports and travel vouchers from traditional paper to electronic. This was progress, according to the e-mails that went out with instructions on how to file, but Jake and everyone else knew that "progress" came with speed bumps, and having these forms kicked back was starting to become "SOP," or standard operating practice. This would be one of his tasks today along with his actual immigration and customs enforcement duties. Of these, Jake would be checking up on some companies with histories of hiring illegal aliens and paying those resident aliens less than minimum wage. Then he'd follow up on any Homeland Security Investigation issues that might have come up.

"Good morning, Rosa," Jake said as he came into the office overlooking the turquoise waters of Biscayne Bay. This was one of the perks of working in the Miami office. Another was the weather and the fact that everyone wanted to visit, especially in the wintertime.

"Good morning, Jake. You've got a meeting later on with Miami-Dade after lunch. It's the one you wanted me to reschedule, and it's at one thirty," she said while fixing his morning coffee. He insisted early on that she not get coffee for him. He wanted an assistant and not a servant in his secretary, but Rosa was a traditionalist and made the best coffee this side of Colombia, so it was hard to argue with her. The homemade muffins she brought in every once in a while didn't hurt either.

"Can I reschedule it?"

"No," she said sternly. "You've rescheduled it twice. Captain Lopez is going to think that you just don't like her."

"I just don't like her," said Jake in a quick, monotone response. "She just gives me the creeps for some reason. Always in your face."

Rosa thought about that response and really had not much to say. She knew all too well that Capt. Monica Lopez of the Metro Dade police force was what some people in decades past would have called a "pushy broad."

"It's your job," said Rosa, knowing that Jake was making a face in the other room while going over the morning folders.

He opened the SIPRNET envelope and read the dispatch from his boss in D.C. Frankfurt, he thought after he read the text. Frankfurt was a logical place for a software salesman to try to recruit new business. But why Sophia? Bulgaria was still trying to come into the mainstream world of Western European business while still being a former Eastern-bloc Soviet puppet state. His gut feeling was to maybe look at this guy a little more closely, but his schedule and main duties with immigration enforcement said no.

"I'm headed to see Lopez and will be on the cell," Jake said as he headed for the elevator to access the parking deck where he had a reserved space.

It was a short ride over to the Metro Dade police headquarters where he was to meet up with Lopez and go over the latest immigration list and "border busters," as they were known. These border busters came by sea and air unlike the ones his friends out west in El Paso and Arizona dealt with daily, who hiked through the desert. Both groups literally risked their lives to make it into the United States. Sometimes he thought they should be given medals for making and surviving the trek rather than being arrested and sent back to where they came from. But that was not his problem. His problem was the stream of folks coming from Haiti, Cuba, and other islands by boat, container, air, and any other way they could make it to the shores of South Florida. Legally if they came by boat and make it to the States, they could stay. If they were intercepted, they were arrested and deported. Some just jumped overboard and drowned themselves as CBP and Coast Guard boats approached rather than having to face returning to a life of hell. Others who tried to smuggle drugs were arrested and spent years in U.S. prisons. Even that, he thought, might be better than the life they had.

Jake pulled his convertible into the parking lot and showed his ID to the gate guard. They never had gates or guards before 9/11, but indeed the world had changed. The guard quickly waved him in, and he parked, got out, and walked a few feet to the door, where he again showed his credentials to the officer at the desk, who called Captain Lopez to announce her visitor. He knew where to go and took a quick elevator ride up to the third floor where Metro Dade SO (Special Operations) had their offices. The elevator doors opened, and he knew right where to find Lopez. Her small office was just a few doors from the bank of elevators, and she shared an assistant whose job it was to support three of the special operations officers.

"She's expecting you," said the civilian assistant. Jake noticed she was rather cute and would have loved to take out to dinner but would never ask because of her boss. This girl, like her boss, never held back her words. "She hates you, you know."

"I know," he said walking by headed to the office.

"You've got a hell of a nerve," said Captain Lopez, not waiting a second to give him shit about something.

"We're on a budget, Monica, and I wear a lot of hats."

"Maybe you can find one small enough to fit your brain," she said under her breath.

"Do you think I can't hear that, or are you just wanting me to think you're a bigger asshole than I already do?"

"Just give me the respect I deserve, and don't blow me off."

"I'm glad we're off to such a great start."

"We got no credit for the organ donor raid in the papers. I nail one of the bad guys myself and not a word about me or my people."

Jake did feel that the press coverage was a little one sided. "I agree Monica, but I can't control the press."

"So what I have for you now are the six illegals I called and left messages about. We found this bunch coming on shore at Cape Florida," she explained.

Cape Florida is a park at the end of Key Biscayne, where locals come to fish and swim. There are actually houses on stilts sitting just offshore. It was not a place were illegal immigrants usually came ashore. They usually landed their makeshift boats on one of the keys and only occasionally on the mainland.

"They landed first at the house of Skip Reid which, as you well know, sits on stilts just off the end of the island," she said knowing that Jake was familiar with Reid, a well-known car dealer in South Florida. He owned one of those houses up on sticks, as the ICE folks knew them. They are about a half a mile or so off Key Biscayne and Cape Florida and required a boat to get to them.

"We picked them up after Reid's housekeeper called and said they tied up to the dock at the house," Lopez said. "That's not technically reaching land, but that's your business, not mine."

"I'm glad you noticed that," he said sarcastically. "You're right. They go back. They should have landed at the Cape instead."

"Are you sure?" she asked.

"Am I sure? Yes, I'm sure! You just said it was my business, not yours. If those houses were considered part of the mainland, we'd have a steady stream of makeshift boats lined up to dock there," Jake sneered.

She ignored his tone. "Are you going to transport?"

"Yup, I'll send a team over, and we'll take it from there," Jake said.

"What about the port situation?"

"What about it?" he asked.

"I don't have the manpower to be at all places at all times. I'm limiting my personnel out there. It's your business anyway," she snarled.

"They're using rent-a-cops at the gates, and retired people are directing traffic. I need your people's trained eyes when we're working turnaround days," he said, trying to make his case to keep the number of Metro Dade special ops officers the same at one of the country's busiest cruise terminals.

"Three and three," she said with the tone that it was not up for negotiation.

"Are you kidding me?"

"Three and three. Anything else today?" she asked in a dismissive tone.

Three and three meant that there would only be three officers for the morning shift and three for the afternoon shift, and that was it. The rest of the security would be what they commonly call "rent-a-cops" or private security personnel who had little or no training in actual law enforcement.

"Plus traffic?"

"Traffic is not me, but downstairs says those officers will be there as usual. I'm special ops, remember?"

"Fine."

"Have a nice day, Agent Stein," she said, knowing that there was not much he could do about how she staffed her special operations. Port security was considered a special operation.

"Goodbye, Monica," he said. "Love you too."

Jake made his way back down to his car and quickly headed out of the parking lot toward U.S. Route 1 south and Coconut Grove, where his father lived in an upscale retirement community with assisted-living nurses checking on him three times a week. One of the reasons Jake wanted the Miami assignment in the first place was to be near his dad, who had just turned eighty. That way he could work and keep a close eye on him. It was tough because his father, Joshua, was an old-school New York Jew. He retired to Miami with enough money to keep him going for years, but he also had some medical issues eating up some of the cash, which he highly resented. Jake was glad to drop by but knew that the conversation was usually not a pleasant one, and his father was cranky about pretty much everything. Jake could buy him a gold Rolex watch, not that he could afford it on his government salary, but knew that his father would somehow find something negative to say about it. The elder Mr. Stein had lost his filter long ago for the words that came out of his mouth, tending to make even family members shy away from spending much time with him.

He pulled into the residential complex and made his way to his father's unit. It was a cute mini-apartment with a small kitchen, bedroom, and living area. Not huge, but perfect for the single, elderly person who may need some additional assistance. Throughout the apartment were call buttons used to bring an immediate response if he were to fall or have a medical problem. Jake's dad had been married four times, but after the last expensive divorce, lost his taste for the institution of marriage.

"Hi, Dad," Jake said while knocking on the door. He had his own key but waited for a response.

"I'm in the can," came the voice of Joshua, who was clearly agitated about something. *Imagine that,* Jake thought, walking though the doorway and into the small unit that had a smell of mothballs.

"I brought you the *Sports Illustrated* college football special edition."

"Clemson is going to suck this year," the elder Stein said to his son as he emerged from the bathroom.

"You can read all about it in here," Jake said while putting down the magazine. "How are you feeling?"

"My knees are a hundred fucking years old, and that gout medicine makes me pee three times an hour."

"You've got to keep taking it or the pain will come back."

"Yeah, yeah, I know," he snarled back.

"You want to go to have some lunch?" asked Jake.

"No. I'm not hungry, thanks to those pills."

"Those pills keep you out of pain, and you've got to eat, so let's grab some lunch down the road," the good son said.

"I'll take a ride, but I won't eat much. You still driving that kiddy car?"

"Classic car, but yes."

"How's that job? You locking up all those spics trying to milk this country dry?" Unlike many of his friends back in Brooklyn, Joshua Stein had become a true conservative, and when sports was not on his television, Fox News Channel was.

"It's all good, Dad. I'm keeping our country safe."

Agent Stein and his sister, Lila, split the duties looking after their father. Lila lived about an hour up the road in Broward County and was married with two kids of her own. Joshua was proud of his grandkids because they excelled at sports, and going to their school games was something that he actually enjoyed, though some of his sideline commentary was known to be less than diplomatic.

The two headed out for a quick lunch before Jake had to be back at the office to assign a couple of ICE agents to go pick up the bunch at the Metro Dade lockup and take them for deportation processing.

Chapter 6

BLUEPRINTS

THE JOB MARKET, like in the rest of the country, was tight in Miami and Dade County, but good help was sometimes still hard to find. Once a manager found decent employees, it was good business to keep them happy, knowing they would keep the business moving. Amanda Curtis knew this all too well as she and her family struggled through a tough economy in which bedding and furniture were far down on the list things people would spend their money on. Putting food on the table was high priority. Buying a couch or new bed was not. Good salespeople were always hard to find. The good ones moved up and onto bigger jobs. The poor performers moved on or changed careers. Sales staff have to hustle to make a buck when money is so tight.

Amanda had three top-notch salespeople working for her at Metro Miami Furniture & Bedding, and she knew how lucky she was to have them. They made 6 percent commission on furniture and 7 percent on bedding. They also helped in the shipping department every once in a while when things got busy. Hamid Khalid grew up in the furniture business, and his family was living up in North Carolina. His Tar Heel roots taught him well; after all, it was the furniture capital of the country. Amanda first met him when he walked in and applied for a job in sales, which, at the time, was not available. Hamid was persistent and would come back to check in with Amanda quite often. Her gut feelings were that this guy would be good in sales. When her top sales rep decided to move back to California to be closer to family, there was an opening. The very first application she went to find was Hamid's. Thankfully for Amanda, he was just working part-time at another bedding company when she called and offered him the full-time sales position with Metro Miami Furniture & Bedding. He immediately accepted the offer and quickly proved himself to be a very good sales professional. His language skills didn't hurt either. He was fluent in English, Spanish, and even Arabic. Amanda thought it was fascinating that he grew up in Turkey, moved to North Carolina as a teen, and learned English so fast. With his family background in furniture, he learned quickly and decided to move south where the weather was warmer. As he wrote up yet another order for a dining room set, Amanda thought that Hamid was indeed a find.

Hamid did grow up in Turkey but never actually lived in North Carolina for more than a month. He moved there on a student visa to attend the University of North Carolina and decided to transfer to Florida International University in Miami to study business. Business to Hamid, however, had nothing to do with profit and loss. His business was one that was never talked about in public, and then only to his partners working on the cruise ship. He also had another associate in Rhode Island with crucial mob connections. Hamid planned to use these to get the things needed to carry out their mission.

"Hamid, great job on the dining room," Amanda said, thinking, once again, just how lucky she was to have this go-getter.

"Thank you, Amanda. We are going to try to move those two leftover couches from last year. A Blue Cross contact said they might be interested for their new lobby in Fort Lauderdale," he said with the confidence of a seasoned sales pro.

"Fantastic!"

Hamid was looking over some of the cruise ship bids that Amanda was working on. Typically each cruise line bid monthly on new bedding for the different ships in their fleet, which called Miami or Port Everglades in Ft. Lauderdale home port. She usually won the bids consisting of a different number of box springs and mattresses each month. They were specially designed beds for the ships, and Amanda had to purchase them from approved manufacturers. Some months they would have only one or two or none. Other months they would fill orders for fifteen or twenty. Those were the months Amanda liked best. She had to sell them to the cruise lines at only 2 percent above her cost, but because of the numbers of units the customers bought every year and the fact that it was guaranteed business, she was glad to get the 2 percent. Hamid's associates who worked on the **Star Orion** would see to it that on the designated sailing they chose, the order would be for at least six to eight box springs and mattresses. Those would be special deliveries that Hamid would see to himself.

Sergio Levta knew that what he had put in motion, he could never return from. His original contact with the man named Mohammad Featha had only been a few weeks earlier, and then just when Sergio started to think nothing was going to happen, a man approached him at the hotel with a routine billing question. During the conversation, though, the man handed Sergio what looked like his bill, but it was actually a nearly identical document with only a few slight changes. This paper had Sergio's name on it and under "hotel services," a long string of numbers and the letters RBS next to them. Sergio's address in the upper right was not his address at all. It was an address in Zurich, Switzerland. The man told Sergio that the address was for the Royal Bank of Scotland in Zurich and that the number was for an account containing 1.5 million U.S. dollars. Only Sergio was authorized to access the account. There was actually a bank card also attached which he could use to draw off the funds. The instructions though, were not written down. They were quietly and simply spoken between the two men. Once he accepted this, Sergio would be contacted within the next seven days with details on how to deliver his side of the bargain.

It didn't take seven days though. A day or so later, he was approached once again at the hotel by the same guest and told to meet a friend named Boris at the pub just a few doors down after work for a vodka. That was the longest afternoon of Sergio's life, knowing that he would soon have to deliver what he promised. It wasn't the fact that he would be betraying his former country that bothered him. They screwed him out of a life he thought he earned, and he couldn't care less about national pride. After all, the Soviet Union didn't even exist anymore. He wasn't bothered that it was a nuclear device that he was helping someone or some group to acquire. What they did with it after they got it was their business. Perhaps the guy was telling the truth, and they only wanted it to even up the sides. It was the fact that they knew him, his family, and that different people he had never met approached him and were fully aware of his education and experience. This made him feel some hesitation. Bottom line, he thought as he wrapped up work for the day, he would be free of this job, and his family would be set for life. That was worth the risk.

He left the hotel around 5:30 p.m. and headed to the pub just a few steps away. Ironically, he stopped here a couple of times a week for a beer or vodka before heading home. This time it was business. He wondered again if they picked this place given the fact he came in from time to time. Up the stairs and into the pub he went while saying hello to a friend going in the other direction who delivered mail for the state. The Chalice Pub was once a church and had turned into what would be the complete opposite to what any religion was all about. There was smoking, drinking, and some under-the-table gambling. Sergio took a seat at the bar and ordered a Stoli on the rocks. He figured he would not have to wait long. He was wrong. Two drinks and an hour and ten minutes later, the bartender asked him if he wanted another drink. Sergio said no thanks. The bartender said this one would be on the man sitting at the table in the corner. Sergio looked over and saw a man sitting reading a newspaper who waved hello like he knew him. It was the same guy who had approached him with the bank account information back at the hotel. Clearly he wanted him to come over. Sergio took his drink and moved to the table with the yet-to-be-named man he didn't recognize except for the hotel encounter.

"Have a seat, Sergio," said the man.

"Thanks for the drink."

"Compliments of our friend, Mr. Featha, who also thanks you for your cooperation. My name is Boris."

Sergio raised his glass, and they drank.

"What's next?" asked Sergio, who couldn't help but think someone was watching them. Actually they were pretty much alone except for a few of people at the bar and one couple near the door. Sergio was still a little paranoid.

"You tell me," Boris said nonchalantly, shrugging his shoulders.

"It's not all that complicated, really. There is a storage facility just outside Moscow where the weapons are kept. I know how the security works and what layers need to be neutralized," explained Sergio.

"We don't use that term. Let's just call it a package. We don't ever talk on the phone or cells. We don't use Skype, Facebook, or Twitter," Boris lectured his new contact.

"I understand."

Boris continued, "We talk only in person. We travel together. We don't talk about business to any outsiders, including your dear Rina. I am in the tour business and also help in the shipping business."

"Fine."

"Moscow? Not Kazakhstan?" Boris asked sounding truly surprised.

"Moscow," said Sergio. "In the former Soviet Union, the leadership, especially senior party officials, were paranoid bastards. They thought the peasants would storm the Kremlin and kill them all. Yes, they had nuclear weapons on missiles pointed at the United States, England, China, and India. They also kept a very small supply of tactical nukes close enough to use on their own people if necessary."

Boris seemed genuinely surprised at this revelation. In the back of his mind, he was thinking of the logistics of getting the "oven" from Moscow back to Georgia and onto a ship for Puerto Rico or Nassau, depending on which would work best. But that was something to worry about another day with other people.

"Then we go to Moscow," Boris stated.

"We go to Moscow," Sergio said, wondering what excuse he would give his wife. Probably that it would be on business to look at other hotel operations.

He had traveled twice before for the hotel to look at booking systems and restaurant operations at sister properties. He would also lie that he was set to receive a giant bonus for developing a new system for the hotel group . . . a system which saved his company a lot of money.

"I need at least a month's notice before we go to Moscow," Boris explained.

"Fine."

"I will confer with my associates, and we will meet back here for a drink at the same time in one month," Boris said.

"Do you have a last name?" Sergio asked still curious about the man sitting across from him as smoke started to drift their way from the cigarette of another customer.

"Just Boris for now. It's better that way," he said as he raised his glass in a toast.

Sergio raised his as well, took a drink, and left the table and pub to go home to see his wife, Rina, who would soon be changing lifestyles.

Miami is one of those cities that people really never forget after a first visit. It's like the tropics meet New York City or Las Vegas. From the famous landmark hotels of South Beach to the suburbs of Dade County, Miami has something for just about everyone and every lifestyle. The ambience hits as soon as people land at Miami International Airport and see the swaying palm trees and feel the humidity of the tropics as soon as they walk out the door. The energy of the city flows all around and can be easily seen in the neon signs and trademark bright tropical hues of pink, white, and blue and felt in the salsa music played on the streets. Even the taller city buildings have glowing neon highlighting them at night.

There was a time when Miami was falling on hard times. The classic old hotels were falling apart, and few wanted to visit or invest money. Thanks to television shows like *Miami Vice* in the eighties and *CSI Miami* along with a slew of other movies and a booming tourism industry, the city had made a remarkable comeback. The cruise industry is one part of that comeback. Business grew along with the size of the ships and number of passengers served each year. Miami was the perfect port to base the new megaships with easy ocean access and close proximity to the Bahamas and Caribe for weekly turnarounds. This was why the State of Florida devoted so much money and infrastructure to the Port of Miami.

Oddly enough, Tom Sundland had never visited the city during his run as a successful actor in a television drama. He knew a few of the actors from *Miami Vice* and used to hang out with Don Johnson every once in a while when Johnson was home on break from filming *Vice*. Excited about his first gig on the *Star Orion*, Tom decided to fly in a couple of days early and see the town. The good news was that the cruise line paid him for the day before and the day after each sailing he was working. With that and a few extra dollars of his own, Tom decided to splurge and booked himself at the National Hotel. The National is one of the famous South Beach places celebrities of the past used to hang out. Today it's a trendy place to stay on the beach for those with money to spend. The signature pool at the National is very long and only a few feet wide. Sort of like a rectangle which runs from the back of the hotel out to the beach. It's where chic upstarts like to lounge before starting a big night on the town. Tom's gay lifestyle was always a closely guarded secret. He had managed to keep details of his personal life to himself and told only a few chosen people. South Beach catered to all lifestyles, all the time. He liked this trip already.

Two days at the National were fantastic for Tom. Two people actually recognized him from his old series playing Sam Primo on *Murder 101*. They were a married couple, but Tom still counted it as two anyway. At this point, he was happy to be recognized at all. He checked out of the National on Saturday morning and took a taxi to the Port of Miami for his first gig on the cruise ship. He was a little nervous not knowing exactly what to expect and had a few butterflies in his stomach. The ride to the port only took about ten minutes because it was located just across the bridge from South Beach. The taxi dropped him and his one piece of luggage off at the Star Caribe passenger terminal that was buzzing with activity, seeing that it was the *Star Orion* turnaround day. He picked up his bag, tipped the driver, and went to the door of the terminal where uniformed security agents were checking tickets and confirmation numbers.

Tom's documents were different than typical passenger tickets. He was a "contract player" and was given a stateroom with small balcony and a temporary ID, allowing him access to the ship's employee deck. The older security guard asked him for his ID and clearly did not recognize him from TV or film. She had to be in her sixties and was probably a part-time employee working to stay busy and to get a discount on cruises for her family.

"Through the metal detectors inside the door and up the escalators to the agents at the counters," she said with a dismissive tone. He hoped that all Star Caribe employees weren't this crass. In a minute he would find out that they were not. Once he went through the metal detectors and up to the next floor, he was told to go direct to the boarding ramp and show his paperwork to the agent. That agent was everything he thought a cruise employee would be. Helpful, friendly, and excited he was here.

"You will have to get a temporary ID down on deck 1 or back out in the lobby. I will take you down there myself. Welcome to the Star Caribe family," the agent said. He was told that a ship's employee representative would be at the terminal to meet him, but he had not seen anyone so far fitting that description in the large airportlike terminal.

"Sounds good. Thanks for helping me out."

The agent escorted Tom past the security people who were standing at kiosks, checking each passenger onto the ship by taking his or her picture and swiping an individual Ocean Pass cruise card which would act as room key, credit card, and identification for the week ahead.

"How long are you with us?" asked the agent named Angel from Orlando. The crew all wore name tags with the state or country they came from. Most of the names he saw so far were from faraway places like Turkey and India.

"A week this time, but I've got a contract for six full weeks between now and the first of the year," said Tom as they made their way into the shining brass-and-glass elevator. This was his first time on a cruise ship, and he was stunned at the size and beauty of the entrance. He looked up at the transparent elevators and giant glass atrium, forgetting for a moment that he was actually boarding a ship.

"We're going down to I-95 which is on deck 1. You have to have a crew card to go down there on the elevators or take the aft stairwell. Yours will allow you to do this once you get it," Angel said as she inserted her card into the elevator's card reader below all the buttons. I-95 was the nickname the crew gave to the main employee passageway running from one end of the ship to the other on the first deck. This was the deck with crew staterooms, a hospital, a medical storage facility, crew dining facilities, crew lounges, food storage lockers, a wine cellar, and much more. There was even a brig, an oceangoing jail. It was truly the backstage of the cruise ship. The deck's floor actually had the classic "Interstate 95" road trippers would see on American highway signs. Once off the elevator, they went a few doors down to the HR office and crew coordinator's desk where Angel dismissed herself. Tom almost wanted to tip her.

"Can I help you?" said the guy with a white uniform and epaulets with one gold stripe on them.

"I'm Tom Sundland, reporting aboard, sir," he said with a little bit of sarcasm. The guy at the desk did not appreciate it. It was turnaround day and his busiest of the week.

"Copy of your contract?"

Tom handed it over with his ID. The guy didn't say much. He started typing away on the computer and in a few minutes asked him to step in front of the camera in order to take his picture.

"9777," said the assistant purser who was not in any mood to play around. "Your card will expire next Saturday, and you need to be off the ship by noon that day or anytime after your contracted appearance and performance."

"Thanks very much."

Tom took his suitcase, rolled it back to the elevator, and pushed the button for deck 9. The elevators were very busy with a new round of passengers finding their cabins, each starting the vacation of a lifetime. For Tom, this was the gig of a lifetime and one that was putting him back on the road to life itself.

When he arrived on the ninth deck, he found cabin number 9777 and opened the door with the new card key he had received from the guy in HR back on deck 1. What he saw when he walked in surprised him. It was a gorgeous large stateroom with a sitting area, private bathroom, flat-screen TV, and a balcony overlooking the Port of Miami (and soon the deep blue Caribbean Sea). On the desk was an envelope with his name on it from the cruise director, who would be his boss for the week. It welcomed him aboard and gave him instructions for a meeting before his first appearance of the week, which was scheduled for the second night of the cruise. Not bad, Tom thought, looking around and getting a feel for the cabin. Getting paid to vacation and play games. Very nice indeed. He couldn't help but snap a couple of pictures with his phone and e-mailed them to his sister in New England, where it snows most of the year.

After a Coast Guard-mandated muster drill in which all of the passengers met at designated lifeboat locations for an emergency practice, Tom decided to head up to deck 14 to check out the sail-away party. The South Florida weather was sunny and warm, and the drinks were free because that was part of his contract. Food too.

Once the elevator door opened, he could hear the steel drum band, indicating that clearly the party had begun. Before he could even get to the bar, a waiter wearing a bright flowered shirt and holding a tray of piña coladas walked up, and Tom gladly took a virgin colada with no rum. The waiters always carried both to please any age or preference. People were standing all around, with some even dancing by the pool as the band played Jimmy Buffet and Bob Marley tunes as well as other island songs. Tom made his way to the outer rail and struck up a conversation with a passenger who looked to be in his twenties.

"Is this your first cruise?" the man asked Tom while sipping his own frozen drink.

"It sure is. Much different from what I expected," said Tom, also sipping his beverage, which sported an umbrella and plenty of fruit.

"I'm Cliff."

"Tom . . ."

"Where you from, Tom?"

"I live in LA."

"Nice. Never been. I've heard it's warm," Cliff said making small talk. "What do you do?"

Being a celebrity at any level from a weekend weatherman to international star comes with a built in radar system. Celebrities know instantly whether or not someone recognizes him or her. Usually from the minute a celebrity meets someone or walks into a room, they know. It's like a sixth sense and usually spot-on. In this case, Tom knew that this guy had no clue he was talking to a seventies icon. Icon might be pushing it, but clearly Tom had been an "A-lister" back in his day.

"I'm in show business," Tom explained knowing that the answer always brought interest.

"Really? What do you do?"

"I'm actually working on the ship this week. Did you see the "Murder on the High Seas" brochure in the cabin with the packet on things to do?"

"Yeah, where you help solve a mystery by working with police as a detective or something like that."

"Exactly. I'm the cop. I played one on TV back in the seventies on a CBS show called *Murder 101.*"

Cliff looked moderately impressed and curious.

"Really? That was a bit before my time, but very cool. Why did you give it up?"

"I didn't give it up. It gave me up. Those things happen in Hollywood. You get on a wave and ride it for a while until it crashes," Tom explained while sipping his very tasty virgin piña colada.

"Maybe I'll play the game," Cliff said, knowing that he most likely would not. It seemed like something geared more for the older folks on the cruise.

"Don't go out of your way. It's my first time on one of these, and I have no idea what I'm doing."

Both men laughed at that honest statement while the ship started pulling away from the pier. With the long blast of the ship's horn, which Tom thought was loud enough to be heard in Europe, his first cruise was under way. They agreed to meet for a few drinks later that night. Cliff was with some friends from college and seemed to enjoy Tom's company.

Ali Ahamid was the quiet type who got things done. An expert operator trained years ago in Iran after moving from his native Saudi Arabia, he was better known in Rhode Island by his alias Frank Castro, who worked at Evergreen Shipping at the Port of Providence. Frank did not have many close friends. Getting close with Dino Tucci took almost eighteen months of very careful networking. He knew whom to contact from the intel he had received before moving from Canada. His code name "Shopper" was seldom used outside a very small circle of people who lived continents away. It took a while to master the Canadian accent, which was not too different from the one he would encounter in Rhode Island where most people don't pronounce the "er" at the end of words. The classic "park the caaa" was a good example. He had to master the Canadian version to build his cover before moving to the Ocean State, as Rhode Island was known.

Frank actually enjoyed the Evergreen job and learned quite a bit about the import-export business and shipping containers. His enthusiasm for racquetball was carefully cultivated because Dino played twice a week at the Providence Racquet Club on the East Side. He joined the same men's league and knew it would be just a matter of time before he was paired with Dino. Once they started playing together, the seeds were planted for the friendship, which Frank hoped would lead to a good source of what was on his shopping list. That list included a medical CT scanner, radioactive pharmaceuticals, and some weapons. The third was the tricky part. He needed to build Dino's confidence and friendship so that when the time came, Dino would not ask too many questions. The CT scanner and pharmaceutical needs had already been given to Dino, and Frank was still waiting for the word on whether his mob friend could deliver the goods. If he couldn't, the whole operation would be jeopardized because the other team members were about to procure the "oven" part of the puzzle in Russia.

If Dino delivered on the first two requests they had talked about over the last few weeks, Frank would pay in cash and wait for a short time before asking for the guns.

Today the two met up for a beer after their evening racquetball matches which both lost to other partners. It was a chilly evening in Rhode Island with light rain and fog, and both men wanted to call it an early night, so they decided to have a drink at the racquet club bar rather than heading to the Hill.

"I sucked today," Dino said while looking over the small menu the bar had for munchies.

"Me too, my friend," said Frank as he took a seat next to Dino at the small bar.

"Sometimes I just hate this game. It's kind of like golfers who just can't help themselves. You just keep coming back for more punishment."

"I don't know much about golf, but this is more of a workout. At least it's real exercise," Frank said.

"True enough, and these beers will ruin any good we just did," Dino chuckled.

There were not too many people around at this time of the evening. A couple of others sat at the other end of the bar, and two were at a table eating some sort of fried food off the menu.

"Any luck with those items I asked you about?" Frank asked as casually as he could.

"Yeah, I can get you both of those. The 'F' one and the 'T' one. I can't pronounce the names of the damn things. And a used CT scanner if you still want that."

"That would be great, thanks."

"Did you know those drugs were radioactive? What the hell are you going to do with them?"

"They're for cancer research in Africa. I do some charity work for an international mission called Worldcare that sends medical supplies and personnel to third-world countries," Frank explained while thinking that this might be a good moment to set up his next request as well.

"So I guess you're the shipping side of that group to get the stuff to where it has to be."

"You bet. It's what I can do to help. The problem is that it's dangerous over there. Some people don't want to help their own countrymen or citizens in some of these places."

"I can imagine," Dino said while taking a sip of his beer.

"Our folks are doing the Lord's work in places around the world and risk their lives doing it. That's sad, and it's up to good people to help them out," Frank went on.

"That's noble."

"I think so. We try to send them what they need on the ground to do some good over there. But like I said, it's pretty dangerous."

Frank could feel that Dino was empathetic to the cause and what he was saying. Soon he would be asking for the last part of his shopping list, but not today. Today was just about following up on the other items and planting the seeds for the rest.

"When will you be able to deliver?" asked Frank.

"My guys say probably within a week or two."

"Wow, that's super. Then I will start preparing the shipping side."

"We will need cash for this, and no names," Dino explained with a much different tone in his voice. This was his business tone. "We'll drop it someplace secure, but payment has to be made at time of delivery."

"Of course. My group is truly thankful and will have the money ready when the items are delivered. Worldcare has many benefactors."

"Good enough. I'll have a final number for you in a couple of days."

The two men sipped their beers and decided not to order from the menu. The food was just not that great, and the choices were very limited. Most of what they offered was frozen premade stuff heated in microwaves. The beer, though, was good and cold and hit the spot after an hour and a half of playing hard racquetball.

It was time for Frank to send a request for funds. These funds would be deposited into Bank of America, Bank of Boston and Attleboro Savings Bank accounts which he controlled under an LLC set up to manage his mother's failing health. He had a ballpark figure in his head from past conversations with Dino. He figured something close to a million for all three items. A CT scanner was way too expensive and traceable. This one would do fine and be the perfect fit for what they wanted to do with it. First they would have to get it to the Republic of Georgia. This was a job custom made for shipping agent Frank Castro.

The weather halfway across the globe in the Republic of Georgia was mild and dry. The Chalice Pub usually stared to fill up after the workday around six or seven with people wanting a little escape for a few hours from whatever life they led. The cigarette smoke was getting thick, and Sergio was worried there were too many people around to talk about the business he was connected with at the moment. Inside, there were a couple of people that he recognized and stopped to say hello to after walking through the door. One worked with him at the hotel, and the other drove a taxi. While talking to these men, he noticed a familiar face at a table not far from the fireplace in the corner. After a few minutes of catching up, Sergio moved on and made his way over to the table where Boris was sitting.

Boris had an interesting look about him. He appeared tough like he had been through a few battles. He was a big, muscular guy with a rough-looking face and a small scar just under his right eye. *Maybe he got that in a bar fight,* Sergio thought, knowing that the answer was probably something more interesting. Boris already had a drink going, and Sergio sat down while a waiter came by to get his drink order.

"Stoli on the rocks," ordered Sergio while slowly looking around to see if anyone was watching him talk to the guy at this table.

"How was your day?" asked Boris like they were old friends.

"Good. Long."

"We have to wait about two to three weeks before we can go to Moscow. This will give you more time to get your pieces in place for our visit," explained Boris who had the smell of vodka on his breath already. Sergio figured he could drink with the best of them.

"Why?"

"That's for me to worry about and handle. But simply put, we're waiting on a delivery by ship due to arrive in that time frame. This will be very helpful with the transport of our package."

"Delivery of what?" Sergio asked, now a bit more curious.

"Our cover will be that we are delivering a CT medical scanner and some drugs overseas," Boris said in a soft voice so that no one could hear what he was explaining to his new partner.

"Really?"

"*Da*. That's right. I have access to a container truck we will drive to Moscow to pick up the package."

"Where will it be delivered?" asked Sergio, trying to understand how this was going to work. It seemed to him that Boris had done his homework. Sergio was worried about how they would transport this package once they had it and whether they would be detected. Once his job of delivery was done, he was out and wanted nothing to do with these people again. His plan was to transfer some of the money to other accounts in the Cayman Islands and move to the United States with his wife and baby on a work visa he would get though a friend who worked for the UN in New York. His buddy had connections with the U.S. State Department and, with Sergio's background in the hospitality business, promised that he could obtain a 180-day work visa.

Boris sipped his drink and ate a few beer nuts. "It will be delivered here to the port with all the appropriate paperwork. We will take it by container truck to Moscow and follow your instructions on how to pick up our package."

"Good enough. I will be working to make things smooth for when we arrive in Moscow. It's just a matter of setting up a few things with the right people. I will need some payoff cash," Sergio explained over the crackling of the fireplace, hoping that this money would not come out of his fees.

"We expected that and will have cash on hand."

"Good."

This was one of the things he did not ask about when originally agreeing to the money offered by Boris. Knowing that his money was protected and that they would pay any other expenses that came with the job was good news to Sergio.

"Why a CT scanner?" asked Sergio as he sipped his Stoli on ice. When this was all over, he would be drinking plenty of Stoli and anything else he wanted in places at one time he could only have dreamed about.

"It's big enough and comes in two pieces, and it emits radioactive signals when in use. We will also have a couple of medical radioisotopes to go along with it."

Sergio asked, "Why do we need the medicines if we won't be treating any actual patients?"

"Once the weapon is inside the CT unit, any radioactivity it emits would be easily explained by those medications being in the same shipment. They will trigger any radiation scanner, making them a perfect cover for our actual cargo," Boris explained.

Now the picture was becoming clear to Sergio, who decided to order another drink after hearing more of the plan. He had described to Boris during their last meeting the type of device they were going after in detail, including his best memory of its measurements. Boris was intent on knowing the weight and size of the device, insisting that the dimensions be exact.

"The package you described can fit inside the bed part of the unit. Even if it goes though radiation detectors, it's for medical use," said Boris confidently.

Brilliant, Sergio thought not wanting to let out too much emotion. Knowing the size of the device they would be getting, he figured roughly in his head that it would fit inside. These were not large weapons in size for the amount of yield they could potentially produce.

"I'm telling my wife I'm going to check out a few hotels the company is interested in."

"That will work," Boris said. "We'll only be gone two days anyway."

Sergio was comforted by his confidence and the logistics that Boris had already put in place. The only thing that worried him was number of people who might know about this plan and his involvement. "These people seem to have their shit together," he said to himself as he finished his second drink.

"We will meet again in one week, but at the hotel," said Boris. "I will check in for a night, and we can discuss our business then."

Boris covered his tracks well and did not want to appear in the same place more than two or three times. He never used his cell phone for "business" but had one for personal use. The two finished their drinks and headed out into the quiet Georgian evening. Sergio had some planning of his own to do.

On his way home, Sergio stopped at the market to pick up a few needed items that Rina had requested in a text message to his phone. The market was usually a busy place where locals could by food, wine, beer, vodka, and other items. They also sold phone cards, cell phones, and accessories. Many people who could not afford a phone with monthly bills would buy cheap devices with activation cards containing a preset number of minutes. That way they could better control the minutes they used. The phones were not very expensive and just provided the basics like voice and text. A kiosk in the store had a couple of different brands of phones and many options when it came to phone cards. He looked over the phones and picked out a generic-looking brand along with a ninety-minute phone card.

Sergio recognized a couple of the people working the checkout lines from past visits and went to the line with a guy he did not know. Typically he used his debit card to make food and other purchases, but today he used cash and bought the phone and card which he needed to move forward on what he was calling his "project."

There were three or four people Sergio could contact in Moscow, people that he used to work with who might be able to help him out. He thought about this carefully and decided to contact the one least likely to ask too many questions and who could use a financial boost. Knowing the situation back in Russia, many former and current employees of the state made very little money compared to the glory days of the USSR. This would work to his advantage in gaining access to the small base not far from the city where he used to work and where his prize was kept. He prayed that nothing had changed since he left and moved to a new life in Georgia.

Peter Koslov and Sergio had been close friends back in the day. Both men had studied together and worked on some of the same programs. Both were let go around the same time. The two kept in touch during the few years since Sergio had moved and he knew, thanks to being Facebook friends, that Peter had gone back to work for the government, but only on a part-time basis. Peter was hired back as a contractor to run safety checks on a couple of nuclear energy plants and perform yearly inspections of a few nuclear weapons stockpiles. One of those was the small base just outside of Moscow that Sergio wanted to access for a few short minutes. It had been a while since he last talked to Peter, and Sergio decided now would be a good time to give him a call. They would read each other's posts and comment on status updates now and then. For this though, he would rather talk on the phone. Facebook and other chat programs were too wide open for others to see.

As he walked down the street heading home from the store, he flipped though his primary phone's contact list for Peter's number. Hopefully it hadn't changed. Putting one phone in his pocket and taking out the new one, he stopped for a few minutes to punch in the codes to activate the phone and the minutes he had purchased back at the store. Like magic, the phone came to life, and he dialed up his old friend in Moscow.

"Da," said a rough voice on the other end of the line.

"Peter, it's Sergio."

"How are you, comrade?" Peter asked, now sounding more like a friend than a tired voice on the other end of the connection.

"I am well. Rina is well, and the baby is getting bigger," Sergio said making small talk.

"Wonderful. I see your pics on Facebook of the baby."

"Thanks. Hey guess what? I might be coming to Moscow for a couple of days to check out some hotel properties. I was hoping we could get together."

"Fantastic. When are you coming?"

Sergio started walking toward his neighborhood and was thinking of the dates that Boris they would probably travel.

"In a few weeks, maybe a month. I will let you know."

"Very good. Do you need a place to stay?"

"No, we'll be there on business, and the hotel will be taking care of my part, thankfully," explained Sergio.

"Excellent. I look forward to beating you in a game of chess," Peter said, thinking of all the nights they worked together, playing chess to pass the time. Both men were good chess players and missed their games.

"Don't count on winning, but count on playing. I will give you a call when we finalize the plans."

"*Da*, very good. I look forward to it. Send my best to Rina, and kiss the baby," said Peter.

"Will do. We'll talk soon."

With that, he closed the phone and put it in his inside jacket pocket. He looked forward to meeting up with his old friend who, no doubt, would give him the critical access he needed in the other chess game he had just started. As he approached his flat and went up the stairs smelling the awful and familiar scent of the garbage container sitting below, he thought that another day at the office was complete. Soon the smell of garbage and the cheap apartment he had now learned to live with would no longer be a factor in his life.

Chapter 7

PORTS OF CALL

S AN JUAN WAS much like any other port servicing all kinds of vessels from around the world. The main supply line for the island residents was shipping, and the container business was important for locals who worked on the waterfront. The cruise business was also a big dollar return for the people of Puerto Rico. Each day a ship was in port meant thousands of tourist dollars flowing into the U.S. territory, where the economy had been hurt over the last few years of a downturn in the global markets. The Star Caribe Line was a big player, with three of their lead ships making port calls weekly. Today was no different. One of the important evolutions of a port visit, beyond selling as many excursions as possible to the guests, was the resupply of items that may be low or out altogether. The ship's supply officer maintained close watch over everything from pickles to steak and anything that a five-star hotel would need for its operation. Typically the resupply would not be very big during the port calls because of the enormous on-load that happened in Miami on turnaround day. Plus the cost was not as controlled when using outside suppliers. Crew members assisting with the on-load are usually granted a few hours shore time in return. Bishar Fouad volunteered the night before to help bring on some of the cases of extra burgers and hot dogs that would be needed for the weekly barbeque held on the cruise line's private island in the Bahamas called Coconut Cay. These were backup burgers the supply officer ordered because running out was not an option. During this cruise, for some reason, people were eating more burgers for lunch at the poolside café on deck 10. Food inventory fluctuations happened from time to time and depended on the weather, number of guests, and a dozen other variables. After the boxes were loaded into the freezing units on deck 1, Bishar was released from duty and headed off the ship. He walked through the maze of shops in the cruise terminal and finally out to the street where he jumped into a cab for a short ride over to the Ritz-Carlton in Isla Verde.

The Ritz was a big complex adjacent to the beach with a large pool out back surrounded by palm trees. It had the usual Ritz grand motor entrance where the cab carrying Bishar pulled up and stopped, allowing the doorman to open the back door for him. He tipped the doorman three dollars and walked into the building through the lobby bustling with people checking in and out. On the other side of the lobby were glass doors leading to the pool and outdoor bar. The bar was positioned between the pool and the beach so that guests could access both easily. The bar was busy as lunch was getting under way and guests were starting their day in the sunshine. Bishar was sure to wear something that would blend in, and the shorts and flowered shirt he chose before leaving the ship fit the bill. As he approached the bar, he saw a familiar face sitting toward the end, watching the women walk by in bikinis and milking the first piña colada of the day. Bishar took the empty seat next to the man he had come to see.

"How's Sellco's favorite sales associate today?" asked Bishar as he looked toward the bartender with a glance that said he wanted to order a drink.

"Not their favorite this month. I had one client leave us for the competition, and that didn't go over very well."

The bartender strolled over, and Bishar ordered a virgin Bloody Mary with extra celery. He liked the taste of the celery after dipping it into the drink.

"Maybe you can get them back."

"I don't care who they buy from," said Abdul-Aziz Fahad as he took another sip of the nonalcoholic tropical delight sitting before him. "I love this weather."

Both men waited for the bartender to reach the other end before talking business.

"I met our friend and gave him the food order we talked about," Bishar said in a lower tone and moving a little closer to his associate so curious ears could not overhear their conversation. "He will be filling it within our time frame and somehow getting the order down to Miami."

"Good. Ali is a good soldier." He used their associate's given name instead of his alias, Frank Castro. "He will get what we need. The other three parts he has ordered will also be shipped soon to our friend in Batumi," said Fahad.

"I have a feeling that our work will be successful and the rewards joyful."

"I too, Bishar. I too."

There was not much more business to talk about as the men ate some of the peanuts the Ritz provided and signaled to the bartender that they would like another round.

"I am making progress at the port for final delivery here. We will need the manifest documents and orders e-mailed at the appropriate times," said Fahad, reaching for another handful of peanuts.

"They will be in place as long as your contact can produce them correctly," said Bishar.

Fahad and Mohammad had a person in Frankfurt who could produce just about any sort of paper or electronic document and make it look authentic. The trick was getting into the Star Caribe intranet and generating a virtually undetectable phony order. Their plan was to produce both a shipping manifest and install order. The manifest would be attached to the CT scanner for delivery to the *Star Orion*, and the install order would be for the medical department to be upgraded with the new technology.

"The copies of the maintenance orders you sent were very helpful for our friend in Frankfurt," explained Fahad. "Both, in fact, were exactly what she was looking for."

"She?"

"That's all you get on that one."

"Now I know why you like to do business in Frankfurt," chuckled Bishar while finishing his drink and taking bites out of the extra celery he had ordered.

The atmosphere at the bar was festive as lunch approached. Salsa music was playing on the speakers as the tropical winds blew in off the ocean. There was a group of men playing volleyball in the pool while others sunbathed on their bright blue chaise lounges. The beach was just steps away through a little gate which fenced off the exclusive resort, which cost patrons around four hundred U.S. dollars a night.

"Once we have hard dates, we will each make reservations. Your move into housekeeping will be helpful."

Bishar nodded in approval. He had finally received the promotion needed to better help the operation ahead.

"I hope the outing in Russia goes well. I understand it is solid," Bishar said, not knowing too much about that side of the operation. He wanted to know more, but each member of the team had only enough knowledge for his own part of the project.

"That is not for us to worry about or discuss," Fahad said quickly, ending that part of the conversation. "My worry today is whether to get one or two pool towels for the afternoon."

"You should be sure to return them. Here they charge for an extra night if they are not returned."

Both men finished their drinks, and it was time for Bishar to get back to his ship, which would sail exactly at 4:00 p.m. with or without him.

"We will talk again on our next visit. Peace be with you," said Bishar, knowing that the two men would meet again but at a different place and time.

"Peace," Fahad said as he got up from the barstool and headed over to the pool to look for just the right chair for a little nap and perhaps a swim. Bishar walked back into the hotel through the spa entrance not far from the outdoor bar and down the corridor on the east side of the hotel, leading to the lobby. He told the doorman he wanted a taxi.

"Where to?" asked the smartly dressed Ritz doorman in his classic brown uniform.

"La terminal de cruceros," said Bishar in Spanish.

It was a busy day for Customs and Border Protection in Dade County, Florida. Agents seized a load of cocaine aboard an Italian container ship and ended up having to go through each of the four hundred and five other containers aboard finding nothing else. The time it took was the killer. Even though they had drug dogs, agents had to hand search for hours. The sheriff's department sent a few officers over for support, but it was up to the federal agents of customs, border patrol and ICE to do the dirty work. It was always interesting to watch the media at work during these operations. Once a stash was found, if it were big enough, a customs public affairs officer would write up a release and invite the media out to see their catch at a specific time. The agents would show up and be paraded in front of the drugs or whatever it was they found to show the taxpayers that their money was not going to waste. Typically only a few agents would get what reporters called "face time" and the glory of the bust while most of the others who worked hours on the search got to go home and see it on TV.

Special Agent Jake Stein did not like to deal with the media and really didn't like appearing on television. While the PAO (public affairs officer) talked to the media, Agent Stein was finishing up some paperwork in his car as a few other agents wrapped up the last of the containers. Because contraband was found inside a container, the entire vessel had to be searched. In the crew berthing spaces below, agents found three lockers containing false bottoms. After further investigation, the bottoms were removed, and in each locker hidden below the deck plate were containers of casino chips. The chips had the names of three Las Vegas hotels. The MGM Grand, Luxor, and Wynn. Each chip was identical to the ones used at the famous hotels, and the values ranged from five to one hundred. Agent Ron Green took a few of the chips off the ship and found Jake sitting in his unmarked government-issued Crown Victoria dockside.

"What do you got?" asked Jake while he folded the last of six reports and put it in the envelope marked classified.

"Chips, lots of them," said Agent Green.

At first, Jake pictured potato chips. The kind you eat. But his training kicked in, and he knew better.

"Casino chips?"

"Yes, sir. Lots of them. From the Luxor, MGM, and one other. I think the Wynn. Here are a couple of samples from the Luxor and MGM."

Jake took them in his hand and examined them carefully. Vegas hotels did many things right. One of them was security in the casino. He knew this from personal visits and DV (distinguished visitor) meetings held there, which he had to attend for work.

"All different denominations?" asked Jake as he noted how real they looked even to his discerning eye.

"Mostly five and twenty-five. Some one hundred."

"Okay. Secure the find where it is. I'll call the Service."

"Yes, sir."

Most people knew the United States Secret Service for the job of protecting the president, but that was only part of their mission. They did much more than that, and one of their specialties was dealing with counterfeiting. When bad money or other high-end counterfeiting was found, the Secret Service came in and took over that part of the investigation. Most new agents spent time working in this part of the business and rotated to other specialties such as cyber crimes or tactical units. Executive protection was the cherry on the sundae all agents wanted, but it took time and experience to get there.

In the back of Jake's mind was his ex and what she did in D.C. Claire was assigned to counterfeiting, and it would be nice to get her to come to Miami on business. If they had been married, she would be working right now in Miami where he was. But that was not to be, and it was a stretch to think that she would actually get sent down seeing that the Service had a field office right there. He called that office and they sent out, as he expected, a junior agent. It took about an hour for the agent to arrive. Jake had command of the scene and therefore had to wait until the scene was cleared before he could head home for the day. It was getting late, and his patience was getting a little thin. Special Agent Janet Conklin pulled up in her government-issued Crown Vic after going through port security. The two cars looked like twins parked together, two G-rides, as they were known to the people who drove them.

"Agent Steen?" she asked after stopping the car and rolling down the window. He hated when people messed up his name. They were off to a poor start.

"Stein, Jake Stein."

"Sorry, my bad."

"No worry. We have some bad chips for you. The crime scene is intact and in the berthing area of the ship," explained Jake.

"Berthing?"

"Sleeping area. They were found under the crew lockers which had false bottoms."

"Copy that, let's go take a look," she said now excited about the find and also the fact that she was outside the office.

Both agents walked up the brow of the ship and into the passage leading to stairs going belowdecks. Following down two sets put them into the crew's berthing area where there were six beds and six lockers standing nearby. The beds, known as racks to the sailors, also had storage below the mattresses, which would lift up. Once the chips were found below the lockers, they were all searched thoroughly. Three of the lockers had the special hidden compartments below. The hole was actually a pretty smart design. False bottom in the locker with a hatch below that went under the floor to a space made for wires and pipes. In the space was a box for whatever the crew wanted to smuggle into and out of any of the dozens of nations they visited yearly.

"Is that all you found?" Agent Conklin asked one of the junior ICE agents securing the scene.

"Yes, ma'am, three stashes, and we opened only one of the bags to get a sample."

"I'm going to take a few pictures and then take custody of the evidence," she said while getting out her small Canon digital camera.

"Do you think they're counterfeit?" asked the junior ICE agent.

"Mostly likely. We won't know until we get back to the office and analyze them. But chances are pretty good."

A few more pictures then Agent Conklin secured the open bag of chips and, with the help of Jake and the other ICE agent, carried them up to her car.

"Do you know Special Agent Claire Wilson, by any chance?"

"D.C. field office?" she asked.

"Yeah. D.C. field office."

"We were classmates at Beltsville and pretty close back then. You know Claire?"

"She's a good friend," Jake said.

They made their way back down the brow and off the ship to their cars. Janet popped her trunk and put two big bags into it while Jake and the other agent did the same.

"We're actually working on a case involving counterfeit chips. This is an interesting find," she said.

Jake found her interesting and almost wanted to see if she wanted to go have coffee some time. *That would be ironic,* he thought. Lose one girlfriend to the Secret Service only to gain another from the same agency. Stranger things had happened.

"I'll give you a call to follow up in a few days if it's okay," said Jake, knowing it was okay, but he wanted to set up another call to this female agent.

"Sure thing, Agent Steen," she said kiddingly.

Jake smiled and got back into his Crown Vic, where he waited for the other agent to come down so that he could declare the scene secure. He noticed an e-mail on his iPhone. It was from Rosa at the office and said he had a SIPRNET message waiting from Felton in D.C.

"Once you're cleared, we can give the ship back to the crew," Jake said to the junior ICE agent walking toward his car.

"It's secure, sir. We're cleared and complete. Locals wanted to take a few more pictures, but that's about it. They're going to keep a marked car here overnight just as a precaution. No leads on who these chips were going to, but we'll work it."

Jake double-checked his paperwork and put it in the folder on the seat, glad that this day was almost over.

"Okay. Scene is secure, and you all are released. I'm heading home after a quick stop at the office."

"Roger that, sir."

Jake put the window up, turned the Crown Vic around, and headed out the port security gate toward downtown and the office. The Miami evening air was thick and muggy, and the traffic was a little lighter now that rush hour was over. He made his way to the office and parked his car in one of the reserved spots marked "government cars only."

After a quick ride up in the elevator, he was back in the office where he felt like he lived sometimes. Rosa had gone home along with the other agents and staffers. He was pretty much alone except for the security guards, who were paid to watch over the building, and a cleaning person or two. He fired up his computer and waited for it to boot up. Once it did, he inserted his CAC, which acted as both an ID and provided secure computer access once recognized, and his personal pin code was entered. Only a couple of people in the office had the security clearance to personally access the SIPRNET account; for most, the intel shop next door had to authorize access. The secure e-mail system was great to communicate sensitive information with others inside and outside the agency, but only certain machines could be used to gain access. After his code was authorized, his inbox had only the one message from Felton in D.C.:

//////TOP SECRET/////SIPRNET/////EYES ONLY//////

TO: J Stein
FR: Felton
SUBJ: PRTC

Jake . . .

    Abdul-Aziz Fahad was back in PR. CBP had his entrance two days ago. He's been in Frankfurt and Bulgaria as well as Islamabad. I'm having PR field office tag this guy and get a little more information on his clients, movements, etc. That's the third time in a few months, which is not too out of the ordinary except that he always comes on a Wednesday and leaves on a Friday. Departed for New York on JetBlue connecting to KLM flt 3 to Frankfurt.

TF

    Jake read the e-mail, responded that he had received it, and then deleted it. **Interesting,** he thought as he logged out of the computer, hoping to get home in time for the west coast Yankees game on TV and an ice-cold beer. Puerto Rico was one of his favorite islands, and he was thinking just the other day that he hadn't made a visit to his team down there lately. As special agent in charge of Miami and now San Juan (until they filled the vacancy), the office fell under his jurisdiction. It was pretty self-sustaining, and he had Wayne Howard, a good agent in charge, running the show down there. Jake thought it just might be time for a field office visit to follow up on this HSI tracking.

    Construction permits were controlled by the City of Providence for those companies that wanted to build within the city limits of Rhode Island's capital city. In some cases, they were tough to get, especially when building in the historic sections of the city. This was not just some case. This was the condo project that Narragansett H&C was planning for the waterfront near the Fox Point section of town. The waterfront had become high-dollar real estate and the preferred address for up-and-coming yuppies. It was also where new restaurants, clubs, and marinas had been popping up. Narragansett H&C had already built a number of different projects in this part of town. One was a restaurant and another a nightclub run by one of the Battellis.

The condo in question was a unit of two hundred, an upscale development that was part park, part retail, and part residence. Modeled after Americana at Brand, a development the Battellis saw on a trip to Los Angeles, this would be Providence's ultimate destination for shopping, dining, entertainment, and luxury living. The design was ready, and the land already purchased months ago by Narragansett, and there was a group of solid investors associated with this special project. The only thing holding up ground breaking was getting the right permits in place to start construction. There had been some push back by a few in the local community who wanted Fox Point to remain just an open park with nothing else to offer. Those voices were quickly quieted after Narragansett settled a small class-action lawsuit brought by a group of East Side residents. This should have paved the way for the permits to be issued to start Oceanside at Fox Point, but two people stood in the way. One was a city councilman and the other an executive with a competing construction company who really did not have the clout for such a project.

Councilman Henry Lombardi had a history of being a pain when it came to city development. He knew who was behind this project and had a poor relationship with the current mayor, who wanted the development completed. Lombardi owned a restaurant in nearby Cranston, where he held court nightly with friends and supporters. He was a lifelong resident of Providence and the first of his family to seek and gain political office. He was clearly eyeing a run for mayor in the future, but he needed time as a councilman to get the experience needed. Lombardi was three years into his first four-year term. So far, he enjoyed politics and the give and take that went along with it. Tonight he would taste the other side of Rhode Island politics.

Twin Lakes was the name of the family Italian restaurant he bought from his father, who started it back in the 1960s. It was not the best location in town, but it was the kind of place that people would find because of the reputation and the food. Mostly it was a place for locals to eat and drink. The wait for a table on weekends would sometimes get up to an hour and a half. That was, of course, if you didn't "subway" the maitre d' with a few dollars, ensuring that your name would be called earlier.

This was a weeknight, and business was pretty good. The wait was around twenty minutes for a table, or people could just sit at the bar and order off the menu there. Located on a small lake in Cranston, the building was old and had a nice front entrance with parking around the building. The back of the restaurant was on the lakefront with big picture windows so guests could enjoy the view while eating some of their favorite Twin Lakes dishes. To access the kitchen and back of the house, as it was known in the restaurant business, there was an employee entrance in the rear of the building.

Dino Tucci and his associates Moe and Sam pulled up to the front and parked. Dino and Moe went into the front entrance while Sam went and stood at the back door. As they walked into the lobby of the restaurant, where the walls were adorned with pictures of celebrities who had eaten there, the smell of garlic made them hungry. The lights inside were very low, and the bar was tucked away from the big windows overlooking the lake. Smoking was allowed in the bar area, where no reservation was required to have a drink and some appetizers. Councilman Lombardi was not expecting a visit from Dino and his associates. The bar area had some tables with small candles in red jars sitting on them along with dishes of goldfish crackers. Henry Lombardi knew Dino from a few meetings they had attended in the past and knew that he worked for Narragansett and the Battelli family. Both Dino and Moe sat at a corner table waiting for Henry to join them. They told the maitre d' to have him join them in the bar.

"Dino, right?" asked Henry as he joined the two men at the table.

"Henry Lombardi, city councilman, nice to see you again," said Dino as he took a goldfish from the bowl. "We have a little problem to solve tonight."

"Problem with the building permits for Oceanside?"

"Smart guy."

"I've got nothing to do with the permit process, but I did ask for a delay to better study the project," explained the councilman as he motioned for the waiter to come get a drink order. "I have the option to do that as a member of council."

"We've been through this with the court settlement and hearings already," Dino was saying as the server came over. "Scotch and soda for both of us," he ordered while not taking an eye off Lombardi.

"Coke for me," said Lombardi as the waiter retreated.

"We've been through this," Dino continued.

"I had some reservations."

Dino waited quietly for a few seconds then said, "We're ready to move and need you to pull your delay request."

The smoke was getting thick in the bar, and the place was warm. Henry Lombardi knew not to mess with these folks, having heard stories of the past.

"What do I get?"

"You get to go home tonight and get to run for office again," Dino said with a chill in his tone.

Moe sat silently. Henry looked at him once or twice, but Moe just sat there.

"We're not fucking around. The delay stops now," said Dino.

"Are you threatening me?"

"No. I'm guaranteeing you will win your next election and have our full support. Or you'll disappear off the face of the planet. Your choice."

Henry knew from stories he had heard that this sort of thing went on all the time in Rhode Island, but he had never expected to experience it firsthand. He had been staying under the radar for years before he ran for office.

"Make the call," Dino ordered.

"They're not in now. It's after hours."

"Make the call," Dino ordered again, but this time with a lower voice and a fierce, unblinking gaze.

Henry knew the head of the permit division personally. He also knew that these guys meant business. Years ago, a city councilman had disappeared after a fight over zoning rights and washed up on the rocks of Port Judith in the southern part of the state a few weeks later. That crime was never solved, but the zoning problems had ended.

"How's your family, Henry?" Dino asked while sitting back in his chair and taking a sip of his Johnnie Walker Black and water. "Two kids, right?"

"Yeah."

"Nice family. A man should watch over his family."

"Yeah."

"Make the call. I'm not telling you again," Dino demanded while sliding the councilman's phone, which was sitting on the table, closer to its owner.

Henry picked up his Android smartphone and pulled up his list of contacts then pushed the button.

"Hi, Jim, this is Henry Lombardi. Give me a call when you can, and go ahead and pull that delay request I have on the Oceanside project. I've looked over everything, and we're good to go. Thanks. Dinner soon."

Dino looked at his friend Moe and nodded. Moe got up and left the table to get his associate, who was still standing outside the back door. The two then departed in the separate car that he driven to the restaurant. Henry just sat there and looked at Dino. Then he spoke.

"I'm going to cash in on that support for reelection."

"We take care of our friends, Henry. You did the right thing."

"If you don't mind, I'm going to go back to the kitchen and check on the back of the house."

With that, Councilman Henry Lombardi got up and headed to the kitchen now knowing how business was really done in Providence. Dino picked up his phone and called Frank Castro to see if he would come over for a drink or dinner. He had some news for him. The CT scanner was ready for delivery. Frank lived just a few miles away and had been busy getting shipping set up for the CT scanner and meds that his Italian friend were procuring for Worldcare. Dino had another drink and checked his e-mail while he waited for Frank to make his way over. He also made a quick phone call to Mr. Battelli to tell him that there would be a construction permit granted the next day or two for the Oceanside development. This was welcome news his boss was waiting for.

About twenty minutes later, Frank Castro walked into the bar and found his racquetball partner and friend sitting alone at the table.

"Great to see you, Frank," Dino said. "I hope you're hungry."

"I am. Thanks for the call. I was going to give you a ring tomorrow actually. Nice that you were right over here."

"I had some business earlier. Let's get a table."

With that both men got up and went back to the maitre d' stand and asked for a table in the dining room. The house was on a twenty- to thirty-minute wait, and the lobby was busy with people waiting to be seated or checking coats. Twin Lakes was a traditional Italian place and still operated a coat check, which has long since disappeared from most restaurants. It was also one of the greatest jobs to have in the place because of the tips and contacts to be made. Many of the state's politicians, business leaders, and power brokers still ate and met at Twin Lakes. Dino was told to wait near the coat check, and about three minutes later, a waiter appeared and told Dino he would escort him and his guest to a table by the huge windows with one of the best views of Spyglass Lake. There was a list of names at the maitre d' stand that would be called as tables came open. Dino's name would never appear on that list. For him, a table would always be ready or made ready.

"We're set to deliver all three items," Dino said as they sat down.

"What are the final numbers?" Frank asked, knowing that he had money wired to his special accounts and hoped it would be enough. He could always ask for more, but that was risky each time they transferred funds.

"Eight fifty."

"For the scanner?"

"No, for everything. All three. The two meds and the scanner. I've got you covered, brother," Dino said, proudly knowing he was doing his friend and a charity a favor. Even though Dino's business often took on a dark tone, he still liked doing good things for people in need. The year before, he had worked with the Battellis to build a new YMCA on Federal Hill in Providence.

"I thought for sure it would be more," a surprised Frank said, trying not to sound too excited about the cost.

"We take care of our friends. Where we bringing this thing?"

"I'll let you know. I'm having the shipping documents sent to me by e-mail, and we'll ship it overseas once we take delivery. This is good news, indeed."

"My pleasure. Cash though."

"Absolutely. I'll have that for you at delivery. No big deal."

Dino took a piece of bread from the basket as a waiter approached. At Twin Lakes, all the waiters were all men. There were no female waitresses. It was tradition here. Both men ordered dinner and another drink. The waiter in black tie quickly departed.

"My people at Worldcare are going to be very grateful. It's a needed machine for a dangerous place," said Frank, who was getting hungry smelling the Italian food being served all around the dining room.

"Glad to help, Frank."

"They budgeted for more, so the left-over dollars might be good for some security items needed," Frank said as he slowly tested how Dino would respond to a request for the last items on his shopping list. "Not sure you can help with those though."

"What kind of security items are you talking about?" Dino asked with a bit of curiosity.

"They need six to eight rifles."

"Rifles? What the hell for?" Dino asked, now very interested in the conversation and the request coming from the guy having dinner with him. "I thought this was some sort of religious organization or something."

"Worldcare is a Christian organization, but there are places in the world where the medical care they give can be looked upon as aiding an enemy. They'll treat anyone. That's in the bylaws. But in Africa and the Sudan, there are people who would do these good doctors and other health care workers harm just for the care they give."

Dino thought about that for a few moments as the waiter reappeared with drinks and more bread. Twin Lakes was also known for the fresh bread they served. People came from around this part of the state to just buy it in loaves.

"What kind of rifles are they looking for?" Dino inquired, not sure that this was something he wanted to help with.

"AR-15s," Frank said coldly, trying to look like it was just another request. "That's what they are looking for anyway."

"How the fuck do you plan to ship those overseas without people asking too many questions?"

Frank sat for a moment before he answered. "Carefully. But we can do it. Remember, that's what I do for a living."

"True enough, but I would hate to see you get in trouble helping these people like this. Medical equipment is one thing. Guns are a different matter altogether," lectured Dino, now sounding like someone who had experience with this sort of thing.

"Easy stuff, really. They come apart and would be shipped in separate containers. Nobody knows about it or gets hurt. My buddy in New York did it for Worldcare in years past and suggested that maybe I should try to help them this year."

Once again the waiter appeared with salads and olive oil for the bread. The conversation halted while the server did his job. The place was busy with the usual clanking of dishes, people talking, and Dean Martin playing in the background.

"I'll be honest with you. I can get what you need, but again it's all cash, and I need to know it's for protecting these people," explained Dino.

Frank was pleased and knew he hit a home run on this one.

"Absolutely. I'll send you a link to a website they operate, and you can see for yourself. Obviously they're not going to show their security people, but you can get an idea of what they face and how they do their jobs. The security is critical for them to maintain their safety and the people they treat," Frank said.

"When do you want them?"

"How long will it take?"

"I can deliver them with the scanner and meds. One delivery."

Jesus, Frank thought. This guy was not kidding around.

"How much?" Frank inquired.

"Our cost, but these things are not discounted. Probably around five C-notes each."

Frank waited a few seconds to reply so as not to look overly enthusiastic, then spoke up.

"Okay. Bring them too. That's a great help and will go a long way to help people in some pretty tough parts of the world."

"Done," Dino declared, now ending the business part of the conversation as dinner appeared on a tray. He wanted to talk about the Red Sox anyway. Frank had to stay and eat and make conversation even though he had much to do to get the money ready and shipping documents for the medical supplies and scanner. The other items he just got his mob friend to sell him would be moved south by a different means of transportation.

Chapter 8

SIDE JOBS

LIKE MANY CITIES of the world lucky enough to have a port, Batumi uses this natural resource to its fullest. The Republic of Georgia is a gateway to the Black Sea, and many people who live there make a living on the waterfront. Times have been tough for this once ancient Greek and later Roman port that dates back to around AD 138 Giant container ships and tankers sail in and out of the port, transporting everything from Middle Eastern oil to handmade rugs and furniture to agricultural products. Joseph Stalin himself made the city his home before the Russian Revolution and rise of the Soviet Union. Today, thanks to the Rose Revolution of 2004 in the capital of Tbilisi, Batumi is a primary and growing city in the now-independent Republic of Georgia. As a coastal city, Batumi residents are used to shipping, but it still lists tourism as a major economic driver in the region.

Boris Stockov was born in and made his primary residence in Tbilisi but had been living for the last couple of months in Batumi. His primary job was as a tour operator, so he found himself in the coastal city quite often, depending on how business was. He had a number of good connections in Batumi when it came to transportation and logistics, to keep his paying customers on the move making the most of their holidays. He also dabbled in intermodal transportation and would jump in as a freelance driver for a friend's small logistics company. When they needed an extra hand, he would drive a container truck out to the port, rail yards or even back to the capital, depending on the situation and how much time he could give this side job. Boris worked hard for his money and did all he could to get ahead. Today Boris was moving a container from the port to the rail yard just outside of

Tbilisi, where he would spend the night at his home before returning the next day with another container.

The standard procedure was that he would be given the shipping order with a container number and information along with customs declarations. He would check the tracking locator to see where it was on the lot, hook up his truck, and go.

"More rain on the way," Boris said to a man who worked for COSCO shipping as he rolled down the window of his truck. COSCO was an acronym for China Ocean Shipping Company, one of the largest shipping companies in the world.

"It's the rainy season, my friend," the man replied as he checked some paperwork Boris handed him that was now starting to get wet from the light rain falling on the port. The shipper checked the match between the container number and the one on the paperwork before signing the clearance to release the container for its next stop in what is usually a long journey for these big metal boxes that move the world's supplies.

"You're clear to roll out. Safe travels."

Boris slowly pulled out of the space and headed to the security gate just a few meters away. Once again Boris rolled down his window and saw the same guard who had checked his credentials on the way in. These guards worked long twelve-hour shifts and had been known to sip more than just the coffee on the job.

"Papers?" ordered the gate guard who was paid by the state and enjoyed government benefits or what benefits were left after the severe cuts all agencies had been going through.

"Good afternoon again, sir," Boris said.

The guard took a second look and recognized Boris, whom he saw from time to time. Boris had given him a couple of Cuban cigars over the holidays, which he very much appreciated.

"Ah, my tour guide friend," said the security specialist, now with a friendlier demeanor.

"Tomorrow the tourists. Today I drive the containers. Got to feed the family."

The guard quickly signed the form and opened the white bar that acted as a gate to allow the truck to pass.

"Same on my end. Take care."

Boris nodded and put the truck into gear and with a loud release of air from the brakes, started to roll out. He was a tough guy who stood six foot four with jet-black hair, and he had fought in Afghanistan for the Soviet Union during their nine-year war back in the eighties. He did two tours of duty with the elite Soviet Special Forces called Spetsnaz and had been wounded twice. In one battle, a bullet hit his leg, which only served to slow down the bodybuilder, who was also an expert shot. He quickly got up and with his issued Kalashnikov AK-47 rifle, charged a barn where six Afghan mujahideen guerrillas were holed up and shooting at his unit. He took out the first three as he ran up a small hill, dodging incoming bullets between trees. Once up to the barn, he kicked in the side door and rolled a Soviet-made F1 fragmentation grenade inside, which exploded and killed the three remaining guerrillas along with a number of goats and a cow. A piece of shrapnel came through the door he was using to take cover and gave him the signature scar he now wore below the right eye.

After the war, he moved back to his native Tbilisi but was not well-educated and struggled with odd jobs before starting the tour company he operated with two other employees. In the former Soviet Union, being a Muslim was nothing people advertised. Religion was only tolerated, and it was not until well after his move back to what is now the Republic of Georgia that he embraced his native religion. He was not a radical though and was selective about certain parts of it, including enjoying alcoholic beverages. He did some business with others who attended his mosque by arranging tours and some local travel. They seemed like reasonable people who paid well. Through one of those business contacts, he met Mohammad Featha, who was looking for someone to go to Moscow, pick up a special package, and return to the port. Mohammad knew of Boris's military background, and the two men met a number of times before an offer was made to do the job. The payment was in U.S. dollars, and Boris had to be trusted. As an ex-soldier, Boris had no great love for the former Soviet state, and the excitement of the transfer returned him to his days in special ops. That kind of adrenaline rush was something he had not experienced in a number of years. With the generous terms of payment and the excitement of the operation, he was in.

Life on board the *Star Orion* was not all fun and games for the ship's crew. They worked mostly seven days a week for the entire four-month contract, which is typical of the industry. Some people came and stayed for only one contract while others worked two contracts a year, and the non-Americans' money was tax-free. There were two main departments to work for on the ship: hotel operations and the deck department. Hotel operations included everything having to do with the guests and guest services. It encompassed the chefs, cabin stewards, housekeeping, cruise staff, entertainers, and waitstaff. The deck department took care of the actual driving and upkeep of the ship itself. People who worked here included painters, anchor operators, line handlers, and engineers.

The master of the ship was in charge. The master was like the mayor of a small floating city, with thousands of people in his care. He or she had a number of first and second officers who also drove the ship from the bridge while at sea. Capt. Bijon Markinson went to sea at the age of sixteen and had been at it ever since. Born in Norway, his entire family was somehow connected to life at sea whether on board ships or supporting the maritime business. His twin brother was also a ship captain with Star Caribe, and, to their knowledge, they were the only set of identical twin captains in the cruise industry. The brothers often joked that they could each board the other's ship and sail for a few weeks without anyone ever knowing. Bijon spent his time divided between operating the 153,000-ton vessel with his officers from the bridge and the mass of paperwork and guest relations that came with the job. The bridge of the ship was a busy place when sailing into and out of ports, but during long legs in the open sea, the officer of the deck who had the con would sometimes have to fight to stay awake. Access to the bridge was strictly controlled by a coded entrance and video camera to see who was coming inside. Only those staff members who needed to know it had the code. Otherwise, if someone had business on the bridge, he or she would be buzzed in. Part of the job in the environmental section was to occasionally enter the bridge and engineering spaces to collect recycling. Imad Patel found himself with this duty from time to time, and the officers and crew liked his sense of humor when he came up. Having a good relationship with the master of the ship was something every crew member wanted. When it came to cabin assignment and other duties, a word from the master of the ship could go a long way. He was helpful in getting his friend Bishar assigned as Imad's roommate during their first contract together.

Today Imad made his environmental rounds, including stopping at the bridge and making small talk with the officers as he collected the recyclables. Knowing that he wasn't allowed to loiter for very long, he went about his business while always taking note of the layout and security systems. After a few minutes, he said his goodbyes and left the bridge for his next stop seven decks below in the engineering control space on deck 1.

Meanwhile, Tom Sundland was excited about trying out his new role in the ship's murder mystery as a police officer working with the passengers who were playing the game of gathering clues to solve a crime. His first duty was to teach them how to secure a crime scene. In the scenario there had been a murder, and the culprit was running around disguised as a passenger. The ship's cruise staff set up an unused cabin as the crime scene complete with a fake body and blood. The body was a dummy the medical staff used for CPR and medical training, but it worked perfectly. The blood was washable theatrical blood the cruise director ordered when thinking up this extracurricular shipboard activity. He knew how guests liked to enjoy different aspects of life on their cruise vacations and came up with this murder mystery idea for those interested in solving puzzles. Star Caribe liked the idea so much that they added a celebrity former television cop to the mix, hoping to entice people to take the cruise for that reason alone.

Tom's passenger group playing the game would meet for an hour during the first two days of the sailing. The game would be over by the third day so as not to interfere with the port visits. Tom had to set up the curriculum and clear it with the Star Caribe entertainment division before he even set foot on the ship. The game concept was the first of its kind in the fleet, and if it was something that guests enjoyed, the company might add it to its other ships. For now though, he was just a part of the pilot program and enjoyed having the chance to design it and take part.

On deck 2, the fake crime scene was in cabin 2052 and the "body" was lying in the entrance to the bathroom. There was blood in many locations, and the place looked like there could have been a struggle. A bloodied knife was on the floor near the porthole window, and some books had been thrown around. The bed was messed up like it had been slept in the night before. In the closet were some men's and women's clothes along with a few hats. Tom had ordered a real fingerprinting kit, which was sent directly to the ship before he boarded. His first order of business was to introduce the group to the crime scene. They were told to assemble in front of the guest services desk on deck 4 at two o'clock and to wait for "Detective Sam Primo" to show up. Tom had to be in full character from the moment he met the guests until the end of the game.

"Who are you people?" Tom asked while walking up to them in his Sam Primo suit and tie complete with a badge hanging from his jacket pocket. "Oh, you're the rookies. Okay, we've got a murder on this ship, and the person who did it is running loose and could kill again." Much to his surprise, there were twenty-two people who showed up for the first of three days of play. "Our crime scene is on deck 2. Let's go."

The group took the stairs down two levels to cabin 2052. Tom explained the basics of securing a crime scene and the step-by-step process of evidence collecting. "Hey, Red, don't touch that door," he barked at a redheaded girl who was taking part in the game. "We haven't dusted it for prints yet. Okay, folks, what are we looking for?"

"A weapon?" asked one older gentleman who seemed to be getting a kick out of Sam Primo's gruff character.

"Very good, Einstein. What's your name?" Tom asked.

"Dave."

"All right, Detective Dave, what else?"

"Prints?"

"True, but not yet. First we have to secure all the evidence so that no one can touch it. We also have to shoot pictures of the body and take note of how things are arranged here in the cabin," he lectured.

Tom walked the group through the beginning process of a murder investigation, and they seemed to really be enjoying the experience. In the back of his mind, he thought that this game concept might just be successful, plus he was having fun. At one point, the guests staying in the cabin next door showed up to get into their bathing suits and clearly had not read the activities list on the daily *Cruise Navigator* newsletter that was left for passengers each night. They must have missed the flyers too.

"Can I help you?" Tom said completely in character to the women trying to access her cabin. "There's been a murder next door."

"Oh my god!" she said gasped, buying the whole thing. The guests playing the game were both inside and outside of the crime scene cabin, and they all stayed in character too. One even asked her if he could check her fingers for blood!

"We're just playing a shipboard murder mystery game," Tom finally whispered much to the relief of the women next door and her husband, who was also thinking it was the real thing.

One of the cruise staff got to play the murderer and had the job of leaving clues in different parts of the ship until they finally caught him or her. In this case, it was a female staffer.

"Look at the clothing, people. Are we after a man or a woman, or do we know?" Tom quizzed his new associates. "The body is clearly that of a man, and there are clothes in this closet for both a man and a woman."

"Woman," said one older lady who recognized Tom's name the minute she saw it on the flyers for the game. She had been a loyal *Murder 101* viewer and had a huge crush on Sam Primo back in the seventies.

"We can't be sure, ma'am. We could have a domestic here or perhaps murder for hire."

"Domestic is a good possibility," said another guest who also seemed to be enjoying the role-playing.

"Why?" Tom asked.

"The message in the dead man's hand says, 'Meet me for some fun after dinner,' and was signed Trixie. The wife's name on the cruise documents on the bedside table is Ann. He might have been cheating on her."

"Good. Very good. We might be looking for an angry wife who knows how to handle a knife. Or Trixie may be Ann's nickname. Cruise paperwork always carries passengers' legal names."

Tom walked the group though the process of dusting for fingerprints before they ended the day's investigating. "Tomorrow, we'll meet here at the crime scene and pick up the investigation. For now, keep an eye open for any clues, and we'll see you back here at two. Two sharp, people." With that, Detective Sam Primo, a.k.a. Tom Sundland, left and went back upstairs to his cabin on deck 9 to change and have something to eat. *Not bad,* he thought as he made his way toward the elevators. Having some fun and getting paid for it. Just like the old days, only instead of a show, it was a ship.

Chapter 9

PARTS DEPARTMENT

MAY IN MOSCOW could still sometimes feel like winter. No one knew this better than Peter Koslov who had to travel around the country as a contract inspector for the government he used to work for and respect. He still worked for them technically, but only as a paid contractor. No benefits, no car, no goodies like in the old days of the Soviet Union. But a job was a job, and he had to look out for his mother and father. Never married, Peter was a bright engineer whose future had been bright before the collapse of the country and change in the way the government did business. He dated on and off but enjoyed the bachelor lifestyle, especially in a town of around eleven million like Moscow, where the women were plentiful. He was a tall fellow with the typical Russian light hair and skin. He enjoyed his beer but, unlike other Russians, was not much of a vodka drinker.

His job was twofold. He was contracted to inspect some of the country's nuclear power plants for safety and to do the same for some of the stockpiles of nuclear weapons, a few of which he had helped design back in the day. That part of the job was easy. They were mainly just sitting in place at various locations, and he had to certify that nothing had changed and no one had touched them. Some were still on warheads sitting in silos, and these were also under the watchful eye of START treaty inspectors. Most of the inspection tours he conducted took him away for a day or two except for the semiannual visit to the small army base just outside city limits, where a few tactical nukes were kept. A lifelong Muscovite, Peter preferred taking the Moscow Metro around town than driving his old car. For the trip over to the Thirty-Fourth Guards of the Moscow Military District, though, he would have to use his car.

The Thirty-Fourth Guards were a field artillery division charged to protect the city and lay within the Moscow Military District. Within the

Thirty-Fourth Guards there was a special detachment of the Twelfth Chief Directorate of the Ministry of Defense, or Twelfth GU MO. One of the most secretive of the state agencies, they were responsible for the safekeeping of the nuclear arsenal. Any base which housed nuclear weapons carried the secret designation known as "Special-Technical Formations." This was one of those. Peter, unknown to anyone including his family, once served in the Nuclear Technical Service Directorate with his friend Sergio. Both men were familiar with this base, also known as "Burr 34," after the Great Russian general colonel Raymondski William Burr. The base housed v/ch 22133, also known as an Object "C" during the former days of the Soviet Union. It was a small and special nuclear arsenal for the defense of Moscow and the Kremlin. His job was to inspect the small special weapons cache and report back to the Twelfth Chief Directorate that everything was in order and accounted for and that no changes needed to be made in the "nuclear registrar," which kept track of all Russian nuclear munitions.

Because of the special weapons at the base, security was high. Along with traditional army security forces, special guards from the Twelfth GU MO kept watch over the facility. They were mostly responsible for the "technical zone," which was the small nuclear depot to which only authorized personnel had access. This climate-controlled facility, ironically enough, had only two guards assigned per shift. The Twelfth GU MO assumed that army security would prevent unauthorized access to the base and, because of budget cutbacks and the small number of "special" munitions housed there, assigned three shifts of only two men each. Because of its size and small number of weapons, Burr 34 was not the typical structure found on most standard nuclear arsenal bases, which were designed for that specific purpose. Those facilities were much more robust, consisting of additional layers of security and units such as helicopters, engineering-technical services, and other precautions.

The guards securing this "technical zone" were familiar with Peter having seen him here about every six months or so when he conducted his inspections. They enjoyed seeing people coming into their small facility every now and then because it broke up the monotonous routine they lived daily. So few people actually came in, that it was actually a challenge for these special guards to stay awake some days. Peter would only spend about a half hour or so checking the security of the weapons, the climate of the facility, the crates where they were housed and tamper-proof locks securing each one. He was charged with opening at least two crates per visit to physically check them on a random basis. He would access a special safe inside the building to get the code to open the locks, and therefore the crates containing the warheads, which were not huge by traditional nuclear standards but, with a variable yield, would lay to waste to a good-sized city and a few suburbs to go along with it.

"Good morning," Peter said to the corporal standing guard at the electric fence surrounding the building itself. It had a single ECP or entry control point, and the guard inside a small booth would have to buzz a visitor in. He knew Peter but checked his credentials anyway just to be sure and in case anyone may be watching him. The days of the "political officer" were past, but there were many moles in the regular army who reported back to higher authority on people they were assigned to watch.

"Good morning, sir. Thank you, sir," the guard said as he buzzed Peter in. With a large clank, the gate released, and the visitor pushed it forward and walked into the small yard surrounding the windowless gray building. For special purposes there was another, much-larger gate just to the left of the smaller one. This would be used for deliveries, maintenance or, God forbid, moving the weapons out of the secure facility for deployment. That gate was on a separate buzzer and was only used once in a great while. It was tested monthly to ensure the gate was not getting rusty and still worked appropriately. Peter walked a few steps over to the main door of the building, which had an electronic release. The drill was that he would insert his secure ID into the card reader while the guard watched for verification. With that, the guard would concur and insert a small key to allow the bolt-action lock to release, therefore opening the door. Peter thanked the guard, who retreated back to the guard shack by the fence and went into the cold, dark cement block building.

There was dim light that was always left on, but he flipped on the main lights to better see where he was going. Ahead of him was a small set of stairs leading down into what looked like a pit to a layperson. It was only around a meter deep and went the length of the building. Inside the pit were wooden crates looking a lot like coffins lined up in a row with letters and numbers on them. There were eight crates in total. Opposite the crates was a small gray safe attached to the wall, and this had a combination lock. As Peter spun the dial to the correct numbers to open the safe's door, he thought it was strange that with all the layers of security that the combination had never changed. He guessed that if a person could get this far, it wouldn't matter anyway whether he had the magic number. As the door made a click sound after the last number, 12, was spun in, it popped open, and Peter reached in and took out the codes for crate numbers 3 and 6. With that, he turned around and opened both crates, which were just the same as they had been the last hundred or so times he checked them. Peter secured each crate, returned the codes to the small safe, and locked it. His next chore was to check the climate control unit to make sure that it was functioning properly and that there were no faults listed on the computer screen that controlled the air-conditioning and heating units. The blower unit was an older type with two large fans housed in two metal lockers standing around six feet tall each, just a little bigger than the crates lying in the pit that they were keeping warm in the winter and cool in the summer. He found no problems with the climate control system. Peter was also responsible for the safekeeping of the weapons, including the building's climate. In financially better days, civil engineers would have been responsible for all things heating and air, but now with fewer people and multiple bases, they were called in only for major problems. Peter or one of his group would have to escort them into the facility should maintenance be needed.

After filling out his paperwork, which would be sent to Moscow, Peter turned the lights off and left the building, making sure the door was secure after it shut behind him. One of the guards also came over to make sure the building was secure then went back to the booth and buzzed Peter out of the facility. He got into his car and headed toward the main gate and into the chilly afternoon with gray skies, thinking that it actually felt like snow while hoping spring would start to kick in soon.

Chapter 10

CONNECTIONS

J UST OUTSIDE THE Rhode Island capital city of Providence, about a fifteen-minute drive down I-95, sits sleepy Seekonk, Massachusetts. Not known for anything really, it was just a bedroom community where people who worked in both Providence and Boston lived and commuted. It was a late May night, and finally the temperatures were starting to come up a bit. Frank Castro hated the cold weather and New England winters. Dino Tucci, on the other hand, was used to it, growing up in the Federal Hill section of Providence. Both men were wearing light jackets as they planned to meet at the agreed-upon time of 9:00 p.m. in a place where Frank had never been before. In fact, when he put the address into his GPS, it only took him to the end of Reed Street; after that, it said he was headed into an unverified area. There was a dirt road off the end of the paved roadway, but Dino had instructed Frank to continue driving on for about one hundred yards to a place called the "Holland Track."

In the back of his mind, as he made his way slowly down the dusty dirt road, was the thought that Dino probably took some of his "clients" down this very path if they failed to pay a debt or needed to disappear. He was told to wait at this location for Dino and his partner to arrive with the shipment of goods that Frank was purchasing. Dino always arrived at a "meet" last, knowing that he could case the receiver for signs of law enforcement or something dirty. If it didn't look or smell right or if something went wrong, he could make a fast escape, controlling the only exit point.

About ten minutes after Frank arrived, the headlights of an unmarked panel truck about the size of a large U-Haul appeared beyond the tree-lined dirt road and slowly came into view as they drove in. Frank's own truck was actually a real U-Haul he rented with cash and would return after he moved his large package to a temporary storage unit before shipping it overseas. The

94

night was black dark, and as the headlights shined on Frank, he was blinded and couldn't see beyond or around the truck slowly moving in his direction. In fact, Frank couldn't even make out who it was but assumed it was his friend with the delivery. As they came closer, Frank began to feel better as he saw Dino's hand wave from the open window of the cab as they stopped just few feet away.

"Hey, Frank, thanks for coming all the way out here," Dino said while shutting down the truck and putting on the parking brake. "Two of my guys are with me. I'm sure the four of us can get these things into your truck."

"You got it, Dino," Frank said as he went around the back of his own truck and lifted the heavy sliding door, trying not to make too much noise. That was hard to do with these metal doors that woke the dead when they were lifted up. Dino and his guys did the same in the back of their truck. The nearest house was about a half mile away, and people were used to seeing kids head out to the open field deep in the woods on some weekend nights. Once the door was opened, they turned on the dome light mounted on the ceiling of the box truck and saw a large wooden crate and one giant crate containing the pieces of a computerized tomography, or CT, scanner.

There were four other unmarked wooden boxes tied down along the inside wall of the box truck. Inside each were two AR-15 semiautomatic assault rifles with no serial numbers. It wasn't that the numbers were scratched out. They were just not on them. There was just a blank space where a serial number would be imprinted. Those numbers follow the life of the weapon and could be associated with a current or past owner, sort of like a VIN number on a vehicle. Frank didn't care if they had the numbers or not, but upon inspection he noticed that these must have left the factory before being assigned serial numbers. Dino also went into his cab and took out a small leather case that one might use to carry shaving supplies. Inside were two tungsten-shielded multidose vials of F-18, or Fluorine-18, and Thallium-201, better known in the medical world as TI-201. Both were radioisotopes.

"Be careful with these. I don't know what the fuck they do, but they're radioactive inside," Dino explained as he handed over the case, not wanting to know much more about how they were going to be used.

"Those are medicines, my friend. They go with the scanner. They're needed for patients who will use machines like this," said Frank as he checked to make sure the case was sealed well. It had a lead lining as an extra protective measure for those who would handle it.

The night was dark and foggy as the men moved the crates from one truck to another carefully, knowing how fragile the machine was. It took only a few minutes to get both CT crates loaded into Frank's U-Haul. Then a member of Dino's crew picked up one of the three boxes with the weapons and handed it down to Frank, who was waiting at the back of the truck.

"There's nothing with these. Just empty clips," said Tony, who was used to helping out Dino on these special deliveries and other duties with the family. "You'll have to get your own caps."

"No worry, these are going to help protect some folks overseas, and they know what to do with them," Frank said as he took the box and moved it toward the U-Haul.

In all, the transfer, which only took around twenty minutes, was much quicker than Frank expected, thanks to the help of Dino and his crew. He went back to his truck; and behind the front seat, in the small space that separated it from the back of the cab, was a camel-colored briefcase. He pulled the case out of the space and carried it over to Dino, who was just getting back into his own truck and chatting with Tony. Frank approached Dino's truck with this final part of the transfer, which his Italian friend was expecting.

"This is a huge help for these folks, and we really appreciate it," Frank said as he handed the case to Dino through the open window of the truck. "You're a great help and good friend."

"My pleasure, Frank. Always glad to help with charities when we can. Be careful with that stuff."

"Will do. Do you want to count it?" Frank asked, referring to the eight hundred thousand dollars cash inside the case.

"Don't have to. I know where you live!" Dino jested, knowing that he indeed did know where Frank lived, and if even a dollar was missing, he would be paying him a visit. "Racquetball soon," he said as he started the diesel engine and put the truck in gear.

"You bet. Later on."

Dino and Tony drove off into the night, back down the dirt road toward the paved street, ending yet another business transaction. Frank also turned his rented U-Haul toward the street with a smile on his face, knowing that he had but two more tasks to complete.

Six time zones away, a chilly wind was blowing at an outdoor café in Frankfurt, where breakfast was being served and a bank notice of fund transfers to three different U.S. banks in the New England area landed in Mohammad Featha's phantom e-mail account. This triggered a notification ping as he sipped his morning coffee, watching the commuters starting their daily shuffle. His soldier was making progress, and this was money well spent.

The morning air in Miami was heavy with humidity, with temperatures in the eighty-degree range at this time of the year as South Floridians moved from spring to the sticky summer months. Jake enjoyed driving his classic car with the top down, but there were a few months of the year when it was only possible: either very early in the morning or at dusk and into the nighttime. This was going to be a special day for him because Claire was flying into town on business to check up on the counterfeit casino chip bust that he and his agents had worked. Even though she lived in D.C. and he in Miami, they kept in pretty close contact and would try to get together if opportunity knocked. He left early for the office to get some paperwork out of the way in order to make time to pick her up at the airport around lunch. As he made his way off South Beach onto 195, the usual morning traffic was true to form and pretty much stop and go as he headed westbound for the city. Jake parked in his usual space and raced up the elevator, only to find Rosa had beat him once again.

"You have Claire coming in at eleven thirty-five, and your dad called, asking for your sister's cell number again," she said as she handed him a cup of coffee, knowing he probably knew all of this, but it was her duty to remind him of such things. "Felton also called from D.C. and would like a few minutes when you get a chance. He said he would text you."

"I don't know what I would do without you, Rosa," Jake said while walking into his office, eyeing the pile of papers she had left on his desk and still hoping that he could get out of there early.

"Just a few small things to sign this morning and some leave requests to approve," she said, following him into the office.

"Cool. I'll be taking Claire to lunch then to the Service field office where she and our guys will talk about the chips."

"Lunch?" she questioned skeptically.

"Lunch. Just lunch," he said back, knowing that she was pulling his strings.

He quickly went through the pile of forms, including some warrant requests that would go to the U.S. Attorney's office and some evidence release forms to return the luggage of tourists who might have been stopped at the airport or cruise terminal for trying to bring items back into the country that were not allowed. On the computer, he quickly went on the CBP portal to approve leave requests for three of his special agents and one civilian cyber guy.

Jake's mind was on Claire and the lunch they would share in just a few hours once she landed. He wanted to take her someplace that was classic Miami and tropical. He was thinking about Mango's, which was on South Beach and had an open porch along with live music at lunch and dinner. He was also decided considering Jaguar Ceviche Spoon Bar for lunch because they'd been there before, and she had mentioned it when she told him about her trip to Miami. She would be staying at the airport Marriott for the two nights of her trip. Jake wanted to make the most of those nights but knew she was hesitant on restarting their former relationship.

"I'm going to be headed to MIA. I'll be on the cell and radio," Jake said to Rosa as he logged off his computer and took his ID out of the reader to put back into his wallet/badge holder.

A few minutes later, he took the elevator down to the parking garage and walked a few steps over to his G-ride parked in its designated spot. He backed up the Crown Vic and headed out through the gate and down to Florida Route 836 West toward MIA, or Miami International Airport. He was a tad early but thought he would take the opportunity to check on some of his field operation agents who worked the airport. They covered both the passenger side as well as cargo.

Outside the car it looked like some towering cumulus clouds were forming to produce Miami's typical daily afternoon showers, he thought as he turned off the highway onto South Le Jeune Road. Traffic was usually tough in this area, with ongoing construction and plenty of barrels to avoid hitting as road crews worked to improve the airport access, which should have been done years ago. The sun was bright and humidity was starting to build as Jake made his way over to the cargo area of Miami International on NW Thirty-Sixth Street. He turned into the Atlas Air terminal where two of his crew were working this morning. Atlas was a huge cargo carrier based in Miami and had become a giant cargo hub for the Southeast U.S. as well as Central and South America. Their training facility was next door to Landmark Aviation, which ran the local FBO, or fixed based operation, where civilian business jets and other aircraft operated. Craig Shultz, Jake's point man on everything cargo at the airport, was training two new ICE agents newly assigned to the office.

Jake pulled up into a parking space and walked over to the Atlas door, where he saw Craig's car. Craig's uncle flew 747-8s for Atlas and was also a great source for keeping an eye open for anything strange moving into or out of MIA. As he opened the door to the building, Craig and the two new agents were walking down the hall headed out. They met in the hallway.

"Special Agent Shultz, how goes the lesson?" Jake asked as the four stopped and chatted for a few minutes in the hallway.

"Just fine, sir. These two guys are getting spun up on everything MIA!"

"Super. I was headed over to pick up a Secret Service agent coming into town to follow up on the casino chips we found."

"Could this be an agent we both know?" asked Craig in a tone that both newbies standing next to him would recognize as a personal moment.

"Why, yes, Agent Schultz, ironically it is."

"Imagine that," Craig said sarcastically.

"Imagine that!" Jake said back.

"How do we look for the rest of the week out this way?" Jake quizzed his colleague, getting the conversation back to business.

"Quiet. Just the usual movements. Field ops has most of it under control. We'll be briefed if anything we need to deal with pops up."

"Very cool. Well I hope you two lads learn a lot from this man. He could write the book on cargo movements."

"Yes, sir," they both said almost at the same time, trying to score with the boss.

"All right, I'm headed over to the PAX terminal to get Claire. See you guys later on."

With that, they headed out the door to their cars. Jake pulled out and headed back around the airport, toward what military and law enforcement typically call the "PAX" or passenger terminal. The great part about driving his government unmarked Crown Vic was that he didn't have to park like civilians do in garages and walk for miles to get to the terminal. He could just pull up anywhere and leave it. Ordinarily the Secret Service would have picked up their own agent at the airport, but this was different, and Jake volunteered to shuttle her down to their office. He walked into the building and headed for Concourse H, where Delta arrivals would be gated. Unlike most who waited for their arriving passengers before the TSA checkpoints, Jake walked up to the supervisor, showed his credentials and special MIA all-access pass, and quickly walked past the lines and through the crew metal detectors which went off but didn't matter for him.

A few minutes later he was standing at the arrival gate for Delta Flight 1151 from DCA, better known as Reagan National Airport in Washington. The MD-88 had just pulled up to the gate, and the Delta agents were opening the door to the Jetway. Tired-looking passengers started coming through the door with their carry-ons and briefcases. First class always got off first, and Jake waited through the first wave of people getting off the aircraft. Finally, after a few more minutes, Special Agent Claire Wilson came through the door and spotted him immediately. His first impression was that her hair was always the same: wavy, dirty blond, and beautiful. She had a knapsack and roll away for the two-night visit with nothing checked. Her eyes, which had attracted him in the first place years ago, were still like magnets.

"Thanks for getting me," she said as she gave him a hug and kiss on the cheek. "A lot warmer here."

"That it is, and I wouldn't have it any other way."

Both agents walked down the concourse and out to the terminal toward his waiting car.

"Glad to see you still know how to park," she chuckled as they walked out the automatic doors of the terminal.

"Just for you, my dear."

"Bullshit. You park like this all the time."

He just loved her directness and missed it every day.

"Lunch or business first?" asked Jake, hoping for the latter.

"We can eat and then head to the field office. I told them that was what I would be doing. We're not supposed to meet until three anyway. They've got some intel processing to use for the meeting. Seems those chips came from what we thought was a closed operation offshore."

He started the Crown Vic and headed back toward the highway and downtown, hoping like hell that she would take the invitation to stay at his place rather than at the government-approved Marriott near the airport. He had mentioned it in an e-mail a few days ago when she said she was coming to town and had not heard back yes or no.

Jake drove toward Coconut Grove and Jaguar Ceviche Spoon Bar. He and Claire had been regulars there on Friday nights a few years back, before she headed off to training and the Service. Jake enjoyed Latin American food, and there was no place better than Miami to get it in the States. Jaguar had Peruvian dishes he and Claire had always enjoyed together. It was a small place but well known in "the Grove" as the locals call it. It was also not too far from his father's place. He parked on Grand Avenue, one of the main drags in the Grove and just a few steps away from the restaurant.

Just as they were walking into the place, his iPhone went off, and he wanted to hit ignore. It was his father calling, as if he knew that they were only a mile or so apart. Knowing it could always be a medical problem or another emergency, he excused himself and took the call as Claire sat down. His dad needed a prescription picked up and asked if Jake could run the errand. Being so close, he said he would right after lunch, but knew he couldn't hang around because Claire had to be downtown at three. His dad would be surprised when Jake pulled up with his ex in the car, Jake thought as he walked back to their table.

"Sorry, had to get that. You never know if it's an emergency," he said as the waiter came over to ask for a drink order. "Diet coke, no ice for me."

"Same, but with ice," she said to the waiter. "How's he doing?"

"About the same. More memory loss, but he's still got a lot of that New York chutzpah!"

"That's good. I wish I could see him."

"Actually, you will. He's got a prescription down the street, and his place is a few blocks away on our way back to town. That's what the call was for."

"Nice. Two Steins in one visit."

"So where you going to stay tonight?" He just had to finally ask, hoping not to hear the Marriott.

"Why don't you just ask, Jake? 'Claire, do want to sleep with me tonight?'" she shot back rapidly.

"I'm not that kind of guy."

"Yes, you are!"

"Okay, yes, I am."

"I'll stay on the beach."

His heart almost came out of his chest. He was so excited but didn't want to show it to her.

"Super. I'll get you the spare keycard I have in the car."

"Just happened to have it in the car?"

"Ironic, isn't it."

Drinks arrived, and they each ordered a light lunch called *chino del chifa*, which was a Peruvian type of stir-fried veggies and rice. The small talk continued for a while, and then the two chatted about the casino chip case. He was looking forward to the night ahead and found it hard to concentrate on anything else.

After they finished lunch and paid the check, he stopped at the CVS drive-though, picked up his dad's prescription, and drove about three minutes to the condo. Jake called ahead and asked him to come outside so that he could drop it off and run along to get Claire back into town for the meeting. As he pulled the Crown Vic up into the parking lot, his dad was sitting on a bench with a Yankees hat on and classic untucked South Florida shirt with flowers on it. Jake rolled down the window and held up the bag with the pills.

"Hey, Dad, here it is, and I've got a surprise for you too," he said while motioning with his head toward the passenger.

"Get out and bring it over here for Christ's sake. I'm an old man."

He put the car in park and both got out just for a second. You could see the surprise on his father's face when he saw Claire.

"Are you two back together?" he asked. The filter had gone out a long time ago, so there was no telling what his dad would or would not say to someone.

"No, just good friends. Claire is in town working on a case."

"Oh, that's right. You protect that asshole we have in the White House."

She spoke up at that point.

"Not exactly, but yes, I'm with the Secret Service, Mr. Stein."

Jake was exasperated and said, "Dad, be respectful of the office and Claire."

"Yeah, yeah. How much was that?"

"I've got it. Just a few bucks, thanks to your Tricare."

"All right. It's hot as hell, and I've got a bridge game coming up. Those people can't play for shit," he said, looking at Claire.

"Be good, Dad. I'll give you a call later on," Jake said while getting back into the car, slightly embarrassed by his father's language.

As they pulled out of the lot, Claire just chuckled.

"What are you laughing at?" Jake asked.

"You."

"Why? I can't control him. He's always like that. You know that."

"That's why I'd be afraid to marry you. You might end up like that," she explained with a bit of a comic tone.

"Who said I would marry you anyway."

The two just shook their heads as he headed back north toward downtown and the Miami field office of the U.S. Secret Service.

Metro Miami Furniture & Bedding had a good month, and once again the store's owner started to enjoy having a little more financial maneuvering room after the downturn in 2008 that put many businesses out to pasture. The store had a large showroom up front with a delivery center in the back. In the delivery center, furniture was trucked in from their suppliers and made ready for the customers, who would either pick it up or, for a fee, Metro Miami Furniture would deliver it to them. There was not much to do with bedding except take it off one truck and put it on another or in the storage area. The company also rented storage units to use as an overflow when room was needed in the back of the store.

Box springs and mattresses came wrapped in plastic and were easy for the staff to handle. Hamid Khalid was up front in the showroom talking to a customer when his phone vibrated, indicating that a text message had come in. After he finished with the customer, he stepped into the bathroom to read the text from his friend in Rhode Island. "Working tomorrow but looking forward to seeing you on my vacation in four weeks," read the text. Hamid knew just what this meant. The pieces were starting to go into motion, and Frank Castro, a.k.a. Ali Ahamid, would be shipping the CT scanner overseas and then would head to Miami in around four weeks to accomplish the second part of his mission.

Three days later on Saturday, Hamid took his lunch break down at Bayside where he decided to get some takeout from the food court and sit on the deck overlooking Biscayne Bay and the Port of Miami. Saturday was a big day in the furniture business because people were not working and could shop. This was why his days off were usually Tuesday and Sunday. Hamid did not want to be away from the shop long, knowing Amanda needed him there for customers. Thankfully Bayside was not too far away, and lunch would only take about forty-five minutes. He wore his red golf shirt and sat at a table near the corner of the deck. He picked the red shirt out this morning purposely for its color.

There were tables all around for people to eat their food and enjoy the view. He was almost finished with his sandwich when finally he noticed another man coming over to sit down near him with a piece of pizza and a drink. The weather was hot and muggy, and the Florida sun was bright. Most people were wearing sunglasses and enjoying a leisurely Saturday. Hamid was reading the weekend edition of *USA Today* during his lunch. He had a few bites of the sandwich left and continued to read the paper until he was finished eating. As he rolled up the sandwich wrapper, he took a few more sips of his Diet Pepsi and stood up to throw away the trash and to return the tray to the top of the trash container. He had left the newspaper on the table with his drink, and the man sitting a few feet away asked if he could look at the sports section.

"Sure, you can have the whole paper," said Hamid as he handed it to him and turned back to get his keys and drink.

"Thanks," said the man who took the paper and went back to his pizza, looking for the sports section.

Hamid just nodded, picked up his drink and keys and headed back to his car. Bishar Fouad, the man who asked for the paper, finished his pizza and also headed back to work. It was turnaround day once again for the *Star Orion*, and his liberty was going to expire in just a couple of hours. As he walked back to the port, he opened the paper to the sports section and found what looked like someone's lunch order folded up inside. "Bringing eight burgers and fries for four people," it read. This was code for eight rifles with ammo arriving in four weeks. Bishar read the note and then ripped it into a bunch of pieces. He threw away about a third of the bits of paper in a trash can, dropped another third into another, and the rest he threw away with the paper before he entered port security.

His next duty back on the ship would be to make sure that four crucial cabins would need new mattresses on a specific turnaround day in the not-too-distant future.

Frank Castro had already done the paperwork and created the documentation to ship a used CT scanner to a broker in the Republic of Georgia for delivery to the Worldcare charity organization. The medical equipment and supplies accompanying it would be shipped in one standard twenty-foot ocean container. Frank was a trusted export broker with Evergreen, and this task was rather easy, seeing that he was one of the approving authorities for the day shift. All he really had to do was schedule a local pickup, and the company would take care of the rest. They would issue a container and load it with the cargo being shipped overseas. In many cases the cargo would be packed in with other shipments in the same container. But because it was a **medhazmat** or medical hazardous material, the scanner and box of radioactive medicines would not be placed with any other cargo. It would arrive seven to ten days later on the other side of the ocean. Once the cargo arrived, it would be delivered to the receiving party at the port, held for pickup, or delivered to an address. In this case, it would be held for pickup at the port of entry in Batumi, Republic of Georgia.

Typically at his job with Evergreen in Providence, Frank would not be scheduling local pickups or deliveries. His job was to handle the containers that were arriving and those ready for export. There were times, however, when he had late-date requests for export of cargo and had to schedule a pickup with the intermodal group who shared the same part of the building. Their office was just across the hall from his. He knew most of the people who worked over there and how long they'd been with the company. On Tuesdays they were usually a bit short staffed, so he picked this day to schedule the special pickup he was arranging.

"Good morning, Sam," Frank said to the new guy who was working alone for just the third or fourth time since joining Evergreen.

"Hi, Frank. What's the good word?" Sam said, not paying too much attention and keeping his head down in the pile of paperwork in front of him.

"Just working like a dog, Sam. Hey, I have a late-date local pickup."

"How local?" Sam asked, still sounding somewhat preoccupied.

"East Providence."

"Tomorrow morning, between eight and twelve," Sam said without even looking up or changing this tone of voice. It sounded to him like an easy add to the morning schedule.

"Super. Here's the waybill and address. You're the man, Sam."

"I know," he said with a little smile while taking the paperwork from Frank and putting it in the box on the right side of his desk marked "scheduled."

The address on the waybill Frank handed Sam for pickup was the U-Haul storage facility located about ten miles away in the town of East Providence. It was not too unusual to have cargo picked up at these types of facilities. Sam didn't give it another thought, but Frank did, knowing that the pickup would occur the next morning and he that had to make sure it was ready. During lunch, he took a ride over to the U-Haul storage and spoke with the person who would be on duty when the Evergreen crew came by for the pickup. This was the same U-Haul dealer where he rented the truck just a week or so earlier.

The self-storage company had a policy allowing the person or company renting the unit to leave written approval authorizing access to third parties. Frank brought a written authorization for pickup from storage unit 3K. The unit was where he had brought the CT scanner and medical supplies the night Dino delivered them. It was convenient that everything was already in crates ready to be shipped. He just had to attach the paperwork to the wooden crates, leave the written authorization with the storage office, and inform them of the pickup. The shipper was Worldcare International Charities, and the authorization for pickup was written on their stationery and signed by a Mr. Tad Azzio. It also bore a notary public stamp and signature. The fact that there was no Mr. Azzio and that an online printing company had manufactured the notary stamp along with the stationery was not even a factor. Frank finished his business and left the small storage office, headed back toward his workplace, where tomorrow yet another export would be containerized and sent overseas. He would message Boris, his contact in Batumi, with the arrival date and tracking number once it was in the system. Frank headed back onto I-195 west, toward downtown Providence, with a feeling of satisfaction and now looking for some lunch before returning to the office.

Chapter 11

GLOBE-TROTTING

THERE ARE MANY different ways to book a vacation, but the Internet is how most people plan their trips to escape the real world. Gone, for the most part, are the corner travel agencies people would visit to plan out their vacations. Agents know the world of travel and have special connections with the airlines, resorts, and cruise companies. Today, though, most people just pull out their laptop and go to Expedia, Orbitz, or direct to the company to book their trip. Such was the case with the people who would be taking a cruise sometime in September on the *Star Orion* out of Miami to the Eastern Caribbean. On the Star Caribe website, guests could check out the ship, book a cabin, schedule shore excursions, sign age waivers, buy drink packages, and much more. It was a one-stop shop for everything their ships offered. The other great thing about booking online was that people could do it from anywhere with a Wi-Fi connection.

It was a chilly day in Brussels, Belgium, considering that it was June, and all the tourists were coming out to shine like spring flowers. Abdul-Aziz Fahad did not have a client here but thought that it would be a good market to crack for the software business he worked for as he took a short walk from the Sheraton Hotel he booked online. There was a misty rain falling and not a sign of the sunshine that was promised on the local weather report that morning. Brussels is a busy city with lots of history, restaurants, and culture. The official language is French, but most people also spoke English and German. Fahad spoke both English and French in addition to his native Arabic and Farsi. For this meeting he would speak English and not a word in his native tongue. He agreed to meet Mohammad at an Irish pub about five or six blocks from the hotel, but off the main drag. He had been there once before and enjoyed the classic Irish food. Unlike in America and other western nations, smoking was allowed in most public places including eateries.

Fahad made his way down a small side street to what looked like a back alley where the Lyons Head Pub was located. He noticed that the place was as small and smoky as he remembered when he opened the door and went inside to look for his boss and spiritual leader. The bar was full and most of the tables taken. The sound of Irish music playing on the sound system echoed throughout. The booths were large and custom handmade of thick wood just for this restaurant. Lyrics of Irish songs were carved into them with some written in Gaelic. Fahad took a quick look around and saw Mohammad sitting in one of them near the kitchen entrance at the back of one of the two dining rooms. He approached the booth and sat on the opposite side, sliding toward the wall. Mohammad slid a bit toward the wall as well for more privacy.

"As-salaam alaikum," Fahad said quietly in almost a whisper, wishing peace be upon his mentor.

Mohammad nodded his head to show his approval.

"Welcome," Mohammad said in a low tone.

A waiter approached and asked the men if they wanted a drink. Mohammad ordered just a bottle of spring water while Fahad ordered a soft drink. The waiter quickly walked off after taking their order and leaving a bowl of peanuts.

"We are progressing on the project," Mohammad started. "You have done well in your duties."

"My team is in place and ready once we have a solid date to work with."

"It is as long as the pieces are in place," Mohammad said with a cautious tone. "I see no reason they won't be by late August or early September. We expect to acquire the 'oven' within two weeks and ship it to Puerto Rico, where you have your arrangements made."

"I do. Our friend in Frankfurt will complete the paper and electronic documentation and be ready for the transfer once it reaches the Port of San Juan. My broker in San Juan has been reliable on both of the test shipments we've completed using the Sellco cover," Fahad said somewhat proudly. He had arranged two dummy shipments for delivery to the port from overseas.

"You have served your faith and will complete your destiny," Mohammad said in a low monotone. "We have also completed travel documents for you and your team. Once the shipment is en route to Puerto Rico and a solid date is set for the transfer, we can book passage."

The waiter approached the booth again with two drinks on his tray and carefully placed them on the table before dismissing himself quickly.

"We will use different travel websites to book the tickets," explained Fahad. "With the documents and names, we should have no problem completing the reservations."

"They will be mailed to you at your Sellco address in Frankfurt and to Hamid in Miami if everything works well in Moscow and Batumi with the shipment."

"With Allah's help and hope," Fahad said quietly. "The orders from Star Caribe for the medical unit installation have to be solid."

"Our friend in Frankfurt and contacts on the ship will coordinate that. Also there is a special crew member who will be of great assistance and make himself known to you."

This was news to Fahad. He was strict on security, and now the head of the operation was telling him he'd have one more team member. *Whoever this person is, he must be a part of the ship's company*, he thought while trying not to act surprised or upset. On another operation just two years ago, he had heard a story that there might have been others involved not known to the primary team. Trust was indeed a rare commodity in the business of jihad.

"Should I have more information on this additional martyr?" asked Fahad, knowing the answer before he asked the question.

"That is all you need to know, my brother. He will be sent from Allah at the appropriate time," preached Mohammad. "He will hand you something with the code words 'Sent from Doha' on it. He will answer to you as leader."

"I will welcome this additional martyr," whispered Abdul.

"Now we order food," said Mohammad as he motioned for the waiter to come back to take an order. Both men were hungry, and this old Irish pub had some of the best classic fish and chips available in Brussels.

Moscow was one of those cities that stuck with you forever after visiting or living there. The history and culture were hard to escape as tourists continued to make their way to the Russian capitol. The very long, bitterly cold winters and usually sunny and dry summers made people want to get outside as much as possible during the good weather months. For Sergio Levta, just being back in the city made him miss the life he once had and brought mixed feelings of disappointment and anger as he parked his rental car not far from Gorky Park. He was nervous about this meeting and what would become of it. He needed his friend's help to complete the task for which he was being paid so handsomely. He also did not want to blow this opportunity or expose himself or the people paying him to any authorities. Sergio was warned by his contact, Boris, back in Batumi that if his friend, Peter, didn't want to play, it could be a fatal mistake. This was indeed a dangerous game he was playing. Boris also authorized Sergio to offer up to one million U.S. dollars to his friend for his assistance.

Peter Koslov was now only making about a quarter of what he did when he was a full-time government employee not too many years ago. This was what Sergio was counting on to be the key in getting his help. Before he could come to Moscow to make contact with Peter, Sergio also had to tell Boris all about his friend, including where he lived, family status, and car he drove. He did not want to ask too many questions about why Boris needed that information. It was just needed before Boris would bless the trip and meeting. What Sergio did not know was that if he reported to Boris, whom he had to contact via phone and code immediately following their lunch, that Peter did not want to play or threatened to tell his bosses, Boris had prearranged Peter's disappearance though an associate.

The sun was shining bright on this June Friday as Sergio walked to their meeting spot near a fountain toward the corner of the park. People were everywhere, getting outside from the dark offices they occupied all morning for some fresh air. He wanted a very public place to chat with his friend whom he hadn't seen in a while and wanted to arrive a few minutes late so that he could see if there were any other people who might be watching them. Paranoid, maybe. Careful, always. He noticed nothing out of the ordinary as he approached Peter from behind and tapped him on the shoulder.

"Long time, my friend," Sergio said as Peter spun around to see his old comrade.

"Da!" said Peter as the two embraced with the typical Muscovite bear hug.

"How are you, my friend?" asked Sergio.

"Fine, just fine. And you? How are Rina and the baby? The pictures on Facebook are always good to see."

"Both are well. She wants to come to Moscow someday to meet you. You should come to Batumi and stay at my hotel," Sergio said trying to start things off and catch up a bit.

"My hotel! Mr. Big Shot," Peter joked as they walked toward some benches that were usually full at this time of the day. There was a free bench not far from a cart selling Indian food.

"I'm only an assistant manager, but it's a job, and I like the hospitality business. It's a lot better than working for the government, in some ways."

"Sure it is. Any job is good these days. Even working for the government part-time is okay. As long as it pays."

That was a good opportunity to ask a few questions of his former comrade. He knew that Peter was a good, loyal Russian, but his loyalty had limits, which in some cases were dictated by economics.

"Are you happy with your current work?" Sergio asked as they sat for a moment on the bench.

"I am. As I said, it would be nice if it was full-time and with my old benefits renewed. Perhaps in the future."

"What if you were offered another opportunity?" inquired Sergio.

"Are you offering me a job, Sergio?"

Both men laughed, and Peter got up to go over to the cart to order some chicken curry and an Indian bread called *nan*.

Sergio waited on the bench, sipping a drink he had bought while walking over, still not sure how best to approach this subject. Peter returned a few minutes later with something to eat.

"Where were we?" Peter asked as he sat down.

"Offering you a job," Sergio said with a little bit of jest in his tone.

"Oh, right. Thanks. I don't want to live in Batumi, my friend," he said with a chuckle.

"Better winters."

"Costs more to live. No symphony or ballet."

"Less traffic," Sergio countered.

"No racing."

"What if you could live in Moscow and have a place on the sea for the summer and a boat to go with it?" Sergio asked, changing his tone to a more serious sound.

"Sure. And someday I'll be head of state."

"I have some friends who would like your help on a project, and they are willing to pay you for it."

"What kind of project?" asked Peter, now wondering what his friend was talking about and whether it was something that he could help with.

"One that pays very well."

"Really? How well?"

"About a million U.S. dollars," said Sergio in a lower, much more serious tone.

Peter stopped eating in midbite, almost choking, and took a sip of his drink. Now he was really wondering why his old friend had showed up in Moscow. Perhaps he was with the black market. He had heard rumors that Sergio did a little dealing on the side. That was nothing too uncommon, given the current economic situation in both of their countries.

"Is this something that is legal?" asked Peter.

Sergio thought for a few seconds before answering. Once he told him what he needed, there was no going back. He would feel extreme guilt if Peter said no and something happened to him.

"You would never have to work again for just providing a little access."

"Access to what?" Peter asked knowing full well what he was talking about. His head started spinning as he thought about what the consequences would be for him if he got caught doing such a thing. The Russian government did not take treason lightly and dealt with it even more swiftly. He had heard rumors about others being offered money by foreigners for information about their stockpiles and programs, but he had figured it was just hearsay.

"You would not be in any way associated with a theft or crime. Mainly it is just providing access for a few minutes. My associate would like to switch out an air-conditioning unit at Burr 34," said Sergio, hoping that using these words and not mentioning the true purpose of their needed access might somehow soften what he was asking.

"An air-conditioning unit?"

"We go in with you, swap out the air-conditioning unit, and leave. Simple really. You used to have facility climate control as part of your checklist, and I assume that hasn't changed since I worked up here," stated Sergio, hoping like hell it hadn't.

"Nothing has changed except the hours and benefits, which were cut when we both lost our jobs."

Sergio took a sip of his drink and decided to get a sandwich from the cart and let this idea sink in for a few minutes. He walked a few steps to the cart and ordered an Indian version of a Greek gyro sandwich while keeping an eye on his friend. The man at the cart took his three rubles, handed him the food, and then Sergio walked back over to the bench and sat down.

"Why come to me for this?" Peter asked.

"I wanted to give you an opportunity for a better life beyond working part-time as a contractor for a government that screwed us both over."

Peter waited a few minutes and ate his lunch without saying anything else. Sergio did the same, worried that he had opened a can of worms and did not know what to do if his friend turned against him. The sound of Peter's silence was deafening even though there was quite a bit of noise, as a man played a sitar for money not far away and lots of people walked by, chatting it up during their lunch hour.

Finally, Peter set down his drink and spoke.

"I wouldn't touch anything?" he asked a little more quietly this time.

"Nothing. Just get us in. I've still got my old ID card, but I'm sure it's not valid anymore. My associate will be with the air-conditioning company. We swap out the air unit with another and drive away."

Peter sat quiet once again for a few minutes. Then he looked up and spoke to his friend. Sergio's stomach was in knots, and his heart was pounding like he had run a six-minute mile.

"How does the money work?"

Sergio instantly had a feeling of relief sweep over him. This was the toughest hurdle he had to jump. If he could get Peter on board, the rest would be just a matter of logistics.

"One-third is wired to an account with your name on it in Zurich, and you get the access code and account number. The rest is wired once the job is completed."

Peter thought for a few more seconds before responding.

"What are you going to do with the 'air conditioner' when you get it?"

"Nothing. It's for clients who will use it to protect their people. If I have a gun and you have a gun, chances are we will not ever use our guns on each other."

This made Peter feel slightly better about considering such a request. He knew deep down inside that this may or may not be the real story, but it made sense in a way, which helped him digest it better.

"I will have to leave after this," Peter said to Sergio, looking him in the eye for the first time in their conversation.

"A million U.S. dollars goes a long way and can take you a long way."

Sergio knew Peter was a good pick because he was single and had no big family ties in Moscow. His sister lived in London and his parents had both died. Sergio and Peter had worked closely back in the day, and he wanted good things for his friend.

"What do I have to do?" Peter quizzed. He didn't want to ask too many questions, knowing there was a risk involved.

"I'll be back with my associate, who is an air-conditioning expert, and we will make contact when ready. I would expect us in a few weeks to a month's time. Once we replace the air-conditioning unit, we will both have plenty of time to move to a better life someplace else," said Sergio with a tone of confidence in his voice.

"I did an inspection there about four months ago, and it will not be due for two months. I am already contracted to perform the next inspection."

"Perfect. That will give you a good month to make your future plans, perhaps finding a new place to live with a new name if you wish. It's not like they will find anything missing for a long time, given the way the inspections are done," Sergio explained.

"I need the one-third first. There is no way I will go through with this without some sort of down payment," Peter said like a businessman.

"My guy understands that. A third of our price will be deposited into the new account, and I will bring you the account information and paperwork when we meet again to complete the transaction. The remainder will be wired in before we go our separate ways," explained Sergio. He had already spoken with Boris, and they both had anticipated the questions and logistics needed to secure Peter's services.

"Agreed," Peter said, thinking that the things were so old that they probably wouldn't fuse anyway. Maybe that was wishful thinking or another way to justify something that some would consider treason. Either way, he would never have to worry about money again in his lifetime if he played his cards right.

The two sat silent once again for a few minutes, finishing off their lunches. After some catching-up conversation, the two shook hands and parted ways, knowing they would see each other again in a matter of weeks, possibly for the last time in both of their lives. It seemed that they would each start anew after their next meeting.

Chasing counterfeit leads was something Special Agent Claire Wilson did as a main job with the Secret Service, but with cutbacks and, more importantly, a giant increase in protectees since 9/11, her primary job often became her secondary job. When a DL, or detail leader, needed additional support, he or she would contact the SAIC (special agent in charge) who would tap into other field offices and branches to augment the request or need. Her open counterfeit cases would have to wait when these requests came in, and she would report for temporary duty as ordered. Thankfully, her trip to Miami was not cancelled, and she was able to follow up on some leads in the phony casino chip case, which was one of fourteen she was working at the moment. She also agreed to stay the two nights with Jake at his place on South Beach and had actually missed him over the years they had been chasing their own careers. Playing hard to get was easy for this girl from Arkansas who was a natural dirty blond and knew she turned heads when walking down the beach. She had to learn to say no to the boys growing up on the Gulf Coast. The good news was that she could be choosy when it came to men and relationships. Something deep down, though, kept coming back to Jake Stein. In her heart she knew that he would wait until she was ready. She just didn't want to show it too often. This business trip was a good test to see if that was still the case. When she boarded the plane to return to Washington in two days, her gut would send a message.

Jake dropped her off at the Miami field office after their lunch, and she was assigned a government car to use for her short visit. Counterfeit casino chips were becoming big business, and Jake's office had handed off the case to the Miami field office after the chips were found that night on the fishing vessel. They had discussed the case a few times over the phone, but typically they would not talk too much about each other's jobs. The day dragged on for both until they met back at his place for the night they both looked forward to.

Morning came around fast, Jake thought, as he drank his early coffee on the balcony with Claire joined him after taking a shower. She had one more workday of a two-night, three-day trip before heading back to D.C.

"I can get you back to the airport tomorrow if you want," he said while pouring her a cup. She still liked it black.

"If you've got time. Otherwise I can get someone at the office to drop me."

She wanted him to drive her to the airport but didn't want to seem too forward. That was strange, seeing that they had just spent two nights together in the same bed. He hadn't lost a thing she thought while sipping her coffee. He still gave her the best she had ever had. Careers be damned, maybe they should get back together, she mused.

"No problem. I'll come and get you around one. That will put you there a good hour before the flight."

"Okay, that will work."

"How's the case of the funny chips coming?" he asked.

"Slow," she said while peeling an orange for a quick fruit breakfast before they both went to work. "We think they're coming from the Dominican Republic. It's good work, and even the people in Vegas can't seem to tell the good ones from the bad ones."

Jake was just getting around to checking his BlackBerry and noticed an e-mail from Rosa, his assistant, saying that he had a SIPRNET message waiting from Felton.

"Hum . . ."

"What?" she asked.

"Nothing, just another SIPRNET from Felton."

"Coming to D.C.?"

"You can only hope," he jested. Truth be known, he would love to come up. Next time he was scheduled for an HSI quarterly, he would ask again to stay with her. Maybe after their last two nights, she would say yes.

"Don't overrate yourself, Special Agent Stein," she chuckled.

Jake continued to look at his e-mail inbox. There was nothing else too out of the ordinary. He just loved having her there and would be unhappy to see her leave the next day. At least they had one more night together.

"We're watching a TC jump around the planet a bit. Not sure it's anything, but I've noticed a pattern. Probably nothing, but we'll keep an eye on it," he said.

"Follow your gut feeling, that's what I always say," she responded, sarcastically as usual. He just loved that tone.

"Oh, really? About the TC or something else?"

"Your professional gut feelings, thank you very much."

With that, the two finished up coffee and she headed out the door with a kiss on the cheek.

"See you for supper. Ride to the airport tomorrow is on."

"Have fun," he said. "Be careful."

"Always."

Jake jumped into his car and headed to the office, knowing that another night of bliss awaited. At least he hoped so. For now, he had some work to do and made his way to the office. Rosa was the best assistant he had ever had. She kept him in check and always moving forward.

He arrived a few minutes after 9:00 a.m., and she gave him a look as he walked into the office.

"What?" he asked while walking to her desk and picking up the daily classified envelope that contained the updated case briefings.

"Long night?" she asked, knowing the answer and wanting to put her boss on the spot for fun.

"In what way?" he snapped back while looking over the envelope.

"You have a sick mind, boss!"

He took the envelope and walked into his office, smiling and thinking of the last two nights. For a while he swore off Claire, thinking that she was all career and what they had years ago would never return. This morning though, he was rethinking that outlook and hoping for perhaps another try at something long term. The commuting distance and fact that she was still torn up with the long hours and career might still stand in the way. Either way, these few nights were a bonus and welcome in his life which had become mostly work and little play.

The computer they used for secure communications and SIPRNET e-mails sat in the intel shop a few doors down from his office. Jake walked over, pushed the doorbell for entrance, and walked in. His clearance and code would allow him access, but when the intel people were working, it was always good to buzz first. He sat at one of the secure computers, shook the mouse to wake it up, inserted his ID/ CAC and typed his password. To get on SIPRNET, he would have to go to a secure website and server and, once again, put in his special SIPRNET password and touch his finger on the print reader sitting next to the system. Once his credentials were read and all was in order, his inbox would appear. Only one message popped up.

//////TOP SECRET/////SIPRNET/////EYES ONLY//////

TO: J Stein
FR: Felton
SUBJ: PRTC

Jake . . .

TC Fahad showed up in Brussels three days ago. Stayed at the Sheridan for one night. I tagged him, and we're getting regular updates from partner countries when available. CIA checked, and there were no clients listed that his company serves there. Also checked for other TC movements in the city, and all were negative. No record of departure, and possible he might have driven out. NSA will also ping him for us.

TF

Interesting, Jake thought. This guy certainly did move around a lot. Before 9/11 and the advent of interagency cooperation, Jake would not have much to do with this sort of intelligence unless it directly related a case he might have been working on with Customs. After September 11 everything changed, and once ICE was reestablished and Homeland Security Investigations stood up, it started to become second nature to follow up on this sort of thing. Thankfully, he had Tom's team in D.C. doing most of the heavy work and handed down the intel to the people in the field who might need it. That reminded him that another quarterly HSI meeting would be coming up, and he was sure that Fahad's movements would be discussed.

Typically it takes six or seven days to cross the ocean by ship from the North American continent to the European continent. In the shipping business, time is money, and any delays because of mechanical problems or weather are not welcome. In this dog-eat-dog business, competition is steep, especially on the intermodal side. The shipment for Worldcare left the Port of Providence bound for the Port of Batumi, Republic of Georgia, via stops in New York, change of shipping line in Algeciras, Spain, and Piraeus, Greece, with arrival almost two weeks later in the Port of Batumi. Boris Stockov was able to track the shipment, thanks to today's technology, right on his smart phone and knew what day it would arrive. Because it consisted of medical supplies and equipment, the container was given special designation and stored in the lower hold of the giant container ships. For this reason, it would be one of the last to come off.

Boris planned his week around the arrival of the container so that he would be free to do some part-time work at his friend's intermodal transfer and shipping brokerage company. When working this job, he would be given a number of waybills and head to the port, railway, or airport to pick up or drop off each container. He knew the process, having done it a number of times over the past few months. One waybill he had in his hand was sent by mail to a postal box rented in the name of Worldcare International. He had the key to the box because he rented it using the organization's name on the rental form and retrieved the paperwork just a few days before. His job was to pick up three containers that day and move them to the rail yard, about ten kilometers away. After that, he was done for the weekend. He started early on this Friday, knowing he had a special job to do and wanted to get the first two containers out of the way before moving the third.

The weather was warm and humid, typical of a summer day in Batumi. The first two pickups went well and relatively smoothly. When he was returning to the port to pick up the third, he drove though the main security gate with hardly a look by the officer who had seen him twice already that day. With a quick wave, he moved his large diesel truck toward the COSCO office. The container yard was hot, dusty, and bustling with activity. Leaving the truck running, he went inside and jumped on the computer at the kiosk used to find container locations and put in the tracking number. In an instant, he found the one marked "Worldcare Intl. (MEDHAZMAT)."

A few minutes later he got back into to his Volvo semitruck, drove over to the correct container trailer, hooked up the fifth wheel and air hose, then slowly pulled up to the COSCO office where he handed off the paperwork before heading to the gate. Once again, the contracted security guard stopped him for the paperwork.

"Last one?" the guard asked as he looked over the forms and the container to make sure they matched.

"*Da*. And ready for the weekend," Boris said, making small talk as he waited for a minute or two. He knew there was nothing inside the container that would cause problems. It was going outbound that would be a little more challenging.

"Good to go, have a nice weekend," the guard said as he waved to the other security officer inside the booth to push the button which lifted the small white gate, allowing access in and out of the port.

The waybill that was on the container was for delivery to the Port of Batumi with transfer to the rail yards for customer pickup. The rail yards also acted as a storage facility for customers who were willing to pay a nightly or weekly rate. Like the port, they were run by the state and had contracted security guards at the gate. He pulled the truck into the entrance and waved to the guard who lifted the gate.

The company he was working for part-time did a fair amount of business with containers and shipping companies, transferring them from place to place. They rented a block area of storage, which was nothing more than a spot in the yard where the company could keep containers they were contracted to move but had to wait for an available truck and driver. They also had three full-sized containers as overflow storage for odds and ends that might not need an entire whole or half container but could be added to others going the same way.

Boris pulled his truck up and backed the container from the States containing the CT scanner and medical supplies into a spot next to the company's storage units. It was a quiet afternoon at the rail yard, and workers were busy loading and unloading a train that just arrived from Kiev. He had the master combination lock code the company used to secure each of their three storage containers, which were around forty-two feet long. Once the lock was released, he opened the door, making a loud sound as the dry hinges moved and the heavy door swung open. An associate was standing about fifty feet away, checking out another container for movement and looked over when Boris whistled to get his attention. Boris waved, asking him to come over for a moment to give him a hand with something.

"Can I help you?" he asked, walking toward Boris in the hot afternoon sun.

"Sure, I just need a hand with a piece of equipment, if you don't mind," Boris asked.

"How big?"

Both men walked to the back of the company's permanent storage container to look inside.

"Just that air unit," Boris explained, hoping he would give him a hand. "It's empty and just hard for one to handle."

"Sure thing."

They went inside the storage container and each took a side of the air conditioner cabinet. They slowly moved it to the container on the trailer attached to his truck with the CT scanner inside.

"Watch the roof," Boris said as the two men moved the bulky cabinet into the back and pushed it to the sidewall where it could be tied down. Once it was in place, Boris thanked his helper, who quickly disappeared into the busy and dusty rail yard. He then picked up the straps he brought with him from home and secured the unit to the cleats attached to the wall of the container. The air-conditioning unit they moved was nothing but an empty shell, except for the fan blade that was seen through the air intake grates on the outside. The motor and other parts had been removed from the inside. Boris had bought it on eBay from a dealer who sold parts for air-conditioning units in Georgia, nearby Turkey, Armenia, and Russia. He was shopping for a particular model used by the Russian government that Peter told Sergio was still used in the special building at Base Burr 34.

Once the unit was secured in the container, he attached the phony paperwork that he had produced on his home computer using as a guide templates he had found online. The paperwork was a work order to replace the current unit at the base with the one he had in the container truck. He also put a similar work order on the crates containing the CT scanner that was in the forward part of the container. The shipping paperwork he would need upon returning to the port had not arrived yet, but he was expecting it in a day or two from Frankfurt. Now it was time for some late lunch and to pick up his partner for this road trip he was about to take. He climbed back into the truck and headed for the gate, and the dust from the rail yard seemed to be coming through the vents.

Chapter 12

SPECIAL DELIVERY

F RANK CASTRO HAD experienced many things during his time in the United States, but had never stepped foot inside an RV. It was not something that he had any interest in and really never gave it a second thought. He'd seen people driving up and down the highways in these mobile play machines. His code name was "the Shopper," and he had completed his mission of acquiring the items he was tasked to get, but there remained one more step to this process. In one of the two storage units he rented for these items were the boxes of weapons that Dino sold him, as well as ammo that he bought as a member of the Rehoboth Rod and Gun Club, where he would sometimes target shoot. Over a twelve-month period, he bought small quantities of .223 rounds, which he used in the AR-15 he rented at the club. The club offered many types of weapons for members to rent for target shooting, which, along with dues, was a revenue stream keeping the club in the black and the holiday parties funded.

Frank had collected ten boxes of fifty rounds which would be loaded into new polymer thirty-round clips he had purchased on eBay using a third-party account he had set up. Everything was in place for the next step: moving the weapons to Miami. He had thought of getting another U-Haul, but that would be risky. It would be better to use a different type of vehicle. A friend who also worked at the port owned a Class C RV, the type with the bed over the cab, and enjoyed taking his family on camping trips around the northeast. Frank looked inside on a few occasions when his colleague wound bring it to work before heading out on a long weekend. He had been surprised at the amount of room inside and was interested in the fact that, unlike commercial vehicles, drivers did not have to stop at weigh stations and were pretty much left alone by law enforcement.

After a Google search on his work computer, he found three dealers who rented these types of recreational vehicles. Only one of the three offered one-way rentals where the RV would be picked up at one location and dropped off at another. Camp America was located in the city of Warwick, Rhode Island, just a few miles south of Providence and just off I-95 near Theodore Francis Green Airport. Frank left work and made his way down to Warwick to see what may be available for a one-way trip to Miami. Spring and summer were the busy months for Camp America when RV rental was at its peak, but much to Frank's delight, this franchise dealer had brought in a few extra units from dealers in nearby Connecticut and New Hampshire. Class C RVs came in a number of different lengths, but Frank didn't care what size it was. The beauty of this plan was that he would not have to use hotels, stop at weigh stations, and could travel quietly down to South Florida with the goods he needed to deliver. He rented twenty-nine-foot motor home and added the additional insurance as well as "comfort packages," which equipped the vehicle with living necessities such as sheets, pillows, knives, forks, etc. Using his American Express card and Rhode Island driver's license, Frank signed the papers for a seven-day, one-way rental to Miami, Florida.

Upon returning to the office, Frank went onto the company Internet site and put a message on Craigslist looking for anyone who would like a free ride to Miami in return for some gas money and fun. By the time his shift was over, the Craigslist post had returned seven possible takers to his offer for a ride to Miami. Four were college students, and three were young professionals looking for some adventure. He only wanted a couple of people so as not to raise any suspicions by traveling alone in a twenty-nine-foot recreational vehicle. Two people would also allow him to keep the back bedroom of the RV all to himself, a necessity because this was where he would store the goods he was transporting. With a phone call, he contacted Jill and Brad, two Providence College students who answered his post. He told them that he was leaving on Sunday, and they were to meet him at the Cracker Barrel Restaurant just a couple of miles away from the Camp America dealership and the airport. Frank planned to pick up the RV on Saturday, take it back to his apartment to pack, then to the U-Haul storage unit that night to pick up the goods bound for Miami.

With the plans in place, he headed off for an evening of racquetball with his friend Dino and maybe a drink after. He hadn't played in about two weeks but was looking forward to the workout. As usual, the place was busy; and after waiting about twenty minutes, the two finally got a free court.

"I'm going to kick your ass," Dino said with a friendly jab to his partner, knowing that the loser bought the drinks after.

"We'll see," Frank said while bouncing the ball on the floor of the court, making the familiar echo. "If I win, I'm also ordering food tonight."

The two men quickly went into action, using the sport to blow off steam from a day's work. Dino quickly dominated the matches, being the better of the two players, hoping for bragging rights and a free dinner. Frank had a lot on his mind and enjoyed the workout, but he didn't concentrate much on his game. The winner would take two out of three matches.

"That's fourteen. One more point and you are done," Dino said, trying to get to fifteen points and win the second match. Frank had scored only eight points in the first match and seven in his current and second match. He would have liked to win the match and tie Dino, but he wasn't playing up to his skill level and was also hungry, having skipped lunch. Within a few seconds, Dino scored his fifteenth point and won two out of three matches. "You owe me drinks and dinner," he said as he wrapped up the evening's play.

"Fair enough," Frank said as they headed to the locker room for a quick shower and change. "Where to?"

"I'm feeling like pizza actually," Dino said.

"Papa Gino's?"

"Sure, why not. They have beer, and we don't have to drive all the way downtown."

A half hour later, they were sitting down for a beer and pizza just across the street from the racquetball club at Papa Gino's, a New England pizza chain famous for their Italian-style flat pizza. The place wasn't too busy because it was a weeknight. The smell of the baking pizza was enough to make anyone hungry just walking into the place. The young waitress brought over their beers and a few breadsticks the manager sent over because he knew Dino was a regular takeout customer.

"You seem quiet tonight," Dino noted as he sipped his brew and broke off a break stick from the basket of six.

"Nah, just tired."

"I hear that. I need to take some time off."

"Same here. Too much going on at work," Frank said as he also took some sips of his beer.

"Hey, how about that underwear bomber trial? What a fucking whack job," Dino said, changing the subject to something that has been in the news of late. A young terrorist tried to detonate a bomb that was incorporated into his underwear a couple of years back and was now just coming to trial in Detroit where the plane had landed.

"He failed to carry out his mission," Frank said as a matter of fact and rather coldly. "Now he goes to jail instead of Allah."

"If I had anything to say about it, he would go directly to Allah without a trial."

"His cause was bigger than himself."

"You sound like you're defending him," Dino said as the pizza arrived hot and steaming.

"Not at all. He did what he thought was right, and that was his decision."

Dino lifted a piece of the pepperoni onto his plate wondering why his friend was thinking like this.

"Fuck him and all of them towel heads as far as I'm concerned," Dino said before taking a first bite.

"Now that's probably why he did it."

"What are you talking about?"

"No one in the West understands people like him."

"What's to understand? The guy's a fucking terrorist."

Frank thought for a minute and remembered that he could not bring his personal opinion out into the open. Not yet at least.

"That he is," Frank said, thinking that he would change the subject to something they both agreed on. "How's your son doing?"

Dino had pizza in his mouth then took a sip of beer and was glad for the change of subject as well. "He's good. Likes his new school and seems to be doing better over there."

Both men continued to enjoy the pepperoni pie and a couple of brews. Little did Dino know that this would be their last evening of racquetball and dinner. Frank's mission awaited, and it was one that he was sure his Italian friend would not appreciate.

The peak of tourism had just past for the island of Puerto Rico now that summer was upon them. Tourists flock to the Caribbean island all winter long to escape cold climate in parts of the United States and Europe. Even if it's for a week, the tropical island is just what the doctor ordered for people needing a break from the reality of their jobs and lives. For others like Abdul-Aziz Fahad, doing business on the island meant frequent visits. As he passed through customs at San Juan International Airport, his German passport was stamped and bags hardly checked. He thanked the young CBP agent working the booth and made his way out to the street level where he would get a cab to the Ritz-Carlton, which was on the beach just a few miles away. His job on this visit was not to coordinate or meet with his soldiers working on the *Star Orion*, but to arrange a broker to receive the shipment he was expecting from the Republic of Georgia in a couple of weeks' time and make sure delivery and transfer was to the correct ship and terminal.

The air was hot and heavy, typical of the deep tropics as the cab driver made his way from the airport to the hotel. The fare was ten dollars, which

Fahad thought was robbery, seeing that it had been a five-minute drive. When they arrived, the doorman opened the car door while the driver got out and took his bag out of the trunk. With a two-dollar tip, Fahad dismissed the driver and walked into the hotel as a bellman grabbed his small rolling suitcase and followed. He knew the hotel, having stayed there a few times in the past. Just inside the main door on the right was the long fancy front desk where they quickly checked him into the hotel and offered a cookie while he was signing for the room.

A few minutes later, out of the corner of his eye, he saw the man who would be helping with this part of his project enter through the front door. They had only met once, but Fahad was exceptional at remembering people and faces. Jose Rio was one of many brokers who worked the Port of San Juan, and the two men had met a few months ago on a previous visit, when Fahad stopped by his office. He knew that Fahad was in the computer software business and needed a piece of equipment imported and then uploaded to a ship. Part of Jose's job as a broker was clearing shipments with local CBP officials.

Jose was told to meet in the lobby bar, which is where he went as Fahad finished up his check-in. A few minutes later, Fahad walked over to the man and reintroduced himself.

"Thank you for meeting me here at the hotel," Fahad said as the two men shook hands. "Would you like a drink?"

"No, thanks, never during the workday," Jose chuckled as the two took a seat a few feet from the giant windows that overlooked the pool and courtyard. Typically, Jose did his job back at the office pushing paperwork with occasional trips to various clients' businesses and warehouses. Meeting at a hotel was a bit unusual, but gaining new customers and keeping old ones meant that he did what it took to get the job done.

"We are excited about doing business with your brokerage and would like to start sometime within the next few weeks," said Fahad.

"Any time is fine with us. We are glad to have new clients and look forward to a long relationship with Sellco."

Fahad took out his briefcase and a few papers which documented the shipment he would be importing and where it needed to go. Paperwork was one of Fahad's specialties. He worked with a woman in Germany who was an expert in documentation work. She could make phony passports, visas, checks, and any other official paperwork imaginable. With the current world climate, documentation work was becoming much more tricky yet it was also lucrative because of that same reason.

"We deal in software and often upgrade equipment that runs specialty programs such as navigational units, medical units, and so on," he said as he explained what it was he wanted Jose to do.

"Very good," Jose said has he listened to his new client.

"One of our specialties is medical imaging machines like x-ray and CT units. We've been doing upgrades for the Star Caribe cruise line on all their medical equipment and will be importing a CT scanner to be installed on the *Star Orion*."

Jose took a few peanuts that were sitting in a dish for the customers' enjoyment as he listened to Fahad. "We've done many medical unit transfers," said Jose. "Some hazmat, some not."

"Wonderful. This should be, as they say, a piece of cake."

Fahad showed Jose the shipping order and documentation along with a picture of the unit that would be coming from Batumi.

"We are shipping out of Batumi, Republic of Georgia, where we overhaul equipment, upgrade units, and make them like new."

This looked pretty easy and standard to Jose, who was glad to add a new client to his list. He knew his boss would be pleased as well.

"When are you expecting shipment?" Jose asked.

"This unit? Within a few weeks."

"Very good."

"There will also be some medications that will be shipped with the unit for trial purposes. They are standard radioisotopes and are listed on the waybill as MEDHAZMAT," Fahad explained.

"No problem. We will receive and hold for delivery until the ship's next port call date, which I believe with *Star Orion* is weekly."

Jose took the paperwork from Fahad and gave him the back copies of each. A check from the Sellco account in Frankfurt accompanied the paperwork and would not be deposited until the shipment arrived at its final destination. The paperwork included the equipment transfer order from Star Caribe, clearing it for delivery on board the ship to be held in storage until the installation team would arrive and upgrade their medical facility. Each Star Caribe ship was being outfitted with CT scanners to complement their x-ray machines, giving passengers top-quality medical care if needed. Fahad knew all of this from the research he had done about eighteen months earlier on the types of medical equipment each cruise line put on their ships. Most had x-ray machines, and a few had CT scanners. With older passengers and more people concerned about being at sea because of questionable health, it was a feather in the cap of the company to have the most advanced technology aboard. Along with documentation expertise, Fahad's German helper was also a computer hacker and had gained access to the Star Caribe and other cruise lines' internal websites to find out more on planned upgrades to the medical facilities of their fleets. There were always upgrades and equipment swaps going on within big cruise lines, and after a little research and computer skill, Star Caribe emerged as the best to exploit.

"Thanks once again for all your help, and we will be in touch about our future cargo coming to the island as well as which line it will be shipped through," said Fahad as he reached out to shake Jose's hand.

"Our pleasure, sir. Have a pleasant stay in San Juan, and let me know if I can help with anything else."

With that, both men parted ways. Fahad's job was done for this trip, but he would make a couple of sales calls to his real clients in town before heading back to Frankfurt. Soon he would be headed to the States as a tourist bound for the vacation of a lifetime on a Star Caribe megaship.

Boris Stockov was not what you would call a people person. He did what he had to do to operate his business and life, but for the most part, he was a loner. He was waiting for a DHL package to be delivered to his flat in Tbilisi, which was coming from Fahad's and Mohammad's document contact in Frankfurt. It contained the phony paperwork he would need to ship the CT scanner from the Port of Batumi to the Port of San Juan and onto the *Star Orion*. He had the tracking number of the package and the DHL app showing him exactly where it was and at what time it would be arriving. On his return trip from Moscow, he would stop and pick it up. There was much to do before then.

After having lunch, he drove his truck a few miles to a gas station just around the corner from the hotel where Sergio worked. The weather was mostly cloudy with a few light showers and somewhat cool for this time of the year, when people in Batumi expected warmer summer weather. He pulled his semitruck into the gas station and saw his partner for this job standing under an overhang near the building, which housed the small minimart. Sergio knew who and what he was looking for and started walking toward the truck. He had a small overnight bag with him and was wearing a light jacket and ball cap. In his mind, he wanted to get this over with and move on to his new life. Already half the money he required was sitting in the Swiss bank. Now he needed to close the deal.

"Good afternoon," he said while opening the passenger door and looking up at Boris in the driver's seat.

"Get in," Boris commanded. Sergio climbed up into the truck and put on his seat belt.

"Chilly," Sergio said, trying to make some conversation with his new partner.

Boris said nothing and started to drive away toward the edge of town where the freeway was located. The two sat in silence for the first hour of the six-hour trip. Finally, Boris spoke.

"Is your contact solid and trustworthy?" he asked.

"He's a pro and has agreed to help us, yes."

Boris was quiet once again for another five minutes.

"I pray he hasn't sold us out," said Boris, almost under his breath.

Sergio waited a few minutes and spoke.

"He's a businessman."

Boris acknowledged this with a nod of the head. About a half hour before reaching the border with Russia, they stopped for a few soft drinks and for Boris to change clothes in the back of the container. Boris put on navy blue overalls with a patch in Russian, indicating that he was an AC repair and deliveryman. When they reached the border with Russia, Boris felt his stomach start to turn. Little did he know that Sergio had the same feeling sitting just to his right. Both men had their passports out, and Boris had the paperwork for the cargo he was carrying. Quite often companies in Eastern Europe would make any extra cargo space available on their trucks to other companies who would save money by leasing the space rather than paying for a whole truck. The road leading up to the border check station was bumpy, so Boris slowed down the big truck to just a few miles per hour to go over the bumps. They were sort of like natural speed bumps.

As they approached the checkpoint, they could see a line of traffic with only two out of four lanes open. The inspection lane for commercial vehicles was off to the right with two trucks ahead of them. The sun had just set, and darkness was taking over. Bright lights at the inspection station filled the early night sky above and, thanks to some ground fog developing, it looked like a dome over the station. Sergio was visibly nervous, but Boris was cool and calm. Really they had nothing that would cause problems going into Russia. It was coming out that the tension would be highest.

"Good evening," the Russian guard said to Boris as he pulled the truck up to the inspection point. "Papers and declarations," he ordered with not much in the way of personality in his voice.

"Medical equipment and an air-conditioning unit, for delivery to points in Moscow," Boris told the guard in a very businesslike tone.

The guard took the papers and went to the back of the truck then returned. Boris expected him to ask to see inside but was shocked that he returned the paperwork and waved them on. Both Boris and Sergio were silent for a few seconds as they drove away and away.

"If it goes like that on the way back, we're golden," Sergio said with a bit of relief in his voice.

"Let's hope so," Boris said, still not making much conversation. "We stay with this Peter tonight then go to the base in the morning?"

"Da."

The drive to Moscow was long and chilly. They arrived a few hours later at Peter's flat, and Sergio asked Boris to wait in the truck while he went to the door to make sure they were still welcome. Peter could always change his mind, and Sergio would be jailed for the rest of his life if he wasn't shot first. He was a little apprehensive as he walked up the steps and rang the doorbell. It took a few minutes, but Peter opened the door and saw his friend standing on the steps. Sergio would know now whether Peter had gone to the authorities or not. Peter looked around before saying anything. Then he looked at Sergio and offered his hand.

"Didn't you say you were bringing an associate?" Peter asked while shaking his friend's hand.

"He's in the truck." Sergio waved to Boris to come on into the apartment. "It's great to see you, my friend."

"Same here. Everything is set for tomorrow. You have the documents for the guards, and I have the pass and codes. Your pass will also still work. It's amazing that they never took it from you or even disabled it," Peter said excitedly.

The three men sat and shared some vodka, thinking about the money they would have when this was all over. Sergio and Peter already had some of the agreed-upon fee for their services. Both Sergio and Boris started to feel better about actually pulling this off.

They bedded down on Peter's couch and floor for the night. The next morning started early, and Sergio had that feeling in his stomach again, like he was going be sick, mostly from anticipation and nervousness. The men donned their overalls and left the apartment with Peter, who was going to lead them to the base and do the talking at the gates.

It was the longest trip of Sergio's life. The ride was about thirty-five minutes with Moscow morning traffic, and he was thinking the entire time that it was too late to back out now. His big worry was that Peter's friendliness was all an act. If he had alerted the authorities, they would all be arrested entering the base. His other worry was that once they get the device onto the truck, it would be found at the border. His head was spinning with many things going on inside as they headed down the highway on another cold, raw Moscow day.

As they approached the base, it all started coming back to Sergio. His years spent with the government, his life in Russia, and how that all ended. Now he was just getting what he was due. Part of him, deep down inside, wished it were still the same. The gate guards were young and looked a bit overwhelmed. There was another truck ahead of them as Peter pulled up in line with Boris following. It was a fuel truck to fill the diesel tanks on base. Peter's car was positioned between the two. Once the fuel truck was cleared, it was their turn. Peter pulled up, flashed his credentials, pointed a couple of times back at the other two men in the truck he was escorting and handed the guard the paperwork to swap out the AC units in the building within the "technical zone." The guard walked over to Boris's and Sergio's truck and instructed them to provide ID and to open the back of the truck. Boris got out of the truck, opened the back while the guard looked inside. All seemed to be in order, and the guard handed to Boris both his and Sergio's IDs. Sergio told the guard he was the technical advisor on the delivery and also showed his old credentials, which the guard instantly recognized as a state official's ID. Quickly the guard waved to his associate in the guardhouse to open the gate and allow them to pass. In a matter of a few minutes, they were inside Burr 34 and headed to the "technical zone" facility.

A few minutes later, they pulled both vehicles up to the gate, which allowed access to the "technical zone" building. Once again, one of the two guards of the Twelfth GU MO came over to Peter and recognized him from past visits. These were the special guards Sergio remembered during his time at the Twelfth Chief Directorate. Thankfully he did not recognize either one.

"Good morning, sir," said the young soldier. "You have some company today?"

"I am here to inspect and also supervise the replacement of part of the climate control system that these two men will be conducting," Peter said with authority. "Here is the paperwork ordering the repair. Another officer of the Twelfth is in the truck with the other gentleman."

"Da."

The guard looked over the paperwork and motioned for his counterpart to open the larger gate, which was for vehicles and not used very often.

"Thank you, sir. Good to see you again."

With that, the men drove their car and truck into the gate and parked near the entrance to the building. Boris backed his truck parallel to the building near the side door that was secured from within. Now Sergio's heart was racing. Time to perform, he said to himself, getting out of the truck. The guard in the house looked toward the main door to the facility for Peter to insert his ID card and punch in his code. With that verification, the guard inserted his key and turned it, which triggered the electric bolt, and the door was released. The process was specifically set up so that no one person could gain access. The guard's key had to be in and turned within a second or two of the correct code being put in.

Sergio and Peter entered the cool, almost dark building, shutting the door behind them. They quickly turned on the lower lights and went to the code box on the wall across from the crates containing the weapons. Finally Sergio spoke.

"Zero, one, five, alpha, twelve?" he asked, as Peter was about to put in his combination.

"Zero, one, five, alpha, twelve," said Peter. "You would think they would change this number." Both men were surprised that the code Sergio used to use was still the correct number.

Peter put in the code, and the box opened. He looked at Sergio as if it were a moment of truth. Both were silent for a few seconds.

"Which one?"

"Does it really matter?"

"No, but I inspected 1 and 5 last time. They won't be due for months."

"One," Sergio said with conviction in his tone.

"One it is," Peter said as he took out the code for crate number 1.

Boris was sitting inside the truck, waiting under the watchful eye of the guards parked by the side door for a signal to get out and open the truck to unload the dummy air-conditioning unit.

Inside, Peter took the code over to crate 1 and opened it up slowly. The prize was revealed at last. The two men glanced at each other before Peter closed the crate while Sergio opened the side door, allowing Boris access to move the AC unit in from the truck. This door was also alarmed and coded but was released from the inside and did not need the guard's key. Ironically the code for this door was kept in an envelope next to the security box.

As they opened the door, Sergio went out to the truck to get Boris to open the back and begin his work. He quickly set up the ramp and as both guards looked on from the guardhouse up front. Boris and Sergio proceeded to roll the AC unit off the back ramp of the container. They moved it around the truck and into the side door of the building, which Peter was standing next to, hoping to look like he was supervising. The guards could clearly see that it was an air-conditioning unit coming off the truck even though it was about fifty yards away. Once inside the building, they closed the door and went to work.

Boris and Sergio slowly laid the unit on its side. Both men stopped for a moment to note how similar they really did look. Good match, Boris thought as he opened the back of the dummy unit. At the same time, Peter went back to the number 1 crate containing the weapon and opened it again. Sergio had been specific when he gave Boris the measurements of the weapon they would be acquiring because it was crucial that it fit into the AC unit shell. It was Sergio's idea to use the cover of the AC swap to get the "oven" out, and he had Peter pass along the measurements and AC type via Facebook messages disguised as asking for some home improvement help. Sergio gave Peter a measuring tape, and Peter measured the length and width of the weapon. He then went back to the AC unit and found that the fit would be tight, but within about two or three centimeters. It was time to move the device from the crate to the AC unit shell.

"You're front, I'm back." Sergio said to Boris as Peter removed the three straps securing it to the crate bottom.

Boris looked up at Sergio then to Peter as the two put their hands on the warhead. "Careful," Boris said in a tone that could almost be comedic given the situation and what they were about to move.

The men lifted the device out of the crate and gently moved it over to the AC shell lying on the floor with the back access door opened.

"Front first," Boris commanded.

"The back is wider, we should put it in first," Sergio said, noting that the pointed top would fit easily but the back might take some maneuvering to get it just right.

"Da," Boris reluctantly said.

The men lowered the back end of the device, which measured four feet, five inches in length, into the air conditioner unit shell.

The fit was snug, but the important part was that it fit. They looked at each other and smiled for a brief second at their accomplishment. Peter then went back to the crate and picked up the wrapping that covered the warhead. They had decided to use some of the pieces of pipe that had been left in the outer room from a real maintenance job as filler in the now-empty warhead crate. Each warhead was covered by gray burlap wrapping, which Peter now had his hands on.

"Get four of those pipe pieces out in the corner of the entrance area, and we'll put them in the crate to cover with the wrapping," Peter said to Sergio. "With a little luck, the next inspector of crate number 1 won't notice a change." He knew, though, that their theft would eventually be noticed and many alarms would sound, but by that time, he would be free and clear and very rich. On the other hand, if the inspector was lazy and did not remove the wrapping, it might never be discovered that the warhead was missing.

Sergio returned a few minutes later with two of the pipes and went back for two more. They were not quite the same length as the warhead but close enough to create a look of bulk underneath the cover.

Both men positioned the four pipe pieces into the crate, and Peter carefully took the gray wrapping and placed it over the pipes. He took the red straps and connected both the front and back as he had found them. They both stood back and looked down into the crate, knowing it didn't quite look the same, but it was better than leaving it empty. With that, they closed the crate, locked the coded bolt, and lifted it back into its proper place.

Boris pulled the hand truck over to the dummy AC unit as Peter took the blankets they had kept inside the now-full shell and wrapped them around the warhead, creating a good bit of padding. They also had straps rigged inside, which he wrapped around the device on the outside of the blankets and secured them. It was similar to how they were stored in the crates sitting a few feet away. Once that was complete, it was time to move the "oven" out the door and into the truck.

It was heavier than they had expected as they lifted it upright and slid the hand truck underneath. As Boris tilted the hand truck back, Peter and Sergio guided it from the front just as they had done on the way in. Peter opened the door. and a cold blast of Russian air came rushing in around them. Slowly they worked the unit over the door lip and outside, heading for the ramp of the box truck. Both guards sitting in the guardhouse took note of the movement, and one decided to walk over. Peter almost passed out. Sergio whispered under his breath to be cool.

"Need help?" the youngest of the guards asked as he was walking closer.

"No, thanks. We're good," Peter said. "Easy fix." His tone was slightly dismissive as the guard waved his hand and turned around, headed back to the comfort of the heated guard shack.

"Let's move," Sergio said softly as all three helped guide the AC unit back up the small ramp into the back of the container. They secured it to the wall of the container as they had done on the drive up but also added secondary straps to the top and bottom. The CT unit was a few feet away. With that, they exited the back of the truck, closed the door, put on the lock, and Peter secured the building's side door from the inside as required. He and Sergio then exited the front, where the guard came out to complete the protocol. In minutes, they were pulling away from the compound headed to the main gate. *One more hurdle*, thought Peter as they headed for what he thought was the finish line of this operation. At the gate, there was a car and a tank truck, which looked like one of those airport septic trucks that empty the holding tanks of airplanes. It was chilly outside, and a light mist was falling onto the windshield as the car was waved on and the tank truck in front of them pulled forward. Once again, all three men had to hide their nervousness and play their roles to a tee. Peter was so nervous that he started shaking just a bit. As the truck in front of them rolled forward, Boris put the rig in gear and pulled up to the guard, who just asked for papers. He handed over the delivery paperwork, and both Peter and Sergio showed their credentials. The guard asked to look into the back of the container, but his was not unusual given that they had been on the special weapons compound.

Boris ordered Peter to get out and open the back, which he did without saying a word to the guard. He disguised his nervous shaking by warming his hands while blowing on them. As soon as he opened the container, the guard raised his hand and said that was enough. The guard peeked in, saw the AC and other cargo like the CT scanner that was set for delivery someplace else, and ordered Peter to close the door and get back into the truck. Clearly the guard was cold too, and wanted to get back inside the main gate house. Boris was handed back his paperwork and waved on. Minutes later they were rolling down the road away from Base Burr 34 with a variable-yield nuclear warhead in the back. The hardest part was done, but the tricky part awaited.

The good thing about an RV unit is that it has plenty of storage. The twenty-nine-foot Class C that Frank rented from Camp America for the one-way trip to Miami had a bedroom in the back and a bed over the cab. The dining room table also folded into a twin bed. The back bed lifted up, and below was plenty of room for storage. The hatch also had a loop for a padlock if one should want to have more security and looked similar to the kind on simple footlockers. The weapons he was transporting came two to a box and the four fit nicely in this space. There was also lots of room under the bedside table, which was where he stored the boxes of ammo that he had purchased over the past few months. With all the items secured, Frank made his way over to the Cracker Barrel just off I-95, where he said he would meet up with his riders. He packed just enough for this trip and upcoming cruise. Everything else was left as is at his rented house in North Providence. There was nothing else there he would ever need again.

"Ready to hit the road?" Frank asked as he pulled the RV up to the sidewalk not far from the long front porch, which adorns all Cracker Barrel Restaurants around the country.

"Totally," answered Brad, who was right out of a college catalog. Tall and tanned, he looked like he surfed for a living. The funny part was that neither he nor Jill, his girlfriend, had ever been to Florida. They were both twenty-one, both students and both ready for a fun time in South Florida before flying home just in time for the start of school.

"You get the top, and she gets the bottom," Frank said not thinking of the connotation of the words he had just said until Brad spoke up.

"That's the way I like it, Frank."

"You know what I mean! No monkey business in my RV!"

"You're the boss," said Brad in a silly way while eyeing Jill, who had her one and only suitcase in one hand and a Mountain Dew in another.

"Do you have a suitcase?" asked Frank, wondering why Brad did not have a bag.

"We packed together. We travel light," explained Jill with a bit of a chuckle. Frank could see that this was going to be an interesting trip.

The two students climbed aboard, and Frank drove across to the gas station next door to top off the tank before hitting the road. Miami was about sixteen hundred miles away, and they were off and running. Jill and Brad may be traveling light, Frank thought, but he was making up for it many times over with the cargo he brought on board hidden in the back.

Taking care of an aging parent is not an easy task, as Jake Stein knew all too well. He had taken a few extra minutes out of his lunch again to head to Coconut Grove to check on his dad who had good and bad days. Today he brought a couple of his favorite hot dogs from a guy who had a food truck on South Dixie Highway. They served burgers and dogs from the window of this crazy-looking blue-and-white step van. These food trucks were starting to become trendy with the younger professional generation who came to work in flip-flops and T-shirts. The hot dogs reminded Jake's dad of his younger days in New York.

"Two with celery salt, onions, and light Guldens," Jake said as he walked up the ramp and onto the porch where Jake Sr. was seated along with a couple of other residents.

"Only two?" asked his dad with a bit of snarl in his voice.

"Okay, three. I got the extra just in case."

"Sit."

Jake came over and sat next to his dad. He started pulling out the hot dogs and fries that were in the takeout box.

"How's that special agent girl?" Jake Sr. asked.

Jake took a bite of his hot dog and a sip of Diet Coke before he responded.

"She's good."

"You sleeping with her?"

"Dad, that's none of your business, and what kind of thing is that to ask your son in front of perfect strangers?"

"They're deaf as a flounder," said the senior Stein, not caring a bit whether anyone heard him.

"Shhh, you can't talk like that. Eat your dog," Jake said like he was talking to a child.

Both father and son sat and ate their hot dogs for a few more minutes in silence before Jake's iPhone started chiming.

"Take it," said his dad.

"It's not a call. It's a text."

"Why don't you just pick up the goddamn phone and talk to people like real human beings?"

"This is quicker, Dad. Otherwise we would have to chat it up, then get to business."

Jake read the text, and instantly his dad knew something was up.

"Bad guys?"

"Nah, well maybe. Not sure on this one. Just a gut feeling on someone we've been watching," explained Jake, who knew his dad loved to hear about his work. He couldn't tell him everything because of security and classified information, but he did share small things he thought his dad would appreciate.

"This guy we're watching keeps showing up in San Juan and has a possible history of ties to a terrorist group. He looks legit, but I smell something from watching his movements from city to city. Might be nothing, but something tells me there's more to it."

Mr. Stein took another bite of his second hot dog and a sip of the vanilla shake, which continued to melt in the hot Florida sun. Then he spoke the only words his son would take to heart that day.

"Follow your gut. I've always told you that. It won't steer you wrong."

Jake thought about that for a minute and took another bite and sip. He was going to send a note to Felton about his theory on this guy but wanted to wait for more evidence. The text he had just received might be enough to make him send that e-mail he was thinking about to Washington. One of his agents in San Juan, Wayne Howard, sent it to him. Apparently from the note, the "FORN," or foreign national, he was watching was back on the island.

> *"FORN you tagged checked into Ritz. Met w/shipping broker in lobby. No other mvts WH."*

Chapter 13

SWITCHING BAIT

THE WEATHER IN Oslo is usually rather cool, and rain is almost always somewhere in the forecast. As Bijon Markinson was wrapping up a four-month vacation from running the *Star Orion*, the sun was shining and the air was fresh, coming through the open window of the flat that he bought a few years back with his brother. Working four months on and four months off, the schedule allowed them to only keep a small place for the time each came home to rest and take their thoughts away from the weight of life at sea. The money both brothers earned was tax free, and the cost of living on the ship was nothing, so they could save quite a bit, allowing them to enjoy time at home or on vacation between contracts. Stefin Markinson lived the same life and alternated with his brother so that he too could use the flat.

Stefin's contract usually ended around two weeks before his brother's started. They would see each other over that time and enjoy some down time together. Bijon was expecting Stefin to arrive this morning but didn't know exactly what time. They didn't know too many people around their flat mostly because of their lifestyle at sea. He was looking forward to seeing his brother and also looking forward to getting back to the ship. Stefin's ship was the *Star Andromeda*, the second in the *Star Orion* class. They joked back and forth about whose ship was better and who had the better crew. Stefin was finishing his second contract after taking a year off to travel the world a bit, which brother Bijon hadn't been crazy about. Bijon was glad his twin brother was back in the groove and done with his little sabbatical.

A few minutes after ten in the morning, a car pulled up out front. It was a taxi, and Bijon could see his brother through the window, paying the driver and collecting his three bags. The wind was blowing a light, cool breeze out of the northeast and as these sailors knew that meant that even though the sun was shining, rain could not be far away. Bijon went to the door to unlock it and welcome his brother home. He was looking forward to getting back to the duties that awaited him aboard *Star Orion*. Many people would welcome four months off at a time, but for Bijon, three to four weeks was time enough to unwind.

"Back from duty?" Bijon said as his brother walked up the stone walkway leading from the street to the two-story townhouse style flat.

"That I am."

Bijon met him at the foot of the steps, and the brothers embraced. Stefin let Bijon get one of his bags left at the end of the walkway by the street where the taxi had dropped him off. They didn't know any of the neighbors and kept pretty quiet during the weeks they were off contract from the cruise line. Mostly they would travel a bit and then return before heading back out to sea. Bijon figured Stefin would hang out for a few weeks and then go off on one of his dive trips. Even though he made his living on the water, Stefin enjoyed sport diving and underwater photography.

"Good trip?" Bijon inquired as he made his way back into the flat. He put the bag down and went directly to the refrigerator, always well stocked with their favorite beers.

"Good, glad to be back."

"Stella?"

"Sure," Stefin said, looking forward to the cold Stella Artois.

"How was handoff and checkout?" Bijon asked, referring to the process of checking on and off the ship for duty.

"Good. Had to finish up some HR issues, and we were also turning over the hotel manager."

"Max Jacobson?" Bijon asked. They both knew most of the hotel managers in the fleet because of how closely they work with them on a daily basis.

"Yeah, he's off for four. Bill Stevens is rotating on."

"Good man," said Bijon. "Straight shooter and knows his stuff."

They chatted for a while in the kitchen of the flat before Stefin decided he wanted to bring his stuff up to his second-floor bedroom. Each of the brothers had his own bedroom and bath. It was a small place, but the price was right, and this was the perfect crash pad for a couple of bachelor sailors. They didn't have much family. Both parents had been killed three years before when an American tourist slammed into their car after leaving a pub in Oslo. The drunk driver was on vacation and had no business being behind the wheel. He was arrested but only spent three months in jail before being released to the American authorities and told never to return to Norway. It was a very tough time for Stefin. He was close to both parents and had experienced bouts of depression and had eventually developed a total aversion to alcohol. When he would see Americans on his ship drinking and partying, it would continue to bring back those horrible memories and inflame his growing anger toward them. After the deaths of his parents, he thought about suicide but never acted on it. Bijon handled the deaths of his parents better, but it was also a crushing blow to his world. During his year off, Stefin spent much of the time in Turkey, trying to find himself and overcome the grief he felt so deeply.

While his brother was upstairs unpacking, Bijon started working on the dishes in the kitchen. A few minutes later Stefin came back downstairs and joined his brother in the small kitchen, which was always dimly lit because there was only a small window over the nook where the table sat. Bijon picked up a plate out of the sink, washed it off, and bent over to put it into the small dishwasher. As he started to stand back up straight, Stefin quietly walked up behind him, took his five-inch diving knife, and drove it into the rear of the base of his neck as blood started to run down his back and onto the floor. The sound was hard to hear with the water running in the sink, but the knife cut though his upper spine and into his throat. Holding his brother's head by the hair, Stefin pulled the knife out and pushed it into his upper back. The only sound Bijon could make out was a gargling noise as blood rushed out of his weakening body. His eyes were wide open with a look of shock and sadness.

"Be at peace with Mom and Dad," Stefin said softly into his brother's right ear as he pulled the knife out once again, turned his brother's dying body around, and ended his life by plunging the knife into his heart. Blood was covering the floor in the small kitchen, so Stefin took off his shoes and walked calmly into the laundry room to get a sheet and blanket set that had never been opened since he bought them on his last break. He walked back over to the kitchen, stripped off his clothes, and wrapped his brother's body, his own clothes, and the knife in the sheet and blanket. Next he took rope that was in a kitchen drawer and tied it around the sheets. Then he dragged the body to the basement access door a few feet away and rolled it down the stairs. The door had both a lock on the handle and a deadbolt. He secured both, cleaned the kitchen, and took a long, hot shower. Out the window, the northern latitude sun was shining, and as he dried himself off, he knew the sea was calling for one last time.

Business was good for Narragansett Home & Construction Company as they continued work on the waterfront developments near India Point in Providence. Business was also good for the other business Dino Tucci was associated with. He worked odd hours and sometimes had very late nights, depending on the mood of his boss and head of the family, Anthony Battelli. The night before, he had been up until almost 4:00 a.m. looking after Anthony as he carried on with cards, women, and booze. Dino dropped the boss off and went home for a few hours of sleep before he had to get up and start his day job. He rolled out of bed and made his way to the bathroom, thanking himself for not drinking very much the night before. When he was looking after the boss, Dino had to stay sharp and take care of business. When he was on his own at night, that was another story. He and his crew had few friends outside the family. They worked together, played together, and did business together. If they had friends outside the family, it was understood that those relationships were different in that family business was never discussed. Dino had very few of these, but Frank was one of them.

Frank and Dino had developed a good and strong friendship. Dino always enjoyed spending time with his racquetball partner, whom he would meet twice a week for league play in East Providence. Dino did a few favors for him and even a little business with the medical equipment and weapons for the overseas charity. He felt they could trust each other and didn't mind even doing what would be considered a small-time transaction in his line of work. Oddly enough, he hadn't heard from Frank for two weeks in a row. No cell call returns, no messages, and worst of all, no racquetball. Dino had to settle for an IT guru for a league partner until Frank returned from wherever he had gone.

Dino had some union business to take care of down at the Port of Providence and figured when he was done, he would stop in to see Frank and find out where he'd been hiding. His partner, Pete, was at his place by Dino's side as they walked into the International Longshoreman's Association to have a conversation with one of the union stewards about a problem they had with a client.

"Good afternoon, Carl," Dino said upon entering the small office of Carl Beck, whose day was about to take a bad turn.

"Hi, Dino, Pete . . . ," Carl acknowledged nervously as the pair looked over at Carl's assistant and told him to scram by flicking their heads toward the door.

"We've got a problem, and you know what that problem is."

"I'm on it."

"No, you're not fucking on it. You weren't fucking on it last week, and now we're going to get on it," Dino said in a not-so-nice manner.

"Dino, they were just following orders from corporate, and we sometimes have to do the same."

"I don't give a fuck who they were answering to. When we said nothing was to move from that bastard company, we meant nothing was to move. Now I hear they had deliveries right off the boat to their warehouse then to the stores. That's a lot of moving in my book."

"The boys are under pressure, but that's the last time until you all say go," Carl said, squirming a bit as he answered.

One of the businesses the Battelli family worked with was not paying its agreed upon "royalty," better known as a kickback, and it was time to put a stop to their operation by ending any deliveries of liquor they ordered coming in by ship at the port.

"That shit stays in the port or on the ship or wherever the fuck it came from," Dino ordered. Pete, as usual, just stood and said nothing.

"It will."

"Carl, if so much as a minibottle gets on one of their trucks, there are going to be some missing cars, flat tires, and a few fires to put out," Dino explained.

Carl remembered the last time when it was the Teamsters who were told by the Battellis not to deliver beer, and a few scabs broke the picket line they had set up to pressure the distributors to come up with better pay. Anyone who broke ranks wound up with slashed tires and some broken bones from mysterious falls down stairwells.

"We'll tell you when to get the booze unloaded and moved off the dock."

"Good enough, Dino. Tell Mr. Battelli hello, and give him our thanks," said Carl, knowing that the money that came in under the table from the family was worth every bit of trouble that would occasionally come up.

Dino nodded his head in response as he and Moe headed for the door. They jumped back into the black Suburban for the short drive over to the Evergreen Shipping offices to say a quick hello to Frank and see when they would play again.

The day had started out cloudy and cool but started to warm a bit as the sun burned off the low cloud deck by the waterfront. Moe drove Dino up to the building, which housed a number of shipping companies, and waited in the car with the engine running while Dino stepped out to see his friend for a few minutes. The metal building was old and the door stuck as Dino opened the one with the Evergreen logo on it.

As he stepped inside, he could smell the aroma of coffee brewing and hear the hum of office workers taking care of the paperwork of the shipping business.

"Can I help you?" asked a young, twenty-something brunette receptionist who instantly caught Dino's eye. He wondered if he had ever seen her dance at the Foxy Lady Men's Club, which he liked to visit and the family owned a piece of.

"Yeah, I'm here to see Frank Castro for a few minutes," said Dino, still eyeing the fine-looking woman sitting at her desk in front of him.

"Frank Castro?"

"Yeah, is he around?"

"He quit about two or three weeks ago," said Carole, as she looked a bit surprised at his question.

"He quit?"

"Yup, surprised us all. Just called in and said he would not be returning to work and that we could send his final paystub to his mailing address. No rhyme or reason."

Dino also had a surprised look on his face. He waited a few seconds then spoke.

"Why? Where did he go?"

"Don't know. No reason. He just up and quit."

For some reason, this did not sit well with Dino. He felt sort of betrayed in a weird way because he thought they were friends. Clearly a plan to leave his job would have been something Frank would have told him. Maybe he changed jobs suddenly, Dino thought.

"So no idea where he's working?"

"Nope. I don't think he's in town either. Johnson, another one of our brokers, saw him at the U-Haul place over in East Providence one morning, then poof, he was gone," she explained.

"Who's Johnson?"

Just at that moment, the door opened with its usual metal-on-metal sound, and a tall cowboy-looking dude walked in.

"I'm Johnson, who's asking?"

"This man is looking for Frank," Carole said as she pointed to Dino, standing there still a bit stunned at the news that his buddy had vanished without saying a word to anyone.

"Yeah, gone. I saw him a few Mondays ago, leaving the U-Haul storage place on Pawtucket Avenue as I was getting coffee next door at the Dunkin' Donuts drive-through. The driveway is right next to Dunkin'," said Johnson.

Dino once again paused to think for a second or two. Johnson continued.

"I had to look twice to see if it was him, and sure enough it was. He was driving an RV out of their gate."

"An RV?"

"Yeah. Pretty good-sized one too. You know, the kind that has the bed over the cab," Johnson explained as he took a sip of the coffee in his hand.

"What the hell would he be doing with an RV?"

"That's what we said," Carole said.

Now Dino was getting pissed. Disrespect was something that he could not tolerate. Frank was by no means a member of the "family," in which case there surely would be consequences, but he didn't appreciate any sort of disrespect, even from outsiders. Bottom line was that this was supposed to be a good friend. Dino took loyalty very, very seriously because that was the environment he grew up in. He demanded it from everyone, inside and outside the family.

"If I find out, I'll let you all know," Dino said as he thanked them and headed toward the noisy metal door and the awaiting Suburban sitting just outside with the motor running.

"Head toward East Providence, take 195," Dino ordered Moe as he put his seat belt on and took a sip of the coffee that was sitting in the drink holder.

"East Providence?" Moe asked.

"East fucking Providence. Don't ask questions," Dino barked, clearly agitated about something, Moe thought.

They jumped on I-95 north for just a couple of short miles before merging onto I-195 east. Both men were silent. Moe was not going to say a word until his boss spoke first. Maybe they had some business over there that needed taking care of. Once in a while Dino would get a call to head somewhere, and Moe would just go with the flow. He never knew what to expect when they arrived.

"Get off at Pawtucket Avenue. We're going to the U-Haul storage place over there."

"I know that place. It's across from Archie's Pizza," said Pete, hoping to find out what it was they were after.

"All you think about is food. You're a true fucking wop," said Dino, still pissed that his friend quit a job, rented an RV, and took off somewhere, especially after he helped him get some off-the-record rifles for that charity overseas. At that moment, it dawned on him. Were those things really for a charity? What did he really know about this guy? Had he been played? All this went through Dino's mind as they turned off onto Pawtucket Avenue. The U-Haul place was about a mile ahead on the right. They pulled into the lot, and there was an office with storage units out back. U-Haul trucks and trailers were spread out on the lot near the office with "Rent Me" signs on them.

"Come inside," Dino commanded.

Moe dutifully obeyed, and both men got out of the truck and entered the little office where a middle-aged gentleman was standing behind the counter, playing solitaire and looking bored at the moment. That was about to change.

"I have a question about a guy who rented a unit here," Dino said as they looked around for other people and cameras. Moe saw two surveillance cameras watching them. Dino was in no mood to take no for an answer today.

"Sure, but all rentals are confidential unless you are on the contract," said Matt, who had worked there for about a year.

Moe pulled a chair over to the wall where a camera was pointed at them. The other was pointed toward the door. He hoisted his six-foot-three frame up onto the chair and yanked the camera wire out of the wall, ending any record this unit might have been keeping of their little visit.

"Do you know who I am?" Dino asked.

The man behind the counter was shaken by Moe taking out the camera and thought it might be a robbery.

"No, sir."

"Good. I just need a little information, and then we'll leave. If you don't give me the information I'm looking for, Moe the Dentist here will pull each of the molars out of your head sort of like he pulled that wire out of the wall."

Matt, the clerk, started sweating and thought about pushing the emergency button that was a few feet away.

"If you push the holdup alarm, which I'm sure you have, you'll be dead before your finger leaves the button."

Matt put his hands up.

"No, man. It's all good. What information do you need?"

"A guy named Frank Castro had a unit in here and showed up a couple of weeks ago with an RV. I want to know what was in the unit."

Matt looked on his computer and pulled up the Castro account. He had four Castros listed, but the one marked *F. Castro* must be the one this guy was looking for. By no means did he want to bring this guy any bad news or hold anything back.

"This is probably the guy," Matt said as he printed out the paperwork on F. Castro and passed it, with shaky hands, to Dino. Moe just stood nearby, looking like he was ready to do anything Dino commanded.

"It doesn't say what was in it?" Dino asked.

"They don't. That's the client's privacy, and I swear that we have no idea what's out there in those things. It's like *Storage Wars*. There's no telling what's out there," Matt explained feeling a little better and less scared.

"What the fuck is *Storage Wars*?"

Moe spoke up, much to the relief of Matt. "It's one of those cable TV shows where people go through storage units and sell things."

Dino dismissed the reference and asked his next question.

"Which unit was his?"

"M-93."

"I want to see it."

"Yes, sir, but if it's locked, we don't keep a key," Matt warned so as not to create any possible disappointment.

Matt grabbed the keys to his golf cart, which was parked just outside the side door of the office, and waved to the men to follow him and hop on. They took a short ride between the units to the M row and quickly found number 93. To the surprise of all three men, the unit did not have a lock on it. Dino got out and opened the door. Inside it was empty except for some small white boxes that were sitting by the right wall of the metal unit that looked a little like a garage. Also sitting in the front corner was a Master padlock left opened on the floor.

Dino picked up one of the boxes. There were eight altogether. They were blank except for the bottom, which read "5.56x45mm NATO cartridge." At that moment he felt a sick feeling in his stomach.

"Where did he go?"

"I have no idea," Matt said, hoping not to piss off this guy any more. "Seriously, man, we just allow access to customers."

Dino knew the clerk would have no idea. He would have to find out where he got the RV to see where it was Frank was going, if the RV people even knew themselves. Like a rental car, once customers leave the lot, they're on their own. Just as long as it's returned on time, unless it's a one-way rental which Dino thought would be the case, seeing that Frank had actually quit his job.

"All right, sorry for the camera mess," Dino said as he pulled out a roll of bills and handed Matt three new one-hundred-dollar bills. "Maybe it just got caught on a ladder or something."

Now Matt was thinking that these guys were pretty cool as he drove them back to the office in the golf cart. Once there, Moe and Dino climbed out and got back into the suburban. Dino took out his new phone and Googled "RV rentals." Three came up. He called all three and asked if they did one-way rentals. Only one said yes and that they were the only ones in Rhode Island offering one-way rentals. He noticed on the website that the rental agency was back near the airport in Warwick and hit "directions from here" on the GPS map function and told Moe to head back toward I-195.

Camp America was on Jefferson Boulevard just about a mile or two from T. F. Green Airport located in the city of Warwick. Dino told Moe to drive to that address. Moe was hoping that the clerk awaiting them at Camp America was more uncooperative than the last guy because he really wanted to tune someone up today. This was getting interesting, he thought as they merged back onto I-95 south.

After a short twenty-minute drive, Moe pulled into the lot where both men saw a number of RV's ready for vacation rentals. The kind with the bed over the cab, just like the guy at the port described, was mostly what they had. Both men went into the office, where there was another customer being waited on. This time Dino decided to play it nice. At least for now.

"Can I help you?" asked another clerk who appeared from the back room.

"Yeah, a friend of mine rented an RV here just week or two ago and said you folks did a fantastic job. We were thinking of doing the same thing," Dino explained.

"Sure thing. How big a unit and for how long?" she asked.

Dino pointed outside the window to one of the RVs that fit the description and said he wanted one like that.

"Is this for a day, few days or a week, or more?"

"For a week, and we want to do a one-way trip."

She looked into her computer to see what was available.

"Did you have a date in mind?"

He made up a random date and told her he would drop it in New Orleans, picking a random city from the top of his head.

"It would be around twenty-six hundred dollars for that week including the camping package for the twenty-nine-foot Class C along with a two-hundred-dollar drop fee for the one-way rental."

He thought that was rather expensive for something you had to drive and clean yourself.

"Well, my friend Frank loved the one you rented him, but said what he paid was much less," Dino said trying to bait her into some information.

"That depends on the size and where he dropped it."

"I'm not sure what size. Can you go back and check to see what he rented?"

"Sure, what was the name?" she asked, always glad to get a new customer in the door.

"Castro, Frank."

The slightly overweight clerk started to bang on a few computer keys and then pulled up the record Dino was looking for.

"Oh, he had a twenty-nine-foot Class C on a one-way to Miami," she said giving Dino all the information he wanted.

"That's right. How many places can you drop it in Miami? That might be a great place to go then fly back."

"There are three, but he dropped it off at the office on South Dixie Highway."

Dino absorbed the information for a few moments as Moe looked on, clearly disappointed that his services would not be needed.

"Let me check with the wife before I make a firm commitment. Miami sounds like a great place, and I know Frank loved the experience."

The clerk nodded her head and turned to the shelf behind her, reaching for brochures advertising the twenty-nine-foot RV to give to this perspective client. Dino thanked her and motioned for Moe to follow him out the door. Frank Castro rented an RV, bought untraceable rifles from him, and went to Miami without telling a soul. Dino knew a rat when he smelled one and was pissed that this guy might have put one over on him. But why? What would this Canadian friend of his want to do with rifles in Miami? Maybe he was on the up and up and sent the rifles to the charity like he said he was going to do then decided to move to a warmer climate. Deep down inside, the guy who grew up in the rackets knew better. He wanted to believe what his friend had told him, but Dino opened his phone and touched the Expedia app to see what flights were available to Miami, Florida.

The weather on the roads though the former Soviet Union, now Russia, was sometimes as bad as the roads themselves. After years of neglect because of government money shortages, potholes and crumbling pavement were common for people who drove these roadways. The government decided to add tolls to help pay for upkeep and to bring some extra money back into the fold. P141 was one of those toll roads and was slightly better than some of the others Boris was driving on headed south to Batumi. The 1,941-kilometer drive was long enough on the way up, but it felt even longer on the way back because of the cargo they were hauling in the back. The cab of the Volvo semitruck was uncomfortable for all three men. Technically it sat three, but three small people, thought Boris. At the suggestion of Boris, Peter was riding back to Batumi with them and would take his leave then, along with his final payment for doing his part.

The tension was still high when they reached the tolls. All three felt their stomachs turn with anticipation as they handed the money over to the toll taker, hoping that he doesn't ask for an inspection. It was the border that concerned Boris as he continued south on the M4 highway, which would take him to the coastal road M27 running along the Black Sea. With long roads, they had plenty of time to think of what they were doing. Boris had played this trip over and over in his head and planned it out well. Every stop he made was predetermined for where it was and who might be around. They stopped in thinly populated areas for the most part, where they would not get much attention and just appear to be another truck pulling a container on the road south. One of those stops was a bit more busy. Tuapse was a port city of around sixty thousand people in Krasnodar Krai, Russia. The temperature this time of the year was usually in the mid to upper twenties Celsius, and the typical July tourists were out in full. The city was just about one hundred kilometers or so north of the Russia-Republic of Georgia border.

Boris pulled the truck off the M27 for some dinner shortly after sunset, which is late at this time of the year at their current latitude. They usually had dinner around 10:00 p.m., so this was nothing too out of the ordinary for the three men. He drove the truck down a few side roads and to a small seafood restaurant he and Sergio had stopped at on the way up. Sergio remembered that the food was good, and Boris seemed to know the owner. Peter was still nervous, knowing what was in the back of the truck, but was looking forward to the food that Sergio was describing.

Boris slowly backed the truck down the small driveway that was adjacent to the building. It was a tight fit, but the truck and container were off the road where Boris and Sergio could do some final adjustments to the cargo before having dinner. They talked about the transfer they were about to do many times and knew what had to be done. Boris unlocked the back of the container and opened one of the two doors, then climbed up and with a flashlight, found the interior light he had installed before leaving for Moscow. He turned on the light and motioned for the other two men to join him in the back and to close the door from the inside.

"Let's start with the scanner bed," said Boris as he pointed to one of the two wooden crates containing the CT scanner. The system had two parts. The first was the actual device, which did the medical scan, and the second was the bed that people would lie on. They were in separate large hard wooden crates for shipping. The bed itself was just a large glorified exam table, but it housed electronics that allowed it to be adjusted in height and length. There was storage inside for items that may be needed such as blankets. Frank Castro had carefully modified this unit before it was shipped. In the storage unit back in Rhode Island, Frank gutted the inside of the bed unit in order to create a space to the dimensions that Sergio had specifically given Boris. Similar to what Boris did with the air-conditioning unit, Frank pretty much made a shell of the bed unit. Now it was time to see if the measurements were correct. If they were not, the entire plan would be in jeopardy. Boris opened the wood crate containing the CT bed unit, and then both he and Peter lifted it out. They were surprised at just how light it was.

"Put it down slowly," Boris said as they moved it to the side of its shipping crate. "The bed is supposed to come off according to my source who did the modification work."

He looked under the bed and sure enough saw four clips that were part of the new modification. They looked like they were factory made and belonged there. Boris unclipped all four and motioned for Sergio to get one side of the bed.

"Lift it slowly," said Boris, trying not to make too much noise. The door of the container was closed over but cracked for air. They lifted the bed unit off its base and put it down on the floor.

"Now the AC, just like before," he ordered.

Both men took hold of the AC unit containing the warhead, unstrapped it from the wall of the container, and carefully laid it on its back. Boris then unclipped the fasteners, which locked the door panel in place and opened it up slowly. Then he reached in and untied the straps, which were wrapped around the blankets covering the warhead. Finally their prize was exposed and ready for transfer.

"Again, just like we did in Moscow," Boris said in almost a whisper.

"I've got the front," said Sergio as he took his place at the head of the weapon.

They lifted together and delicately removed the warhead from the air-conditioning unit shell and placed it slowly down into the base of the CT scanner bed. For an instant, Boris thought it wouldn't fit from the angle he was seeing, but he felt a strong sense of relief as they got closer and started lowering the warhead into the bed's base unit. It fit. Perfectly. Actually it was slightly smaller than expected, but that was fine because they were going to be wrapping it with blankets and four bags of kitty litter. The litter was a backup diversion for bomb sniffing dogs that might inspect the unit. As a CT scanner and with the additional radioactive medicines shipping with it, any alarm would be bypassed, but he liked to have redundancies.

"Let's get the straps tightened up," Boris ordered after they wrapped the unit in the same blankets the men had used in the air-conditioning unit.

"My work is almost done," said Sergio, now getting even hungrier. Peter just stood and watched the two men while keeping an eye on the door for any movement outside. It was dark, but they did not want to leave anything to chance.

"All right, let's put the bed back on," Boris said, looking down, satisfied with their packing job. The bed was lifted a few seconds later and slowly lowered to the top of the base where Boris snapped all four fasteners. There were no locks on these fasteners, which Boris thought was a mistake. Locks, however, would have looked out of place, which was the reason they were left off.

Next the all three men lifted the bed unit up and slowly lowered it back into its shipping crate. It was much heavier now. Then all three carefully lifted the crate back to the front corner of the container, secured the cover, and strapped it back down to the wall and floor as it had been. For now, their job was complete, and all three men had worked up a good appetite. They secured the container doors and walked the few steps to the restaurant next to their parking spot in the alley.

Most of the customers were locals and walked to the small neighborhood bistro. Some people parked out front. The men entered the restaurant from the rear where Boris's friend, Aglaya, was busy in the kitchen. She was a sexy blond with a figure that would stop any man in his tracks. Her name in Russian actually meant "beauty," or "splendor." Boris introduced Peter and reintroduced Sergio. After hugging Boris, she kissed the other two men on the cheek and went back to stir her soup on the gas stove.

"I hope you boys are hungry," she said, looking over with eyes that would cut though a man's heart.

"Starved," said Boris. "Not too much further to get back to Batumi."

She continued to work on dinner for the two occupied tables up front where paying customers were finishing up their salads.

"I'll set you boys up downstairs with some pasta and meatballs," said Aglaya, pointing to the stairs that went to what looked like a small wine cellar.

Boris went down the stairs, where there were three additional empty tables and bottles of wine in racks. She used this for special parties and overflow when upstairs was full. The only problem was that customers had to go through the kitchen to get down there, but that was part of the charm, she thought. Sergio and Peter followed Boris down the stairs, feeling the cooler, slightly musty air below, and were ready for a good meal. Boris looked over the wines and pulled out a bottle of Khvanchkara red semisweet. There was a corkscrew sitting on the table next to theirs, and he quickly went to work on the bottle. A few seconds later, he poured each man a half glass. He lifted his glass in a toast.

"To success so far," he said.

"Don't jinx it," laughed Sergio as he also lifted his glass.

Aglaya started a mixer up above in the kitchen and headed down the stairs with bread to check on her friend and his comrades.

"Ah, bread. My wife makes a fabulous sourdough," explained Sergio.

Aglaya put down the bread and said the pasta would be ready in a few minutes. She turned back toward the stairs as both Sergio and Peter dove into the loaf. When she knew they were getting bread with their backs to her, she turned back around with a silenced 9 mm Glock in her right hand and shot both men in the back of the head. The only sound was the mixer upstairs and the men's bodies hitting the table and rolling to the floor. No one upstairs heard anything else. Boris walked over and kissed Aglaya on the mouth then made sure each man was indeed dead. Aglaya put the pistol back on the wine shelf and went upstairs to turn off the mixer and serve pasta to the customers up front.

Boris took another sip of wine and then wrapped up each body in the blankets that were left for just this purpose by his associate in a dark corner of the basement. She returned a few minutes later with pasta for two. Boris took the pasta from her hand, set it on one of the other tables, then quickly embraced her while both started taking each other's clothes off. Seconds later, Boris had her up on the same table where they had just murdered two people. Somehow this added to the passion of their lovemaking. She was alone in the restaurant and, on the way downstairs, had shut the door to for the quick encounter that she had dreamed about for the last month or so.

Later that night, Boris had arranged for a fisherman friend of Aglaya's to take the bodies, now wrapped in blankets and chains, on his fishing boat and dump them in the Black Sea. He was told they were deer carcasses used for meat in the restaurant, and his generous fee guaranteed that he wouldn't ask any questions.

It was dawn before Boris could get back on the road to Batumi. Aglaya had no idea what he was carrying in the truck, but she knew he did work on the black market. She liked him, and he paid cash for her services. Her background in the former Soviet KGB and now-Russian black market made her good catch for him. They parted with a kiss and promise to meet again soon.

Boris headed south on the M27 toward the border crossing, which was his second-to-last hurdle. The inspection station at the border crossing was not going to be busy because he picked nighttime to go through. The more people in line, however, the quicker the border guards worked. That was his only regret for traveling late. His paperwork was in order, and he just had to play it cool. As he drove toward the border crossing, a soldier waved him into the inspection area to the right. There were six trucks ahead of him as he opened his phone and checked messages while waiting for his turn. The guards were working fast with the trucks ahead, and he hoped it would be the same with him. They were not making the drivers get out, which was always a plus.

The truck in front of him pulled up to the inspector, and Boris started to sweat. *It's all in the role-playing*, he told himself as his turn approached. A few seconds later, the air brakes of the truck in front of him let off a loud swish sound, and it started to roll away. The young guard waved Boris up to the inspection point before requesting papers and cargo documentation.

"Any hazardous material or a large amount of cash?" asked the uniformed man who looked more like a boy.

"No, sir. Just an air-conditioning unit and medical equipment."

The inspector looked over the paperwork and scanned Boris's passport. The reading said, "Clear," which told the inspector that Boris was not wanted or a criminal. He then asked for the keys to the lock on the container doors in the back of the truck. Boris shut down the truck and handed the keys to the inspector, who went around back. After opening the lock and then one side of the back door of the container, the inspector looked inside, then quickly shut the door and put the lock back on.

Boris couldn't see him in the rear mirror and read the newspaper, trying to look like this was all routine to the other inspectors who were around and dealing with other travelers. A few seconds later he could see the inspector come from behind the truck in his rearview mirror and knew from the look on the guy's face that he was good to go.

"Drive carefully, and welcome to the Republic of Georgia," said the inspector as Boris was handed the paperwork.

"Good day," Boris said while putting the truck in gear and then pulling away, headed south toward Batumi.

A few hours later, Boris was back in Batumi and the shipyard where he had started. He came through the gate with little notice from the gate guard, who knew him and waved him though. Slowly, he pulled his truck and container back to the corner of the dusty yard to his company's space, where he could work without much notice. He opened his container and unstrapped the air conditioner unit shell. It was not too heavy, but it was bulky as he slid it side to side to move it from the wall of the container that it was attached to. He decided to go outside and look for a hand to move it into one of their storage containers a few feet away.

Minutes later, he returned with a yard worker, and both men made quick work of moving the air-conditioning unit into the company's storage container. The worker even made a comment on how light this unit was for being an air conditioner, and Boris responded by saying it was just used for spare parts.

He then loaded ten boxes of computers and software he had been storing in the unit next door, all marked "Sellco-SJU," meaning shipment to Sellco REP, San Juan, Puerto Rico. The waybill and customs declaration said the same for the container itself but included the CT scanner along with the secure lockbox containing Fluorine-18 and Thallium-201 radioisotopes. Both shipping documents were attached to each crate of the CT unit and to the small lockbox that was traveling with it. On those documents the "ship to" address read, *Sellco REP Port of San Juan///Hold for Transfer to Vessel:* Star Orion.

Washington in summer could be hot and sticky, but this first Wednesday in August, there was a taste of fall in the air. Special Agent Jake Stein walked through the lobby of the Hyatt Regency, to which he had become accustomed, thanks to his quarterly Homeland Security Investigations meetings, and headed for the escalator taking guests up to the street level above. At the top of the escalator, the double doors automatically opened, and he walked out onto New Jersey Avenue for the short walk over to Union Station, where he would be meeting his ex-, possibly current, maybe future girlfriend for a quick coffee as she came into town for the start of her work day at the Secret Service Washington field office. Jake wouldn't pass up an opportunity to get together and was hoping for a closer encounter later on that night before he headed back to Miami on the morning Delta flight out of DCA.

Union Station was bustling with commuters headed to Capitol Hill, D.C. law offices, embassies, and many other places of employment. He entered though the south doors and went directly to Au Bon Pain located just inside. The place was jammed with people getting their morning caffeine fix and pastries to go. He looked around and did not see Claire. They had agreed on 6:30 a.m., but he was a little early, misjudging the time it would take to walk there from his hotel just a couple of streets away. Jake knew what she liked and ordered for both of them as he eyed a place to sit down.

With two coffees in hand, he landed at a table not far from the door, having just been vacated by an elderly couple waiting for the Amtrak to New York. He could tell this by looking at their suitcases and bag tags. Always the detective, he thought. A few minutes later he could see Claire coming through the terminal hall headed for where he was. Jake held up his arm to get her attention, and the excitement of being with her again started to build up inside him.

"How are you?" she asked as she got through the crowd and closer to him. They embraced, and she kissed him on the cheek. Not exactly where he wanted the kiss, but he would work up to that.

"Fine, got in late last night," said Jake handing her the coffee he had purchased.

"I thought this meeting was next week."

"It was, but Felton has to travel and wanted to move it up a week," Jake said as he unwrapped a cheese filled Danish. "Want a bite?"

"I'm good."

"Yes, you are. Want come to my hotel and have sex tonight?" he said in a lowered, almost-whispered tone.

"Slow down, cowboy."

"I figured I would get that on my agenda right away."

"Dinner, yes, we'll see on the rest," said Claire, trying not to smile too much.

The two sipped their coffees while Jake dipped his pastry into his before eating a bite.

"That's disgusting," she exclaimed while looking at people around them hoping not to be too embarrassed.

"It's delicious. Sure you don't want a bite?"

"Not now, not ever."

He laughed at that, knowing full well that they were teasing each other.

"How's chasing counterfeiters?"

"Good, we tracked down the chip makers your folks intercepted. They were offshore in the Dominican Republic, making perfect replicas of chips from four big casinos in Vegas."

"Nice job."

Jake looked at his watch and knew he had to start heading down the street for the seven thirty meeting.

"Dinner at six?"

"Sure, where?"

"Hyatt?"

She nodded, and they both got up to part ways. This time she kissed him on the mouth, and her eyes said it all. She was in for dinner and might just stay the night. This made Jake's day, and it had just started. Special Agent Claire Wilson headed off to her part of the government while Jake headed off to his.

Ten minutes later, Jake was once again on the fifth floor of 101 South Capitol in secure conference room three with his other field office counterparts, making small talk, waiting on the boss to arrive.

"Have a seat," said Col. Tim Felton, entering the room and headed for his place at the head of the long conference room table. All the members had left their iPhones, BlackBerrys, iPads, and any other electronic devices in cubbyholes outside the door. Felton's assistant pushed a button, and the lights lowered while a projector fired up today's PowerPoint briefing.

"Quiet quarter, but a few new items out there," said Felton as he flipped through a number of slides, calling on each member to brief their own. Each member would securely e-mail his or her brief via secure SIPRNET to be included in the presentation.

Danny Williams of the Boston field office was wrapping up, and Jake prepared to speak next.

"Miami and San Juan," Felton said.

"We've been watching a couple of things that might be worth passing on to our intel partners. This one in particular." A picture of Fahad leaving customs in Puerto Rico flashed up on the screen.

"Former TC Abdul-Aziz Fahad has been in and out of San Juan a lot lately along with some other spots, including Brussels and Frankfurt. He works for Sellco Software and Computers but has had ties to some of our friends in Pakistan, Turkey, and Afghanistan. I tagged him, and one of my guys followed him to a meeting at the Ritz-Carlton with an island shipping agent."

Jake paused for a minute.

"He's selling software, shipping it for clients. Are the clients legit?" asked Felton.

"All perfectly legit."

"So."

"So they don't have clients in Brussels or Turkey. Why would he be going there?"

"To get more clients?"

"Perhaps. But another odd thing is that one of my guys said that every time he's in San Juan, it's the same day the cruise ships call, and he has friends working on one or a few of them."

Felton and the others thought about this for a minute or two.

"How do they know that?" Felton asked, now a little more intrigued.

"He was watching Fahad having lunch at the Hilton, and a funny thing happened when he was leaving. The doorman seemed to know them both, as if they'd been there before. So my guy asks the doorman who they were, and the doorman said he knew the guy with Fahad because they both spoke Farsi and chatted a couple of times. Apparently the doorman said Fahad's lunch partner worked on the cruise ships," Jake explained.

All of the agents in the room thought about that for a few seconds. Why would this guy be meeting with a cruise ship staffer, and why did he only come to the island during cruise ship port visits?

"That's interesting. Let's keep this guy tagged and see where it goes. Is this the only guy he's met with?" quizzed Felton.

"That's all we know of."

"Okay, no other intel on this Fahad?"

"No, sir. Just what we have from past meetings and his history as a former or possible TC. Cold after that."

Felton took a sip of his coffee and looked at the briefing folder in front of him containing paper versions of the slides now projecting on the screen.

"Keep us posted. Might be something. Might be nothing. Looks like CIA and FBI have nothing on this guy from what you have here."

"That's correct, sir. I've checked with both agencies but will continue to monitor."

"Good enough."

"Oh, Claire says the chip bust we made on the boat turned out to be a big deal with counterfeiters offshore. They worked with Interpol and busted the ring."

"Nice work. Good interagency cooperation."

With that, they moved on, and soon the meeting was over. Each agent collected his or her belongings, left the conference room, and picked up phones and pagers outside the door while chatting it up with each other.

Jake had some immigration paperwork to drop off upstairs at the INS office one floor above and headed for the elevator. Special Agent Danny Williams was also headed out. "Going up?" he asked Jake.

"Just dropping some INS paperwork off upstairs. Lunch?"

"Sure," said Frank.

After Jake paid a short visit to his brothers up at the INS office, the two headed out to lunch on Massachusetts Avenue.

The funny part of these meetings was that he would always end up with about half a day with nothing to do in D.C. Often he would hit one of the Smithsonian museums or just read a book. His flight left the next morning, so he had even more time this visit. After lunch, he took a nap and got ready for dinner with Claire.

She was right on time, as usual. They met in the restaurant that was just off the lobby and offered the usual hotel dinner fare. He dressed in jeans and a golf shirt, and she was wearing a short red skirt and cotton top. In the back of his mind, he wondered if she dressed that way just for him.

"How about a drink for a girl?" she asked walking over to the table. "Or are you too cheap?"

Oh, how he loved it when she talked this way, he thought.

"I thought you were buying?"

The waiter walked over to take their drink order, seeing that she had arrived and the table for two was complete.

"Gin and tonic," Claire ordered.

"Scotch and water," Jake added.

"You're leaving in the morning?" she asked, knowing the answer.

"Ten thirty flight direct to MIA," he answered, meaning Miami International Airport.

The waiter returned after a quick trip to the bar with both drinks and some napkins.

"Would you like to order?" he asked, standing at their table.

"How about the spinach dip appetizer?" Jake asked while getting a nod of approval from Claire.

"Sure thing. Do you want to keep the menus for dinner?"

"Fine, thanks."

The waiter headed off to put in the order and to give them some time to look over the menus.

"I was glad to see you in Miami," said Jake, trying to get the conversation going his way.

"Same, Stein. Your dad looked good."

"He doesn't change much. Some medical issues. Very cranky."

"I could tell," she chuckled.

They both looked at the menu to decide on dinner.

"You look great, as usual," Jake said while looking at the chicken selections.

"So do you."

"I think we should get back together."

She sat for a moment or two before answering that and sipped her drink.

"You don't waste time."

"I've already wasted a lot of time. We're not getting any younger."

She took another sip. "Speak for yourself, Stein," she said, calling him by his last name as she usually did. "It's complicated with two cities, two careers, two sets of parents, you know."

"We can uncomplicate it," he insisted.

She didn't say anything for a few minutes. They had been down this road before. It ended in disappointment when he decided to move to Miami and she put career ahead of any sort of relationship. That was when she was applying to the Service. After getting accepted, she was busy getting ready to go to training, and they had been going out for more than a year before he was promoted and moved.

"Commuter relationships just don't work," she finally said.

"Maybe you can move to Miami or I can transfer back here."

"I'm not moving unless they move me. You can't transfer now. You've got too much seniority down there, and there are no GS-13 HSI slots up here for you. Plus, you couldn't function without Rosa, and she's not budging."

They sipped their drinks for a little while and finally decided to put that conversation off for another time and to enjoy each other's company.

"I'm not too hungry," he said with a devilish look in his eyes.

"Get the check," said Special Agent Claire Wilson.

They paid the check and quickly went back to his fourth-floor room. Thanks to his frequent flier and Hyatt points, he had a room upgrade, which amounted to a slightly bigger room with minibar and garden tub in the bathroom. Once in the room, they started kissing each other and fell back onto the soft king bed. Minutes later, they were both naked as she ripped open a condom and went to work on him. Her body melted inside as he entered her and his sweat washed across her breasts as the two rolled as one. This is the bliss she remembered and secretly longed for. For Jake, this was what he dreamt of during those lonely nights alone in his Miami condo. They let the hours slip by, slowly making love and drinking from the minibar a few feet away.

At 6:00 a.m. Jake's iPhone alarm started making that dreaded noise no one likes to hear after a short night's sleep. He rolled over and saw Claire's naked back. He wished he had the whole day to spend with her. Unfortunately they both had to get up because their government jobs would not wait, and soon the e-mails and messages would start trickling in.

"I'll come down for a visit," Claire said as she put her red high heels back on.

"I'll come back up," Jake said as he buckled his pants and brushed his slowly graying hair.

"Apparently you already did," she joked while finishing getting herself together.

They took a moment, embraced and kissed before she headed out the door, and he finished packing for the trip back to Miami. He was looking forward to the next HSI meeting in a couple of months. She walked away, trying to think of a good reason to visit him in Miami. Last night had made it well worth all the trouble it took to travel these days.

Ali Ahamid had never been further south than New York City while living the life of Frank Castro in Rhode Island. He wanted to take a little time and see some of the sights he had watched on television or read about while growing up. His trip in the RV to Miami gave him just the excuse to take his time and enjoy the ride. Plus his two companions were all about stopping along the way. They had a few more weeks left of summer and wanted to make the best of it. His rental agreement was for two weeks on the one-way rental, so he had until then to return the unit.

They took I-95 south and went around New York but decided to go through Washington, D.C., to see the monuments. The irony ran deep, Frank thought, as he played tourist and took mental notes, maneuvering the RV by the Washington Monument, the Capitol, and even saw the back of the White House from the Ellipse. He was careful to stay far enough away as not to create any second looks by playing tourist. His secret cargo was well hidden, but he did not want risk any of the upcoming operation.

After D.C., the three headed south in the RV, stopping to camp for a couple of nights each in Virginia, North Carolina, Georgia, and St. Augustine, Florida. He did not realize just how far a drive it was to South Florida. They arrived after eight nights on the road, tired but thankful for the experience. He had grown to enjoy Brad and Jill's company as they explored the East Coast of the United States. He dropped them at the Fairfield Inn just a few miles from the Miami International Airport, where they would stay for a couple of nights before flying home to New England.

Now it was time to get down to business and he contacted Hamid Khalid on Facebook and set up a lunch meeting. Hamid was "second leader," meaning he was number two in command of the operation. Frank secured a campsite for two nights at the Miami Everglades Campgrounds in Southwest Dade. He thought it would be far enough away from the city to keep a low profile. He was right. It was about as close to the Everglades as you could get without actually getting in.

Hamid told his boss, Amanda, at Metro Miami Furniture & Bedding that he would be reaching out to a few potential clients after lunch and headed out to meet Frank. An hour and ten minutes later, Hamid pulled his pickup truck into the campground and found Site 31A after getting a map from the guy at the gate.

"Peace be with you," Frank said as he came out of the RV and approached Hamid's truck.

"And to you, my soldier."

"We have everything our brothers on the ship requested in their signals."

Hamid smiled and followed Frank into the air-conditioned RV, where they could have a private conversation.

"My plan is solid. We have to transfer the weapons at a self-storage unit I have rented not far from the port before you return the RV," Hamid said with deep conviction in his voice.

"We can meet tomorrow," Frank said, not knowing what Hamid's schedule was.

"We can meet tomorrow night. I have to work at the store during the day. I have the mattresses ready at the storage unit."

With that, the two ate some food that Frank had made and discussed how things were going to unfold. Then Hamid left to go back to work.

A little more than twenty-four hours later, Frank followed his GPS directions to the Dixie Self-Storage just a few miles south of the city on South Dixie Highway. It was 8:00 p.m., and they had agreed to meet after the facility closed its office at seven and when it started to get dark outside. Frank waited just down the street for Hamid to show up in his pickup. That way they could both pull in together with Hamid's gate code.

Hamid was punctual and signaled Frank to follow him to the storage facility entrance, where he put in his code and the gate opened. Both men pulled their vehicles through the large opening, with Frank following in the RV. It was just after dusk, and the area was lighted by floodlights positioned every five units. There were also surveillance cameras at the end of each row, but with the lower light levels at night, these had little resolution all the way to the opposite end. Hamid made sure to request an end unit on the opposite side from the camera position. He also parked his car so that the headlights would face the camera, the glare ending any chance they could be seen.

He opened the rolling door of the garage-sized unit as Frank positioned the RV with the door facing away from the camera. Hamid was impressed with the way Frank had stored the cargo under the back bed frame and in the other spaces available in the RV.

The men moved all four boxes out of the RV and into the storage unit. They did the same with the four boxes of ammunition. Inside the storage unit sat four special-ordered mattresses and four box springs. They were unwrapped and standing side by side against the wall of the unit. All of the materials that Hamid needed for this part of the operation had been gathered slowly over the last four months. He closed the storage unit door from the inside so that the men could work in privacy.

They carefully took each AR-15 out of its wooden shipping box and wrapped each in small bubble wrap plastic. The process did not take very long, and in a short time, all eight weapons were sitting on the floor wrapped in plastic bubbles. Next, Hamid took each weapon and wrapped it once in a white sheet matching the color of the mattresses.

"You've done well, my brother," said Frank, admiring the meticulous advance work Hamid had completed.

"Thank you. Let's do the first mattress," he answered, pointing to the one leaning on the wall of the unit.

Frank laid the mattress on its side. The entire side had been cut along one edge and flipped open like a door exposing the inside. Hamid had carefully carved out the center of the foam padding of each mattresses and removed enough stuffing to make room for a single weapon.

"Slide the weapon inside," Hamid ordered. "Slowly."

Frank took the weapon, now wrapped in bubble plastic, and one white sheet and pushed it into the center of the mattress. The goal was to get it into the center and surround it with the foam stuffing that had been removed. The new foam mattresses were perfect for what they were trying to accomplish. They were special-sized bedding designed specifically for the cruise industry, which could sleep one person or be pushed together to make a double. He ordered extra sets of two, ensuring they would have enough stock for future cruise business. The ammo was loaded into the extra clips Frank had purchased online and wrapped separately in bubble plastic then placed next to the weapon in the middle of the mattress.

"That's close to the middle," Frank said, admiring his work.

"Good. Now we take the foam and pack it in around and on top of the weapon."

About ten minutes later, the first of eight was complete. The toughest part would be to restitch the edges and return the original plastic wrap as it had been. The tasks took all night, and by 5:00 a.m. they had four completed sets of two.

"We have worked hard and done well," Hamid said as he took a sip of the iced tea he had brought along, knowing how hot it would be even at night working inside of the storage unit. The ice in the drink had ago long melted away.

"I will return the RV later today and take a cab to your apartment," Frank said as they planned the next step.

"Very good."

With that, the two closed and locked the storage unit and left as the sun was coming up over South Dade County. It was not too unusual for people to be working inside the units late at night or early in the morning. Many sales professionals kept their samples along with other goods they used for work inside the units. They would come and go with little or no notice. Hamid had been seen many times going to and from the unit Amanda rented for Metro Miami Furniture & Bedding's overflow inventory.

Frank drove the RV back to the campground and slept for about five hours before he packed up his belongings, checked out of his site, and drove to the Camp America dealer on South Dixie Highway, where he returned the unit with two days to spare on his one-way rental. Hamid sent him a text and said to meet at his work address so that they could have dinner before returning to his apartment later that evening.

"Can we help you with a ride or shuttle to the airport," asked the clerk who checked him in and completed the rental forms.

"I'm going into the city if someone is going that way," said Frank, always looking to save a buck.

"Sure, what address?"

"Metro Miami Furniture & Bedding on Biscayne Boulevard," he answered.

"Not a problem. We'll run you right up there."

A few minutes later Frank climbed into the van the RV company used as a courtesy shuttle and was on his way back to meet Hamid, thinking how beautiful this part of the United States was. At least for now.

Chapter 14

MOVING PARTS

M OHAMMAD FEATHA NEVER met any of his soldiers at the same place twice and rarely met with them more than two times each. As leader, Abdul-Aziz Fahad was an exception because of the coordination that was going on between different soldiers who had little communication with each other and the fact that he had mentored the future martyr. Some he would not even meet until the operation was under way. Mohammad was nervous about this operation the closer they came to executing it because so many things could go wrong. Always poker faced and never showing emotion, he thought about the different aspects of what was about to happen as he ate his panini sandwich sitting on the edge of the *Fountain of the Four Rivers* in the middle of the Piazza Navona on this late summer afternoon in Rome. The atmosphere was busy with tourists and locals competing for spaces to sit as artists displayed their goods and painted away. The smell of bread baking at nearby restaurants filled the humid air.

He could see his lead soldier approaching from the south entrance to the piazza and made eye contact while ever searching for a tail or someone who might be watching. Fahad made his way toward the fountain with a bag in his hand containing a sandwich he had bought on the way over from a street vendor not far away.

"Peace," said Fahad as he pulled his sandwich out of the bag.

"And to you," Mohammad answered.

The two ate a few bites of their lunches before Mohammad spoke again.

"We have much success to be thankful for."

The sun was beating down, and Fahad nodded his head in agreement wearing his Louis Vuitton designer sunglasses.

"Our shipment is at sea from Batumi, and we have a date set for delivery," continued Mohammad.

161

"What is that date?" Fahad asked.

"September 3 for delivery to San Juan and September 5 for delivery to the ship."

Fahad thought that these dates would work fine. It was a little more than three weeks away and would give him time to get back to San Juan and finalize the shipment with his broker, then head to Miami to board the ship himself. Clearly Mohammad had solid confirmation of the "oven" shipment or he would not have called this meeting.

"Then our sailing will be booked for the second from Miami," said Fahad.

"Correct. You may contact your soldiers in Florida and on the ship to confirm that date."

Fahad took another bite of his sandwich and a sip of the drink he had.

"We will make final arrangements and carry out the will of Allah."

Mohammad nodded in agreement, and the two spoke no more words. They finished their lunches and took one good look at each other before embracing, knowing it would likely be for the last time on this earth. With the sounds of a violinist standing in the corner of the Piazza Navona playing for change, the two men walked in opposite directions toward their own destinies.

Hamid had a busy week at the furniture company and went back to his apartment to meet Frank, who was staying with him. The two were planning on going out to get some dinner. When he arrived, he found Frank sitting at the kitchen table with a large pepperoni pizza. Frank told him it had been delivered about a half hour earlier.

"This came to the door, and the driver said it was paid for," Frank said to his superior, not quite knowing whether Hamid had sent it or not. He thought they were going out. "The driver said happy early birthday and handed me this note."

Hamid took the note that was on the back of a pizza order form used at all Pizza Hut restaurants. There was a large square that was designated for special requests or instructions. Inside the square it read, "Happy early September 2 birthday. Enjoy, Sam."

Hamid looked at Frank, and his face took on a serious expression. "We sail on Saturday, September 2, and will make reservations tonight on different websites."

"That is good news. This is from our leader, I assume."

"It is. Good news, indeed."

Hamid had much work to do. He had the dummy paperwork ready to deliver the mattresses he had been preparing to the ship, but he needed to finalize those arrangements. He also had to signal his soldiers working on board during their next turnaround day, which was coming up in forty-eight hours.

"I will work on Expedia," Frank said as he went to get out his laptop.

Both men got started on their computers, booking a one-week cruise on the September 2 sailing of the *Star Orion* out of Miami. No airfare would be needed. They requested single cabins on deck 7 forward if possible.

Eighteen hundred miles away in Frankfurt, Germany, Fahad was doing the same: booking passage for two on the *Star Orion*'s September 2 sailing. In order to blend in with the other passenger reservations, he booked his for Mr. and Mrs. Jose Fuentes. This would be the name he would travel to the United States under and use to embark out of the Port of Miami. His Costa Rican passport had already been prepared by Mohammad's document woman who had done so well with the shipping documents over the past few months. The cover story would be that his wife would be joining him on the ship on the day of departure. She would cancel at the last minute due to a work conflict, but he would sail to join the friends they were vacationing with, seeing that it was already paid for in advance. After a few clicks of the mouse on both sides of the Atlantic, the bookings for the September 2 sailing of the *Star Orion* had just gone up by four.

Two days later, Hamid went to Bayside Marketplace for lunch at the Latin American Café where he had enjoyed some fantastic Cuban fare in the past. Before entering the restaurant, he stopped to read his *Miami Herald* newspaper just outside the building on a bench overlooking the waterfront. The weather was typical for late summer in Miami; it was hot and humid, with afternoon showers and thunderstorms likely, according to the forecast he noted on the front page of the paper. It was just before 11:00 a.m., and there were no rain showers in sight. The sun was bright as midday approached, and he was wearing a New York Yankees hat, which kept his face shaded but also sent a signal to his associates who would be close by within the hour.

Around eleven twenty-five, Imad Patel emerged from the crowded walkway leading to the area near where Hamid was reading and stopped to tie his shoe. He was dressed in comfortable khaki shorts with a button-down, short-sleeve, light blue island-style shirt but was not wearing a hat. The absence of the hat signaled to Hamid that he had no information or message to pass on this visit. Hamid looked at Imad then at the door to the Cuban restaurant just a few feet away. Imad knew the drill. The Yankees hat Hamid was wearing signaled that he did have information to pass. Hamid folded his newspaper and walked inside the Latin American Café and asked for a table for one. A few minutes later, Imad did the same. They would not sit together, but Imad would follow Hamid's lead, knowing that a message would be passed. They had four ways of passing messages and never used the same one twice in a row. Sitting down at a table meant that they would meet in the restroom on the signal of the senior soldier, which in this case was Hamid.

The restaurant was crowded with the usual sounds of glasses clinking and people chatting filling the air along with the scent of Cuban cuisine. A waiter showed up at Hamid's table a few minutes after he sat down and asked for a drink order. Hamid decided on an iced tea and ordered an appetizer of chips and salsa. Their salsa was freshly made, and he had ordered it during past visits on his own time.

Sitting four tables away, Imad also ordered a drink and a chicken dish called *arroz con pollo*. He was closer to the outside tables facing the marina and pulled out his iPad to check on the latest news headlines. The iPad was his newest electronic device and one that he had been saving up to buy. On the ship he had a laptop, but the addition of the iPad brought him a much better and different online and multimedia experience.

After the waiter delivered his appetizer, Hamid got up to use the restroom and wash his hands. About a minute or two later, Imad put his iPad into its case, picked it up, and did the same. The restroom was located at the back of the restaurant, around the corner from the bar. It had one stall and two urinals for customers to relieve themselves. As Imad entered the restroom, he was pleased that the only other person using it at the moment was Hamid. Without saying a word, he walked to the urinal next to the one Hamid was currently using. Both men continued to finish their business and moved over to the single sink to wash their hands. Hamid went first, then backed away to allow Imad to wash while he pushed the button for the air-dry machine. Seconds later Imad finished washing and also pushed the button for the air dryer. While Imad dried his hands, Hamid took a small book of matches out of his pocket and dropped it on the floor. Imad bent down and picked it up and put it in his own pocket. The whole sequence of events took less than two minutes, and both men exited the restroom one right after another.

Imad sat back down at this table, and a few minutes later his *arroz con pollo* arrived. He ordered another drink from the waiter, but this time it was a screwdriver. He did not drink much alcohol, but he was excited about the words he had just read on the back of the matchbook cover and wanted to have a small personal celebration before heading back to work on the ship. The small note read, "Room 902." Imad would inform his partner that their operation would kick off on September 2, which was the second day of the ninth month, as noted in the message. There was much to finalize back on the *Star Orion,* he thought as he sipped his drink and pondered what needed to be done back on board.

Being an out-of-work actor is worse than just being unemployed because if you have had some success in show business, the public perception is that you are washed up. After Tom Sundland's fall from grace years ago and slow climb back to sobriety, he was enjoying the smaller gigs and the fact that he was able to do more than one project at a time. The cruise ship gig was something that he did not want to do at first because he had heard horror stories from other performers who had bad experiences. But as he stood in the security line waiting to board the *Star Orion* for another three-week engagement, he thought this was the best thing he had done in years. After giving it a try, signing up again was a no-brainer. He was booked for the August 26, September 2, and September 9 sailings reviving his Sam Primo character once again. To his amazement was the number of people who used to watch his old show, *Murder 101*, either when it was on network TV or later in syndication. The cruise line actually sold DVDs of the series in their gift shop and ran reruns on one of the ship's television channels during the weeks he worked on board. It was so successful, that this time they decided to expand the classic TV-themed cruise to include two other former stars from both a comedy and another seventies drama. As Tom stood in the security line just outside the terminal, he saw Rex Nelson looking lost on the sidewalk. Clearly it was Rex's first gig on a ship.

"Looking for someone?" Tom said after he stepped out of line to go over to help a former colleague whom he hadn't seen in years.

"Oh my god. I heard you were also on this boat!" Rex said as he shook Tom's hand and they embraced. "Long, long time."

"Too long. How are you, my friend?"

"Doing good. Better now. Getting some work and smelling the roses a bit more," said Rex as he looked around like he was waiting for someone.

"You'll love this gig. I tried it once, and now I won't say no when they call."

"Really? I was a little nervous at first," said Rex, still looking around.

Tom figured that Rex had never been aboard and thought the timing was good that they ran into each other.

"You looking for someone?"

"Yeah, the lady at the agency said that someone from the ship would meet me once I cleared security."

"They'll meet you upstairs, but this is the line for security. We all have to go through it. We have a separate brow, though, once we get checked through."

"Brow?" asked Rex having never stepped foot on anything bigger than his dad's eighteen-foot Boston Whaler years ago.

"Gangplank. The thing you walk on to get aboard ship. Then there's a crew security check, which is pretty quick."

Rex nodded his head and smiled.

"There's a lot to learn, my friend, but it's all good," said Tom as he pointed to show Rex where they needed to stand.

As the two made their way through the first security checkpoint, which was similar to the TSA security posts airports have, they collected their bags and headed up the escalator to the crew entrance which was just off the main terminal, where hundreds of vacationers were checking in and getting their sea passes.

"She said to look for a lady named Tammy who would have a sign with my name on it," Rex explained.

"Tammy Thompson. She's a sweetheart and your go-to person for everything while on board. She coordinates all the contracted talent on this ship," Tom said, sounding like an old pro even though it was only his third contract.

The two headed down the hallway marked "Crew Only," where Tammy was approaching from the opposite direction.

"You found my new friend," she said to Tom as they got closer.

"I did. We knew each other back in the day."

Rex introduced himself to Tammy, who handed him a badge and asked to see his contract paperwork. She verified that he was indeed contracted for three sailings and checked Tom's as well.

"You both are going to have a lot of fun," she explained while handing back the paperwork. "We also have Diane Lutz, who is doing some special stand-up nights for the three weeks."

Neither man knew Lutz personally but remembered her seventies sitcom called *The Flying J*.

"Does the ship move much?" Rex asked. He was a little nervous about going to sea and getting seasick.

"Like a cork in a bottle," answered Tom with a chuckle in his voice. "We almost rolled all the way over the last time I did one of these!"

"He's full of it," Tammy said giving Tom the eye. "You might feel some motion, but it so big, it's not very much."

Rex figured Tom was giving him the business. After seeing the enormous white ship before him, he started to get excited about the experience ahead.

"The good news is that we can head into the ports and have some fun," Tom explained. "Nassau, San Juan, and St. Thomas."

Some ships alternated their port calls and itineraries every other week from Eastern Caribbean to Western Caribbean. *Star Orion* kept the same schedule for the nine months she would spend in the Eastern Caribbean before heading to the Mediterranean for the late spring and summer months. The ship had been back on this schedule for about a month or so after the crossing from Europe.

"Can you take Rex to check in on deck 1?" Tammy asked Tom, who had done this drill twice before.

"Sure thing."

Tom and Rex headed a little further down the hallway to the crew brow, where they presented their temporary credentials and paperwork before being allowed to cross over onto the ship. Once on board, at the end of the brow, there was yet another security checkpoint for crew coming and going.

"You have to go through this spot when getting on and off at the ports. Make sure you always carry your ship ID and driver's license," said Tom as he put his spare change into the round dish so he could walk through the metal detector.

Once they cleared crew security, Tom headed for deck 1, where he and Rex would get their cabin assignments for the three-week contract. Unlike regular crew members, who lived on deck 1, as guest entertainers they would be given regular cabins someplace on the ship and could enjoy many of the amenities, including the pool and buffets.

"I'm 7009," Tom said to Rex as they looked at where they would be living on the ship.

"7020," Rex answered. Both men would be just down the hall from each other which, Rex thought, would be good if they wanted to hang out.

"My show days are Tuesday and Friday and yours might be the same, but check with Tammy," explained Tom. They would each do two "shows" per week, either on the same days or different days. Once per week, all three would be together for an audience Q&A session in one of the ship's lounges. Tom was surprised at just how many people showed up the first time he did his. The sessions were heavily promoted on the ship's television station, and with three celebrities from the seventies, were bound to have big attendance.

They finished up the check-in process by taking another picture for their IDs, which would also act as their stateroom key cards, and headed up the elevators to deck 7. Passengers were just starting the embarkation procedures and soon would be filling the hallways and restaurants of the 150,000-ton vessel.

Meanwhile, one deck above them, Capt. Stefin Markinson finished unpacking and hung his mess dress dinner uniform in the closet of the cabin, which was supposed to be occupied by his twin brother for the next four months. Clipped on the white Star Caribe uniform shirt he was wearing was his brother's ID, which, so far, no one had questioned. The new captain reported aboard with not much fanfare and relieved a more junior captain who had just finished up his first contract as master of the ship. Stefin knew most of the other captains in the fleet except for a few of the newer ones who had been promoted to the top job earlier that year. He looked over the "hand off" paperwork the departing captain had gone over with him and pulled up the departure checklist on his laptop to get ready for the sail out. In his file of documents was an order and notice from Star Caribe that their sick bay would receive some new equipment, including a CT scanning machine. This he would give to his lead doctor and deck coordinator so that they would have a heads-up. The document had been generated in Frankfurt and arrived via a FedEx package, which was waiting when he arrived at his brother's flat back in Oslo.

His cabin was on the port side of the ship just a few feet away from the bridge, and it was about the size of one of the suites on board. On this trip, the hotel manager was also a newly promoted officer and had joined *Star Orion* after being an assistant on two other company ships. Thankfully, neither he nor his brother had worked with him before.

"Two thousand six hundred fifty-two aboard, Captain, waiting on another sixty or so," said Jon Watson as he presented his first hotel manager's report, which is given to the master of the ship before sailing.

"Very well, Jon, congratulations."

"Thank you, sir. It truly feels good."

The weather on this Miami day was hot and muggy as the departure hour of 5:00 p.m. drew closer. When the guest services manager reported all passengers aboard to the hotel manager, they would report to the ship's master. The deck crew would then stand by to secure the gangways and make ready for sea and anchor detail.

At four thirty-five the hotel manager received a call on his shipboard cell phone with the final count.

"Two thousand seven hundred five for the final count, Captain," said new hotel director Watson.

"Very well. Engineering, we'll need power for all four pods," the captain said after pushing a button marked *CHENG,* which stands for "chief engineer," on the small console that was attached to his chair. A few seconds later he had his reply that all systems were go as he prepared to sail his ship out of the Port of Miami under his brother's name. He worried that perhaps the harbor pilot assigned to his departure may recognize that he was not his brother, but once again fate was on his side as one of only three female harbor pilots entered the bridge. He had not worked with this woman in the past and hoped that two weeks from this date, he would have the same luck in order to carry out his mission.

The term "Google it" is pretty much universal when people look for information these days. It was exactly what Moe said to Dino when he was asking whether Moe had heard of the charity called "Worldcare." In his

The first and last line

office at Narragansett H&C, he searched the Internet and found a German nonprofit organization based in Frankfurt. The website said that the charity supported faith organizations around the world with donations to aid in health care. To him, it looked legit, at least at first. The odd thing about the website was that there was no way to donate to the cause and no mailing address listed. It looked almost like a site that had been under construction and never completed. The domain had a dot dk address for Germany but under the *Contact Us* tab, there was just an info e-mail button which when clicked on, directed you back to the home page.

When searching for news or articles about Worldcare, nothing came up. He then searched "Frank Castro, Worldcare," and again, nothing came up. There were lots of people named Frank Castro, but none had anything to do with the guy to whom he had sold weapons and trusted as a good friend. The more he investigated, the more pissed off he was getting. Dino Tucci was not someone you would want to disrespect or piss off. His boss, Anthony Battelli, had even less patience for disrespect of deception. Anthony took any slight to one of his earners as a slap in his own face.

With coffee sitting on the desk and cinnamon Dunkin' Donut in his hand, he continued to check the Internet while also getting his plan together for the day. Anthony and his driver entered the building and stopped by Dino's desk on the way to the boss's big office.

"You're early," said Anthony to one of his better *capos*. Dino looked up, took a sip of his coffee, and answered his boss.

"Wanted to look at this thing with Frank again."

"You still obsessed with that Castro guy? Fuck 'em."

Frank just looked at the screen and then back at Anthony, who had no idea he had sold this guy weapons.

"If this guy fucking lied to me, I'll hunt the bastard down."

Anthony treated Dino like a son and would always protect him. He and all the members of his crew were as close as a real family could be. They ate together, spent holidays together, laughed together, and cried together.

"Do what you need to do," Anthony said, putting a blessing on whatever it was Dino wanted to do to fix the situation. They had connections in many major cities across the country. Dino nodded his head while Anthony moved on to his own office to start the day. Even with the contacts he might have in Miami, most of whom were in the drug business, this was something he wanted to get to the bottom of himself.

"I'm worried about those ARs I sold him," Frank said to Moe, who was his usual silent self.

"So what?" Moe said nonchalantly.

"So I don't get lied to, and who the fuck knows what he did with them?"

"He sent them to that organization. That's all you need to know."

"Why'd he disappear off the map then?"

"He wanted a vacation?" Moe asked, knowing that his immediate boss was not about to drop this.

Dino gave him a dirty look, and that ended the conversation. He got up, took his coffee, and pointed to the door. Moe knew that they were on the move and opened the office door and the door of the Suburban sitting only a few feet away. It was hot and muggy for a Rhode Island morning in late August, and Dino had to check on a problem that the family had with one of the local used car dealers who wasn't playing the game according to Battelli family rules. Anthony Battelli had his hands in many businesses, including moving used cars at a few lots in Rhode Island and Southeastern Massachusetts. Recovered stolen cars would sometimes end up at the auctions where insurance companies would sell them to recover some of the costs they incurred replacing them. Various brands of vehicles were worth much more than others, and it was up to the managers of Battelli's lots to bid on the good ones then turn them for serious profit. Another arm of the family would even steal the cars and hide them until insurance paid off the owners, then miraculously the cars would be found a few months later and end up at auction where his people would buy them.

The trouble with the lot on Taunton Avenue, just over the East Providence line in Seekonk, was that the manager had let an outside associate outbid him on a couple of cars, which the guy would then turn around and sell privately. After the sale, they would simply split the profits. Apparently this had been going on for over a year to the tune of over a million dollars. The auctioneer wanted to score some points, so he tipped off the family by informing the manager of one of Battelli's other lots in Cranston, Rhode Island. Mr. Battelli was not happy.

Traffic was usually busy along Taunton Avenue, which was also U.S. Route 44, where many car dealers, both new and used, did business. They pulled into the lot unannounced and drove over to the office, which was a small building toward the back. Moe then put the Suburban in park and got out and into the backseat while Dino got out and went inside.

"Dino!" said Marvin Taylor, who had managed this property for the last two years after spending twenty-four months in federal prison for operating a chop shop on Boston's South Shore. Battelli did a favor for his friend who ran a crew in Southey by taking him in and away from that territory. The job also allowed Marvin early work release from the federal pen.

"Marvin. Let's take a ride. Junior can handle things for a little while," Dino said, looking over at the assistant manager, who was all of twenty-five years old.

"Okay, sure, Dino," Marvin said in a nervous tone. He figured no one would ever find out about his extracurricular activities making a few extra bucks on the side.

Both men walked outside and toward the Suburban. Dino got into the driver's side and Marvin the passenger side. Junior looked on through the window from the office as they pulled out and took a right onto Taunton Avenue headed toward the small town of Rehoboth.

The Suburban had factory dark tinted windows but Dino had the driver's and passenger's windows also tinted after market. The amount of tint was slightly darker than Rhode Island law permitted, but no one ever said anything to him about it.

"How's business?" Dino asked Marvin, who had his hand on the door handle and felt like there was something wrong.

"Good, Dino. The numbers are good this month."

Moe was sitting just behind Marvin and quietly pulled out a syringe he had in his computer bag sitting on the floor in front of him. He slowly removed the needle cap and let it fall on the floor.

"We're happy with the numbers, Marvin. Anthony wanted you to know that too."

Marvin couldn't figure this meeting out but felt slightly relieved to hear Dino say that.

"Good to know," Marvin replied.

"See that house over there?" Dino asked pointing to a random house that was just off the right side of the car as they continued to drive down Route 44.

Marvin looked toward the right, and as he did, Moe took one of his huge hands and pulled Marvin's head back. He then drove the syringe into the left side of his neck with the other.

Marvin had been nervous, but this was nothing he expected. As the succinylcholine invaded the vein in his neck, his last thirty seconds of having any bodily control gave him a sick feeling in his stomach. He immediately started to lose all control of his limbs, hands, legs, and feet. The drug paralyzed the patient's muscles, rendering him immobile but at the same time kept him conscious. A person under the influence of this drug could still feel everything, but he could not move or make a sound.

Moe put the syringe cap back onto the needle and returned it to his laptop bag. The rest of the twenty-minute ride to an old rock quarry in Rehoboth was silent.

The quarry had been abandoned for years, but kids still liked to play near the pond that sat at the bottom of what looked sort of like a manmade amphitheater. On the north side of the quarry, there was only one road in and out. It was a paved for about the first half mile, then dirt for the rest of the way. In total, it was probably around a mile and a half into the quarry from the secondary road they had turned onto from of Route 44. There were woods all around for miles.

Dino stopped the Suburban at the end of the road, near the edge of the quarry. There were still piles of crushed rock all around from years past when limestone was a hot commodity.

"We used to fish out here years ago, Moe," Dino said as he put the vehicle in park. Moe had been to this location in the past and humored his boss, hearing the same story over again.

The amount of succinylcholine Moe had given Marvin was enough to keep him totally paralyzed for around an hour. Moe dragged Marvin out of the car and bound his hands and his feet with black gaffer's tape just in case the drug wore off too soon.

Dino motioned for Moe to go to the back of the Suburban and get his pliers from the toolbox. He returned a few seconds later.

"Prop him up on the side of that tree," Dino ordered while he and Moe dragged Marvin around six feet to the big pine that was reaching into the sky.

"Marvin, can you move your leg?" Dino said as he slapped his leg a few times to test it.

He was trying, but it was almost impossible.

"Come on, Marvin, try moving your leg," Dino said a second time.

Then Moe went back to the Suburban, got a bottle of water that was sitting in the drink holder between the front seats, and returned.

"Try this," Moe said.

Dino took the bottle of water, opened it, then poured it over Marvin's body and saw no muscular movement. Marvin could feel the water and reacted by letting out a small squeak, but could not move a limb.

"You with us, Marvin?" Dino asked again.

Marvin desperately tried to talk, but the drug would not allow him to speak. His brain functioned, but his body did not.

"We're not going to kill you, Marvin. Don't worry."

Dino waited a few more minutes and then asked Marvin a few questions.

"We know you're working with that Keith guy, buying and selling under the table. Anyone else, or just him?"

Marvin took a breath and looked up at Dino, who was standing over him. He tried to mouth the word "no." He tried to move his head back and forth to indicate no. He could not communicate. His brain said to say something, but his muscles were frozen.

"Feel this?" Dino asked as he pinched his cheek with his fingers.

Marvin made a very slight noise, indicating he could indeed feel the pinch. Still, he was powerless to do anything.

After being tipped off, Dino had watched Marvin carefully for a couple of months to see if this guy had set up a used auto ring or whether it was just one or two goons working together. He was convinced of the latter but wanted to hear it for himself.

"A few Beamers, a Mercedes, and a Jag, just to name a few. That's not what I call small money," Dino explained. "Almost a million stolen from the family so far by our estimate."

"Aaah," was all Marvin could say, but it sounded like a whisper. He had literally shit his pants by now. All three men could smell it. Dino had seen this before in others.

"No, you can still work for us, Marvin, but I want the other managers to know that this sort of bullshit won't be tolerated."

Marvin looked up at Dino and tried to nod. It was like a horrifying out-of-body experience. He could feel things like pain, but could not move any part of his body.

Dino started to walk away toward the Suburban, where he had his coffee and a small box of Dunkin' Donuts. He opened the passenger door, reached in for the coffee and a donut, then he turned back to look at Marvin sitting at the bottom of the tree with Moe standing over him.

"I know you won't do it again, Marvin," Dino said as he looked at Moe, nodded and took a bite of his Boston Kreme donut.

Moe pulled the pliers out of his pocket, and Marvin's eyes opened as wide as they could with fear. He had heard stories of this guy in the past but never witnessed anything himself. Now he was about to not only witness it, but also feel it.

"Oooooh," Marvin gurgled. He was powerless to talk, move, or do just about anything except continue to lose control of his bowels and bladder.

"Open wide," Moe said, trying to sound like a dentist would.

"Faaaaaaaa," Marvin tried to scream. His brain was saying, "No . . . fuck no," but the only sound was that of a very small animal.

Moe took his pliers and one by one pulled out all of Marvin's bottom teeth while letting him wait in excruciating pain between extractions. He and Dino were actually a little surprised that the guy didn't pass out. When Moe the Dentist, was done, he took out a dirty dishrag they had brought along, wet it down with the water from the bottle, and stuck it in Marvin's mouth to help with the bleeding.

Dino took a knife, walked back over, and, after giving his now-partially toothless associate time to think that his life may be about to end after all, cut the tape holding Marvin's hands and feet, freeing him.

Marvin could breathe through his nose, but he could still not move a muscle.

"I expect you at work tomorrow," Dino warned as he and Moe headed back toward the Suburban. "This shit will wear off soon, and you can walk to the road or call for a ride." Dino threw down the cell phone Marvin had dropped when injected with the drug.

Both men got into the SUV with Moe in the driver's seat. Before he put the key in the ignition, he stuffed a balled-up handkerchief in his pocket.

"What you got there, Moe?" Dino asked.

Moe looked a little sheepish. "His teeth. I'll clean 'em up, and add 'em to my collection."

Dino stared for a second then laughed. "You're a sick bastard, you know that? I'm glad you're on our side."

They pulled out with wheels spinning, leaving a cloud of dust and rocks washing over Marvin like a sandstorm. An hour or so later, the drug wore off, and slowly Marvin regained muscle control. He indeed had a long painful walk back to the main road to think about his actions.

Dino continued to sip his coffee and decided on his next step in the Frank Castro mystery as Moe drove down the dirt road heading back toward the office. When they returned, Dino decided to go back on the Expedia website and book the ticket he had saved to Miami for Wednesday. It had been a long time since his last vacation, and a few days in Florida might be good for him, Dino thought as he started to count some of the money his crew had brought in over the last twenty-four hours.

Chapter 15

PAID TIME OFF

SUMMER IN WASHINGTON, D.C., was usually rather hot, but this year the nation's capital was suffering through a string of record warm days in the upper nineties. Along the mall, the crowds seemed to thin a bit after lunch, during the hottest part of the day, as the tourists headed for the air-conditioned museums. As part of her daily routine, Special Agent Claire Wilson liked to run her mile and a half around noon before having a light lunch. With the temperatures so hot, she decided to only run three times a week until the weather cooled off a bit.

After her run, she walked over to the food court on F Street not far from her desk at the Washington field office of the United States Secret Service. It was an easy place to get a salad and drink some water. Her colleague and friend, Janet Conklin, from the Miami field office was in town, finishing up a home office visit and some paperwork from counterfeit cases she had been working. Janet had sent her a text to see if she wanted to meet up for a quick bite. The two had gone through training together and were part of the same Beltsville graduating class.

"It feels more like Miami here than it does back at home," Janet said as she approached Claire, who was standing in line waiting to order a salad.

The two hugged each other.

"So great to see you," Claire said. "Don't get too close. I've been running!"

"I'm glad you got my text. I really wanted to hook up for lunch or something," Janet explained as she stepped up to the counter to order.

A few minutes later, both ladies took their plastic cups to the soda fountain to pour a drink then find a place to sit. As was the case on most days, the food court on F Street was jammed with people trying to get a bite in the midst of busy schedules. They found a table for two and sat down, waiting for their order number to be called.

"I have been slammed on this trip," Janet said, starting the conversation, anxious to get caught up on each other's busy lives.

"I'm sure. It was great to see you in Miami. You're doing good work down there."

Just then, a man with strong Greek accent called their number, and Claire got up to pick up the salads. She returned with both hands full.

"I miss D.C. food," Janet chuckled, looking at the size of the salads in Claire's hands.

"I miss Miami's beaches," Claire said.

"I'll bet that's not all!"

Claire smiled, knowing exactly what her friend sitting across the table was talking about.

"I do miss Jake. I didn't for a while during training and fieldwork, you know. But after his visits here and my trip down there, it's complicated."

They ate their salads for a few minutes before Janet spoke.

"You two seemed really good together when we had supper down there."

Claire nodded in agreement. Then she lowered the tone of her voice a bit as if to talk about something classified.

"I did something for his birthday coming up. It's the big three-oh, and we've been talking about taking a trip together."

Janet looked surprised and tried not to act it.

"Really?" she said.

"So he has the big birthday coming up on September 8, and I was thinking of doing something really special that would show that I'm back into the idea of a full-time relationship."

They took bites of their food as Janet looked on, curious to find out what her friend had done.

"I talked to Rosa, his secretary, and she also thought it was a great idea. Then I called Felton and asked him to help me conspire," Claire explained carefully.

Janet grew more curious by the minute, trying to eat and listen.

"What did you do, Claire?"

"I booked us a vacation during the week of his thirtieth, and he has no idea about it!"

Janet almost choked on her lettuce and had to take a sip of the Diet Pepsi sitting in front of her.

"Are you kidding me?" Janet exclaimed. She was thrilled for her friend.

"Nope. Felton put in the leave paperwork, and Rosa cleared his schedule. I'm flying down on Friday night to have dinner and surprise him. We have reservations in the Grove, then on Saturday we leave for seven fabulous days in the Caribbean on a cruise!"

Janet put her fork down, got up, and hugged her friend. The two were giddy like high school girls talking about their first prom date.

"You better not go and get married without me," Janet ordered.

"Oh no, nothing like that. I wanted something easy that left from right there in Miami and not too expensive, so I booked one of the ships right there."

Claire had not told a soul about her birthday plans for Jake. She didn't want anyone to tip him off and didn't want to give the other agents in the office ammunition to poke fun at her.

"He thinks I'm coming down just for the weekend just to have a birthday dinner on Friday," Claire said.

"I can give you a ride to the ship that morning if that would help," Janet offered to her friend.

Claire thought about that for a minute.

"That would be great. Jake could leave his car at home and save some money on parking."

Janet lived in Hollywood, Florida, about thirty minutes north of Jake's place on Miami Beach.

"It's the least I can do," said Janet as they continued to eat their lunch.

The two continued to talk while crowds of people piled into the food court for lunch. The place was getting loud and busy.

"I hope he's not mad," Claire said.

"Are you kidding me? He's going to be so thrilled. This is perfect."

That was just what Claire wanted to hear. She wanted to do something special for his thirtieth birthday but was afraid that he might not want to go away for a whole week. Jake was a fast burner, as they said in the ranks of Homeland Security. He had risen to special agent in charge of a field office after only seven years with DHS. She knew he was a workaholic and didn't take much time off. Maybe this was just what they both needed to get their relationship back on track and headed for the long term, she thought as they finished their lunch.

The airport in San Juan was just a few miles from the beach where some of the resorts were located, attracting people from all over the world to escape their lives for a week or two of sunshine and margaritas. The Courtyard Marriott was on Isla Verde Beach just a few doors down from the Ritz-Carlton. It was the off season, and the hotel was only half occupied; some of those were airline employees who used the property for their federally mandated crew rest.

Jose Rio entered through the lobby and made his way down the hall toward the door that led to the beach and pool. He was told to meet his contact at the pool bar once again. He thought it was strange that this guy would only meet at hotels and not come by the office, but keeping clients happy was part of his job. The weather was normal for this time of year in the tropics with high humidity, and a good breeze blowing in off the bright aqua blue ocean just a few feet away.

"Hola, señor," Abdul-Aziz Fahad said as Jose approached the part of the bar where his client was sitting.

"Hola, como esta?"

"Fine, my friend. Fine," Fahad said in a chipper tone.

"Your transfer is all set once the shipment arrives in San Juan next week," Jose said as he went over the paperwork before him that was generated when he received an electronic copy of the waybill from the COSCO shipping office in Batumi. Boris had been meticulous when it came to making sure the papers were in order whether forged or real documents. He had also sent along copies of the Star Caribe paperwork ordering the upgrades to the medical facility on board the *Star Orion,* which Fahad gave to his broker. As the shipping broker, Jose would clear all the paperwork with local Customs and Border Protection field operations officers before the shipment arrived in order to expedite the clearances needed later on.

"I am off to see another client and will be in touch on other Sellco shipments in the future," Fahad said as he shook Jose's hand.

"Our pleasure. Safe travels," Jose said as the two ended the meeting, and Fahad walked back toward the lobby in order to cut through to the parking lot where his rental car was parked. He would call on two other clients in San Juan then return to the Courtyard Marriott for the night.

The next morning he woke early and went into the bathroom to shave his mustache and dye his hair in order to match the picture on the Costa Rican passport he was carrying. He had express checkout, so he did not have to go back to the front desk. All he had to do was pack his things and head out the door to the car, which he would return to the Avis rental agency just a few miles away then board their airport shuttle bus. Looking in every way like the typical vacation traveler, Fahad made his way to the American Airlines counter to check in for his trip to Miami under the name Jose Fuentes.

Life at sea was not for those who needed huge networks of close friends with busy social lives. It was not for those who wanted to stay in close relationships or anyone wanting a traditional family unit. Most seagoing men and women try for normal things in life like marriage, but the failure rate is high. Neither Stefin Markinson nor his twin brother had ever married, and the women they dated knew that they were sharing them with their first love, the sea. Bijon had a large network of friends and a few girlfriends, but Stefin's group was much smaller. He had only a few close friends, and of those, a few also worked on various vessels as officers.

Carleen Foulton was a friend he had met during a visit to the emergency room on one of his breaks between sea duty. He had been out fishing by himself near the town of Fetsund at a favorite spot along the river Glomma about thirty kilometers from his flat in Oslo when he slipped from a pier and cut a three-inch gash in his leg. Knowing that the wound required a couple of stitches and that he should probably get a tetanus shot, he went to the hospital in the town of Lillestrom. It was there that the two met and actually ended up dating for a couple of months until she realized that the sea would win out in any relationship. They ended up becoming close friends and saw each other once or twice during his breaks from Star Caribe. They were both avid divers, and she also liked to fish.

Carleen knew he was rotating off the ship because he had seen Bijon in the market and actually thought it was Stefin. The two had laughed as Bijon set her straight and filled her in on his brother's plans. Typically Stefin would e-mail or call once he got settled back in town and caught up on his life back on land. She thought it was strange that she had not heard from him since the e-mail, figuring that he would have been home for at least three or four weeks. She e-mailed and sent a few text messages but got nothing in response.

Her sister, Christine, lived just a few kilometers from his flat in Oslo, and she decided, after having lunch at her house, to drop by and pay him an impromptu visit. She arrived at Stefin and Bijon's flat knowing he would be alone, as his brother returned to his ship on opposite working schedules. The weather was cloudy but comfortable as she approached the front door and rang the bell. No answer. She rang again and then tried knocking. Still nothing. Perhaps he was in town or out on a diving trip, she thought as she peered through the small windows that were on each side of the door.

A few minutes later a postman arrived with mail and said hello as he stuffed a few pieces into the box by the street. He then asked her if she could tell Stefin that his box was full. Carleen walked down the walkway to the mailbox and the postman showed her how overstuffed it was.

"That's odd," she said upon seeing the box with so much untouched mail.

If he was going on a dive trip, she would have had at least some Facebook messages, pictures, or status updates. Now that she thought about it, she had not seen him on Facebook in a few weeks.

"I'll tell him," Carleen said as the postman finished with the box and prepared to move on. She returned to the front door and saw through the window that the kitchen window was half opened. Surely, she thought, he must be around or not far away. She decided to go around to the back of the townhouse and knock on the back door. Perhaps he was in the basement working on something. The back of each townhouse was exactly the same. They each had a small patio and back kitchen door. As Carleen walked up to the door, she could see that in addition to the kitchen window being open, the small window for the bathroom was also wide open.

She knocked on the door and peered inside where the sunlight was shining through the half-opened window, lighting up the entire kitchen area. Inside she saw that the basement door was open. Carleen had been in Stefin's house a few times, and in the basement the twins had a bar set up and big-screen television to watch football matches. "Hello, Stefin?" she said, knocking again. There was a bucket and mop sitting just outside the door on the patio, and Carleen figured that perhaps he had been cleaning the house. The bucket was empty and the mop was hard; so it must have been a while ago, she thought as she pushed it aside. Just for sport, she tried the door. It opened. He must have left it unlocked.

She cracked the door and once again announced herself in case he was in the basement or up in his bedroom. Still no response. As she opened the door further, she smelled something that she had never smelled before. An odd but awful smell, like something had been left out of the refrigerator and was going bad. Again, she thought, it was just like a typical bachelor to leave food out in the open. Looking over at the counter, there was no food. In fact, it was quite clean. That was also odd, she thought.

Just a few steps away, the basement door was fully opened. Maybe he was working on something down stairs that smelled really bad. That would explain the open windows. She walked over to the door, looked down the stairs, and stopped in horror. Her stomach started to turn because of what she was looking at. Her heart started beating like she was running a marathon. At the bottom of the stairs was what appeared to be something wrapped up in sheets and tied around and around. The smell was twice as bad as she stepped down onto the first stair. With a sense of urgency and fear, she got out her cell phone and tried to dial 112 (Norway's version of 911). She was so nervous that she dropped the phone, and it landed about four steps down. Carleen then proceeded down the four steps to retrieve the phone, and as she got closer to the bottom, she could see what looked like bloodstains on the sheets wrapping what clearly was a body. After picking up the phone, she backed up the stairs quickly, went out of the kitchen to the back yard, and dialed 112. Within fifteen minutes, Oslo police had arrived, and the flat she had visited on a number of fun occasions was now a crime scene.

Rosa Lee knew that Jake would be in for a short time this morning, but he spent lunch on most Tuesdays with his father over in Coconut Grove. She also knew that Jake's dad could be a handful for her boss at times and empathized, given her own situation with her mother, who had moved in with her just a few months ago after being diagnosed with Alzheimer's. Taking care of aging parents was something most baby boomers were going through, and many could relate.

When Jake would get a SIPRNET message, it would generate a nonclassified e-mail sent to both his and Rosa's regular Outlook inbox saying that he had message traffic waiting. Rosa was not cleared for SIPRNET, but the e-mail alert allowed her to make sure Jake was checking it. She had another reminder on her calendar for this twenty-ninth day of August and that was to remind him to call his ex-girl, current-girl, or whatever she was at the moment to wish her a happy birthday.

"Hi, Rosa," Jake said as he walked into the office. Light rain fell just outside their window.

"Call Claire for her birthday, and a SIPRNET message is waiting," she said smartly while looking at the morning online version of the *Miami Herald.*

"Already done. I called her on the way to the office this morning. She's still coming down to celebrate my thirtieth."

"That's a big step, isn't it? How 'together' are you two?"

Jake inserted his CAC government ID into the computer and logged on. He was under Rosa's microscope, and he hadn't even had a cup of coffee this morning. He wanted to cut down on the caffeine just a bit, so he started giving up his first cup at home and now would instead wait to have his first at the office. Besides, Rosa made some good coffee with her own blend that she would fix for him in a few minutes.

"Trying to get things back to where they were before she went off to training and broke it off," he said after looking over a few e-mails he had already seen on his iPhone. Jake then took his CAC out of his main computer and headed for the intel office next door.

"Good idea. Maybe she'll come around and marry you. Then again, maybe not. She's focused on the Service," Rosa said as he walked by her desk.

"That's encouraging." Jake said sarcastically walking out the door. Over in the intel shop there was only one message, and it was from Felton in Washington.

//////TOP SECRET/////SIPRNET/////EYES ONLY//////

TO: J Stein
FR: Felton
SUBJ: PRTC

Jake . . .

TC Fahad back in SJ. NSA ping also confirmed him on the ground in PR. Arrived 28 Aug via Lufthansa to London, then British Airways to SJ. Still on the island. No departure scheduled or hotel info. Maybe your boys can check those Sellco clients to see what he's up to.

Cheers,
TF

He looked at his calendar and noted that the last few times this guy was in Puerto Rico, he was there on the same days the cruise ships called. He remembered this because of the intel he had from one of his agents, Wayne Howard, who had seen him having lunch with a cruise ship employee whom they could not identify. On another occasion, Howard reported that he had met with a shipping broker at the Ritz. Not all that unusual for a guy selling products that needed to be shipped to the island. They had also checked out Sellco, and it looked clean.

"Get me Howard in San Juan," Jake said to Rosa as he walked back into their office, and she handed him his coffee.

"Yes, sir."

A few minutes later his phone rang, and he picked it up.

"Hi, Wayne," he said into the phone while thinking about the SIPRNET message he just saw.

"Hi, Jake."

"I just got a note from Felton that the TC we were pinging is back on your turf and hasn't left yet. I want you to go over to the two clients we know he has there and ask what types of products he has sold them and when they take delivery and shipment info, etc."

The line was quiet for a few seconds as Jake heard his agent writing down the instructions on the other end.

"Yeah, I remember you asked us to look up who he had for clients here from one of his arrivals. I forgot who they were, but we got the transcript from the CBP arrival lane agent's conversation and will look it up. He's traveling on a German passport and calls Frankfurt home."

When a person flies into the country, he or she goes through the usual customs procedures and actually speaks with an agent before being admitted and getting a passport stamp. Each airport has a different number of lanes that passengers file through, with some having more than others. Puerto Rico is not a huge entry point, and only has three lanes for international arrivals to filter through.

"Super, Wayne. Did you say German passport? He's from Pakistan."

"Might be a dual," Wayne said referring to a dual citizenship. This would be easy to check, Jake thought, making a note to follow up on it.

"Okay, thanks for the info. I still need to get down there and check up on you guys."

Jake had been trying to schedule a visit, seeing that their field office was temporarily his responsibility because of the vacancy needing to be filled. Management meetings, along with the additional duties, kept getting in the way.

"You keep saying that! We're just a stepchild. We know it," Wayne said with a chuckle in his voice.

"Just let me know about the TC. Talk soon, Wayne." With that, Jake hung up the phone.

He worked for around three more hours on employee evaluations, which were coming due, before getting into his car and heading south to Coconut Grove to have a bite to eat with his father.

Neither he nor his father was very religious, but he offered to take him to temple during the Jewish holidays. He would accept the gesture sometimes, but not always. There was no rhyme or reason. It just depended on the senior Stein's mood at the moment. As a family growing up in Brooklyn, they would faithfully attend, and all four of the Stein children would also take part in religious education. Jake and his three sisters were proud of their Jewish heritage, and he had even spent some time in Israel at an international conference on customs procedures.

Today Jake figured he would take his dad out someplace nice instead of eating at the assisted-living facility. Thankfully his dad embraced cellular technology and kept his phone close so that when Jake or his sisters would call, he would answer right away. After calling ahead, the senior Stein was waiting on the bench near the main entrance, ready to go as Jake pulled up in his convertible.

"This car is so fucking low," Mr. Stein said after opening the door and bending down to get inside the classic Jag XKE.

"It's a classic," Jake said.

"Yeah . . . yeah . . . yeah . . . Bullshit."

Once the senior Stein was belted in, Jake pulled away and headed toward South Dixie Highway and Coral Gables, where there was a T.G.I. Friday's restaurant that his dad seemed to like. Mr. Stein senior was a meat-and-potatoes kind of guy and had no like or patience for fancy food or restaurants.

"Claire called and said she was going to come down for a weekend to celebrate my thirtieth," said Jake, trying to change the subject and make some pleasant conversation. "I think she's planning a dinner somewhere."

"Make sure you pay," said his dad.

"It's my birthday!"

"You should still pay. Does this car have a muffler?"

Jake rolled his eyes a bit.

"It's supposed to sound like this. It's a classic Jag."

The two were very different people. Some even questioned whether Mr. Stein senior was Jake's actual father because they were that much different from each other.

Ten minutes later, Jake pulled up to the restaurant and they went inside for some lunch and conversation. Jake's mind was one-third on the conversation, one third on Claire, and one-third on what Wayne might find out in San Juan.

The senior housekeeper on board *Star Orion* was going over the Wednesday reports from her army of stewards who serviced and kept the cabins of the three-thousand-plus passengers clean and in top condition. Wednesday reports were important in planning to order anything that might be needed during their Saturday turnaround day. There were fourteen cabins needing refrigerator checks, five needing new patio chairs for the balconies, and seven needed bedding swaps. Each steward would make notes on anything that needed to be fixed and send them up daily with their reports. She went onto her Star Caribe intranet website and filled out the appropriate form which would generate orders from headquarters for the bedding and chairs. Those turned into purchase orders, which were sent directly to the suppliers who had the current contracts at the home port of each ship.

Bishar Fouad had spent a few months working his way up to housekeeping and had become a junior cabin steward while his partner, Imad, stayed in the environmental section. Both areas worked to the advantage of their overall mission. His twenty cabins were along the middle of deck 7, and his keycard worked for all the cabins he was responsible for, which gave him access anytime he was needed. He made a note in his Wednesday report that cabin

7620, 7624, 7632, and 7636 had category "D" bedding. Any cabin with category D bedding would be switched out on the next turnaround day. In past reports, he had reported that the bedding in these cabins was category B then C. He saw in the Wednesday report notes that his cabins with category D beds had been noted by the head housekeeper and would be replaced. Because they were his responsibility, he would take part in the switch out on turnaround day.

Bishar met Imad on the aft outdoor crew deck where those who smoked could do so. It was late, and most of the crew members who were not working were in their cabins either using Skype to talk to loved ones at home or getting much-needed rest. At sea, time seemed to stand still, and the days ran together.

"Category D beds being replaced in four of my cabins," Bishar said to Imad as they sipped their late-night tea. The two had been cabinmates for this contract along with one other in the past.

"I'm sure that will be a busy day," Imad replied. They were careful where and when they talked about their mission. They would never talk about it in their cabin or any public part of the ship except this small area, where the wind was usually strong and there was low light for the one camera that watched this part of the crew deck.

"Volunteer for the human chain on Saturday. I will be supervising the bedding switch out for my cabins and will make sure we work together for the load out and load in," Bishar said. Bedding replacement started with the old beds being brought down out of the cabin on the freight elevator to deck 1 and then off the ship. Then the new bedding would be brought onto the ship and up to the cabins, where the steward responsible for that section checked the quality and set it up. Assigned and volunteer crew members would form a human chain to move the beds from the truck then onto the ship where two others would continue the transfer to the cabin.

"Already done. I'm on the list," Imad said.

The two continued to sip their tea and did not say much more. Both were tired and needed to rest for the busy week they would have ahead. After finishing their tea, they retired to the cabin where they would sleep through the night and dream about how the world would change after they completed their mission.

Amanda Curtis was going over paperwork and looking forward to a few days off once the busy season for furniture was over. For now she was just happy for business being as good as it had been. Hiring Hamid and another salesperson who came from the Jacksonville area continued to pay off. They were starting to outgrow their warehouse and would soon need to look for a larger facility to keep inventory on hand for both the wholesale and resale side of the house. A few months before, Hamid had suggested using a few storage units for recurring orders they would be picking up, such as hotels and the cruise contracts. This idea worked out perfectly for Metro Miami Furniture & Bedding.

"Got seven sets and five of the Zubryd patio chairs for *Star Orion* on Saturday," she told Hamid as he arrived at work. He was nervous about the order and knew that it would be in on Thursday, which was the usual drill for the cruise contracts. It was a relief for him to hear it from Amanda though.

"I'm leaving early on Saturday, but we'll get it in the morning," he said.

"I know. Thanks for that. Once it's done, you're good to head out and start your vacation."

A week before, Hamid had put in for a few days off, and she was happy to oblige after all the hard work he had done and the new business he brought in.

"Seven sets should be okay. We have twenty on hand at the moment," he said, checking over some paperwork, knowing that four of those sets would be his own custom-made handiwork.

"You and your friend Frank going to do something with your time off?" Amanda asked. She thought perhaps Hamid might be gay, seeing that he never talked about a girlfriend or really socialized very much. Since Frank Castro had arrived around ten days earlier, they had spent quite a bit of time together.

"We're going to take a cruise," Hamid said, thinking that the cover would work for now, and it wouldn't matter once the mission was completed.

"Well, you spend enough time with the business side of the industry. I hope they gave you a professional discount."

He chuckled and wanted to change the subject.

"Not really. Only actual employees get discounts."

"You two should have fun, and please don't think about this place at all on your vacation. Except for when you go to bed, of course," Amanda said.

If she only knew how true those words actually were, he thought, as he worked to finish up a delivery order for a dining room he had sold to an elderly couple who had just moved to South Florida.

He went on Facebook to see how his friends were doing and to double-check if a particular friend had checked in. About two months ago, he friended Jose Fuentes and watched his status updates carefully. He knew Jose, a.k.a. Abdul-Aziz Fahad, their mission leader, would be arriving in Miami sometime this week. As he signed on, he went to Jose's wall, and sure enough it said he checked in at Miami International Airport two days before. He hadn't been on Facebook for a couple of days but knew things were in motion. Hamid and Frank had no idea where their mission leader was staying in the Miami area, but they didn't have to. The plan was in motion, and that was all they needed to know. Now it was just a matter of all the components coming together. Just one glitch, and the whole mission would be over. It was a complex operation with many moving parts, and both men knew that destiny would arrive if it was Allah's will.

Chapter 16

TURNAROUND DAY

S ATURDAY, SEPTEMBER 2, started out early for Hamid Khalid and Frank Castro. It was five o'clock in the morning, and both men knew what they had to do. For Frank, it was rather simple. He would take a cab to the Port of Miami and board *Star Orion* just like any other passenger meeting friends and going on a cruise. For Hamid, it was more complicated. After leaving Frank with a hug for good luck, he left his apartment for the last time and headed down to the Dixie Self-Storage unit in the company truck he had taken home the night before. It was common for him to take the truck home if he had a port delivery the next day. To keep the costs of doing business as low as possible, Hamid and a couple of the other salespeople would also help deliver orders. It was Hamid's idea and one that Amanda welcomed. The company had a few delivery people who worked part-time for hourly wages to handle moving most of the big stuff, but his plan kept the cost of doing business lower, as was the case today. Instead of two delivery people, Hamid would meet one at the storage facility and get the Star Caribe order transferred. Typically they would be done by 9:00 a.m. because of the hours the cruise line required deliveries to take place.

At 5:30 a.m., Hamid pulled into the Dixie Self-Storage and saw that Richard Lorenzo was already there and waiting for him. Hamid put in the code, and the gate opened slowly and loudly. For a minute, Hamid thought that the entire neighborhood would hear them, but it didn't matter. Managers of the storage unit were used to seeing the furniture folks coming and going.

Hamid pulled the truck slowly onto the storage lot and made his way over to the unit he would be opening up. His furniture company rented two of the units for inventory, and Hamid had rented one for his own use. Richard did not know which was which as he pulled up slowly behind Hamid's truck.

It was a hot September morning in Miami, and the sun was still below the horizon. Hamid got out of his truck and opened his storage unit while Richard walked up to give him a hand. Simple work for the most part.

"We have seven sets of beds and five chairs to transfer," Hamid said to Richard, who just nodded in agreement. Both men were rather tired, but Hamid had his game face on today.

Inside the unit that Hamid opened up were four sets of two beds each. They were wrapped in the typical fashion and looked just like any of the others that the men had delivered to the ships before. They made fast work out of moving the beds onto the truck. Hamid kept a careful watch to see whether Richard noticed anything different in the handling of the wrapped beds. This would be the first test of many that day.

"Where are the chairs?" Richard asked as Hamid pointed to another unit on the opposite side of the small driveway that separated each row.

"We have three more bed sets, and then the chairs," Hamid said. He felt a sense of relief as the two walked a few feet across to the real Metro Miami Furniture unit to get the other beds. So far, nothing was out of the ordinary.

Hamid opened the unit, and the two men quickly transferred three more sets of bedding. There were two per set and all wrapped in plastic. Hamid had the order in a folder along with stickers used to designate which stateroom they would be sent to. Similar to passenger bags, the beds would be pretagged to make the on-load quicker at the port. He put the seventh-deck-cabin-numbered stickers on the first four sets they loaded on the truck from the first storage unit and did the same with the additional three sets, which were bound for the fourth deck.

Once the beds were transferred, they went to a third storage unit just a few doors down and pulled out five metal deck chairs, also wrapped in plastic. Just as he did with the beds, he put the stickers on the chairs, indicating which cabin they would be sent to.

Hamid and his assistant Richard were done in less than thirty minutes. By 6:00 a.m., Richard climbed into the company truck for the drive down to the port. Hamid would drop him back off after the delivery to pick up his car then drop the truck back at the shop before starting his much-anticipated vacation.

An hour earlier, the pilot boat from the Port of Miami met up with the *Star Orion* just off the coast of Florida to transfer the harbor pilot, who would help guide the ship back to its berth. It was a breezy morning, and the seas were running around two to three feet. The ship's master and the harbor pilot worked closely together, using the experience of the pilot to best navigate the tight waterway leading to the passenger terminals. At the end of the waterway was a giant turning basin where the ships would turn completely around so that their starboard side would be facing the terminals, and they would be pointed toward the sea for a quick departure later that day.

Once pier side, the controlled chaos of turnaround day would begin. Waiting would be semitrucks full of food, fuel, supplies, and more. There would also be garbage trucks and an army of International Longshoreman's Association union stevedores who would load and unload. They all would arrive before dawn to get cleared into the port, and their supplies would be off-loaded onto the pier for security inspection before being transferred onto the ship by forklifts.

Inside the ship, passengers would be getting their last buffet meal before disembarking according to the color of their outgoing luggage tags. Most passengers were out of their cabins before 7:00 a.m. so that the stewards could start to prepare for the next round of guests who would start boarding around noon or just before. The passageways of all passenger decks were crowded and elevators jammed with the departing guests. At around ten thirty in the morning, the guest services manager would start to wrap up the disembarkation and begin to look for what they called the "zero count." The zero count was when all passengers were off the ship. The guest services manager would then call the hotel manager, who would inform the master of the ship that zero count had been achieved and for a very short time, the ship was empty of paying customers.

On deck 7, Bishar Fouad started his morning rounds and tagged four doors with purple stickers, indicating that the beds would be swapped out and needed transfer down to deck 1. The list of cabins with major changes like bedding or furniture would also be in the hands of the head housekeeper and deck lieutenant, who coordinated the crew members needed to accomplish the task. Imad Patel had volunteered for the human chain today and positioned himself on deck 1 for the additional work, which would lead to extra liberty time on future turnaround days.

Outside the terminal was the usual hustle and bustle of all the moving parts that happened almost simultaneously to get the ship ready to sail at 4:30 p.m. The security gate leading to terminal 3, where *Star Orion* was tied up, had two other trucks waiting for clearance to enter when Hamid pulled up in line with his Metro Miami Furniture & Bedding box truck. As Hamid waited his turn, he prepared the paperwork to show to the gate guard, Hector Lopez, whom he recognized from past deliveries. He had not delivered to the port in over a month because he skipped the last one purposely to avoid looking overly anxious. The wind was blowing a bit this morning, and the driver of truck in front of him dropped some of his paperwork, which went flying out of the cab into the wind. Hamid jumped out of his truck to catch a couple of the papers and walked it back to the security guard and driver parked in front of him. Both the guard and the driver were thankful for the help. Once that truck cleared, Hamid pulled up and had a few chuckles with the guard about the incident. Richard got out of the passenger side of the truck and went back to open the box for the security guard from Tactical Security Services, or TSS, to look inside. TSS was contracted to the port and handled many of the security functions including the bomb-sniffing dogs that would roam the freight being onloaded onto the ship.

Just as Richard was closing the door and the security guard turned to walk back to the cab where Hamid was sitting, a Dade County sheriff's deputy came walking over. They also had jurisdiction over the port but dealt more with the passenger side. He had a white piece of paper in his hand, and for a second Hamid had a bad feeling in his stomach. He wasn't sure what this was about because this hadn't happened the other times he delivered to the port.

The deputy stopped Hector, the TSS security agent, and they chatted for a few seconds next to the truck. Hamid tried to look in the mirror to see what they were talking about but did not want to appear nervous or out of the ordinary. A few seconds later the deputy handed the paper to the TSS guard and started to walk away.

"You're all set," said Hector as he handed Hamid back his paperwork and cleared him to enter the port and move his box truck shipside. Apparently the deputy found one of the forms lost in the wind sitting close to his cruiser next to the terminal and returned it to the guard.

Hamid thanked him and slowly drove toward the gleaming white *Star Orion* cruise ship, sitting about fifty yards away, next to the terminal. The standard procedure would be to pull up and wait for the stevedore in charge to put him in a queue for off-load. Because they were not palletized, the beds would be off-loaded directly from the truck to the ship via the human chain that would pass them from one set of two people to the next. He would back his truck up to the brow of the ship leading to deck 1, and then a member of the ship's security team would join the head housekeeper to inspect the bedding.

TSS had two bomb dogs assigned to three ships during turnaround days. The TSS K-9 unit would patrol up and down the pier, and the agent would attach to each pallet an orange sticker, indicating that it was clear to load and had been inspected for bombs.

"Three minutes, then you're cleared to the brow," one of the stevedores said to Hamid as he waited in the truck. A few seconds later, the head housekeeper appeared and walked toward him.

"I have seven sets and five chairs coming," she said, looking at her paperwork.

"That's what I have. How are you doing?" Hamid said as he tried to make some small talk.

"Same old, same old," she said, giving him a look that in nonverbal communication meant that she was about ready for her contract to end and start a long-awaited break.

"Come on back," the stevedore ordered as the head housekeeper stepped back away from the truck and headed toward the brow connecting the ship to the pier. All deliveries were done on deck 1 with direct access to the pier. Passengers would be loaded through the passageway leading to deck 4, which looked much like a Jetway the airliners used.

Hamid backed the truck up to the brow and got out of the cab, as did Richard. The two met at the rear of the truck, and they opened the back. A few seconds later, the TSS K-9 guy started to walk toward them. Hamid did not recognize this guy from past visits. As he got closer, Hamid saw that he was a she. They didn't say anything as he and Richard jumped up into the truck to begin the process of unloading the beds to the waiting chain of crew members who would transfer them to the cabins. The first to be transferred were the five chairs, which was quick and easy, requiring only a single person to walk them in. Next came the first set of beds. Richard and Hamid lifted the set of two off the truck and down to the waiting stevedores who would hand them off to crewmembers. The TSS agent walked the dog past the first set and then took an orange sticker and stuck it to the side of the plastic. The stevedores handed them off to the crew members, who moved them onto the ship and right around the metal detector, which were not wide enough to scan the beds and the crew members that carried them. It was a bonus that they already had the orange stickers on them.

As they got to the fourth set of beds, Hamid held his breath. He also looked toward the ship and did not see either Bishar or Imad, who were also working that side of the operation.

Hamid and Richard lifted the fourth set, this one headed for deck 7, off the truck while the TSS agent walked the dog by. She took an orange sticker and placed it on the plastic and the process continued. He did not want to look into the ship too much, but Hamid watched as this set moved down the human chain and past the metal detectors. He assumed Imad was someplace on the inside, helping move the beds.

The TSS agent turned her attention to a pallet that was being unloaded from another truck a few feet away. Before she did this, she walked back over to the furniture truck with her dog and asked Hector to bring each set close to the edge of the back of the truck so that she could tag them all quickly and move on.

All seven sets of beds were off-loaded, inspected, and sent aboard *Star Orion*. Inside the ship, Imad was on the delivery side of the crew and positioned himself to help with the fourth set. He and another volunteer returned to get the seventh set. Each was delivered to its designated cabin. Up on deck 7, Bishar was busy taking the plastic off the beds and quickly making them up for the next guests to use upon embarkation. He noted the right side of all four sets had a slightly different sewing pattern and looked different from the ones he was used to seeing from the factory. As a precaution, he made the beds, and then would lie across them to see if he felt anything different. Nothing. *That's amazing,* he thought. This was a tribute to the work his fellow Soldiers of Faith had done.

Imad, having finished his special duty moving the beds, spoke only a few words to his friend Bishar, who was busy working on the cabins.

"Are we good?" he asked, looking into cabin 7624 as Bishar finished making up his last bed.

"We're good. Perfect, thanks."

With that, Imad went back down to his cabin on deck 1 to get ready to report to his duty station in a few hours to finish the off-load of any trash that might have been missed earlier by his teammates in the environmental section.

Bishar put a copy of the *Star Navigator*, the ship's daily newspaper and events listing, on the bedside table for the incoming passengers, finishing his work on this cabin. As he closed the door behind himself and moved down the deck 7 passageway toward his cleaning locker, he stopped to make a note on the daily report, which would go up to the head housekeeper. He wrote, "Cabins complete. Cat "D" beds in 7620, 7624, 7632, and 7636 replaced."

Work had been busy for Dino Tucci and his associates as they kept all the moving parts of the Battelli family businesses in check. He finally blocked some time off to find out what happened to his friend, or ex-friend, Frank Castro. He was intent on finding out whether or not he was being played and taken advantage of. After doing some investigation over the past three weeks, he had found out a little more about Frank, but kept running into dead ends. He had a cop friend, who helped him out once in a while, check into Frank's background. The odd part Dino and the cop noticed was that there was not much history with this guy. Dino knew he was from Canada originally but moved to the States years ago. He got his social security number from the Evergreen folks at the port, and it showed that he had been born in Nebraska. That made no sense at all, unless they moved from there to Canada, then back to the States. But how was Frank a Canadian citizen, as he claimed? He checked for some family in Omaha, but found nothing. In fact, the most disturbing thing he found was that he really found almost nothing at all.

Dino wanted to fly to Miami and confront him personally, knowing that was where he had returned the RV unit and thinking he could probably track Frank down. Weighing on his mind this whole time was the fact that he had sold him those weapons, thinking they were being sent overseas to Worldcare with that CT scanner they bought. The people at Evergreen said they had only one shipment to an organization called Worldcare, and Frank had handled the transaction. They told him it was a piece of medical equipment, and that was all. Whether he sent the weapons in that shipment or sold them or kept them, Dino just did not know. Frank's mysterious disappearance and that missing detail gave him a gut feeling that just felt wrong.

With a long weekend and an airline ticket, Dino finally landed in Miami on Friday and went directly to the RV rental agency on South Dixie Highway. He got into town two days later than he originally wanted to because of pressing business back home. It was just after 2:00 p.m. when he pulled his rental car up to the main office building on the lot. As he walked inside the air-conditioned office, his sunglasses fogged up after leaving the heavy humidity of the Miami afternoon. The manager happened to be working that afternoon, and he was the same guy Dino had spoken with on the telephone.

"Castro, Castro," the manager said as he clicked though the files on the computer sitting on the counter. "Castro, Frank. One way from Warwick, Rhode Island."

"That's it. Did he give any forwarding address or a place where he might be contacted here locally?" Frank asked like a seasoned investigator. He had been questioned so many times by cops in the past himself, he knew how to ask.

"No, sir. Just this cell phone number on the paperwork and a work number with the Rhode Island address."

Dino had the cell number, which for the last three weeks or so had been going straight to voice mail.

"I remember when he dropped the unit off because he left a bunch of towels inside, and I had to get them out," the manager explained.

Dino thought about that for a few minutes. It was nothing too unusual, he assumed. The manager continued.

"We gave him a ride to Metro Miami Furniture or something like that down on Biscayne."

Dino pulled out his phone, called up the notes app, and typed in "Metro Miami Furniture."

"Are they local?"

"Yeah, I see their ads sometimes in the paper," said the manager, who thought Dino was something other than just a friend.

The two men talked for a few more minutes, and Dino figured he had gotten just about all the information he could from this man. Once he got back into his car, he Googled Metro Miami Furniture and found the location and address, then tapped the map for directions.

He thought perhaps that he would find Frank or someone who knew where he might be at the furniture store. The whole thing was strange, and Dino Tucci was going to get to the bottom of it. He would not be made a fool of.

He arrived at the furniture company about forty-five minutes later. Both Amanda and Hamid were out of the store at the time. Hamid, ironically, was down at the storage unit checking on inventory for the current and future cruise orders, and Amanda had taken the afternoon to meet with two possible corporate client leads.

Two people were working inside the store and neither had ever heard of a Frank Castro. They suggested returning when some of the other employees or the owner was around to see if they might know the person.

With that, he left the furniture store and headed down to South Beach, where he was going to stay while in the Miami area. He had been here before and loved this part of the city. Technically, where he was headed was the City of Miami Beach, but everyone just referred to it as "South Beach." He planned to return to the shop to follow up on his search for Frank and to ask the others who worked there about him the next day. For now, he wanted to check in and get ready for meeting an old friend from high school for dinner. His weekend was going to be busy, as he planned to check in with two families that the Battellis did business with in this part of the country. It was always good to make personal contracts in his line of work.

The Betsy Ross is a classic art deco hotel dating back to the glory days of Miami Beach. For Dino, it was the only place he liked to stay when in town on business or pleasure. He checked into the hotel located just across the street from the beach and close to bars and restaurants. Dinner and drinks with his buddy who had been his classmate at LaSalle High School back in Providence lasted well into the early morning hours. On Saturday he got out of bed and headed straight for a Starbucks, a short walk from the hotel, for a morning coffee. He was booked through Sunday night and planned to return to Rhode Island on Monday or Tuesday at the latest.

After coffee and returning for a good hot shower, Dino made his way back to the lobby and had the valet fetch his rental car. A few minutes later, the white Camaro was brought to the door, and Dino gave the driver a twenty-dollar bill. It was the best tip the valet had received in a month.

His first stop was a local beer distributorship, where he met with Sly Predo. Sly was his counterpart and a *capo* with the Morelli family of South Florida. They owned the Budweiser rights to all of South Florida along with many other businesses and enterprises. The two had been professional friends for years and even vacationed once together in the Bahamas on a fishing junket. Sly offered Dino any help that he might need while staying in his territory. Both men enjoyed the short visit before Dino left for another trip over to Metro Miami Furniture & Bedding to see if someone may have knowledge of the whereabouts of Frank Castro.

It was close to 11:00 a.m. when he arrived. The store closed early on Saturdays, and Amanda Curtis was in the office. Hamid was once again out of the office on a sales delivery. Dino walked through the showroom toward the back of the store where the salespeople had their offices and where a customer service counter was located.

"I'm Dino Tucci, and I was here yesterday looking for a Frank Castro who was picked up at an RV rental agency and dropped off here about ten days ago," he said to one of the newer sales associates standing behind the counter.

"Let me get Amanda," the associate said. A few minutes later he returned with Amanda, who was wondering who this big guy was.

"I'm Amanda Curtis, managing partner," she said, reaching for his hand to shake.

"Dino Tucci. I'm looking for a guy named Frank Castro. He was last seen being dropped off here around ten days ago by an RV rental agent."

Amanda had met Frank a number of times during his stay with Hamid.

"Are you a police officer?" she asked, not knowing who this guy was or why he might be looking for Frank.

"No, just a friend from Providence. Frank did some work for me up there, and I wanted to make sure he was paid."

Amanda thought for a minute before speaking.

"I met Frank a couple of times. He is a friend of one of my senior salespeople, and they were hanging out together. I think Frank is vacationing with him."

Bingo, thought Dino. Finally a lead to the missing Frank Castro.

"Do you know where he is staying?"

"No, not exactly."

At that moment, Dino got a text from one of his people in Providence and switched the phone to silent mode.

"What do you mean 'not exactly'?" Dino quizzed Amanda.

"I thought he was staying with Hamid, who works for me. I believe they are planning a vacation together, and you might have missed them anyway."

Dino was relieved that he had a lead but troubled about missing them.

"Why is that?"

"They're leaving today on a cruise. Hamid worked this morning, delivering to the port, and the two were going to meet back there and actually enjoy some time off," she explained.

Dino noted all of this.

"I think Frank is not his actual name," said Amanda.

"I beg your pardon?"

"Frank. I think his actual name is Ahamid. Or something like that," she told him.

Now Dino had a knot in his stomach and started to get pissed.

"Why do you say that?" Dino asked.

"Hamid called him that and the name Ali every once in a while. Frank used his car and dropped him off now and then. I remember him talking in some other language. I think it was Russian or Hebrew."

Dino now knew there was something terribly wrong with this picture.

"When do you expect them back?"

Amanda turned her computer around and pulled up a picture of the *Star Orion*.

"They're going out today on this ship and will be back in a week. I think they are a couple."

Dino asked a few more questions and thanked Amanda for her time. He went back outside and started his car to get the air conditioner going while he made a phone call to someone he knew could help him out and owed him a large number of favors.

"Keith, I need a special favor," Dino said after he dialed a number in Boston. Keith Moore was a special agent with the FBI. Dino saved his life one day when there was a hostage situation at the Walpole State Prison just down the road from Gillette Stadium, where the New England Patriots play. One of the prisoners had taken hostages in the infirmary then released them only when Keith said he would hand himself over as a hostage. The guy holding the gun was Gino Montelli, a former member of Dino's crew, who got into drugs and ended up getting pinched for possession and distribution. Gino used one of the phones in the medical unit and called Dino, hoping for some help after he made his escape with the hostage. Dino negotiated with Gino, and the standoff ended peacefully. Keith knew that Dino was a made man, and their relationship was one of mutual respect. He also knew the mob boss had saved his life.

"What is it, Dino?" Keith said coldly. He wanted very little contact with him but owed him his life, literally.

"Check this name for me best you can," Dino said and then spelled the name Amanda gave him. "Ahamid. First name Al or Ali."

"I'll call you back," Keith said then hung up the telephone.

While he waited, he searched cruises for the *Star Orion* and saw that they departed every Saturday out of the Port of Miami. Out of curiosity, he looked to see about availability for today's departure. The website said there was same day booking available, but it had to be done by 3:00 p.m. at the port. He looked at his watch, which read 11:45 a.m. A few minutes later, his phone rang.

"Yeah," he said, which was Dino's standard answer to a phone call.

"How do you know this guy?" Keith said on the other line.

"I think he's fucking with me. Says his name is Frank Castro. Then disappears into thin air. I fly down here to Miami to find him and he's gone, but someone said he was referred to by that name," Dino explained.

"His name is Ali Ahamid, and he was last seen living in Yemen four years ago. He's on the TWL."

"What's the TWL?"

"Terror watch list," Agent Keith Moore said coldly. "Might have been involved in the embassy bombing in Egypt in the nineties. Not much after that, according to what I'm looking at."

Dino was silent for a few seconds on the other end of the phone call. Then he spoke, "All right Keith. Thanks."

"If you know this is the same guy, I need a call back."

"Will do. Thanks for the intel."

Dino ended the call and once again sat for a few moments. He had mixed emotions. He was severely pissed at this guy and now feeling that he might have been played in order for him to carry out some sort of terror plot. He looked at his watch again, and it was close to noon. He quickly backed the rental car out of the parking lot and jumped back on I-95 south to I-195 to cross the bridge over to Miami Beach and the Betsy Ross Hotel, where he had all his clothes and travel gear. During the entire drive back to the hotel, he was trying to put two and two together.

Dino Tucci lived a life of organized crime and felt no remorse for anything he did. It was business. Committing a crime against the country he loved was a different story though. On 9/11, he wanted to bring those hijackers to justice himself if he could. He felt powerless just watching those towers fall and all those Americans die. Dino didn't know what Frank or Ali or whatever his real name was up to, but he'd be damned if this guy will commit some kind of terrorist act.

At twelve thirty he arrived at the Betsy Ross and told the valet that he would only be a few minutes and tipped him another twenty to keep the car up front. Thirty minutes later, he was back down in the lobby with his suitcase and backpack standing at the reception area checking out. The doorman tipped off the valet that he was getting ready to leave, and they had his car right up at the door with the engine running by the time he walked outside. Another twenty-dollar-bill subway, Dino's term for a tip, and he was off driving down Lincoln Road, toward the car rental office Avis had on the Beach side of Miami.

Dino dropped the car at the Avis office and paid the sixty-dollar penalty for not returning it to the main rental return at the airport. Then he got into a cab and told the driver to take him to the Port of Miami. He decided he would take the cruise, figure out what the hell this was all about, and then maybe fly back from one of the stops. Or, if he was enjoying himself, he might just stay the entire week and return to Miami. If this guy were planning something, he would be there to stop it.

It was around one thirty when he arrived at the Port of Miami. He honestly had never been aboard a cruise ship, and the driver asked him which he was sailing on. Dino answered, "*Star Orion*," which the driver knew well. Terminal 3. The driver pulled around to the drop-off lane, and Dino looked out the window at the size of the ship that he was about to board. First, he needed a ticket. It was rare that passengers bought tickets at the pier, but last-minute bargain hunters were common at this time of the year after school started back.

Dino got out of the cab, tipped the driver, and walked into the terminal toward the security screening station, where the man asked for his tickets. When he said he was going to buy one, the man checked his ID then allowed him to proceed to lane G upstairs, where last-minute cruisers could purchase tickets.

"First cruise?" the Star Caribe representative asked as he walked up to her station. Lane G was all but empty. In fact, the terminal was starting to thin out as passengers arrived and boarded the vessel.

"Yes. Never cruised before. Wanted to give it a try."

He presented her with his ID while she checked to see what might be available.

"Inside or outside?" she asked, noting that he looked a little nervous.

"Inside or outside what?"

"Cabin. Would you like an inside or outside? I have a few inside left and a number of outside, depending on your deck preference."

"What do you suggest?"

She typed a few keys on her computer and then looked up and asked another question.

"Are you going to be double occupancy or single?"

He just held up his index finger to indicate one.

She went back to her computer and then looked up to give him a choice.

"I have an outside balcony on deck 5 for eight hundred and ninety-nine. I also have a junior suite on deck 8 for sixteen ninety-nine."

Dino really didn't care. He always traveled first class.

"Give me the suite," he said, pulling out his platinum American Express card. Around Providence he always paid in cash. They did business in cash.

But when he traveled for the family or for personal reasons, he had to use a card like everyone else.

"It's a junior suite, but I can check to see if a royal suite might be available."

Dino figured that she was working on commission, but he was in a hurry to get this done.

"No, the junior suite is fine."

She typed some of his document information into the computer and then asked for his passport. Thankfully Dino always traveled with his passport in his backpack from his trips to Italy and Canada.

"You are just going to love this experience," the representative said with a smile then handed back his passport, driver's license, and credit card. "Now I have to take your picture."

He did his best to smile while she adjusted the small camera on her workstation and took his image for the "ocean pass," which would act as his onboard charge card, cabin door key, and security pass when getting on and off the ship.

"Junior suite 8052, Mr. Tucci," she said as she handed him his ocean pass along with a ship diagram to show him where his cabin was located. "The junior suite allows you access to some special privileges which are listed on your ocean pass holder."

"I'm traveling with some friends, and I was wondering if they have checked aboard yet," he asked.

"What are their names, so I can check?"

"Frank Castro?"

She typed on her computer once again and waited for a few seconds before looking back up at Dino.

"No Frank Castro just yet. But I can't see reservations, just confirmations of those who already have checked in."

"How about Ahamid Ali or Ali Ahamid?"

She checked again and found nothing.

"They may have reservations, but unless they have checked in, I won't have them in my system."

Dino thought for a minute.

"Can you search for just first names?"

"I can put a name in and see if it pops up," she said, trying to be as cooperative as possible with this last-minute customer.

"Try the name Hamid," he said, and he spelled out just as Amanda had done.

She typed in Hamid, and nothing came up. For a few minutes, Dino thought that maybe he booked himself on the wrong ship or that they decided against the trip altogether.

"We still have two hours before we close out, and they might be running late. Check with guest services on deck 4 after departure or this evening, and they can check again."

"Thanks very much," he said as he collected his bags and headed toward the passenger gangway one floor above. As he went up the escalator, he thought about how he would confront Frank, if and when he found him. Maybe he should just observe for a while to see what was going on. With over three thousand passengers on the ship, he thought that it might take a couple of days just to find him. Hopefully, later that evening he would get some help from the guest services people.

At the top of the escalator, he walked up to the security checkpoint a few feet away, and the guard instructed him to insert his ocean pass into the slot. Within a second, a chime sounded and his picture popped up on the computer monitor on the opposite side of the kiosk that the guard was standing behind. The guard welcomed him aboard, and Dino walked across the gangway onto the *Star Orion*. He wondered what Frank could possibly be planning by booking a cruise vacation. This was the mystery he was determined to figure out, and he just spent almost two grand to do so. He took out his phone and called back to the office in Providence to tell Moe that he would be back in a week or sooner. They were expecting him in a day or two, but Moe didn't ask any questions. He never did. The boss kept telling him to take a vacation anyway. Now was his chance to get away from it all for a little while and take care of some unfinished business at the same time.

Around 1,050 miles southeast of Miami, the Hapag-Lloyd container ship MV *Bremen Express* was closing in on Puerto Rico after a six-day passage from the Port of Gibraltar. Before entering the Mona Passage en route to the Panama Canal, the giant ship would make a scheduled port call to San Juan for supplies and to off-load and onload containers. The COSCO container with Boris's special shipment inside would be off-loaded later in the afternoon and stored for content transfer to the *Star Orion* when she arrived in San Juan on Tuesday for the weekly port call. Because it was shipped and marked MEDHAZMAT, it would be off stored in a special area designated for such things. Shipping broker Jose Rio would receive the tracking e-mails once it was off-loaded. He would also be alerted to what storage yard it would be housed in as he monitored all of his client's shipments to keep them updated them on the progress.

The huge ninety-seven-thousand-ton container ship made its way toward Puerto Nuevo located near the southern end of San Juan Bay, where most of the cargo piers were located. The ship tied up at wharf C for the twenty hours that it would remain in port. On the pier were hundreds of stevedores waiting to operate cranes and trucks to move the containers around like a big game of Lego.

Jose was expecting inbound and outbound cargo today on three vessels. One of those was **Bremen Express** with shipments for six of his clients. Two from that ship were being held for transfer to other ships, and one of those was a MEDHAZMAT. He was having late coffee and a quick break at the small shop just down from the port entrance after a long morning of chasing cargo from the first ship of the day, which had arrived at 5:00 a.m. His Samsung Galaxy vibrated, and Jose pulled it out of the right pocket of the shorts he was wearing. It said he had new mail, which he clicked on with one hand while taking a sip of the hot coffee in the other, being careful not to spill it on his new smartphone.

COSCO//SHIPPING NOTIFICATION//**TRACKING NUMBER4521671JC//VSL DGZL OFF-LOAD 1422Z//HOLDING88G XFT 090512 VSL NSSP

It was his notification that one of his clients' shipping containers and contents had been off-loaded from the vessel DGZL, or **Bremen Express**, and would be kept in holding area 88G until transfer on September 5 to the vessel **Star Orion** once it cleared customs.

Jose's assistant was working the dock at the moment and would have handled the customs paperwork for that off-load. Hatzel Silva was new to the brokerage and just starting to work on his own. Jose wanted to make sure things were going smoothly, so he took his coffee to go and got into his car for the five-minute drive back to the port.

The weather was typical of San Juan, and a few showers had fallen, leaving the air heavy with humidity. His glasses fogged up as he got out of his air-conditioned BMW and walked over to the dockside customs office where other brokers were gathered and where he would find Hatzel.

"Still waiting," Hatzel said to his boss as he approached. "One is off-loaded, and the other five are still being worked."

"I got the e-mail on the first one."

In a few minutes, four more similar e-mails would arrive in both men's inboxes, indicating that now five of their customers' containers were off the ship, awaiting customs clearance and inspection.

Jose knew just about everyone who worked at the Port of San Juan. He was a native islander, and he was the third generation of his family to be in the shipping business.

"Just got the last one," Hatzel said. "You want me to handle them?"

"Sure thing."

With that, Hatzel took his folder of paperwork over to the customs desk, and the officer told him to go to zone 4 for clearance. There were four zones on this pier where customs officers would clear cargo. Zones 1 and 2 were for roll-on and -off cargo like cars and construction equipment. Zones 3 and 4 were for containers, which would also be driven though an x-ray/radiation detector once back on wheels before being cleared.

Hatzel and Jose got into their company truck and drove over to zone 4. There they had to wait in line for others to be cleared that were off-loaded. Not all containers had to be inspected. Actually, only a small number were physically searched. Because one of theirs was a MEDHAZMAT, it might be looked at more carefully.

Twenty minutes later, their COSCO container pulled up for inspection. The officer took the paperwork from Hatzel as the two made small talk. Jose watched to see if Hatzel was doing a good job for his clients. About two minutes later, the officer instructed Hatzel to open the back of the container. The officer jumped up into the container while Hatzel stayed on the ground. Brokers were not allowed inside any containers or boxes before they were cleared. A few seconds later, the officer appeared at the back of the container and jumped off, instructing Hatzel to close it up and secure the back. He then put a "MEDHAZMAT CLEARED" sticker on the door and told the driver to move thought the x-ray/radiation detector. He also walked over and showed the x-ray operator the paperwork.

Hatzel walked back over to Jose as the yard driver of the truck slowly pulled between the two large white walls that looked a little like a car wash unit. The truck stopped when the red light came on, but then the x-ray operator illuminated the green light and waved for him to continue to slowly pull through. The officer controlling the unit received a radiation indicator light and looked back at the paperwork. With the MEDHAZMAT designation and CT scanner listed on the cargo manifest, he reset the radiation indicator.

In all, the process took about ten minutes. The customs officer stamped and signed the paperwork and handed copies back to Hatzel, who then walked back over to Jose.

"Nice job," Jose told his new employee. "Was that your first hazmat?"

"Yes, sir. The only thing the guy suggested was that the small hazmat package containing"—he looked down at his paperwork—"medical radioisotopes, or whatever the hell they are, be better secured to the big crate containing the CT scanner."

Jose just nodded. He didn't pack this container, and it didn't matter now because it would be transferred in a few days anyway.

"What's next?" Jose asked.

"Another COSCO box with tires," Hatzel said as the yard driver pulled away and headed toward storage area 88G, used for hazardous materials awaiting transfer. Almost three thousand miles away, Boris received an automatic e-mail from Jose's office saying that his Sellco shipment was in San Juan and awaiting transfer to the *Star Orion* on Tuesday, September 5. Abdul-Aziz Fahad also received the same e-mail in his Sellco account.

Jake was thrilled when Claire called him and said that she would be coming to Miami for a long weekend to celebrate his thirtieth birthday. He was also surprised, seeing that he had asked her to come down a few times in the last couple of months, and she was just too busy or perhaps didn't want to. She told him to pick her up at the airport and that they would have a very special weekend together. By "very special," Jake was thinking on a number of different levels.

The plane was on time, and Jake parked his Crown Vic in the official vehicle space just outside the Delta terminal at Miami International Airport. He went inside to meet her, still excited about the nice birthday surprise. When she arrived, the two embraced, and Claire told him that she had to stop at baggage claim. That was strange, Jake thought, because she always traveled light and never checked her bags. Whatever, Jake thought, as they made their way downstairs to the bag carousel. The important thing was that she was here, and they had the whole weekend.

Claire's bag came down the conveyor belt, and she pointed it out to Jake for pickup. It was a regular-sized suitcase, which, thanks to his experience with customs, he could tell was packed to the max. "You coming to stay?" he joked as he lifted the roller suitcase onto its wheels and started heading back to the car.

She had made a reservation at Jaguar in the Grove for that evening. It was one of their favorite spots.

"I'll clean up, and you can pick me up after you get out of work. The reservation is for six o'clock," she said as they got into the car for the twenty-minute ride out to his condo on the beach. "Let's take the Jag to Jaguar."

He dropped her off at his place then quickly went back to work. Later that evening he returned, and the two got into his XKE, which already had the top down. Jake had been driving it the night before and sometimes kept it down to air out. He actually had a cover for the classic car and planned to put it back on after the weekend was over. They drove over to Coconut Grove, and he let the valet park the car while he and Claire went inside for the early dinner. Jake couldn't figure why she wanted to eat so early, but maybe she had other plans after. He could only hope.

"I'm so glad we could do this," she said after ordering drinks and an appetizer. "I wanted to do something special for your birthday."

"You think you're glad? I'm pleasantly surprised at the whole thing. Let's go down to Largo tomorrow," he suggested for Saturday.

"I have a better idea."

The waiter dropped off the drinks and some multicolored chips with Cuban sauce for dipping. They picked up their glasses, had a silent toast, then took a sip.

"What's that?"

"How about we go to San Juan and St. Thomas?"

Jake had to think for a second. The visit. The big luggage. *She's done something*, he thought quickly.

"San Juan?"

She chuckled and took out her iPhone then dialed a number. When it was ringing, she handed him the phone.

"Hello, boss," said a familiar voice on the other end.

"Rosa?"

"You're officially on vacation," Rosa said, trying not to laugh too hard.

Jake just looked up at Claire. She was grinning from ear to ear and held up some type of travel documents.

"Are you kidding?" Jake asked into the phone and toward his girlfriend sitting across from the table.

"Felton granted your leave, and Claire's booked the trip. Your birthday surprise is a week in the Caribbean!"

Claire got out of her chair and went to give him a hug. He stood, and they embraced for a moment before sitting back down.

"I didn't think you'd believe me," Claire said pointing to the phone. "She's still on the line by the way!"

"Rosa?" Jake said.

"Yes, boss, I'm hanging up now. I'll see you in a week. Don't do anything I wouldn't do!"

With that, Rosa hung up the phone, and Jake took a long drink from the glass in front of him.

"I can't believe it," he said.

"Believe it. We leave in the morning on the *Star Orion* for seven wonderful and restful days."

"You called Felton?"

"Yup. Rosa too, and we worked it all out."

The waiter returned to the table, and they both ordered their favorite dishes. Jake was still pretty surprised by Claire's gesture and planning. He had never been on a cruise before, and the two had actually talked about possibly taking one, but that had been a long time ago.

"Janet is going to pick us up at your place tomorrow around lunch and drop us at the port," she said.

"You thought of everything, haven't you?"

"That I did. It goes with the job!"

He chuckled and couldn't help but think of what seven days off would feel like, especially with Claire. The two finished their dinner and headed back to his place. He had to tie up some loose ends and get packing.

Around noon the next day, Janet picked up the two and dropped them at the Port of Miami. It was Jake's first cruise, and he did not know what to expect. It was busy and very crowded, but he noticed how smoothly Star Caribe moved people though security and onto the ship. Claire had booked an outside stateroom with its own balcony on deck 9. It was a few extra dollars, but she wanted his thirtieth to be something very special.

After presenting their passports and government IDs, the two were given their ocean passes and boarded the ship. Clearly the desk agent recognized that they were federal law enforcement officers and gave them a booklet usually reserved for gold and platinum cruise members containing coupons for free drinks and such. It was a nice gesture, they thought, as the shop's photographers snapped their pictures like paparazzi.

"Maybe I should call Wayne and the boys in San Juan while we're there for a few hours," Jake said.

"Forget it. You're off. No work."

Jake chuckled and knew that she was looking out for him. He would check e-mail though. He couldn't be totally cut off from the digital world for seven days. Even Claire would probably give in to checking Facebook and e-mail, he thought, as a man walked up and handed him a fruity drink. Jake Stein was finally taking a break, thanks to the woman he had considered proposing to a few years ago . . . a woman he thought he had lost.

Chapter 17

SAIL-AWAY PARTY

E VERY STAR CARIBE cruise started off with a sail-away party at around 5:00 p.m. as the ship got under way on the first leg of her seven-day cruise. Once the lifeboat drill was complete, and the master of the ship ordered the release of all lines, the cruise officially began as the 150,000-ton vessel slowly got under way.

The party was up on deck 11, commonly known as the pool deck, where the passengers gathered for music, drinks, and fun. This was another beautiful, hot afternoon in Miami, with partly sunny skies and few hit-and-miss tropical rain showers that had been drifting in from the ocean toward Biscayne Bay. Caribbean music filled the air as one of the ship's bands played poolside, and waiters walked around with trays full of piña coladas in special keepsake Star Caribe glasses for those who bought them.

Tom Sundland and Rex Nelson were holding court at the aft pool bar with a few fans who recognized both actors. Rex was settling into the routine and finding out just how wonderful this gig was. He was sad that it only lasted three weeks but had already e-mailed his agent, asking for more. Because they were contracted entertainers, they could mingle with the passengers and were even encouraged to do so. The marketing folks back in Miami wanted to do more of these retro-themed cruises.

Three decks below, on deck 7, Bishar Fouad welcomed his new guests who were occupying their cabins for the first time. Most just dropped their stuff and headed up to the sail-away party after the lifeboat drill. He paid special attention to cabins 7620, 7624, 7632, and 7636, hoping that the passengers noticed nothing different with the beds. So far, no complaints.

On the bridge, Capt. Stefin Markinson was supervising the departure while allowing his first officer to work with the pilot, maneuvering the giant ship through the narrow channel heading out to sea. There were a few faces he recognized from past cruises, but in this business, every tour was a different experience, and people came and went. No one so far had even given him a second look. To them, he was who his nametag said he was—Capt. Bijon Markinson.

Back on deck 11, the party continued as people mingled, ate, and drank rum-filled cocktails while the band played on. A week before, Hamid had received a Facebook message from his friend Jose Fuentes, telling him how wonderful the cruise would be that they were both taking. In the note, he suggested that they meet at the bar in the solarium section of the pool deck during the sail-away party. He also said to bring any other friends who might have taken the trip together.

Abdul-Aziz Fahad's cover as Fuentes was working well so far. His expertly prepared phony passport passed its last test as he moved though security and check-in. The story of his wife's illness keeping her from sailing with their group of friends so moved the Star Caribe representative, that she upgraded his cabin to an outside with a balcony. They were in the business of keeping guests happy, and she was glad to put him in 8833, knowing that his wife would be unable to join him.

The solarium section of the pool deck was for adults only and had its own pool and two hot tubs. There was also a bar facing the pool where guests were already starting to sun themselves on the deck chairs. Fahad got off the elevator and walked around the corner into the solarium, heading toward the bar, when he spotted one of his team members already having a beer. He did not see any other members of the team. As he approached Hamid, who was sitting on the first bar stool, he saw another man approaching from the opposite direction. Fahad had met Hamid on two other occasions back in Frankfurt as they started to put the details of the operation together. The other members of the team were vetted by Mohammad Featha personally and purposely never met each other. Fahad assumed the man who was heading their way was another member. Perhaps it was the man with code name "the Shopper."

"Hamid, you old man," Fahad said as walked up while putting out his hand to shake. There would be no traditional peace greetings or other languages, which could compromise their cover while in public.

"I knew you would show up," Hamid said. "What are you drinking?"

"Beer for me," Fahad said as the other man walked up.

"Jose, this is Frank Castro. One of my business partners I told you about."

The two men shook hands as the bartender handed Fahad a cold Bud longneck and asked Frank what he wanted to drink. Frank ordered the same thing.

"How are you, my friend?" Fahad asked.

"I'm well and excited about this trip," Hamid said. Frank just stood and sipped his beer, having never met the man before him, who was their leader. He did all his dealing with Hamid, who reported back to Fahad.

"Same here. Did you have an easy time checking in?"

"We sure did. I had to work this morning, then dropped off my truck and headed back to check in as a passenger."

"I took a cab over, but it was pretty easy. I came a bit later than most passengers, but it was perfect timing to meet up with Hamid, who had to work early," said Frank as he sipped his cold beer.

"We have four more friends on the ship this week as well."

Hamid had a slight look of surprise on his face as his leader spoke.

"Four more friends?" Hamid said with a curious tone.

"You bet. The two you guys know, an associate who knows a lot about computers and communications systems, and a fourth who I'm told will be joining us."

Hamid and Frank nodded their heads, not knowing who these additional team members would be. Their leader kept each team member pretty much isolated as far as communications went, and each person knew some parts of the plan, but not all. This was one of those pieces of the puzzle that was just now starting to come together.

The irony was that not even Fahad knew who their last team member would be. He only knew that Mohammad had told him to expect an additional member, who would be a key part of executing the mission. Mohammad told him back in Rome that he would be contacted on the ship with a coded message to confirm his identity. Fahad did not know whether it would be another passenger or a member of the crew. He would just have to wait to find out. The three sipped their beers and chatted for a while about how each had been doing over the last few years while the sail-away party was in full swing.

Seven decks below them, Dino Tucci waited in line at the guest services desk on deck 4. People would come there to book shore excursions, settle their bills, make any complaints they might have, and any number of other issues. It was the seagoing version of a hotel's front desk.

"Next," the young lady in the sharp uniform with one stripe on her epaulet, indicating that she was a junior member of the guest services team.

"I am wondering if some member of my group have checked in," Dino said to the women who looked more like a girl.

"I would be glad to check. Give me one of the names."

"Frank Castro."

She pounded a few keys on the computer sitting in front of her for a few seconds.

"Mr. Castro is aboard. I can't give you his cabin number, but I can dial it on the phone for you if you would like to speak with him."

"No, that's fine. I'm sure we'll find each other. You can't go too far on a boat," he told her with a little chuckle in his voice.

"Is there anyone else?"

Dino thought for a moment.

"I have a first name of one of our folks, but not last."

She typed a couple more keys. "I can do a name search and see what comes up."

"Hamid?"

Once again she typed the five letters of the name and waited a few seconds.

"My machine is slow. Oh, here we are. There is one name that came up under that search. A Mr. Hamid Khalid also checked in."

Now Dino felt his stomach twist. Something was clearly going on. At least he had found Frank, but what to do next? He thanked the women at the desk and walked away, starting to feel the movement of the ship under his feet. It was a subtle, strange feeling he had never had before on a strange trip, a trip whose ending he just wasn't sure about.

Nassau is one of the busiest cruise ports in the world with ships calling on the Bahamian capital daily. The economy of the Bahamas relies on tourism, so local merchants work with the cruise and travel industries to make it as easy as possible to do business on the tropical islands that made up the British territory. Nassau itself is on the island of New Providence, which is a relatively small island with the airport on one side and capital city on the other. Just across from Nassau is Paradise Island, home to the famous and extravagant Atlantis resort and water park.

Every week the *Star Orion* arrived in Nassau on Sunday at noon for a twelve-hour port visit. Most passengers disembarked to shop, go to the beach, or take one of the many excursions that the cruise line offered. With two other cruise ships in port at the same time, the amount of people walking, and shopping along Bay Street jammed the small sidewalks.

On board, crew members used this time when there were few passengers around to do their weekly lifeboat and fire drills required by the company and the U.S. Coast Guard. On the bridge, the first or second officer would usually have the watch while the captain did paperwork and worked with the hotel manager on other matters. Captain Markinson wrapped up his daily hotel operations meeting and called down for some tea to be delivered to his in port cabin located just a few steps off the bridge. When he was done with the tea, he decided to take his weekly walk around the ship to check on various departments. It was good for the skipper to be seen by the crew, who usually didn't have a chance to spend much, if any, time with him. Plus he could get a good look at how they were performing and even meet some of the passengers.

He took the elevator down to deck four and spent a few minutes walking through the casino as the crew cleaned the place getting it ready for a busy night of gambling at sea. Some passengers cruised just for the chance to gamble, much to the delight of Star Caribe and all of the other cruise lines, which make much of their profit from this part of the business.

Next he stopped by guest services to see how the guest services manager was doing with the current weekly group of passengers. There was only one passenger being helped at the desk at the moment, and two other guest services personnel were on duty with nothing much to do while most of their guests explored Nassau. Captain Markinson picked the younger of the two just standing around and walked over to him.

"Yes, Captain?" the young and nervous guest services specialist said to his boss.

"I had a nice note from one of the passengers and wanted to thank him for his compliments. What cabin is Mr. Jose Fuentes in?"

"One moment, sir," the young man from the Philippines said with a thick accent as he typed into his computer. "Mr. Fuentes is in cabin 6383, sir."

"Thank you. Good job, everyone. Keep up the good work," Captain Markinson said as he picked up one of the free candies out of a dish and walked toward the bank of elevators about thirty feet away. He got on the elevator and pushed the button for deck 6.

Seconds later, he got off the elevator and entered the portside passageway of deck 6 looking for 6383. Even as the captain, he had to look at the diagram on the wall to see where it was located. He had picked the wrong side and crossed over to starboard before heading forward toward the cabin he was looking for. It was dead quiet in the hallways. He expected to see a cabin attendant or two, but they were all finished with this part of the ship, seeing that it was later in the afternoon.

Whether his mission leader was in the cabin or not was a gamble, but it was time to make contact. He walked up to the cabin and knocked on the door. Seconds later the door opened; and Abdul-Aziz Fahad, a.k.a. Jose Fuentes, was clearly surprised to see the captain of the ship standing there.

"Hello, Mr. Fuentes, I just stopped by to thank you for sailing with us and to see how your experience has been so far," the master of the ship said.

"Thank you, Captain, it's been marvelous so far. I just wish my wife could have joined me," Jose said, staying in complete character. He had been on a couple of cruises under different names to see how the ship operated and had

212 W. F. Walsh

never seen the captain stop by a passenger cabin. This was a little odd and more than a little concerning.

"We wanted to make sure you have the best service possible, and your cabin was drawn as a random number for a personal visit by the captain."

Fahad thought for a second that perhaps it was part of the cruise.

The captain continued, "As part of our effort, we invite you to have a bottle of wine or champagne on us." The captain handed Fahad an envelope with a certificate inside for the free wine.

"Thank you, Captain. That's very nice. I'm sure it will go to good use."

Fahad opened the envelope and pulled out the certificate card, thinking that it was a nice gesture on the part of the cruise line. As he opened the certificate card, there was a small piece of paper inside with three words on it. His demeanor changed in an instant, and his heart started pounding when he read it. His usually dark complexion turned slightly pale. He looked up in shock at the captain standing in front of him.

The card read, "Sent from Doha."

"I invite you to sit at my table during Friday's formal night in the dining room," Captain Markinson said to his mission leader, who was still clearly in a state of shock.

"I would be honored to. We have much to talk about. I will let my other friends know about this fine gesture." Fahad kept his composure and character in check.

Suddenly a family was approaching, moving down the hall toward them with shopping bags full of goods bought in Nassau.

"I will be on the bridge standing watch all night on Friday after the dinner. I will see you then." With that, the captain shook his hand and headed in the opposite direction, down the passageway from where the family was advancing. Fuentes, a.k.a. Fahad, retreated back inside his cabin, still speechless over the visit and the man sent from Mohammad Featha to help in their mission. The ship departed Nassau exactly at midnight bound for San Juan, Puerto Rico. They would spend the entire next day at sea before making port on Wednesday.

Dino Tucci had still not made contact with Frank Castro and wanted to wait to see what was going on before he decided how to approach him. There were many questions this guy was going to answer for Dino before his trip was over. He figured Frank had gone into Nassau for the port visit and that he would eyeball him on Tuesday, which was to be spent entirely at sea. He wanted to watch from a distance to better judge what was really going on here.

—∞∘〰◈〰∘∞—

Sea days were busy for the crew of *Star Orion*. All events for the next day were listed on the *Star Navigator* left nightly in each cabin during turndown for the passengers to see what was going to be offered. Dino decided once again to have breakfast in his cabin because he wasn't ready to confront Frank and did not want to be seen in the dining rooms or up at the buffet restaurant called Ocean View. He purposely hadn't shaved since leaving the Betsy Ross Hotel on Saturday. With his heavy beard growing out for a few days and a floppy hat with sunglasses, Dino felt he would not be spotted first. In some ways, he thought, now heading for the elevator and the pool deck, this whole thing was a little like a spy novel. He just did not know how it would end. One thing was for sure: he would not be made a fool of, and Frank Castro would somehow come clean.

On the pool deck, the sun was shining, and once again the band was playing Caribbean music as the waiters circulated through the crowd with trays full of tropical drinks. The place was packed and almost all the deck chairs taken, both on the pool deck itself and the upper sun deck just above. Dino figured he would go to the upper sun deck, get a drink, and, like an eagle looking for his prey, watch down on the crowd below.

He found a vacant lounge chair and bought one of the tropical drinks called a San Juan Smash from the waiter, dressed in a flowered shirt, who was walking by. Thankfully, he had brought a book to read and settled down for a couple of hours. While reading his book, Dino couldn't help but think that this didn't suck. There were ladies all around in bathing suits, drinks on demand, island music, and a cool ocean breeze. He just might have to try one of these cruises again.

As he looked up from reading, he saw a hot redhead and an equally hot blonde sunning themselves by the pool below. Apparently they had just arrived, or he somehow had missed seeing them earlier. Back in Providence, he wouldn't hesitate to introduce himself. Just as he was starting to look back at the book he had on his lap, something caught his eye further away. Dino had pretty good vision, and through his sunglasses, he squinted a bit. On the opposite side of the pool, from the girls he had just been admiring, were Frank Castro and some other guy walking around, looking for a place to sit. Bingo! He had him in his sights. A few minutes later, another guy joined them.

That familiar feeling of being pissed started to come over him, but Dino knew he had to play by different rules on this boat. Otherwise he would have gone down there, grabbed this guy by his neck, and asked him what the fuck was going on.

This was the time for waiting and watching. He did not recognize the other two but assumed one of them was the guy named Hamid. Looking at them together also gave him a sick feeling in his stomach. They did look like terrorists, Dino thought. He did not want to profile them, but after what his FBI guy in Boston told him, it made perfect sense.

Over the next couple of hours, he watched from a distance, and nothing seemed out of the ordinary. They looked like just a few guys enjoying the pool and the sun on their vacation. Dino decided to have dinner in his cabin, not wanting to risk being spotted. The more he could watch from afar, the better chance he had of finding out what was going on.

Chapter 18

PORT OF CALL

THE AMAZING THING about cruising was that when people woke up in the morning, they were always surprised that the ship was already docked at another port of call. *Star Orion* arrived at the San Juan pilot buoy at 5:00 a.m., was docked by 6:30 a.m., and cleared customs by 7:00 a.m. It was a standard Wednesday port visit for the crew and yet another place to explore for the over three thousand passengers still eager to spend money.

While the passengers disembarked from deck 1 aft, the crew opened the cargo doors forward. San Juan was a resupply port should they run out of anything that might be needed for the second half of the cruise. It was also a fueling port, and one that the company used for personnel to join or leave the ship in emergencies. Occasionally they would use this port to onload equipment that needed replacing. Because the ship was here for fifteen hours, the crew also had opportunity to do maintenance or safety drills.

Captain Markinson left the bridge and joined his hotel director and first deck officer for the port brief, typically taking only a few minutes. Each would talk about any changes or issues that might have come up so far and any on-loads they were expecting. Both the captain and the first deck officer already had the paperwork for the day's deliveries, including a new piece of medical equipment they were expecting.

"Three personnel departing for emergency leave," the hotel manager said while looking over his notes. "Onloading additional bananas, beef patties, and a few other things the executive chef added to the critical list."

Captain Markinson continued to listen for a few minutes then asked for the deck report.

"Off-load compacted trash and two bad fire hoses. Onload two new fire hoses, number 2 garbage disposal motor, and a new piece of medical equipment for the hospital," said the first deck officer.

"Where's that going to be kept? We don't install that ourselves, do we?"

"No, sir. The paperwork says someone will come in from Miami for a week to install and train the med folks. We will stow it in the medical storage locker on deck 1 until then."

The captain thought that the documents forged in Frankfurt and electronically smuggled into the ship's corporate e-mail traffic were brilliant. The e-mail went directly to the deck department and, when returned, went back to what appeared to be the home office in Miami, but it was actually a clone account overseas.

"Very well," the captain said, ending the quick meeting and heading for his cabin, where breakfast should be waiting.

Across the port at holding area 88G, a transfer truck pulled into the lot to hook up to COSCO container 1671JC, containing a shipment bound for the *Star Orion*. The transfer paperwork was generated automatically when it showed up on the daily yard movement plan. Once the transfer was complete, an autogenerated message would be sent to the broker, who would notify and charge their client accordingly.

Because the container was carrying a medical hazardous material, the driver had to sign a special release form showing that it had been removed from the holding area when he gave the security guard at the gate the transfer paperwork.

Ten minutes later, the transfer truck arrived at the passenger piers located along the San Antonio Canal, where the *Star Orion* was tied up. It was coming up on noon, and most of the passengers who were going ashore were already off the ship. The pier would be rather quiet until later in the day, when the process would be reversed and the passengers started returning.

Standing at the beginning of the pier where the security checkpoints were located was the third deck officer, who had been given the duty of supervising on-loads and off-loads during this port call. Most trucks were not allowed down the pier and had to be unloaded by forklift. The forklift drivers would then deliver the pallets of cargo to the ship. Security would sweep the pallets just outside the cargo bay doors before they were allowed to proceed onto the ship itself. There were two port security officers working the pier, and one had a bomb dog.

The transfer driver put on his flashing lights and got out of the truck to open the container he was pulling. This was a secure container because of the medical hazmat classification, and he had to use a combination to open the lock. The combination code was included in the paperwork supplied by the shipping broker who leased the container.

As the driver opened the lock and back door of the container, the third deck officer signaled a stevedore that they were ready to off-load two pallets. A forklift driver turned his attention to them and drove over for a pickup. Inside were two large wooden crates sitting on pallets. Both had plastic document holders stuck on the side with shipping paperwork enclosed. The truck driver handed his transfer paperwork to the third deck officer, who then climbed up into the back of the container to verify by checking the paperwork attached to both crates. Stamped on the crates was MEDHAZMAT, indicating special handling and that there were hazardous materials enclosed.

The third deck officer gave a thumbs-up signal to the stevedores, and minutes later both pallets were picked up, brought down the pier, and positioned just outside the cargo bay doors of the ship. The ship's supply officer was busy at this end, checking in the extra provisions he had ordered. A few minutes later, the port security officer with the dog walked over and put yellow stickers on the pallet containing the provisions and both pallets marked MEDHAZMAT, clearing them for on-load. Boris had packed four six-pound bags of kitty litter around the weapon once it was secure, wrapped and covered inside the CT scanner bed shell as an extra precaution against bomb-sniffing dogs.

On deck 1, forklifts belonging to the ship were used to move cargo within the holding areas on board. They were also used to pick up cleared cargo from off the pier and bring it onto the vessel. The main passageway running the entire length of the ship on deck 1 was nicknamed I-95, after the United States highway running north and south on the East Coast. At times, it felt like the actual I-95, or Grand Central Station, as some members of the crew called it.

A forklift came off the ship through the cargo bay doors and onto the pier to pick up the provisions pallet and delivered it to refrigerated hold number 1. There were three refrigerated holds on the ship positioned forward, midship, and aft for easy access from each galley above.

In the environmental section, Imad Patel was a couple of hours into his shift, and it was time to take his break. He would sometimes leave the ship and step out onto the pier, using the crew brow while in port to get some fresh air. Today he walked down the I-95 passageway toward the aft cargo door, where the crew's brow was located. Crew members would almost always enter or exit the ship from a separate entrance than that of the passengers, even during port visits. The cargo bay doors were large enough to allow for the easy movement of forklifts on one side and a crew security checkpoint on the other when fully opened.

As he put his ID into the kiosk for the Star Caribe security agent to check him off, he heard the sound of a propane-fueled engine approach and watched the ship's forklift leave the cargo bay, heading for two pallets sitting on the pier next to where the third deck officer was positioned.

Standing by the railing five decks above on the promenade level, looking down at the pier, were Fahad, Frank Castro, and Hamid Khalid, who had stopped their daily jog to take a rest and observe.

It took less than a minute for the forklift driver to pick up the first pallet containing one of two wooden crates marked MEDHAZMAT, turn around, and head back into the cargo bay. The driver took a left inside the ship and transported the pallet and crate down the I-95 passageway to the far end where the ship's hospital was located. There four crew members unstrapped the crate from the pallet, lifted it off, and, using a dolly, moved it two doors down to the secure medical holding area used for emergency overflow, equipment, and extra medical supplies. They carefully placed the crate in the back of corner of a second room separated by a half wall and repeated the process with the second crate. In a few minutes, the head medical officer arrived and signed the company order attached to the shipping documents, indicating that medical personnel had received the shipment. The paperwork instructed the head medical officer to open the second crate, extract the small package containing the radioactive medicines used for the scanner, and secure them separately with other medications in the medical facility.

Once both crates had been taken onto the ship, the three men on the promenade deck above continued their jog. At the same time, Imad finished his break on the pier and headed back onto the ship toward the environmental department, where he would continue crushing cans and recyclables into small flat packages.

Twenty-five minutes later, the third deck officer finished with the stevedores and radioed the bridge that all on- and off-loads for the day were complete. The officer of the deck relayed this news to the captain, who was in his cabin doing paperwork. The captain smiled as he hung up the phone and took a sip of his green tea, knowing that his long-awaited revenge against the system was closer to reality.

Police and investigators in Oslo had a tough time finding next of kin for the person they found stabbed to death at the foot of the stairs at the Markinson residence. Carleen Foulton told them all they needed to know about the brothers who shared the condo. As it all unfolded, she was shocked and sad at the same time. She figured she had lost a good friend. It was up to authorities to tell his only other living relative, his twin brother, about the murder, she thought.

She told police that the body had to be Stefin's because he was rotating off his ship and coming back from his job at sea. The medical examiner had a different take on the situation. It seems that after tests on the body and matching dental records, it was Bijon, and not Stefin, who was murdered. They also determined that the body had been there for a month to six weeks. After sweeping the house for fingerprints and the usual investigational techniques looking for forced entry, they could only place the two brothers in the house at the time of the killing, making the other twin instantly a person of interest in the case. There was no murder weapon found.

Police protocol dictated that they would inform the living brother of the murder and question him at the same time. This was all but impossible because of the unique situation, with Stefin being at sea, so they contacted his employer who in this case was Star Caribe.

Six time zones away, in Miami, the assistant director of human resources for Star Caribe started his day with a cup of coffee and troubling phone call.

"Edward Reynolds," he answered, upbeat, trying to start his Thursday off on a positive note. He was looking forward to the weekend ahead.

A strongly accented voice was on the line. "This is Captain Borgjston of the Oslo, Norway police, and I have some confidential news for your head of human resources."

Instantly Edward sat up in his chair as the fog of the morning was lifted. "She is on vacation this week, and I am acting director."

"We have some bad news about one of your employees. Mr. Bijon Markinson was found murdered a few days ago at his flat in Oslo."

This was a first for Edward. He had heard stories of getting these types of calls from friends who did the same job at other companies. They were usually sad stories.

"What happened?" Edward asked as he quickly logged onto his Star Caribe computer to look up who and where this person was in the company.

"It seems he was murdered. Stabbed to death, though the case is still open and under investigation. We would like to question his brother, who also works for your company."

At that moment, Bijon's picture and employee profile opened up on the screen in front of Edward. It indicated that Bijon was currently contracted and master of the *Star Orion* for another three months or so. This was a personnel matter, and he did not let the officer on the other line know what he was reading.

"What's his brother's name?" Edward asked, getting ready to search the computer.

"Stefin."

Edward quickly typed in Stefin's name, and his profile popped up just as his twin brother's had a few moments ago. This time it said that his was currently off contract but signed to start another starting on December 8, about three months away.

"And you said it was Bijon who was found murdered? I just want to confirm," Edward continued.

"Yes. Bijon Markinson. We would like to contact his brother or have you contact him for us."

This was not adding up, Edward thought as he quickly called up the operations page on the Star Caribe intranet site to see where the *Orion* was at the moment.

"I can make the notification for you, Captain, through our channels, but you will have to wait for him to get back to port to talk to him yourself. We will ask him to call you over sat phone, but I can't guarantee that he will. It depends on his workload and where they are located."

The captain wrote down some contact information for Edward and agreed that it was their best course of action.

"That will do fine, and we will look forward to hearing from you both as we continue with the investigation," the captain said on the overseas call.

With that, they ended the conversation, and Edward then dialed the secretary of the CEO and informed her that he needed to see Mr. John Monaghan right away.

A few minutes later, Edward walked into the executive suite of Star Caribe, where Mr. Monaghan's secretary told him to go right in. He had met Mr. Monaghan on a number of occasions but did not have much daily interaction with the chief executive officer. His boss, the vice president and director of human resources, did and spoke highly of the guy.

"Mr. Monaghan, I think we have a problem with one of our captains," Edward started off.

"Call me Red," he said at first, putting Edward at ease. "What's up?"

"You need to know that Capt. Bijon Markinson was murdered at his home in Oslo four or five weeks ago. The police just found his body though. I just got off the phone with an investigator."

As Edward did when the police called, the CEO instantly sat up and turned to his computer to look up Markinson. He knew who he was and that his identical twin also served on Star Caribe ships, but he didn't know them personally.

"Are you kidding? What happened?"

"It seems he was stabbed to death, and they suspect the other Captain Markinson."

Trying to digest all this, Red started reading the employee profile of Bijon, followed by his brother Stefin's. Then the chief executive stopped dead in his tracks.

"It says Bijon is on contract and on *Star Orion* and Stefin is off," Red announced.

Edward paused for a few seconds, and then he spoke.

"That's the problem, sir. Bijon is dead."

Red got up and went over to the bar sitting a few feet away in his large office overlooking Miami's Biscayne Bay. He poured himself a cup of coffee and offered one to Edward. He took a sip of the black coffee, walked back to his desk, and looked Edward in the eye.

"Then who the hell is driving the ship?"

St. Thomas is a favorite stop of the cruise industry because it's a friendly port and a United States territory. Most passengers buy liquor and jewelry during their twelve-hour visit to the island while others hit the beaches or golf courses. Jake and Claire were doing neither, having visited the island on business in the past. They decided to stay on the ship and enjoy all that it had to offer.

In San Juan the day before, they went to lunch with his friend and fellow agent, Wayne Howard. Jake said he would not talk business on this trip, but he couldn't resist the opportunity to get some lunch with his friend who technically worked for him. At lunch, Wayne decided to have some fun and paid the chef to come out and sing happy birthday while the hostess got on the PA and did the same. For the usually quiet Jake Stein, this was a funny and embarrassing moment indeed.

In just a few moments of business while Claire was in the restroom, Wayne informed Jake that none of the three Sellco clients had bought anything in months from the TC named Fahad and that he was still on the island. No exit had been recorded. Wayne told him that he would be checking through the import-export documents just to be sure and would e-mail him results by the time he got back to work.

So far, this vacation had been just what the doctor ordered, thought Claire, as they stood on the pool deck for the sail out of St. Thomas. It was dark, and the stars were coming out as the *Star Orion* slowly backed away from the pier, headed out to sea.

Seven decks below, Dino Tucci sat at the blackjack table in the casino with a baseball cap on and glasses he had bought during the port visit to Nassau. Thankfully, Frank Castro was not a gambler and, having tracked him across the ship, Dino knew that he spent no time here. Dino liked to gamble and had the money to do so. He was playing at the twenty-five-dollar-minimum table, which meant there were big dollars at stake every time the dealer started a new game. He was actually enjoying the cruise and figured he would confront Frank and his friends on the last night of the trip. They only had two nights left and one full day at sea tomorrow.

Tom Sundland had two autograph session appearances each week of his current three-week contract and two *Murder 101* games played with passengers who elected to sign up. His friend, Rex Nelson, had the same sort of schedule. The retro TV franchise was a winner with the actors and the cruise line.

His second game of the week was always on Friday, which was a sea day with no port visit, as the ship sailed back toward Florida. Tom had all his game scenarios approved by Star Caribe before his contract started, and with more and more experience, he was getting pretty good at putting them together. The toughest thing for Tom Sundland was staying away from the booze. He had been down that path once and almost ended up dead. He liked his new start, the gigs his agent was starting to get for him, and freedom to explore other options.

Rex, on the other hand, was still a bit of a wild card. He looked at the cruise gig as a step down but something to keep him employed between television shows. Unfortunately for Rex, the television work had all but disappeared after his show was cancelled. His ego didn't disappear, though, and the meet and greets with passengers kept that very much in place.

"I've got one more show tonight," Tom said, knowing that Rex also had one more for this week. They called them shows even though they were highly interactive roll playing "whodunnit" games.

"Me too, thankfully," Rex said sipping his morning coffee as the sea passed twelve stories below, where the men were sitting just forward on the upper pool deck. The two would meet there for coffee or to read a book before the afternoon autograph and Q&A sessions.

"Thankfully? How the hell can you go wrong with this gig?" asked Tom.

"I like it, don't get me wrong, but I can do bigger things."

Tom took a sip of his coffee before responding to that line.

"And I can't?"

"No, no. You're amazing. The passengers love your shows and taking part in them. You will do huge things in the future. I didn't mean it that way."

Tom nodded as Rex sipped his coffee, knowing that he had sort of insulted his friend who was, literally, in the same boat as himself.

"FX is going to pilot this new comedy based on a truck stop, and Andrew thinks I've got a good shot at reading for it," said Rex.

"Nice. What do you think of Andrew so far?"

"Best I've ever worked with. He knows his stuff and just about everyone in town."

Andrew Kelleher was one of the up-and-coming agents in Hollywood. He was getting serious buzz in the trades for two of his clients who had won Oscars the year before. They were new to the business and Andrew got them both parts in a movie that ended up being the darling of the year. When an actor thanks an agent at the podium while holding a shiny new Oscar, the phone will start to ring and keep on ringing. Rex had signed with Andrew the year before the Oscar wins and had a three-year deal at 10 percent. The only problem Rex seemed to have was his reputation on the set from years ago and trying to break a typecast.

"That's good news, Rex," Tom said, wishing his friend well. Tom had considered trying to get Andrew to represent him as well through his connection with Rex, but he would wait until his current agent's contract was up.

Both men were looking forward to getting back to the West Coast after their three-week engagement was over the following week. Tom would return to Star Caribe in the future, but he was not sure whether his friend Rex would. It was nice to sit high up above the sea and relax all the while getting paid for it, Tom thought, as he picked up a book he was reading while feeling the salt air rush by.

Special Agent Wayne Howard started his Friday with a three-mile run and was glad the weekend had just about arrived. He had enjoyed catching up with his boss and friend for lunch two days before and especially enjoyed meeting Claire. The two were great together, he thought, as he made his way from his car to the office with a donut in one hand and laptop bag swung around his shoulder. His service weapon was on his left belt, seeing that he was a lefty, and occasionally the powdered sugar from the donut would fall on the gun and holster. This would bring teasing jabs from his friends who told him he looked like he was in Scarface with cocaine dust all over his gun.

Inside he fired up his work computer after inserting his government CAC and checked his e-mail. Wayne had requested the import reports for the last month to check on a couple of items. One was whether Sellco had any current or past imports. Already the clients checked out and said that they had not done business with the Sellco rep for quite some time. Being a good investigator, he looked at Fahad's movements in and out of Puerto Rico over the past year and noted that he had been there quite a bit for having only two or three clients that on the island. Today he wanted to cross-check the import documents against what the Sellco clients had told him during his visit.

When he did the cross search for the company named Sellco, he was surprised to see one item dated the week before pop up. According to the clients he interviewed, they had not bought anything from this company for months. Perhaps the company had new clients on the island. He clicked on the item and read the import documents. Sellco imported a CT scanner for transfer to a Star Caribe vessel. Wayne printed off the document and then did a more in depth search for Sellco imports. There were six other items that dated back three years, but none in the last fifteen months. Of those, the imports were all computer-related hardware. Nothing medical.

Wayne thought that perhaps Sellco also sold medical computer equipment or something similar. He went to the Sellco website, and there was nothing at all related to anything medical. Things with this transfer were not adding up. He looked back at the documents and saw that the broker was Jose Rio and included a contact phone number. Wayne decided to give Mr. Rio a call.

"Hello," said Jose, who was back on the piers and also ready for the weekend ahead.

"Mr. Rio, this is Special Agent Wayne Howard from ICE. I have a question about one of your clients."

Jose immediately stopped what he was doing to give the federal agent his complete attention. After all, these guys could make or break an import-export broker.

"Yes, sir, which one?"

"You imported a CT scanner for a company called Sellco last week, and transferred it to the *Star Orion* this week."

"Yes, sir, I remember that. It was a MEDHAZMAT."

Wayne made a note of that on the pad in front of him and continued to question the broker.

"Who was the Sellco rep?"

Jose would have to look back at his records to remember the guy's exact name, but remembered his last name.

"It was a Mr. Fahad, I believe. Not sure of the first name, but I can look it up."

Wayne also wrote down the name Fahad on the pad and asked Jose for the complete spelling of the Sellco rep's name, whom he now had questions about. Jose said he would get the information and call him back in a few minutes.

While he waited for the call back, Wayne confirmed that Fahad had arrived in San Juan but had not left the island. His history showed one- and two-day stays, but his current visit was now going on three weeks.

A few minutes later, his phone rang, and Jose Rio had the full name of the Sellco rep who hired his brokerage firm.

"The rep was Abdul-Aziz Fahad, and the import was from Batumi, Republic of Georgia," Jose reported to Wayne.

"I see the outbound port on the paperwork along with the transfers. No name associated with it. Has Mr. Fahad contacted you in the last couple of days?"

Jose thought for a second then spoke. "Not since we met a couple of weeks ago at the Marriott."

"He didn't meet you at your office?"

"No. As a matter of fact, except for the first one, all of our meetings have been at hotels. The Marriott and the Ritz. He never came back to the office, which I thought was strange," Jose answered.

Wayne also thought this was starting to sound odd, and he definitely began to smell something going on here. He thanked Jose for his help and told him he might be calling back for more information. Next he picked up the phone and called field operations at the airport. He told them he wanted to do a face match for the last three weeks of departures. A face match would take his Fahad's current passport picture and look for matches on video surveillance tapes to see if he left Puerto Rico under a different name. Field ops got right on the job and told Wayne they would call him back with the results when they had them.

The documents sitting on his desk indicated a cargo transfer to the *Star Orion*. He decided to call the cruise line's headquarters in Miami to ask them about the transfer. What had started as a routine follow-up was turning into a full-fledged investigation, and he had a gut feeling that there was something terribly wrong. After speaking to the Star Caribe operations people, who had no record of the transfer and no order for a CT scanner, he ended the call with a promise to call back when he knew more. According to the cruise line, they were adding this technology to most of their new, larger ships, but *Star Orion* was not due for any medical upgrades at the moment.

Twenty minutes later, operations called back.

"Howard," Wayne answered.

"Wayne, we have a match on your face," said CBP supervisor Al Ksen.

"What do you have, Al?" Wayne asked.

The voice on the other end of the phone sounded all business.

"Your guy left for Miami on American Airlines 224 under the name Jose Fuentes using a Costa Rican passport. He entered MIA the same day. Video of departure and arrival confirmed."

For a minute, Wayne had visions of the 9/11 terrorists going through airports on the way to hijack airplanes. Now he had a confirmed terrorist collaborator shipping things to cruise ships and using different names and passports.

"Okay, Al. Time to get the big boys involved in this. SIPRNET that stuff right over and copy to Felton in D.C.," Wayne ordered.

Typically Wayne would go up the chain of command and contact Jake in Miami with this information. Jake would then move it up the chain to Felton, and other agencies would get involved. There was one small problem: Jake Stein was vacationing on the very ship they were talking about, and he was completely out of pocket.

He picked up the phone to call Felton in D.C. direct. This time, he used the STU-III secure telephone unit they had in their office to give the briefing. The two spoke for about ten minutes.

On the other end of the secure call, Tim Felton ended the conversation with Wayne in San Juan. Next he picked up his unsecure telephone and called Star Caribe headquarters in Miami. On a call like this one, there was only one person he needed to talk to, and that was the chief executive officer of the cruise line.

"John Monaghan's office," a female voice said on the other end of the phone.

"Mr. Monaghan, please. This is HSI Executive Associate Director Tim Felton calling from Washington on a national security matter."

The secretary on the other end almost spit out the Diet Coke she was sipping and quickly got her boss on the phone. She had noticed that over the last two days people were acting strangely, and meetings were happening without her scheduling them. Maybe this had something to do with that entire hubbub.

"This is Red Monaghan."

"Mr. Monaghan, this is Director Tim Felton from Homeland Security Investigations and ICE in Washington. We have evidence that something might have been smuggled onto one of your ships and that a possible terrorist collaborator is involved. I am going to need a list of passengers and crew members currently on the *Star Orion*. A warrant will be issued if needed, but we would rather work with you to resolve this issue quickly."

Red Monaghan had been busy over the last twenty-four hours, trying to figure out what was going on with the captain of the ship in question and the murder investigation in Oslo. Now this call. Something clearly was amiss.

"Anything you need, sir. My folks will e-mail it right up to you."

"We appreciate it, Mr. Monaghan."

Red took a deep breath then spoke again. "We might have another issue associated with that ship."

Tim was about to end the call in order to continue looking into this mystery unfolding in front of him.

"What's that?" Tim asked then took a sip of the tea he had poured.

"The current captain at sea operating the *Star Orion* is Bijon Markinson of Oslo, Norway. Yesterday my HR people received a call from the Oslo Police, saying that Captain Markinson was found dead in the basement of his flat in Oslo."

Tim was leaning back in his swivel desk chair and immediately sat upright and pulled closer to the desk, picking up his pen.

"Are you kidding me?" Tim asked. "Then who is in charge of the ship?"

"Bijon has an identical twin brother, Stefin, whom we cannot find at the moment. Stefin is also a captain with our company and rotated off a sister ship a month ago."

Using the pad in front of him, Tim started taking notes, realizing that this was getting bigger by the minute.

"Have you contacted the *Star Orion* to see who is in charge?"

Red took a few seconds then answered.

"We made a preliminary call to the chief engineer and hotel director but didn't tell them what was going on in Oslo. We asked some normal operational questions then asked how Bijon was doing. Both said he was fine."

Tim knew right away that the twin brother was clearly in charge of the ship. Red Monaghan came to the same conclusion earlier that morning after making the phone calls but didn't want to make any moves before knowing how best to handle this odd situation. At first Red thought it was just a domestic dispute of some sort and would be handled as a personnel matter. Now it was looking like something altogether different and was taking a scary turn.

"Mr. Monaghan, I am sending some agents to your office and will need complete access to your personnel files. I also need you to keep a very tight lid on this for now until we figure out what the hell is going on," Tim ordered.

"Whatever you need, Director," Red answered. "No one knows right now what we know."

With that, Tim ended the call then picked up his phone again and told his secretary to get him the watch officer at the National Counterterrorism Center.

Chapter 19

OPTIONS

FRANK CASTRO, HAMID Khalid, and Abdul-Aziz Fahad had spent the week like any other small group of friends from college getting together for a reunion of sorts. They enjoyed the pool, port visits, and many of the other amenities the *Star Orion* offered. Today, they decided to meet for a late breakfast in the Clipper dining room located on deck 11 just aft of the swimming pools. The Clipper offered a buffet breakfast daily, and each man made himself a plate. They then sat together in the far rear of the restaurant, next to the giant glass windows overlooking the back of the ship, with a view of its wake cutting into the blue ocean waters. Most of the big breakfast crowd had already eaten and made their way to the pool or other places on the ship to enjoy the last day at sea. Fahad planned the breakfast meeting that way so that the three could talk quietly.

This Friday was the day they had waited and trained for. It was the day that Allah's will would be carried out and that each had reconciled himself to savor. Their mission was under way, and now the final plan was getting ready to be put into action. Each man knew the outline of the plan but now would get the final details from their leader.

"Our additional martyr has contacted me and, as promised by Featha, will be key to our plan tonight," Fahad said as he took a sip of his black coffee. The other two men leaned close to the table and listened intently.

"He is the captain of the ship."

With that news, neither Frank nor Hamid could hide the look of surprise on their faces and sat back in their chairs to absorb what had just been told to them. Fahad then outlined the final parts of the plan and asked each if they had any questions. He then changed the subject, and the three men ate a good breakfast, looking forward to the forty-eight hours ahead of them.

Ten decks below, Bishar Fouad and Imad Patel met on the aft crew smoking deck and also finalized the plan and orders Fahad had relayed earlier in the week. Bishar had the same reaction the others experienced when told that their captain was part of the team. His job would be to secure the medical locker and prepare the weapon. Bishar knew that this would be his destiny. In a previous life, he was a soldier of the Russian army attached to a field artillery unit. His specialty was "special weapons," and he was trained in the deployment and use of the tactical nuclear warheads. As the Soviet war in Afghanistan raged, he was pulled out of his specialty and put into a conventional army unit sent to fight the mujahideen. As a young soldier he did his duty, but he sympathized with the very people he was sent to fight. After the war was over in 1989, his conscripted army service ended; and Bishar moved to Pakistan, where he started a life of religion and a path toward radicalism.

Dino Tucci decided he would confront Frank Castro the night before the cruise ended. He had been watching his movements throughout the ship during the week and still had a gut feeling that something was wrong. He watched him stay with the same fellows he came aboard with, including the one his cop friend told him was on the terror watch list. He wondered all week how that guy could have gotten aboard in the first place, but figured he might be using another name. Dino had a bunch of questions Frank was going to answer before getting off this ship.

During the week, Dino ran into Tom Sundland and attended one of his meet-and-greet sessions. He did not take part in the *Murder 101* mystery games, but he has grown up watching the show in the seventies. In Dino's line of work back home, he was not intimidated by anyone. In this case, though, he was just a little bit starstruck. Tom also enjoyed Dino's company, and the two met for drinks a couple of times during the week. Rex Nelson also joined them between hosting his own mystery games. All three men were sailing alone and seemed to hit it off. Tom and Rex knew that Dino was from Providence and in the construction business. Little did they know that his other job was closer to some of the characters that used to appear on their television shows.

After Tom and Rex's last mystery game, the three planned to meet for drinks in the casino bar. It would be the last time they would be able to get together before Dino disembarked and headed home to Providence the next morning. Dino figured he would have some drinks with these guys then go up and surprise Frank with a little "question-and-silence session," as he called them. Who knew he would make friends with a couple of the stars he grew up watching on television?

The National Counterterrorism Center is a clearinghouse for intelligence on everything that has to do with terrorists and possible operations against the United States. It's a top-secret part of the national security apparatus, and even its exact location is secret. The watch officer in the Joint Operations Center took Col. Tim Felton's call seriously, seeing that it was coming from an executive associate director. He then contacted three key members of the Joint Terrorism Task Force. Within minutes, a conference call with all five people was initiated.

"Go ahead and give a quick brief, Director Felton, everyone is on the line," said the watch officer over the secure telephone connection. They did not have time to put together a videoconference because of the urgency of the situation.

"We believe that a terrorist collaborator has smuggled some sort of device onto a Star Caribe ship during a port call to San Juan. The same ship's captain was murdered four weeks ago at his home in Oslo. We believe that the captain's twin brother is in command of the ship, posing as his brother and part of this operation. The acting SAC in San Juan did a face match, and the TC was seen departing Puerto Rico for Miami under an alias, using a Costa Rican passport. MIA has matched the face entering the country, but, since then, we have lost him. We believe he might be on the ship as a passenger. We have the passenger and crew manifests being sent to us as we speak."

There was silence on the line for a few seconds.

"This is Amy Ford from the CIA. What sort of device?"

Felton turned to his notes. Typically CIA would not be part of the Joint Terrorism Task Force, but because of the international reach of this investigation, he wanted her on the call.

"It was a medical CT scanner imported from Batumi, Republic of Georgia, by a company called Sellco."

A few seconds passed, and you could hear each person jotting down notes.

"Anything on Sellco? Oh, sorry, this is Burt Lefebvre from the FBI."

Felton again looked at his notes then spoke. "Sellco is a legit company, and this guy works for them. We confirmed his employment. The problem is that they don't sell medical equipment, and this was shipped as a medical hazmat because of the radioisotopes that were sent along with it."

Amy from the CIA spoke again after taking this all in. "So to bottom line this intel, a TC imports a radioactive medical device or whatever from a third-world country then uses dummy documents from the cruise line to get it on the ship being driven by a dead captain."

All four people on the call were silent. Then Felton spoke up.

"Yeah. And to make it even more interesting, my Miami SAC is vacationing on the same ship with his girlfriend, who is a Secret Service agent at the Washington field office."

Once again the group waited for a few seconds before someone else spoke up.

"This is Amy again from the CIA. You have to get them a message to check this shit out. If the passenger or crew manifest comes back with other operatives on it, we've got serious problems."

Felton answered. "Agreed. I will e-mail him a message on his civilian e-mail, which I hope he's checking, and copy Claire, the girlfriend. I will code word the message."

Because they all knew that Jake would not be able to see his government or secure e-mail on the ship, a message would have to go out on civilian e-mail servers. Code wording meant that a special word or words would be attached to the body of the e-mail letting the recipient know it was an authentic flash message.

"When is the ship due into port?" asked Burt from the FBI.

"Tomorrow morning," answered Felton. "The cruise line is keeping this quiet for now, and communications with the ship are normal."

Under his breath, all four members of the conference call could hear Burt whisper the word "shit."

"Time to get Dean involved in this," said Amy from the CIA. She knew from past experiences that in crunch situations, open communications with the White House was key to good decision making. Christopher Dean was the current national security advisor to President John O'Connell.

"Copy that. HIS will make the call to Dean. Let's talk again in a couple of hours when I get the manifests and we can see who the hell is on that ship," Felton said, ending the call and turning to his e-mail, waiting for the lists from Star Caribe headquarters to arrive.

Friday afternoon on the *Star Orion* was busy, as people were getting ready for the last formal night of the cruise. Passengers dressed like they were going to the prom while the photographers set up in key areas to document their experience and hopefully sell lots of photo packages. Traditionally, the captain would don his mess dress uniform and invite a few lucky passengers to dine at his round table situated in the middle of the extravagant main dining room. It was going to be the last night of the cruise, and people wanted to make the most of it.

Jake Stein and Claire Wilson were well into vacation mode. They were going to be celebrating his thirtieth birthday during dinner, and she wanted to order a cake and bottle Champagne at their table. She stopped by the guest services desk on deck 4 to make those arrangements to surprise Jake later that night. Then she was going to head to her room, but she decided to break her own rule about staying off Facebook, e-mail, etc. for the entire week. She wanted to send a confirmation e-mail to Janet back in Miami to make sure they had a ride when the ship returned in the morning. She also wanted to make sure that everything was okay with her mom, who had minor surgery a few weeks before they left. Star Caribe ships had wireless in-cabin Internet for those willing to pay. For others, they had an Internet café set up on deck 6. She got off the elevator and walked a few feet to the Internet café, where only two people were online. Using her ocean pass, she swiped the card reader attached to a workstation and logged into her Yahoo account, knowing it was expensive at two bucks a minute.

Staying off the Internet and out of digital touch from the real world was harder to do than she had imagined. This was okay, though, because it had to do with confirming travel plans, she thought, as she tried to justify being online. A few seconds went by, and her e-mail popped up with 142 new messages. She fired off a confirmation e-mail to Janet, her Miami counterpart, about picking them up the next morning. Calling from the ship would be much more expensive. She scanned the e-mails for anything from her mom but saw nothing. Typically her mom would only e-mail when it was really important.

Right before she was about to sign off, she saw a message dated today from a government account with the subject marked "Flash." She recognized the term instantly but knew that in her agency and most others, civilian e-mail was never used for most official business. She looked at the sender before opening the e-mail, thinking perhaps it was some sort of spam. Then she saw the name Felton. Maybe something was wrong with Jake's time off, she thought. But why "Flash" in the subject? She went ahead and clicked on the e-mail.

TO: J Stein
CC: C Wilson
FR: Felton
SUBJ: FLASH

Jake . . .

We have reason to believe a device was smuggled onto the ship you are aboard. TC Fahad believed to also be aboard posb under alias Jose Fuentes. Checking manifests for other possible operatives. Also believe captain may be involved. Nothing confirmed at this point. Quietly investigate and report back when able. CC to Special Agent Claire Wilson, USSS. Trinity Church. Repeat: Trinity Church.

Felton

Claire read this message and immediately printed it out on the HP printer sitting a few feet away. She then closed the account and logged off the Internet. Taking the message off the printer, she headed for their cabin and now had her game face on. This had to be real. If this were some sort of a spoof for Jake's birthday, she would take out her service weapon when she got home and shoot someone. A few minutes later, she arrived at their cabin on deck 8 and opened the door. Jake was sitting on the balcony reading a book and enjoying his last day of vacation.

"Jake, I went to send an e-mail to Janet to confirm our pickup tomorrow," she started to say before he interrupted her.

"I knew you'd give in first! I knew it," he laughed, knowing they both took a vow to stay off e-mail and Facebook.

"Jake, listen. I got this from Felton."

Instantly his demeanor changed. Why would Felton be sending his girlfriend an e-mail? He took the e-mail from her hand and quickly read it. Then he looked up at her.

"Trinity Church," he said.

"What the hell is Trinity Church?" she asked, not wanting to play games at this point.

"It's a code word message. Trinity Church is that little church near the World Trade Center and our current code word for authenticating messages if we have to use a civilian or unsecure server."

Claire sat down in the chair next to the small vanity.

"Shit. I've seen traffic on this guy. He's been in and out of San Juan."

Claire sat quietly. Then Jake spoke again.

"No weapons, no support, and we might have some kind of terrorist op going on right around us," he said to his girlfriend, who knew that their vacation was now over.

"I've seen nothing unusual, but what's usual on one of these things?" she asked.

"Good question. And what kind of device?"

Jake decided to start with the alias name Felton gave him in the e-mail. *So much for a birthday celebration,* Claire thought, as they walked out of their cabin, closed the door and headed to the guest services desk to see where Mr. Fuentes might be.

Afternoon was moving along in Washington, D.C., and the Friday commute home would be under way soon. Most people who worked inside the Beltway knew that the Friday afternoon rush always started early, with many trying to get a head start on their weekend. Tim Felton's weekend would have to wait as he and his counterparts from the Joint Terrorism Task Force figured out what was going on with this cruise ship headed toward Miami.

He dispatched two agents from Jake's office in Miami to the Star Caribe offices to personally question the CEO and others in the company about everything having to do with the ship's operations. He also received the e-mail he was expecting, with the current crew and passenger manifests. Quickly he forwarded the manifests to the other members of the task force. Sharing intel was something new since 9/11 and a plus when it came to most investigations. While he would be checking the names on the list, they would be doing the same. One agency may have intel on someone that another might not. At this point, time was critical, and Tim Felton knew he had to get to the bottom of this.

He and another agent split the list. Tim would enter the names of the crew, and Special Agent Darryl Huger would check the passengers against the terror watch list and run them though the National Security Agency secure database. He knew one name that was already a suspected terrorist or terrorist collaborator. Thirty minutes into his search, the name Bishar Fouad popped up. Former Soviet Army soldier suspected of training Taliban soldiers and of being a Taliban sympathizer, last known living in Pakistan. *How the hell did this guy get a job on a cruise ship?*, Tim thought as he took notes on the pad next to his computer. As he continued down the alphabetized list, he came upon the name Patel. Like the others, he entered the name and waited a few seconds for the search to either clear the name like most of the others or find something on this guy. The search took slightly longer than the others. A few seconds later, Imad Patel popped up. It seemed he was once on a terror watch list, but he had been taken off the list three years earlier. The job he had was in the environmental section of the ship. Tim wrote his name next to Fahad's as a possible suspect. He continued down the list.

Special Agent Huger was doing the same with the passenger list a few feet away. He was into Ks when the name Hamid Khalid came up. Khalid was not on a current or past terror watch list, but was a suspect in the U.S. Embassy bombing in Rome back in 1995. He was also a suspected member of a radical terror group working out of the Philippines in the early to midnineties. Khalid moved to Canada, then to North Carolina, and finally last known living in Miami. No connection with any terrorist group since 1995. *This guy could be a sleeper,* Huger thought as he jotted down some information on his own pad.

Both the crew and passenger manifests had pictures attached to the names, thanks to today's technology. Tim asked NSA to run the pictures though their database for possible alias matches. His STU-III secure telephone rang, and he had a gut feeling this would be a call related to the search.

"Felton," Tim answered.

"Director Felton, this is Brad Miller at NSA. We have some image matches for the two lists you sent over. Are you ready to copy?"

Tim sat up and pulled his pad closer. "Ready to copy."

"Passenger last name Fuentes is cover for Abdul-Aziz Fahad. Terrorist collaborator. I'll send the sheets on all of these guys over SIPRNET, but I'll just list what we found."

Tim knew Fahad would show up. This face-recognition intel software was priceless in determining what type of organization might be involved.

"Continue," Tim ordered.

"Passenger Castro, Frank, a.k.a. Ali Ahamid. Passenger Hamid Khalid. Crew member Imad Patel. Crew member Bishar Fouad. Crew member Kamal Lahab. All known or possible TCs."

Across the river at CIA and down the street at the FBI, his counterparts were coming up with the same list of names. Small additions or subtractions to their background sheets were expected, depending on the depth of each agency's intel, but clearly this was an organized operation well under way.

"SIPRNET those sheets right over to me and copy to Lefebvre at FBI and Ford at CIA," Tim ordered.

"Will do, sir."

With that, Tim ended the secure call and then picked up the unsecure line. "Get me Chris Dean at the White House," he ordered.

Every minute that went by, the *Star Orion* was getting closer and closer to Miami. The ship was set to meet the pilot boat at 05:30 a.m. Saturday, almost fifteen hours away. Jake Stein went to the guest services desk to inquire about Mr. Jose Fuentes. He had to be careful not to reveal that he and Claire were federal agents. If the captain was involved in this operation, others might be as well. He had no idea what he was up against and whether he could do anything at all. Now was the time for some quick investigating.

The guest services clerk confirmed Mr. Fuentes was aboard but could not say what cabin he was staying in because of company policy. She offered to dial him on the phone, but Jake said no thanks. He then asked whether the captain would be at dinner, and she said he would be at both the early and late seatings and available for pictures.

"We've got two targets to watch. One we know, and another we need to find. Best thing to do will be go to dinner as normal and watch the captain," Jake said to Claire as they walked away and headed back to their cabin. Nothing out of the ordinary had been observed on their walk down to guest services.

"If they're working together, maybe Fuentes/Fahad will make contact with him," she suggested.

"Exactly. Let's get dressed for dinner."

They both got into the elevator and clearly still had their game faces on.

Chris Dean started his day trying to wrap up business for the week and had plans to head out of the office early to start a weekend outside the Beltway. He enjoyed the sport of kite surfing when he could finally break away from his mobile phone and the national security apparatus, at least for a few hours. Unfortunately these were rare opportunities. The phone call from Tim Felton changed his agenda for the afternoon and clearly would end any plans of getting out of town early. He told Tim and the others on the Joint Terrorism Task Force to come over right away and also asked Amy from the CIA to join them. All the members of the task force were gathering information on the intelligence they had and looking for more, using the assets of their respective agencies.

Tim had been to the White House on a number of occasions, but each time he still had chills when he walked up to the appointment gate next to West Executive Drive. His name was on the expedite list, and after presenting his credentials, he was given an appointment badge to wear around his neck with a red "A" on the front. He walked out of the guardhouse and headed toward the West Wing entrance on the north side of the White House. As he walked up the hill, a couple of reporters and photographers were setting up for their evening news live shots just to his right in an area they called Pebble Beach. They called it that because for years it had been covered with small rocks and pebbles instead of traditional grass, which could not survive the daily stampede of the media circus.

As he approached the West Wing entrance, a marine opened the door, and Tim walked into the West Wing Reception Room, where Dean had told him to meet. Upon arrival, he met up with Amy from the CIA and the two waited for Burt Lefebvre from the FBI and Brad Miller from the NSA. Five minutes later, both men arrived, and Tim told the receptionist that the JTTF was there to see Mr. Dean.

After a few minutes' wait, Chris Dean appeared, and the group headed for Chris's office just around the corner. Each member of the JTTF briefed Dean on what they knew and what they suspected was going on. He had an overview from their previous conversations, but now with the new intel sitting in front of them, the picture was becoming much more clear and much more ominous.

"There's nothing definite about a WMD, but there's something going on here. The evidence points to a WMD. To our knowledge, there are no WMDs in the Republic of Georgia," Dean said.

Amy spoke up from CIA, "The shipper was a no-go. The name came up empty. Probably a ghost name."

The group looked at their notes.

"The cruise line said no medical machines were ordered for this ship. The paperwork from the broker in San Juan was all phony," said Felton. "The origin was also dry, and Sellco has no record of it."

Dean looked at his watch. It was now early evening, and the clock was ticking. The chief of staff now needed to be included into the loop. Possibly the president as well. He picked up his phone and dialed a couple of digits.

"This is Dean, we need a few minutes," he said to the chief of staff, who herself was about to call it a week. He gave her heads-up that the JTTF was working something but no real details until he knew what the story was. He hung up the phone and instructed the others to follow him a few short steps down the hall. Much to the surprise of most people who have never stepped foot in the EOP, or Executive Office of the President, better known as the West Wing, it's rather small.

"What do we have?" said Dr. Karen Leslie, PhD and chief of staff to the president of the United States. Dean briefed Dr. Leslie on the intel they had been gathering throughout the afternoon. She was a Yale-educated lawyer who got into politics later in life than most career types. At age fifty-four, she was a no-nonsense leader who had been a key player in the election of President John O'Connell just two years earlier. This was a job she was made for, and she excelled at it.

She listened thoughtfully then got up and walked through a door, which connected her with the Oval Office. Only a few people had walk-in privileges, and she was one of them. She returned a few seconds later and picked up the phone.

"I need to see the president. Is he in the residence?" she asked, knowing that's where he probably was. Much to her surprise, he was not upstairs. A few seconds later, her phone rang back; and his secretary informed her that he was out on the South Lawn with his family's new Norwegian elkhound, which had been a gift, ironically enough, from the king of Sweden. Dr. Leslie got up again and walked though the Oval to the doors leading out to the Rose Garden and South Lawn. The Secret Service agents with the president knew she would be walking over.

"Mr. President, we might have a problem on a cruise ship headed for Miami," she explained as one of the agents scooped up the rambunctious puppy. "The *Star Orion* might have active terrorists on board and a possible WMD." The conversation lasted about two or three minutes, and she then returned to her office where the members of the JTTF who were still assembled.

"We're going to the Sitroom with this. He's going to meet us there." With that, the group got up and headed a few feet down the hall and around the corner. An officer of the Uniformed Division of the Secret Service stood as they approached his desk before going down the stairs. The Situation Room is more of a complex rather than just a room with secure communications. The Sitroom watch officer met them as they entered and joined them at conference table. Typically, other members of the National Security Council would be called as well, but Dean wanted to wait to see how the chief of staff and the president wanted to handle this.

Ten minutes later, the president entered the room, and everyone stood as he made his way to his seat at the head of the conference table. On the wall facing the president were large flat-screen televisions and secure videoconference cameras.

"Do we know where the ship currently is?" asked President O'Connell.

Dean looked at his notes and answered, "Yes, sir, it's in international waters approximately twenty-five to thirty miles off the west coast of Andros Island in the Bahamas, bound for Miami. ETA in Miami is seven o'clock tomorrow morning."

Felton spoke next.

"Sir, Star Caribe, the cruise line, maintains GPS location of all their ships and is relaying coordinates hourly to us at this time. They are cooperating fully, and we have two agents at their ops center in Miami."

The president looked at the briefing notes sitting in front of him prepared by Dean and his team as the intel was being put together. Dean spoke next. "As far as ISR [intelligence, surveillance and reconnaissance] assets, we are tasking the NGA [National Geospatial-Intelligence Agency] to track the ship and get us some pics before the sun sets."

A few seconds later, one of the large TV screens on the wall facing the president came alive with a map of the Bahamas and South Florida. The other screen had the logo of the White House until it changed to a montage of pictures.

"These are the possible terrorists that are currently on the ship and in your notes, Mr. President," said Amy from the CIA. "We've got good ID on all of them, and confidence is high that there is an op under way."

The president looked up and took all this in. Then he spoke, "And the captain is in on it?"

"Yes, sir, we think so. Given the intel we have on the twin brother from the Oslo PD and history we've quickly put together from the cruise line, it all makes sense," said Felton.

A few seconds later, the STU-III rang, and the watch officer, who had retreated to his own office, answered. He then buzzed into the conference room.

"Mr. President, Secretary Pratt is on the line," the voice said out of the speaker sitting a few feet in front of the president. The president leaned forward and pushed the line with the blinking red light.

"Ron, you up on all this?" said the president.

"I'm coming up to speed, Mr. President."

The tension in the room was beginning to mount as the group realized that they might be looking at some sort of terrorist strike only hours away.

"What do we have down there, in case this is a real problem?" asked President O'Connell.

"Sir, not much. I have the cutter *Vigilant* around thirty miles away and COMSUBFOR Atlantic has the *Pittsburgh* doing workups just south of Key West," said Secretary of Defense Ron Pratt.

"Let's get them closer and find out what that device is that was brought aboard the ship," ordered the president.

"Already ordered, sir," said the voice out of the box. Currently the SECDEF [Secretary of Defense] was in his office at the Pentagon.

The president looked back down at his notes. Then spoke again.

"What does the CIA have on this device? Do we need to ask our friends if they have any missing nukes?"

Amy from the CIA spoke, "If it is a nuke, it's either black market or stolen. If we ask, we show our hand."

"We don't have a hand to show," said President O'Connell. "Who gives a shit if they know there might be a WMD on a ship. For all we know, it's homemade."

Felton raised his hand and spoke up.

"Sir, it was exported from Georgia. Russia is the closest nuke power. We need to ask them if they have a missing weapon."

President O'Connell nodded in agreement.

"He's right, Karen," the president said to his chief of staff, who at this point had been silent and taking it all in. "Have State give them a ring. It's so late in the game, it's probably worthless, but it can't hurt."

Dean spoke next. "It would take at least a few days for them to check their entire inventory, but if they already have a record of a missing weapon, we might luck out."

The body language of the group indicated all agreed with this statement.

"If they admit it at all. They might deny it if there is something missing," Amy said.

"What if it is a nuke?" asked Burt from the FBI. "If we storm the ship, they might set the damn thing off, killing everyone on the ship and depending on where they are, people on nearby islands or in South Florida."

The president took a sip of his drink while his chief of staff spoke up.

"One step at a time, Burt. Let's see what we are dealing with first," Karen said.

The entire group knew from the intel they'd been gathering that whatever was brought onto the ship in Puerto Rico was marked a MEDHAZMAT and had some sort of radioactive material. No one wanted to admit it out loud, but they all knew what that meant.

There were two seatings for dinner each night on the *Star Orion*: the early seating at 5:00 p.m. and the late seating at eight. Claire had chosen the late seating on the recommendation of a friend when she booked the cruise. The two left their cabin for the main dining room with a much different demeanor than they'd had for the previous nights of the cruise. Now they were very much at work.

Their table was on the port side, first level of the three-story dining room that looked like something you would have seen on the *Titanic*. It had a grand wooden staircase where a string quartet serenaded diners from a landing about half way up. In the center of the first level of the dining room was the large round captain's table. The table had ten place settings, including the captain's. His place was marked with a gold nameplate while each of the other place settings had a white card bearing the Star Caribe logo along with the lucky guest's name that had been chosen at random or otherwise. Star Caribe rewarded some of their frequent guests holding platinum status from over thirty sailings the privilege of dining with the captain. Some weeks there were a number of platinum frequent cruisers on board while other weeks only a few. In that case, the hotel manager would pick guests at random for the experience.

Jake noted that there were six people sitting at the captain's table, waiting for the master of the ship to arrive. He looked at their faces carefully, but being around thirty feet away, near the windows, his view was limited. For a minute while walking in, he thought he might have recognized one of them.

After they sat down, the captain arrived in his mess dress uniform and took his place at his table.

"Only six takers?" Jake asked Claire.

"Maybe more will show up," she said as they looked at the three empty place settings.

A few minutes later, the head waiter arrived to announce the daily chef's specials to Claire and Jake and to take drink orders. Each week, the waiters would try to memorize the drinks their passengers favored and bring them without being asked in order to get bigger tips.

"All men," Jake said as he sipped his water and reached for a piece of bread.

"They're not talking much," Claire said quietly. "Captain looks pretty serious."

Jake decided to do some recon and go to the rest room in order to walk closer to the captain's table. He noted the guy sitting closest to the captain and indeed recognized him from the pictures he had seen during intel briefings. The others he did not recognize, but clearly they were all either Hispanic or Middle Eastern, even the guy who obviously dyed his hair dark blond. After he finished in the bathroom, he took a different path back to his table to report to his girlfriend what he had seen.

"I recognize the guy sitting to his right," Jake said to Claire. "He's a known TC and, I think, a guy we were watching going in and out of San Juan a lot."

Claire took a sip of her drink. No alcohol for her tonight, she thought, as the Diet Coke fizzed in front of her.

"There's six of them and two of us," she said. Thankfully they had a table for two and could talk quietly. Another tip from the frequent cruiser friend was to ask for a table for two if possible. Tonight that tip was paying off.

"Seven," he said correcting her. "Captain makes seven."

They ate like it was any other last night on a cruise ship. The last thing he wanted was to give away his identity. Shortly after dessert, the captain stood up from his table, shook the hands of the men sitting around him, then he retreated to the doorway of the dining room to take some pictures with other passengers. The men who had eaten with him waited a few minutes, then they also got up and left the dining room.

Jake and Claire did the same. Jake followed the guy he recognized while he told Claire to follow any one of the others. She picked Frank Castro, who headed with one of the other men to the art show on deck 3. She noted that they did not say much to each other and started looking at random paintings hanging for sale in the makeshift gallery. Her job as a Secret Service agent at home was to look for things out of the ordinary when it came to people in crowds. She was trained well at the academy in Beltsville.

One deck above the art exhibit, she noticed a man also watching the guy she was tailing. This man had not been at dinner; at least he hadn't been part of the six who ate with the captain. This was getting odd, she thought as she pretended to look at the art offerings. She wanted to take a picture of the two guys she was tailing and have Jake e-mail it back to D.C. This was an easy thing to do, seeing that others were taking photos of the art exhibit. The tricky part was getting to a point where it looked like she was snapping a picture of a painting while shooting a good image of her suspects.

The pictures were aligned in four rows of about twenty feet long each. They took up most of the space in this half art gallery-half photo shop. She walked down the second aisle, noting that her subjects were on the next row and about four pictures down. This gave her the perfect opportunity to snap a shot or two of the painting in front of her at an angle that would allow a clear shot of the subjects. She clicked off three photos with her iPhone and continued looking.

Both of her subjects left the art exhibit and headed toward the elevators, and she did the same. They entered the elevator with three other people, and Claire squeezed in at the last second. Not knowing what deck button had they pushed, she just looked at the panel of numbers as if hers was already pushed. The elevator stopped on deck 4, and two people got off. Next the elevator stopped on deck 5, and she noted that they were positioning themselves to get off. The door opened, and she took a gamble and stepped off. Both of her subjects followed and headed around the corner to the Typhoon Bar. She did the same and entered the bar, where a piano player was dressed like Elton John, singing the pop star's hits. Both subjects took seats at the bar and ordered drinks. She sat in the darkest corner and told the approaching waitress she'd wait a few minutes to order a drink.

Five minutes later, she noted that the same guy who had been watching her subjects from above in the gallery entered from the opposite direction and sat in the far corner of the lounge. Now something was up, she thought as she watched both her subjects from dinner and the guy in the opposite dark corner. Maybe they were working together. Claire wanted to get a picture of this third subject but did not have the chance. Jake had said to meet back at their cabin in one hour to compare notes.

The bar was busy, and Elton John had switched to Billy Joel when Claire decided to head back to her cabin to report what she had seen. Both her subjects and the third guy were still sitting in the same places. She headed back to the elevator and met Jake in their cabin five minutes later.

"My guys went to aft end of deck 7 and just talked," Jake said. "It's the outside deck, and you can see the wake of the ship off the back end."

She pulled out a bottle of water from the small refrigerator they had in their cabin and also gave her report. "Mine went to the art gallery. There was a third guy watching my guys."

He thought about that for a minute as Claire explained what she saw.

"A third guy? One of the others from dinner?" Jake asked.

"Nope. Never saw this guy at dinner. He was clearly watching them and tailed them to the Typhoon Bar."

Jake sat down on the bed and loosened the bow tie he was still wearing with his white dinner Jacket.

"Did you get a picture?"

She took out her iPhone and pulled up the pictures she had shot in the art gallery.

"Good shots," she reported.

Jake did not recognize the faces of the men in the photograph. He only recognized the guy he was following. "We need to e-mail these back to the office for a face match and ID."

Claire agreed, and after each changed clothes into something more comfortable, they left their cabin for the Internet café two decks below. They arrived and noted only one person online who looked to be finishing up.

"It ain't working, just went down," the man said, clearly aggravated by the inconvenience. Both Jake and Claire looked at each other. This was odd. Perhaps it was a signal problem. "I tried to make a phone call as well, and they said that system is down too."

Claire and Jake thanked the man and decided to head to the guest services desk to see if all communications were down on the ship. They took the elevator down two more decks and stood in line at the guest services desk. On the last night of the cruise, many passengers settle their bills and work out discrepancies they have noted on the electronic checkout available on the television in each cabin. Once they got to the head of the line, they asked about the Internet and phone service.

"Both are down sir and have been for about an hour. We're sorry for the inconvenience," said the clerk, who Jake thought looked all of fifteen years old. They were about to walk away when the young clerk said something else that stopped them in their tracks. "Our corporate system is down too, and we can't even check credit cards or talk to the home office."

Jake thanked him again and the two headed back to the Typhoon Bar to see if the subjects Claire had been tailing were still there.

On deck 1, Kamal Lahab had been at work in his IT office when the call came from the staff captain, who was Captain Markinson's second in command, that the ship had lost Internet and phone satellite communications. He ordered Kamal to look into the situation and report back. Outages were not uncommon at sea during storms or other atmospheric events that interfered with even their state-of-the-art communication equipment. This was a call, however, that he had expected. Lahab had developed and written computer code that would ensure that all Internet and satellite communications would be rendered useless. He also wrote a code that jammed the ships in-house and corporate intranet sites, essentially cutting the ship off from home base. The only communications available off the ship were the VHF radios on the bridge and in the engineering spaces. The ship's security center had also lost its communication link to the outside world. They had two portable satellite phones for emergencies or power failures. In this case, power was not the issue. The issue was loss of signal for the ship's system. Devon Forest, the ship's security manager, figured that it would soon return to normal.

Lahab was an expert in cyber security and fancied himself a pretty good code writer. His mission was small but critical, and now he just had to monitor internal systems. He had joined Star Caribe two years earlier, and his assignment to this ship was why it was picked to be the vessel to deliver the "oven," as they called it. Fahad knew Lahab's assignment and mission but kept his identity from the other team members for the sake of operational security.

President O'Connell had returned to the residence for a few minutes to change into more casual clothes and check on his wife while the group waited for more intel. Four others had joined the group in the Situation Room, including the secretary of Energy, who brought along one of their expert physicists. The director of Central Intelligence or DCI, as he was known, also arrived. Amy was still in the room, but now she sat in a chair along the wall behind her boss. At this point, the president wanted his top people at the table. All of the members of the JTTF continued to get updates from their agencies, and the National Security Agency was also represented in the room when the president returned.

"Where are we?" asked President O'Connell as he entered the room and everyone stood. The chief of staff spoke for the group.

"Sir, we have some new intel and an update from earlier." Karen looked at her notes and continued. "Tim said his people at the Star Caribe operations center report that the ship's DPS, or dynamic positioning system, which is sort of an autopilot and anchor at the same time, has stopped reporting their current position. It can keep the ship in one position without using the anchor, but it also reports the ship's speed, position, and other information back to home base every few minutes."

Karen looked at Felton to pick up the briefing. The director of Homeland Security had not arrived, and he was their senior rep at the moment.

"Sir, apparently Star Caribe ops lost contact with the ship. Their internal intranet and satellite phones are not responding. They think the whole system has been cut off at the source. Also no response from our guy whom we e-mailed on the ship."

The president took a sip of the drink sitting in front of him and asked, "How close to Miami do they have to get to cause real damage if it is a nuke?"

Secretary of Energy Kyle Yoon, the first Korean American cabinet-level appointee, answered the question. "Sir, it depends on what type of weapon we are talking about and what the yield is. If it's, say, ten kilotons, they just have to be within around ten miles to level the city."

At this point, everyone in the room was quiet. A few seconds later, the intercom also came on, and the Situation Room watch officer said the DCI had a secure call waiting. Michaels picked up the STU-III in the center of the table and pushed the blinking red button to connect.

"This is Director Michaels," he said into the speakerphone. "Everyone, including the president, is on the call."

You could almost hear the nervousness in the voice on the other end, whether it was from intimidation because of the people listening in the Situation Room or the news he was about to tell his boss.

"Sir, our contact in Moscow has reported back. It was around midnight his time when we initially called with our inquiry, and I'm sure he had to run it up the flagpole before getting some answers. I think the urgency of the call and the current situation has opened them up a bit more than usual," said Jim Mills, who worked for the director of operations.

The DCI had his pen out, and everyone was listening intently. "Go ahead, Jim," Michaels ordered.

"It took about an hour and a half for them to get back to us, but they have been investigating the case of a missing tactical nuclear weapon from a classified storage area. They would not say where that storage area was. We know where most of their weapons are stored, but there are a number of different locations," Jim said.

The tension in the room could be cut with a knife when that news came in. Jim continued. "Apparently it's a variant of the ZBV4 tactical nuke used for both artillery or short-range missile systems. It's also a VY weapon."

The president looked at the DCI and the others in the room and asked a question. "What's a VY weapon?"

"Variable yield, sir," Jim said on the other end of the phone. "Our folks seem to think it's a five to eighty."

The secretary of Energy let out an expletive under his breath.

"Kyle?" the president said, looking in his direction. "What the hell is that?"

"It means the weapon could be set to detonate a yield from five to eighty kilotons. Eighty would take out most of South Florida."

The president and the others were quiet for a few seconds, taking in the troubling information coming in from Central Intelligence.

"Sir, they won't give us any details on the missing weapon other than that. The fact that they admitted it in the first place is surprising," Jim's voice could be heard saying from the secure speakerphone.

The DCI spoke next. "Sir, we don't know if this is the weapon on the ship, but something radioactive was shipped from Batumi, Republic of Georgia. Odds are it's the Russian weapon."

A few seconds later, Jim's voice from the speakerphone could be heard again. "Sir, the only other valuable piece of intel they gave us is that one of their former scientists and inspectors who monitored the nukes a few years ago was seen in surveillance video at the border crossing from Russia to Georgia in a truck driven by a former Russian soldier. They said they are investigating, and that's about all they'll say."

The president continued to take notes while trying to think about what his next move would be. He spoke looking at his director of Central Intelligence. "So they just shipped this thing like it's a FedEx package? How'd we miss this one, Donald?"

Clearly the DCI was uncomfortable, knowing that somehow there had been a lack of security and intelligence in this matter.

"Sir, our intel is that it was shipped as a CT medical scanner. If it is a weapon, it's disguised somehow," he told the president.

Everyone started to look at his or her notes when the president spoke again.

"What are we thinking with this, Karen?" he said to his chief of staff.

She looked at the speakerphone and spoke. "John, what have your folks been working up?" She knew the secretary of Defense had asked his people for some possible scenarios.

"Mr. President, we have two possible responses. The first is getting a Seal team on the ship and taking control of the vessel. They would drop in by chopper or board from a chase boat launched from the cutter *Vigilant*."

President O'Connell was a man of few words when weighing a decision. He liked to listen to all possible actions before asking questions. "What's the second?" he asked his SECDEF.

"Sir, the other much more radical and immediate," John said over the speakerphone.

"Go on."

"Mr. President, the second action would be what we're calling the 'umbrella option.'"

He looked up at the others in the room. They were all puzzled, except for the secretary of Energy and the physicist who was with him.

"The 'umbrella option'?" asked President O'Connell.

The SECDEF continued, "Sir, this ship is getting closer and closer to Miami. If they explode the device close enough, we could lose the entire city. The *Pittsburgh* is en route so that if we confirm there is a nuke aboard, we sink the ship so fast that if they pull the trigger, the water would act like an umbrella and suppress at least some of the blast. If it is indeed the device in question, there is a built-in minimum countdown to detonation, allowing for a small window to get the thing as deep as possible."

The room was silent. The president waited a moment then spoke. "Like taking down airliners on 9/11. The safety of many outweighs the lives of a few." He couldn't believe he was almost quoting Star Trek, but that was what they were telling him.

"Sir, our first concern is always people's lives. The Seal option may be a moot point, given the time it will take to get them geared up, briefed, and headed to the target. We put two 315th Airlift Wing C-17s on Bravo Alert at Joint Base, Charleston, in case you decide to go that way. But the 'umbrella option' might be a very real possibility to spare South Florida a nuclear terrorist strike," said the SECDEF on the speakerphone.

The secretary of Energy spoke next. "Mr. President, the 'umbrella option' works only if the blast is below water. Dr. Adam Scott here can explain." Dr. Scott was a well-known expert in nuclear physics on loan to the Department of Energy from the University of North Carolina in Chapel Hill. He had also consulted at the DOE for a number of years on nuclear fallout distribution, and he still held a top-secret clearance.

"That's correct, Mr. President," Dr. Scott explained. "The deeper the blast occurs, the more the water will absorb the energy, sort of like getting caught rising into the canopy of a giant umbrella. Five hundred feet or deeper is ideal."

The president waited about a minute to speak next. The group was silent, waiting for his decision. He rose and spoke his next order. "John, prepare for both options."

Chapter 20

TOT (TIME ON TARGET)

T HE LAST NIGHT of the cruise was well under way with the usual shows, parties, and the final formal night. On the bridge of the *Star Orion*, two staff officers and a helmsman were standing their watch on a quiet but cloudy night in the tropics. The ship was on autopilot, and they had briefed the Miami arrival just a few hours ago with Captain Markinson, who then went to do his duty greeting passengers and hosting the formal night. They were aware of the communications problem and knew that IT and the CHENG were working the situation. It was taking longer than usual, one of the staff officers thought as he sipped his tea. Staying awake during late nights at sea was a challenge for all who stood watch.

Seven decks below, the engineering watch officer also fought the urge to doze off. The chief engineer had come into the control room during the initial computer and communication malfunction, then left for dinner in the crew's mess.

On deck 7, Bishar Fouad, Imad Patel, Abdul-Aziz Fahad, Hamid Khalid, and Frank Castro, a.k.a. Ali Ahamid, assembled in the ship's library located near the midship elevators. The library was empty at this time of night while most people partied in other parts of the ship. Fahad went over the plan once again with his team, and then all joined for a few seconds of prayer. Moments later Bishar Fouad and Imad Patel left the group and walked down the starboard passageway toward cabins 7620, 7624, 7632, and 7636. A few minutes later, Fahad also walked down the passageway toward the cabins but stopped around twenty feet from where the other two men were getting ready to enter the first cabin.

Bishar Fouad took out his cabin steward key card, inserted it into the lock of cabin 7620, and with the sound of an electronic tweet, the door unlocked. He knocked and announced himself as he did many times as a cabin steward turning down the beds. This time, he would not be making cute animals out of towels that the passengers had come to expect nightly. Two people were staying in this cabin, and neither was there at the moment. Fouad and Patel quickly stripped off the blankets from the beds, which had been pushed together to make a queen. Each man then took out a six-inch hunting knife and cut into the side of each mattresses. They pulled out the foam from each, and, in a few minutes, reached the bubble-wrapped AR-15 assault rifles. Bishar Fouad had left a large gray laundry bag and a plastic suit bag on the shelf of the closets in each of the four cabins during his daily cleaning. He put one of the rifles into the large laundry bag and the other into the suit bag. The suit bag seemed to fit the weapon better, but both would work.

Quickly the two men stuffed the mattresses with the foam and bubble wrap but didn't worry about the gash down the side. Fouad made up the bed and left it as it had been. The only problem was that the feel of the bed may be different, but neither man cared. They left the cabin and moved to 7024. It was still very quiet in the passageway as Fahad kept a lookout, still standing about twenty feet away. Fouad put his ear close to the cabin door and heard the television going. He knew there were two people staying in this cabin, and it was unfortunate for them that they were not late-night partiers. He knocked on the door and was about to use his master key when the door cracked open.

"Excuse me, sir. We have to take a look at your bathroom for a possible sink leak," he said to the man, looking though the crack in the door wearing a bathrobe. The man agreed and opened the door as both men entered and saw his wife or girlfriend lying on the bed, watching television. Fouad told the man he would show him where the problems had been in the bathroom sink. He let the man enter the bathroom first and followed, shutting the door. Seconds later he took a towel off the rack, covered the victim's mouth, pulled out his hunting knife, and stabbed the man in the back. At the same time, Imad approached the woman and asked her if he could look at the light fixture behind her head. She was also in a bathrobe and sat up to get out of the bed. As she stood, he picked up the pillow and, with her back to him, pulled out his own hunting knife and stabbed her multiple times in the back while holding the pillow against her face.

Both men then dragged the woman's body into the bathroom and closed the door, leaving both victims inside. Seconds later, they cut open the mattresses and repeated the process of retrieving the weapons. This batch also had the additional bubble-wrapped clips of ammunition. They put both the weapons and the clips into the laundry and suit bags but left the beds and stuffing ripped apart, knowing no one would be back in this cabin.

Abdul-Aziz Fahad walked over and collected the laundry bags and suit bags containing the weapons while his men repeated the process on the third cabin. Once again, they found that the cabin was empty and retrieved the weapons while remaking the beds as best they could. The last cabin was empty as well, and they entered and started to unstuff the mattresses. A few minutes later, Fahad saw two people approaching the cabin from the opposite direction. He quickly approached them and said that two men were working on a problem with their sink. He asked if they could come back in about a half hour. They decided to go up and get another drink, not knowing that their lives, at least for the moment, had been spared.

With the weapons removed from the last cabin, all three men retreated to the library, where the others were waiting. Each member was given either a laundry bag or suit bag with a weapon inside. Fahad separated the magazines and put two in each bag. He and Frank Castro each had an extra bags, which would be given to the captain and Kamal Lahab.

It was getting close to 11:00 p.m., and each team of two had their assignments. Bishar Fahad and Imad Patel headed for the medical clinic and locker on deck 1. As employees, no one would question their movement. The other four members headed aft toward the rear stairwell and walked down five floors to deck 2, where Captain Markinson met them at exactly 11:00 p.m.

Without words, the remaining four men descended down the staircase to deck 1 where the captain would escort them to the engineering spaces. They approached the engineering center, and the captain entered a code, opening the door. Each man had either a laundry bag or suit bag with a weapon inside. The captain walked in first, and the others followed behind. Inside was a small operations center where the engineers monitored all of the ship's systems. Adjacent to the operations center was the IT center, where Kamal Lahab had been working late. At exactly 11:00 p.m., he disabled the ship's internal security camera network.

The men entered the engineering control room, where two watch officers were on duty. One had just finished running the engineering prearrival checklist while the other ate a sandwich and thumbed through a magazine. When the captain walked in, they both stood up with a look of surprise on their faces. Perhaps the captain was giving a private tour, one of the men thought, as he quickly put his sandwich down.

Hamid Khalid handed a suit bag over to Kamal Lahab when he came out of his small area to greet the visitors. Frank Castro and Hamid opened their bags and pulled out their loaded AR-15 assault weapons. Both watch officers' eyes opened wide with shock at what was unfolding. Seconds later, with absolutely no emotion, Hamid fired two shots into each man, killing them both instantly. The control room was heavily insulated, and the sound of the gunshots went no further.

Access to the engineering control room was limited to those who worked there and deck officers who had business with engineering. Kamal Lahab had changed all the access codes to the control room for everyone but himself and the captain. He also changed the codes for the medical storage locker, which was more like a two-room mini warehouse with medicines and medical equipment and where Bishar Fouad and Imad Patel were headed.

A few minutes later the captain, Fahad, and Hamid left the engineering control room heading for the bridge, carrying their laundry and suit bags, ready to complete their mission. Frank Castro headed for the medical storage facility to ensure the other Soldiers of Faith completed their mission when the time came.

Dino Tucci continued to follow Frank and his friends from a safe distance. When he saw them enter the library and meet with the two *Star Orion* crew members, Dino smelled something wrong. He backed off a bit from his surveillance because he couldn't go into the library due to its limited space, and he couldn't follow them down the passageways without being noticed. Whatever was going on, he was determined to stop it.

He walked across to the elevator and decided to go down one deck. On the *Star Orion*, the elevators were all glass, and people could be seen getting on and off as they went up and down the decks. On this final night of the cruise, people were making the most of their time left on the ship, and the elevators were very busy. The smell of alcohol and perfume hit him as he entered the elevator and squeezed in for the ride. A few seconds later the elevator stopped at deck 6, and the automatic door opened, allowing Dino and some others to step off. Waiting to get on were Jake and Claire. Instantly Claire noticed Dino getting off and held Jake's arm as he started to step forward to board the elevator. "Let's get another drink, darling," she said to Jake.

The two backed away from the elevator and went around the corner from the crowd for a moment.

"That's the guy who was following my targets earlier," she told Jake in a low voice while looking in the direction of Dino who was standing on the other side of the atrium. "I don't think he's with them, but he is definitely watching them."

Jake looked over and saw that clearly the guy was looking up toward the glass elevators. "Let's just ask him. Maybe he's CIA or another agency," he said to Claire. There really was no other play here. So the two made their way over to the other side of the atrium and approached Dino.

"Excuse me, I saw you today and yesterday with that other group of men. Are you traveling with them?" Claire asked in a nice, soft manner. Jake just looked on while eyeing the elevator himself for movement of the others.

Dino was clearly surprised by the question and now wondered just who these people were.

"Who wants to know?" Dino asked with a hint of his Italian temper starting to show.

"We're federal agents on vacation, and one of those guys is someone we might know," she explained.

On one level, Dino was relieved that there was someone else is on board who might help if these guys were to pull something. On the other hand, he was the guy who had sold them guns and a medical machine on the black market.

"A friend in your line of work told me that one of those guys is a suspected terrorist. I was friends with the guy he's with and think they're both terrorists of some sort."

This was getting complicated, Jake thought, as he decided to also ask a few questions.

"What do you do?" Jake finally asked.

"I'm in construction in Providence, Rhode Island. I know Frank Castro and have good knowledge that these guys are up to no good. When I found that out, I followed him onto the ship."

Jake and Claire thought about this for a few seconds without speaking again. The three continued to monitor the people getting on and off the elevator. Both Jake and Claire felt that Dino either had some past law enforcement background or might have been in the military.

"Your friend is right. I don't know the name Frank Castro, but the guy he's with is on our watch list," Jake explained.

"What are we going to do about it?" Dino asked.

"First, we have to find them again. Communications is out on the ship, so we can't access telephones or Internet. I suspect they have something to do with that."

Dino hadn't realized that the Internet system was down. He was not the wired-in type. "I didn't know about the phones," he added.

"The captain might be involved in this as well," Claire said, getting back into the conversation.

Dino was surprised at this piece of information and thought for a moment before speaking again. "If that's the case, we can't trust the security folks on board. And what are they going to do with a ship anyway? Hold all of us hostages?"

At this point, Jake figured he had nothing to lose by keeping anything from Dino. He was convinced by now that Dino had nothing to do with these guys but might be helpful in how they dealt with the situation.

"A device of some sort may have been smuggled aboard the ship in San Juan," Jake explained. "With e-mail and communication down, I can't get any more information on what my folks in Miami might have found out."

"What kind of device?" Dino asked.

"We don't know at this point, but I would assume a bomb of some sort or even a WMD."

Dino knew what the initials WMD meant and had a sickening feeling in his stomach.

"Tom Sundland will help us out," Dino offered. "He's a good guy and trustworthy."

Claire spoke up. "The actor?"

"Yeah, he played a cop on television and knows how to handle tough situations. Plus he works on the ship and knows his way around. We'll need someone who knows the ship."

The three stood for a few moments as they sized each other up. Jake was trying to put a plan together in his head.

"We have two issues. First, if they take over the bridge, we have to get control back to one of the other officers. Second, we need to find out where this device is located and secure it," Jake said.

Claire knew that this was a tall order. It was a huge ship, she thought as she tried to pull ideas from her own experience and training.

"We know where the bridge is and can start there," Jake said.

Dino looked down at the floor and was quiet for a few moments. Jake and Claire noticed a change in his demeanor. Something obviously was on his mind.

"What is it, Dino?"

He was silent for a few more seconds, then he spoke in a soft, low monotone. "Can you make a bomb out of a medical CT scanner?"

Both Jake and Claire were taken aback by this question out of the blue.

"A CT scanner?" Claire asked.

Dino needed to come clean. Too much was riding on this. He would deal with any legal consequences later on.

"I sold Frank Castro, the guy I was watching who is with the guy you two are watching, a CT scanner for what I thought was an overseas medical nonprofit." He decided not to add that he had also sold Frank some weapons.

"To be honest, I don't know, but we have to assume that it can be done, and that's what they have here on the ship," Jake said.

Claire thought for a moment and then brought up a good point. "If it's a medical machine, then wouldn't it be in the medical center or sick bay or whatever they call it on a boat?"

Both men looked at each other.

"I hate it when women are right," Dino said out loud while Jake thought the same thing.

The three decided to head for a place where they could see what was happening on the bridge. Then their plan was to find the ship's medical center. Tom Sundland would be definitely helpful with this because of his experience working on the ship, Jake thought as they walked off together toward the elevator. Dino was right about that.

Hours earlier, the officers and crew of the USS *Pittsburgh* had been just south of the Florida Keys, finishing lunch between workup drills, getting ready for the sub's upcoming deployment, when Capt. Rusty Pearson received a flash message on the ELF, or extremely low-frequency receiver. The message ordered him to take his ship at her fastest speed to position 25.7 north latitude, 79.9 west longitude, or just southeast of Miami, and wait for further instructions.

Nine hours later, they arrived at the coordinates sent to them in the message and hovered at periscope depth, wondering what was going on. The position was in the vicinity of the Miami Terrace Reef. The depth ran from around six hundred to two thousand feet. Captain Pearson figured it might have something to do with either Cuban refugees or some sort of drug interdiction. He ordered the HF, or high-frequency antenna, be raised so that they could have two-way communications with COMSUBFOR (Commander, Submarine Forces).

The coordinates placed them 120 miles or so off the coast of Miami. The crew knew there was something strange going on when the captain suddenly broke off from doing workup drills and told them over the 1MC that they were headed at flank speed to those coordinates. What they were to do when they arrived was a mystery not only to the crew, but also to the captain.

Capt. Stefin Markinson knew that his brother would have disagreed with what he was doing, but it was too late to worry about that now. Posing as his twin brother, Bijon, and wearing his nametag and ID, he would make a statement against America then join him in eternity as a reward. He made his way to the bridge entrance on deck 7 and punched the code to open the door. A camera was pointing down at everyone on the bridge, but it was disabled at the moment, thanks to Kamal Lahab's handy computer hacking. The door to the bridge could be opened either by buzzer from inside the bridge or by code input by an authorized member of the crew. The captain punched in his four-number code, and instantly the door made a loud clank and cracked open.

It was quiet and dark as he walked through the door with Hamid Khalid and Abdul-Aziz Fahad in tow, each holding a laundry bag and suit bag with weapons inside. The bridge was deathly quiet, and the weather was fantastic. Sitting in the captain's chair was the senior watch officer, and standing a few feet away was the junior watch officer. They were talking about American football when the bridge entrance door light illuminated with the loud sound of the door being released. The only light inside was from the low glow of the radars, GPS screens, and other instrumentation along with a few red navigational lights in the ceiling. Unlike the movies and contrary to what most people think, the bridge is only manned by two, or sometimes three, people while the ship was on autopilot late at night.

"Good evening," Captain Markinson said to the senior watch officer.

"Captain's on the bridge," the junior watch officer announced while at the same time wondering why the captain had what looked like two passengers with baggage with him.

"Good evening, Captain," the senior watch officer of the deck said while climbing out of his boss's chair.

"What is our position?" Captain Markinson asked the junior officer standing a few feet away.

While their attention on was reporting to the captain, Fahad and Hamid untied and zipped their respective bags and quietly pulled out the AR-15s. Each man readied and cocked his weapon.

"What the fuck?" said the junior watch officer. Until this moment, his back had been to the visitors while focusing on the captain, then he heard that telltale sound and turned around to look.

The captain took a few steps away from the two watch officers, who now had the look of fear in their eyes. In the seconds it took their brains to process what was going on in front of them, Fahad and Hamid put two bullets into their chests, killing them instantly.

The captain then picked up the phone on the console in front of his chair. "This is the captain, the bridge is secure," he said.

"Engineering is secure," Kamal Lahab said into the telephone.

The captain hung up the phone and looked at the instruments in front of him, knowing that his ship was on autopilot, which he would now monitor.

Back on deck 1, Bishar Fouad and Imad Patel used the new code Kamal Lahab had given them to open the secure door of the medical locker and storage area. With a click of the lock, the door released, and both men went inside, closing and locking the door behind them. It was relatively dark until Imad turned on the second light switch, illuminating the storage area, which smelled a little like a hospital. They quickly took their weapons out of the bags, loaded and cocked them. A few minutes later, they walked to the back of the second room, where two giant wooden crates were sitting in the corner. Bishar started to open up the crate marked with the number 2 along with "MEDHAZMAT" stamped across all sides. Meanwhile, Imad picked up the phone to call the bridge. "Medical facility secure," he said to the captain on the other end. A few minutes later came a buzz at the door from Frank Castro, who would be assisting the two and making sure they carried out their mission. Imad opened the door and let him in.

Bishar and Imad had work to do. They had to open the crate, take the bed apparatus apart, and ready the weapon. Imad's job was to assist Bishar, who planned on programming the minimum short-timed fuse and setting the highest yield available for detonation. Once the device was programmed and its timer engaged, their orders were to stand guard and protect it until zero hour. Frank Castro was there in case either of them had cold feet.

Tom Sundland was in his cabin, getting ready to go out and get a few late-night drinks before getting some shut-eye. He'd had a fantastic day at his last meet-and-greet session with the largest turnout of people so far playing their **Murder 101** mystery game. He had tried to make a Skype call back to his sister in the States, but the Internet was still down. Suddenly there was a knock on his cabin door. He opened it and recognized Dino right away. The others he did not know.

"Tom, we need your help with something right away," Dino said in a serious tone. "Let us come in for a second, and we can explain." With that, Tom opened his door wide and invited Dino and the other strangers inside. Dino introduced Jake and Claire, and they ran though what was going on. Tom was taken aback and had to make sure it was not some sort of joke.

"Listen, I don't know anything about law enforcement except the little I've learned from doing the show and research," he explained.

Jake spoke up. "We know. But we need you to show us the best ways of getting around the ship and also for backup if we have to take these people out."

"Looks like we're outnumbered and outgunned."

Jake nodded his head in agreement as did Claire. The four left Tom's cabin and headed for the bridge overlook on deck 10. From there, Tom said they could look down into the bridge wing and try to see who was in charge and driving the ship. To see inside the bridge was tough from that angle, but it was possible. The only problem was that it was nighttime and very dark. Thankfully, cruise ships put out plenty of lights to show off their vessel during night operations. So far, the captain had maintained the exterior lighting, hoping to keep things as close to normal as possible.

"Let's check out the port side," Jake said as they got off the elevator on deck 10. The deck was not too busy this late at night except for a few people in the hot tubs and a couple of kids in the pool trying to squeeze in one last swim before disembarking in the morning. The four walked to the portside rail and moved forward toward the bow to look over the side, down onto the bridge wing.

"Can't see shit," Dino said quietly. The top of the bridge wing was two decks below them. They also couldn't see through the main bridge windows because the design faced the bow of the ship and was forward and below them. The main bridge windows were aligned completely across from one side of the ship to the other in an almost-crescent arch.

"The roof of the bridge looks pretty flat," Jake said, looking forward of where they were standing. "If I can get down there and quietly look over into the bridge, we can get a better picture who's driving the ship."

Claire spoke up. They weren't married, but she suddenly felt like she might lose him.

"That's too risky, Jake," she said. "If you fall, you could slip right off the ship and into the sea."

"It's pretty flat except for the edges, and it's only two decks down."

"Jake, what if they see you?"

He looked around for a few seconds and saw a fire hose locker against the bulkhead a few feet away. There were no people around because it was getting late, and this was usually a quiet part of the deck forward of where the pool was located.

Tom and Dino remained quiet. After all, they thought, he was the fed with the training. Jake opened the fire locker and pulled out the inch-and-a-half hose that was wrapped into a tight oval. He had Dino help him tie one side to the rail close to the center of the ship. The top of the bridge sloped down on both the right and left sides, so if he slipped, he would keep right on going off the side.

"I'm going to rappel down to the top of the bridge and slide toward the front on my belly. Then I can look down into the windows from above," he explained.

"You better hope they don't spot you," Tom said, weighing in on the plan now.

"I'll peek in through the windows toward the right side right before it starts to slope away."

He gave Claire a kiss on the mouth, grabbed the end of fire hose, and quietly lowered it down to the roof of the bridge two decks below. Between the roof of the bridge and the deck they were standing on was another deck in between, with portholes looking forward. Jake positioned the fire hose to run between the large cabin windows so that he could not be spotted by anyone inside.

"Be careful, Jake," Claire said as he climbed over the railing and lowered himself down on the fire hose. Then she looked at Tom. "If anyone comes over, tell them you're rehearsing part of your show and to keep away."

A few seconds later, Jake gently touched down on the top of the bridge and flattened out onto his stomach to begin sliding forward and toward the right. The slope he needed to avoid was hard to see from his point of view because of the darkness. If he started to slide, that would be it. He would slide off and fall ten stories into the sea below. There was nothing to hold onto. He quietly inched forward and started to get closer to the front where the edge was. The wind was blowing around fifteen to twenty knots, which was something he hadn't think about until now. Thankfully, the ship was not tossing very much due to its enormous size.

It took about three minutes for him to slide all the way forward and toward the right where he wanted to be. The slope started about a foot away and to his right. A sudden move that way would be fatal. He inched closer to the front and stopped just short of the edge. He could see the windshield wiper motors sticking up in front of him. It was pitch black except for spotlights that shined on the sides of the ship and up into the superstructure above him.

Jake slowly pulled a few inches forward until his left cheek was touching the metal of the windshield wiper motor, which felt cold to his skin. One more slight push with his legs, and he could look over the edge and down into the bridge windows. He looked for about two seconds and saw the glow of red lights and one person sitting in the captain's chair. He retreated for a few seconds then repeated the process. This time he saw two other men with what looked like M16 rifles and two bodies on the floor. Once again, he quickly pulled up and back. That was enough. He slowly slid himself back toward the center and rear of the roof where the fire hose was hanging. Then he stood up, tugged on the line to make sure it was still secure, looked at his friends above and gave a thumbs-up. With the bench-pressed, toned muscles in his arms, Jake pulled himself up to the top of the line and over the rail, back onto the deck.

"Two guys with M16s plus the captain," Jake reported to the others. "Two possible KIAs on the floor."

"Holy shit," Dino said. "I fucking knew it. I'll shoot that bastard in the eyes,"

Jake looked at Dino and for a second and thought that maybe he had experience with this sort of thing. No time to wonder though. *Time for action,* he thought as he wrapped up the hose and put it back in the fire locker.

"Tom, where's the medical station or hospital or whatever they call it on a boat?" Jake asked.

"It's down on deck 1, why?"

"That's what we're going to have to secure. They can drive the ship all they want, but the device has to be secured."

"Jesus," Tom said under his breath.

"Let's go," Jake ordered to his small group.

The Situation Room was beginning to get crowded as more of the national security team started to arrive. So far, the media had not caught on to the fact that something big was going on. That was perfectly fine with the people in this room because they needed to keep a cap on what could be a panic situation in the city of Miami and all of South Florida. On one of the plasma screens on the left wall was a small countdown clock, which had been set to the time *Star Orion* would be arriving at the pilot station just off the coast of Miami. The clock read six hours, fifteen minutes, and twenty seconds and continued to count down.

"Sir, the cutter *Vigilant* is tracking the movements of the *Star Orion* about fifteen miles south of her. Both ships are able to see each other on radar, but it's nothing out of the ordinary and shouldn't spook whoever is driving the cruise ship. The *Pittsburgh* has arrived on station and is ready to respond to our orders. She can move as needed depending on the target's movement," said Secretary of Defense Ron Pratt, who had driven over from the Pentagon during a short break in the meetings while more intelligence was coming in.

"Mr. President, we've confirmed the movement of this man Abdul-Aziz Fahad from our records over the last couple of years, and the pattern clearly points to a terror plot. Our agents in San Juan continue to follow up on the software company he worked for. Here are the pictures of him entering Miami last week using an alias, and this is a picture of him that Star Caribe sent over. Their SOP is to send the home office a final passenger manifest including pics taken for their security system," explained Tim Felton.

"Anything more from our Russian friends?" asked President O'Connell.

"Mr. President, no, sir. Nothing new from Moscow since the missing weapon report and intel on the truck driver, but that's about all we expect. It's an embarrassment for them, and they'll no doubt go dark on this whole situation," said Director Michaels of the CIA.

"Time?"

"Mr. President, this clock is the time left before the ship gets to the pilot station off the coast of Miami Beach, about six hours or so," said Dr. Karen Leslie, chief of staff, pointing to the side monitor.

"Can we get a team on board?"

"Sir, not enough time for Seals, but a boarding team from the *Vigilant* is possible. They have worked up a plan to approach from the rear and sneak onto the ship to try to gain control. If they try to fight it out, and the bad guys decide to detonate the device, it would do great harm to the northern Bahamas. It could potentially spread radiation across their islands and possibly parts of South Florida seeing that the ship is getting so close," the SECDEF said.

The president sat back in his chair and thought for a minute or two. The others around the table were silent. The tension in the room was once again so thick, you could almost cut it with a knife.

"Ron, get the Coast Guard going. I'll give them two hours. After that, we go with the umbrella option. Have the *Pittsburgh* intercept and track, but they don't shoot unless I give the order from here," ordered President O'Connell.

"Yes, sir," said the SECDEF, who, like everyone else in the room, knew that if that Coast Guard boarding team couldn't get the job done, they would be doomed along with the rest of the passengers and crew. If the *Pittsburgh* had to sink the ship, the good guys would perish along with the bad.

Meanwhile, the monitor the clock continued to count down.

Chapter 21

SEMPER PARATUS

O NE THOUSAND THREE hundred fifty miles south of Washington, D.C., the Coast Guard cutter *Vigilant* was trailing and monitoring the *Star Orion* from a range of around fifteen miles, as ordered. The crew was looking forward to returning to their home base at Port Canaveral the next morning, but things were about to change when the captain got new orders.

"All ahead flank," ordered Capt. Brian Lewis. "I want to close to about five miles. Battle stations surface." The officer of the deck repeated the order as the ship came to life with the general quarters alarm ringing in the background. "Rig the ship for black ops." He wanted to minimize all lights and communications to stay hidden as much as possible.

The captain then left the bridge and headed below to personally brief the boarding party. This mission was different. He knew from the first communication from Washington that a boarding party might be necessary and had ordered one assembled. Now he needed to make sure they knew what was at stake. He gave them a quick overview of what was going on. He also briefed the young officer in charge of the boarding party that there might be two friendly agents on board also briefed in on the situation.

The TAO, or tactical action officer, had downloaded a detailed deck plan for the *Star Orion* and brought copies of it to the brief to distribute. He had taken a good look at it along with pictures of the ship to determine the best approach for the team. He also handed out sheets with the pictures of the suspected terrorists sent from Washington. For good measure, he also shared pictures from the federal IDs of Special Agents Jake Stein and Claire Wilson.

"The goal here is stealth and speed," said the TAO to the group of eight who would board the ship. "The approach to portside aft is key. There is a covered outdoor crew break area on the starboard side of deck 3 and a maintenance staging area on the opposite port side. A metal wall separates the two areas. If you approach at an angle, the separation wall will block any view from the crew break area. Passenger cabins and balconies face either starboard or port, but only a few face aft. It's late, and most passengers will be in their cabins asleep, but we can't rule out being spotted."

The boarding team took a good look at the handouts. The captain spoke next. "Our job is to gain control of the vessel and the device which the CIA seems to think is in the medical facility on deck 1. We have to assume that the terrorists are armed. We also don't want to alarm the passengers. A tricky combination."

Unlike the Navy Seals, their small Zodiac rubber boats were orange, not black. Thankfully there was no moon and some clouds, which should help hide them until they got to within fifty yards of the *Star Orion*. At that point, the ship's lights would begin to reach them.

"We will drop and orbit," said the TAO to the group who knew that this meant that the Zodiacs would break away after dropping them off and trail in the darkness until they were ready to be picked up. "If passengers ask what we are doing, just tell them it's part of a drill or something." All the men thought that might be a bit of a stretch, seeing that they would be dressed in black and carrying weapons.

The captain gave a final few words. "This is a critical national security mission, and we are counting on you to carry it out and show just what the Coast Guard is capable of. Good luck and Godspeed."

With that, the two boarding teams did their final preparations to launch as the USCGC *Vigilant* closed on the *Star Orion*.

The medical facility and medical storage locker were on deck 1, where passengers were forbidden to be unless they were coming to use the hospital or the forward or aft passageways off the ship during port visits. Tom led Jake and the others down to deck 1. Jake had a plan to at least get a look at what they were facing by pretending to be seasick and visit the hospital. The others would tag along in support, with Tom as their escort.

The four approached the doors of the medical facility or ship's hospital, as it was known. The doors were closed. To the right and about thirty feet down the passageway, Jake could see another set of double doors with red crosses on them. These were clearly bigger doors with security code pads, and above them he could see a sign reading "medical storage locker." There was also a yellow warning sign on the door itself, which read "authorized personnel only." He saw no movement or sign of anyone on the outside, but it was what was going on inside that he needed to deal with. He wanted to get a good look at the doors and layout before stepping into the medical facility.

Dino opened the door to the medical facility, which was manned twenty-four hours a day by either a nurse or a doctor. At first they saw no one at the small reception area, then a nurse came walking up from the back and asked if she could help them.

Dino and Tom made up stories of seasickness and back strain to buy time while Jake and Claire took a look around to see if there might be access to the medical storage locker from inside the hospital. No such luck. The facilities were two separate rooms and spaces. The only access into the storeroom was by medical personnel or someone ranking high enough to have the code to open the door. Jake was at a dead end and decided to ask the nurse where the chief medical officer was at the moment. It was time to flash his and Claire's credentials and get some assistance. The nurse was intimidated by the urgency of Jake's request to talk to the medical officer and by his credentials as a federal officer. It was a bit of a risk, but Jake figured that the staff involvement in the terror operation was probably limited to a few people the captain trusted.

The nurse picked up a nearby phone and punched four digits into the dial pad. She spoke to the doctor and apologized for waking him up before handing the phone to Jake. After a brief explanation for the call, Jake hung up the phone and told the others that the medical officer would be down in a few minutes to assist them. Perhaps they could gain access to the medical storage facility next door, he thought as he sipped a drink of water from the cooler in the small reception area. What his small group would do if they did gain access was another question. After all, the people inside were heavily armed and might have some sort of WMD.

The communication officer on board the USS *Pittsburgh* had never seen so much flash traffic being sent to them from COMSUBFOR. He would see the messages before handing them off to Capt. Rusty Pearson and knew something big was going on. Now there were new messages coming direct from the Pentagon. They were standing by on station at the coordinates originally given to them over twelve hours ago.

"New heading, one nine zero. Depth three hundred feet," Captain Pearson ordered as he came walking back into the control room with the executive officer, or XO. "All ahead flank."

"All ahead flank. Aye, sir. My heading is coming to one niner zero at three hundred feet," said the young helmsman, who was all of nineteen years old, repeating his commanding officer's orders.

The captain continued to look at the new orders he had in his hand and moved to the chart plot sitting just a few feet away. He and the XO looked at the new coordinates on the orders and figured the time it would take to get there.

"We're not too far off," the XO said to his boss, who clearly was under pressure and had sweat beading up on his forehead, just below the rim of his ball cap.

"The box says about fifty-three minutes," Captain Pearson said back to his number two. "I want you to personally go down and make sure we have two good fish ready to fly. We will go to battle stations torpedo in about thirty minutes."

"Aye, sir." The XO quickly departed the control room. Tension was beginning to build throughout the ship. They had been to battle stations, no drill, twice in twelve hours. Now the ship was moving again at flank speed on a heading due south at condition one.

Two fast orange Zodiac Hurricane RIBs (rigid inflatable boats) were launched from the United States Coast Guard Cutter *Vigilant* with a boarding party of four in each. They were the latest boats the Coast Guard had for intercepting drug runners or conducting search and rescue operations. Three Mercury three-hundred horsepower Verado engines gave the coxswain driving the lead boat power enough to push the limit on speed to almost forty knots. Both boats were blacked out and ran about one hundred yards apart to paint a much smaller radar picture if they were picked up by the *Star Orion's* aft radar system. The men and women of the boarding party were armed with SIG-Sauer P229R forty-caliber side arms and Colt M4 carbines, plus two members carried C-4 explosives. They knew what had to be done. One team of four would secure the bridge while the other would secure the weapon, which their intel said would be somewhere in the medical center.

It was almost two o'clock in the morning, and the order for the boarding had been given about an hour earlier. The preparations and intel briefings took about an hour of precious time that continued to click by as the *Star Orion* got ever closer to the Port of Miami.

The boats slowed as they approached the rear port quarter of the 150,000-ton cruise ship sailing along on autopilot at around fourteen knots. Some cloud cover kept any moonlight at bay, and the tactical environment almost pitch black until they were getting closer to the ship's lights. The coxswain driving the lead Zodiac could now see the deck they were targeting for a boarding. He carefully approached so that the opposite side of the same deck would not be visible to them, therefore keeping the crew recreation deck blind to their approach.

Picking up some wake, the coxswain slowed even more as the boarding party readied their equipment. As they approached slowly to within around twenty feet of the vessel, the boarding leader signaled to her man carrying the M4 grappling-hook gun to fire. Seconds later a single shot rang out as the hook streamed toward the maintenance deck three stories off the water on deck 3. The hook landed on the deck with a large clank while the boarding leader, Ensign Kyla McClellan, pulled the rope tight enough to get a solid hold.

The coxswain pushed his throttles forward a bit to close in to around five feet of the vessel and keeping station at the same speed of around fourteen knots. Quickly all four members climbed up the rope to the covered outdoor maintenance deck.

Minutes later the second Zodiac approached, and four more coastguardsmen moved from one boat, to the other, to the line, and up to the ship. In all, the whole clandestine boarding process took around ten minutes. Both Zodiacs quickly backed off and slipped away into the darkness to shadow the huge cruise ship as their boarding teams went to work.

All of the members of the boarding party were wearing black tactical uniforms and black jackets. Each member quickly readied weapons then took off their jackets. The jackets were clearly not needed in the warm tropical climate, but used to cover their M4s as they moved throughout the ship, possibly being seen by passengers. Ensign McClellan gave her final orders to both teams. She was leading Team Alpha while Senior Chief Petty Officer Patrick Kingston led Team Bravo. They moved out within about two minutes of each other. Both teams of four left the deck and went into a side door leading to the rear staircase. The rear staircase of the ship went to all decks from the top to the bottom. Team Alpha went down the stairs toward deck 1 and the medical facility while team two went up toward the pool deck. The stairs were used by some of the passengers to go up and down one or two decks at a time; however, most people used the forward and aft elevators.

At a little after 2:00 a.m., most people were already in their cabins, either sleeping or putting their luggage into the passageways for the crew to collect and move to deck 1 and eventually off the ship in the morning. The team leaders had the ship's diagram in their hands and quickly moved toward their objective.

Boarding Team Bravo quickly made it up to the pool deck and walked forward toward the front of the ship. They had discussed the best way of accessing the bridge, and it was not though the main bridge entrance on deck 7. That entrance had two security doors to be buzzed through by the bridge personnel along with security cameras. The team assumed that security cameras were working and did not know the terrorists had disabled them.

Each team also had two-way communication with the other and with the cutter *Vigilant,* where the captain and crew monitored their progress in the combat information center.

Senior Chief Petty Officer Kingston signaled Team Bravo to stop at the forward rail of the upper pool deck.

"You're starboard bridge wing and we're port," he said in a whisper to two of this team members quietly, pointing to both sides of the ship. His plan was to have two men rappel down and land quietly on each bridge wing to coordinate their assault. Two men would enter from each side of the bridge and take out the bad guys.

On the bridge, Captain Markinson was sitting in his chair, monitoring the autopilot and had ordered the next watch to start two hours later than usual. This assured that he would be alone on the bridge with Abdul-Aziz Fahad and Hamid until they were close enough to the pilot buoy just off the entrance to Government Cut, which led to the main channel into the port. *Star Orion* would be third in a line of three returning ships that morning. This worked to the advantage of their plan. After picking up and killing the harbor pilot, they would drive the ship through Government Cut and up into the main channel, picking up speed and detonating the device. The bridge was dark, with only the glow of instruments and monitors along with low red lightning.

Two decks above, as Boarding Team Bravo split into two and proceeded to each side of the ship, the wind was picking up. Senior Chief Kingston and his partner tied off their lines on the starboard side while watching the other two men on the port side do the same. Once they were ready, he signaled to the others to descend using the small LED map light hanging from his pocket.

Nine decks below, Boarding Team Alpha continued down the aft staircase to deck 1. On the way, they passed a few passengers who thought they might be part of the ship's security crew. The jackets they each draped over their M4s hid the team's weapons. Ensign Kyla McClellan and her team of four had no idea how to find or secure this possible WMD they were after. She had the intel brief, knew about where it was located, but not how to deal with it. Almost two years out of the United States Coast Guard Academy in New London, Connecticut, this mission was her toughest so far.

They also did not know whether the ship's security department was in on the plot but assumed they were because the captain was. Both the medical department and security department were on deck 1, where the team was currently headed.

Once the team arrived at deck 2, Ensign McClellan put her hand up and had the other three members wait while she alone went down the last flight of stairs to recon deck 1. Quietly she stepped down the last stair, stepping onto deck 1, facing the main middle passageway the crew members nicknamed I-95. The medical facility door was just a few feet down the passageway on the left. The medical locker storage entrance was further down. The door to the ship's security office was about halfway down on the right. She could see crew members busy a little further down from the security office, wearing white jumpsuits with the Star Caribe logo on the back. They were moving baggage onto large carts from the midship staff service elevator. Her first target, she thought to herself, would be to enter and secure the medical facility. Quietly she walked back up the steps to her three waiting team members and briefed what she saw one deck below.

"The door to the medical facility is closed, and there is a security camera outside. We'll descend to deck 1, put two and two on the door, and then enter. If it's locked, Jim will hold my weapon, and I'll play passenger needing medical attention. Once someone opens the door, we're in. Do not fire unless fired upon," she ordered.

Boarding Team Alpha then quietly took the steps down to deck 1. All four members peered into the long main passageway and saw the crewmembers handling baggage about halfway down. The crew was far enough away and too busy to even notice the boarding team stepping quietly down the side of the hallway and surrounding the entrance to the medical facility with two on each side. Ensign McClellan looked at her teammates, nodded, and then tried the door. It was locked. She took her weapon off her shoulder, handed it to her partner, Jim, then stood in front of the door and rang the buzzer.

Inside the medical nurse looked at Jake and asked what she should do. The security cameras were all out, so she could not see who was buzzing. She was so nervous, she wanted to cry.

"Just go and open the door like you're open for business," Jake said in a calm, quiet manner, thinking more terrorists might be outside. "Claire and Tom, take the right side, and Dino and I will take the left. If it's a bad guy, we'll take him down and secure any weapons."

The nurse went to the reception desk where the button to buzz the door open was located. She knew she could drop below the desk if any shooting took place. Her hand was literally shaking as she went to press the button and buzz in the person at the door.

With a loud buzz, the door released, and within seconds all four members of Boarding Team Alpha came in announcing themselves with weapons ready to fire.

"United States Coast Guard," Ensign McClellan said with her game face on.

Jake was shocked and relieved. He put his hands up and made sure the others had done the same. "We're on your team. Federal agents," he said, stepping out into the small reception area of the medical center.

"I need to see some credentials," Ensign McClellan ordered. "Slowly."

Jake and Claire pulled out their federal IDs and badges, presenting them to the Coast Guard boarding team and took a deep breath. "These people are with me, and we are damn glad to see you," he said while pointing to Dino and Tom. Ensign McClellan recognized Stein and Wilson from the photos she'd been advanced, and she had to take his word that the other two men were indeed on their side.

All four members of Boarding Team Alpha lowered their weapons and also took a few deep breaths.

"What you're looking for is in the medical storage facility next door," Jake said. "With at least two armed terrorists ready to light it off. Now maybe we can take some time and figure out how to secure it."

Ensign Kyla McClellan put her weapon down and took out the paper diagram of the ship she had in her back pocket. She looked up at Jake and delivered some sobering news. "We were given two hours by the SECDEF to secure this ship and that weapon. The USS *Pittsburgh* is taking up station, and if we don't get it done, they will put two torpedoes into this ship and sink it."

Jake and Claire looked at each other. Claire was pale. Tom and Dino looked like they might be sick.

"How much time left?" Dino managed to ask.

"Thirty-five minutes," Ensign McClellan answered.

Up on deck 11, Boarding Team Bravo began their rappel down to the bridge wing two decks below. The bridge wing was open, with a small roof covering it, extending from the main pilothouse. It had a console with engine controls and was where the captain would drive the ship to the pier. Sticking out from the bridge, the bridge wing allowed a full view of the entire side of the ship.

Kingston and his partner quietly descended and landed gently on the top of the bridge wing. He could see his teammates on the opposite bridge wing do the same. Their hearts were racing, and the clock was ticking. Each man readied his weapon, taking the safety off and making final adjustments. There was a metal ladder descending down to the floor of the bridge wing from the roof. The senior chief signaled the others with his light once again, slung his weapon into a shooting position with his right hand and arm while holding the rail of the ladder with his left. He knew he would be exposed for at least a few seconds until he made it to the bottom of the ladder. He would be ready to fire, climbing down the ladder, but he would rather be in a position behind the control console to assess the situation first.

Step by step, he descended with stealth, thanks to the soft rubber on the bottom of his boots. His partner did the same right behind and just above him. The bridge was lighted just enough so that he could see the captain and two other men in the middle of the pilothouse. This was good news for him and his team. From that vantage point, it would be hard to see all the way out to the wings in the darkness.

Once all four men were on the bridge wing, the senior chief keyed the mic on his two-way radio three times, fast signaling his partners to move. Two men entered from each side with weapons pointed at their targets in the center of the pilothouse. Red dots from the team's laser sights instantly appeared on the chests of Fahad, Captain Markinson, and Hamid Khalid.

"United States Coast Guard!" Senior Chief Kingston announced, clearly taking the three men by surprise. Fahad was the only man holding a weapon and quickly raised it. Kingston squeezed off two rounds, instantly hitting Fahad in the chest. Fahad fell back into one of the large black chairs used for the watch officer and pulled the trigger on his own AR-15, firing off a single blast toward the senior chief and his partner. Petty Officer Sean Daily was hit in forehead and collapsed onto a blue console containing instruments and a computer screen. His body then slid to the floor.

Hamid Khalid grabbed his weapon and turned it toward the two men approaching from the starboard side. His was cocked and ready to fire, but before he could pull the trigger, both men fired off two rounds each. Hamid felt the bullets burn into his skin and rip his insides apart. He lost all feeling of movement and fell to the floor of the bridge, dropping his weapon. In the last seconds of his life, he looked up at the Coast Guard petty officer standing above him. He shook his head, and said a few ominous words.

"It doesn't matter. We're close enough." Blood was flowing from his nose and mouth. His eyes were wide open and slowly stopped blinking as his heart stopped beating.

Captain Markinson was in shock and raised his hands to surrender. Senior Chief Kingston quickly put him in handcuffs. Then he keyed the mic attached to his left shoulder. "Team Bravo MC, bridge is secure, one member down," he said, signaling the others and the cutter *Vigilant* that his mission was complete and had one casualty. All the members of the boarding party wore bulletproof vests, but the lone bullet Fahad fired hit Petty Officer Daily in the forehead, instantly killing him.

———∘oo-)◉(-oo∘———

Ensign McClellan heard in her earpiece what had just happened on the bridge. She relayed that news to her team and the others. Her fear was that these people would detonate whatever it was they had if they were spooked or attacked. The ship was getting closer and closer to Miami, and the USS *Pittsburgh* had their orders. There was little time to plan.

"I say we go in with C-4 and take them out," she said, looking over at Jake. He had no rank to pull, and it was up to her how the team would handle the entrance to the medical storage locker. She respected his and Claire's positions, though, and wanted their opinions.

"They could blow us all to hell if we do that," Dino said with his uninvited thoughts on the situation.

"We know their names. Why not talk our way in?" Ensign McClellan suggested. "The security cams are down. They would have to open the door if it was one of their own."

Jake thought about this for a few seconds. "How many are there?"

"I've got six on my list plus the captain."

"Six?"

"Yeah, but there were only two on the bridge with him. That makes four inside," she said. Then she squeezed the radio mic attached to her shoulder. "Alpha team leader to Bravo team leader."

A few seconds later, Senior Chief Kingston responded in her earpiece.

"Get me an ID on one of those two you hit," she ordered. A few seconds later, she took out her sheet with pictures and names and circled one.

"Fahad," she said, looking over to Jake. "And by the way, we're down to twenty minutes."

Jake thought then spoke. "It's the only chance to distract at least one of them. If we lure him to crack the door and step outside, he's out of the picture, then we go in."

Claire then spoke up, saying out loud what the others were thinking. "If it's a timed detonation, then it doesn't really matter anyway."

Dino answered, "Fuck 'em. I'll be damned if we don't at least try. I'll do it. I know one of those bastards, and if he's in there, he'll be shocked to see me standing outside. I want to take him down."

Jake took the sheet of paper out of Ensign McClellan's hands with the picture of Fahad circled on it. "Dino's right. Let's get it on."

The crew of the USS *Pittsburgh* was trained to do their job better than any navy in the world. Today, that training might kill a bunch of their fellow countrymen and those from around thirty different nations represented and working on board the *Star Orion*.

"Periscope depth, Mr. Thompson," ordered Capt. Rusty Pearson. "Close to two thousand yards."

The Los Angeles-class submarine was now at battle stations torpedo and slowly approaching the *Star Orion* while slowing to ten knots. They were tracking the cruise liner using passive sonar, and now the captain wanted to come up and take a look. It was dark topside, but they were close enough to see at least the lights of the target ship.

Tension was high, and all hands were quiet except for those needing to speak.

"Up scope," Captain Pearson ordered. Quickly the periscope rose, and the captain lowered the two folding handles in order for him to move it left and right. He looked into the sight and turned slowly clockwise. Suddenly he stopped. Then he slowly moved further to the right and stopped again.

"I see the target and the ship ahead of them. I can barely make out the first cruise ship, but *Star Orion* is still third in line," explained the captain as he spoke to those in the control room. They were recording what he was seeing, as well, for playback if necessary.

"The *Vigilant* is on the opposite side and out of range."

He looked for a few more seconds and asked the XO if he wanted a look. The XO looked through the viewfinder then backed off.

"Mark my bearing. Down scope," ordered the eighteen-year veteran of the submarine service now commanding his first boat. "WEPS, what's the time?"

"Twelve minutes, sir," said the weapons officer over the intercom, watching the clock closely for his boss.

"WEPS, two fish ready to shoot?"

"Tubes loaded, sir," he replied back after confirming with his machinist mates that the two Mark 48 ADCAP (Advanced Capability) torpedoes were ready. They would target just under the middle of the ship for the most effective strike. The two powerful Mark 48 ADCAPs would essentially split the ship in half, sinking it quickly.

The captain looked over at the XO. They both knew what was at stake. This had never been done in the history of submarine warfare. Sinking an unarmed civilian cruise ship with torpedoes was unprecedented.

"We just need a shoot order now," he said to the XO. Then he pushed another button on his intercom box. "Float the buoy and raise the HF stick," he ordered to ensure that he had both VLF (very low frequency) radio and HF (high frequency). "Comm, make sure we have an open channel with Washington. If the order comes, I will verify with the XO."

"Aye, sir," replied the sub's communication division officer.

The captain looked at the clock on the wall of the control room showing Zulu time and thought about how he might have to explain this to his kids someday.

Dino Tucci was used to handing out punishment for deeds against the family like missed payments, performance issues, and whatever else his boss told him needed adjusting. What these people were doing was an act against his country, plus knowing he had been tricked into aiding and abetting, boiled his blood. Now he got to do what he had wanted to do all week, especially if Castro was inside the medical storage locker with the others.

"Once you knock and tell him you have a message, they'll call up to the bridge to confirm. Our guys up there have the captain standing by to confirm. Then they'll open the door," said Ensign McClellan to Dino as they prepared to carry out their plan. "We're down to ten minutes before the deadline."

They left the medical office and walked a few feet down the passageway to the entrance to the medical storage facility. Once again, Tom was sent down the passageway to let the crew members further away know that they were rehearsing his scenario game for his next contract. Two members of Team Alpha with Jake on one side and two members with Claire on the other approached the door. Two members of the boarding team members gave Jake and Claire each a side arm.

Dino stood in front of the door and looked at Jake, who nodded. Then Dino knocked loudly on the door.

Inside, all three men were surprised to hear a knock at the door. They were prepared to kill anyone who interfered with their mission at this point. Bishar was sitting on the floor next to the weapon, having just programmed in a fifteen-second short fuse. Once the "execute" button was pushed on the small screen, the programmed detonation order would be carried out. The only way to stop it would be to have the program escape code, which was different for each weapon by one number. Bishar didn't have that number. It didn't matter for what they were doing. Once "execute" was pushed, there was no going back. He just needed to set the time and yield.

Imad and Frank Castro approached the door. Imad spoke. "Yes?"

"I have a message and orders from Fahad," Dino said in a command voice that none of the men recognized.

"Call the bridge and ask him," ordered Bishar still sitting on the floor with the weapon. He did not want to move from this position.

Imad picked up the phone on the wall just a few feet away from the door and dialed the four-digit code for the bridge. The captain, with a coastguardsman's gun to his head, answered and confirmed that he had sent a messenger with critical new instructions too long to go over on the phone.

While Imad was talking to the captain inside the medical storage facility, crew members began to notice the men and women gathered around the door on the outside. They thought there was something wrong. A couple of them started to walk toward them and could see the guns. Tom approached the crew and explained that it was part of his *Murder 101* game and to stay away. They recognized Tom from the last few weeks and returned to what they were doing.

The double door had a keypad to access from the outside and button release from the inside. Dino heard the button pushed on the other side of the door and the locks released. Seconds later, the right side of the double door cracked open and Frank Castro's (a.k.a. Ali Ahamid's) eyes almost came out of their sockets when he saw Dino standing there.

"Hi, Frank," Dino said sarcastically while reaching in with his hand and grabbing Frank by the shirt. The door almost closed on Dino's arm until Ensign McClellan pushed it open with her entire body, almost falling to the floor. Dino had such a grip on Frank's shirt that it started ripping as he pulled him toward the outside of the door. Frank was unarmed. "You're so fucked," Dino said while punching his ex-friend in the stomach and forcing him to the floor. Then he kicked him in the balls three times for good measure. Frank was so much pain, he was barely able to breathe.

What seemed like hours took only seconds as the rest of the boarding party burst through the double door with weapons drawn. Jake saw Imad grab his AR-15 that was leaning up against the wall. He pointed his pistol toward Imad and pulled the trigger three times, hitting his target. The force of the bullets impacting his body pushed Imad up against the wall before he started to slide back down toward the floor, creating a huge red bloodstain, thanks to the exit wounds in his back.

Bishar was in the back of the medical storage facility sitting next to the device but more than an arm's length from the control panel, which was still open and exposed. He reached for the AR-15 sitting next to him when he heard the men burst through the door in the next room. He cocked his weapon.

Ensign McClellan and two of her teammates rounded the slight corner leading to the back room of the facility and saw Bishar. He fired two rounds but missed the coastguardsmen, who quickly backed off. All he needed to do was reach in and hit the "execute" button on the control panel. He didn't care about getting shot as long as the armed weapon's detonation timer was enabled.

Eighteen hundred miles north in the Situation Room of the White House, the president and his national security staff listened to the radio calls from the team relayed though the USCGC *Vigilant*. There had been silence since they got word that the bridge of the ship was secure and that they had lost one coastguardsman. Boarding Team Alpha had made an initial call that they were going to take the medical storage facility, but nothing since.

The ship had closed to within thirty miles of Miami and continued to steam toward the city.

"Why haven't they stopped? We have control of the bridge, don't we?" asked the president.

"We don't know, sir. Unless they lost control of the bridge," said the SECDEF.

The president looked around the room.

"The *Vigilant* can take out the Azipods, sir, if you give the order. It will take a few extra minutes to get in a little closer," explained SECDEF Pratt.

"We don't have time. It's getting too close to Miami. If they light that thing off, it could take out most of Dade County," CIA Director Donald Michaels said. His agency had further intelligence from Russia received over during the last two hours, thanks to surveillance video they had reviewed, indicating that Boris Stockov had indeed smuggled the weapon out.

The president had little choice left.

The communications officer on the USS *Pittsburgh* received an EAM (emergency action message) both in electronic message form on the ELF and verbal message over NESTOR (secure high-frequency radio). The captain had his orders and read them out loud. The XO also read the message and verified the order.

"Flood tubes 1 and 2," he ordered while putting the paper with the message on it down on the navigation table. "I want to close to 1,500 yards."

Bishar struggled with his AR-15 in one hand while trying to slide about two feet back in order to reach the control panel on the weapon. Jake and Claire joined Ensign McClellan and her team, moving about halfway back inside the medical storage facility to where a small wall turned a slight corner and separated the two rooms. Jake peered around the corner and saw that Bishar was trying to get to the device. He took a deep breath, stepped out into full view, and fired two shots toward Bishar, with one round missing to the right and the other hitting his shoulder.

With the impact of the bullet, Bishar dropped his AR-15. Pain was running throughout his body from his shattered shoulder as blood gushed out of the hole the bullet had ripped. Jake dropped back for a second or two behind the corner. If Bishar still had his rifle in his hands, he could shoot though the thin wall and hit every member of the boarding team along with Jake and Claire.

Thirty seconds later, Jake stepped out from behind the wall. Bishar was using his good arm to reach as far back as he could, bringing his hand to within inches of the control panel on the nuclear weapon. Bishar could now see the "execute" button on the screen. He continued to reach toward it.

Jake aimed his borrowed SIG Sauer pistol at Bishar's head and pulled the trigger twice. The back of Bishar's head exploded outward and splattered across the floor, all over the side of the nuclear device he was reaching for.

Ensign McClellan and the other members of Boarding Team Alpha raced to Bishar's body and kicked the AR-15 assault rifle away. Jake also moved up and looked at the panel inside the opened hatch of the tactical nuclear weapon sitting in front of them. On the small screen, in Russian, it read "armed" and there were two buttons on the right side labeled "execute" and "terminate." Jake looked at Claire and the boarding team, reached in and pushed the button marked "terminate." The screen flashed twice and changed from "armed" to "ready/enable."

Ensign McClellan keyed her radio microphone. "Weapon safe, weapon safe, weapon safe." This transmission was received on the *Vigilant* and instantly relayed by satellite to the Situation Room in Washington.

Secretary of Defense Ron Pratt stood up and yelled, "Belay that order, belay that order," into the speakerphone sitting in front of him. The president stood up as well once he heard that the weapon was safe. His heart was racing, thinking that it might be too late.

The communication channel was open in the control room of the USS *Pittsburgh* as they were 1,700 yards out from the *Star Orion* and closing to 1,500 yards. Capt. Rusty Pearson was also listening to the range count from the sonar technician.

"Seventeen hundred yards and closing, sir," said the sonar tech.

"Flood, equalze and open the outer doors tubes one and two," said the captain who had sweat running down his back and on his forehead. "Stand by to shoot."

"Sixteen hundred yards and closing, sir. Target still bearing one niner five."

Immediately following that range report, the NESTOR high-frequency radio came to life. "Belay that order, belay that order," they heard. The captain and XO looked up at the speakers and then toward each other. Next the communications division officer came over the speaker of the 1MC used to connect all the members of the fire control party. "Belay, belay, belay," he said breathing heavily.

"All stop," the captain ordered. "Tracking party, stand fast."

The captain and the XO confirmed the order and shook each other's hand, then emotion took over, and the two briefly embraced. Everyone in the control room started shaking each other's hands. The crew could hear the relief in Captain Pearson's voice when he picked up the 1MC and spoke. "This is the captain. Close the outer doors tubes one and two; drain tubes one and two. Secure from battle stations torpedo. This is the captain, carry on."

On the bridge of the *Star Orion*, Capt. Stefin Markinson informed Senior Chief Patrick Kingston that there was one more terrorist in the engineering control center. The senior chief radioed Ensign McClellan who told Jake and the others. Dino walked over to Frank Castro, a.k.a. Ali Ahamid, who was sitting up against the wall in handcuffs. He reached down, picked him up by the hair, then led him to Jake.

"Let's take Frank down there and have him call and get the bastard to open the door," Dino said to Jake.

Jake and Ensign McClellan agreed, and they moved to the entrance to the engineering control center. Under armed escort, Dino took Frank by the hair once again and followed. They needed to secure that center because it controlled many of the ship's systems. That's why back on the bridge when Captain Markinson tried to slow and stop the ship after the Coast Guard rushed in, he could not gain throttle control.

Just outside the door of the engineering control room, Dino picked up the phone and put it up to Frank's ear. Frank then spoke a few words of Arabic to Kamal Lahab. Seconds later, the door lock buzzed and the team moved in with weapons drawn. Kamal was shocked to see the armed boarding team members and his associate in handcuffs. He raised his hands and was quickly taken into custody.

The ship finally came to a stop. Outside, more Coast Guard personnel boarded from the *Vigilant* and from Coast Guard Station Miami Beach. After taking full control of the ship, Coast Guard personnel searched for and found the staff captain shot dead in his cabin along with two other deck officers.

Inside the ship's security office, four personnel were also found dead. Capt. Stefin Markinson told the Coast Guard that Fahad and Khalid left him alone on the bridge for a short time while they eliminated those key members of the ship's crew. Passengers were assembled according to the color on their bag tags issued the night before in various parts of the ship as typical for any cruise, but this time they were each questioned and screened by members of the Joint Homeland Security Task Force.

Jake and Claire made finally contact with their respective bosses, who told them how proud they were of the two and for them to take a real vacation.

"I'm never going on another vacation with you," Claire said as the two stood on the pool deck. The sun broke over the horizon starting to reflect on the glass buildings of Miami, now coming into view.

"Never?"

"Vacationing with you is no fun, Jake Stein," she said with the hint of a chuckle in her voice.

"What if it were a honeymoon?" Jake asked.

Claire looked at him. One thing she had learned over the past twenty-four hours was that life was too short. Now she had a better appreciation of time spent together.

"Only if it's a honeymoon!" she said. The two embraced and fell into a passionate kiss just as Dino and Tom approached, ending the romantic moment. After all they had been through, Jake still didn't know what Dino did for a living.

"What is it you do in Providence, Dino?" Jake asked. Dino handed him a cup of coffee.

"I'm in construction," he said to Jake and the others as they sipped their coffee.

Chapter 22

BREAKING NEWS

JAKE'S IPHONE WAS working again now that they were close enough to shore, and his mailbox was filling up with a week's worth of e-mails. It would be a while before they got off the ship, he thought as he started to scroll down through the e-mails. Claire was doing the same.

His CNN news alert went off. Claire's Fox News alert also went off at almost the same time. They both read the news alerts, then looked at each other.

It read, *BREAKING NEWS—Los Angeles—A major explosion has occurred near the Port of Long Beach, larger than anything seen before, setting off major fires. Phone reports say many buildings and structures have collapsed. Witnesses said the blast could be seen from as far away as San Diego during the predawn hours. Sources report that the origin of the explosion seemed to be a large cruise ship.*

The End

Author Biography

W. F. WALSH is a two-time Emmy Award-winning television personality and has spent over twenty years in television news and entertainment. As a producer, Walsh has been awarded five Telly Awards for his work on various programs from news to reality.

He is also a lieutenant colonel in the United States Air Force Reserve and has served on military missions to both Iraq and Afghanistan, among many other locations around the world. He has been awarded the Meritorious Service Medal, the Air Force Commendation Medal, the Navy and Marine Corps Achievement Medal, the Air Force Achievement Medal, and the Global War on Terror Medal, among others.

He holds a master's degree for military operational art and science from the United States Air Force Air University and a bachelor of science degree from Emerson College in Boston, Massachusetts.

Originally from the State of Rhode Island, W. F. Walsh now makes his home near Charleston, South Carolina, with his wife, Janet, and their two children, Frank and Amy.

Made in the USA
Lexington, KY
21 June 2013